ADVANCE PRAISE
BREA. ___ . . . . .

Nobody lives forever. Or do they? Hop on board. *Ballast Point Breakdown* opens with the wind tearing at your face as you bounce across San Diego Bay in the moonlight, hurtling toward a fiery collision of the past and the present. Guitar playing Private Eye Rolly Waters finds that the truth has a way of floating to the surface and that other things are perhaps best forgotten.

> *G.M. Ford, Author of the Leo Waterman series*

This is Fayman firing on all cylinders.

> *Bill Fitzhugh, Author of* HUMAN RESOURCES *and* PEST CONTROL

As a San Diego author and some-time musician, *Ballast Point Breakdown* spoke to me on so many levels — the unique San Diego settings, the dolphins (!!) and of course, the musician jokes (How many guitarists DOES it take to screw in a lightbulb, anyway?). But you don't have to be a San Diego musician to enjoy this twisty mystery.

> *Lisa Brackmann, Author of* ROCK PAPER TIGER *and* BLACK SWAN RISING

Musician turned private eye Rolly Waters isn't your average gumshoe. In Fayman's skilled hands Waters is clever, funny and intrepid. But he's much more, a scarred hero who carries the guilt from a decades old tragedy that makes him a real, fleshed-out character who you root and fear for as he follows clues no matter how dark an alley they lead him down." Bravo, Mr. Fayman!"

> *Matt Coyle, Author of the award-winning Rick Cahill crime series*

Private Eye Roland Waters investigates with the cool, laconic style of the blues guitarist he is.

> *Matt Goldman, NYT Bestselling Author and Shamus Award Nominee*

**Praise for the Rolly Waters Mysteries** *Border Field Blues* **and** *Desert City Diva:*

A powerful new voice on the crime-fiction scene, Corey Lynn Fayman delivers a potent dose of sex, drugs, and rock 'n' roll.
  *ForeWord Reviews*

A rollicking and fast-paced crime novel.
  *San Francisco Book Reviews*

Readers will enjoy the broadly drawn characters and the rough and tumble borderland setting.
  *Publishers Weekly*

Sparse dialogue and riveting scenes make this mystery impossible to put down.
  *ForeWord Reviews*

Fans of wisecracking California crime solvers will enjoy this working-class PI with a poet's soul.
  *Booklist*

A weird, but welcome, addition to the pantheon of literary PIs. A delightfully strange spin on the noir genre.
  *Foreword Reviews*

Offbeat characters and popular musical lore distinguish this decidedly unusual tale.
  *Publishers Weekly*

The dialogue is the real attraction. It is sparse but ricochets with witty abandon. This bare-bones style evokes the natural desolateness of the desert backdrop beautifully, allowing the story to thunder on to a shocking conclusion.
  *Foreword Review*

# BALLAST POINT
# BREAKDOWN

# BALLAST POINT
# BREAKDOWN

COREY LYNN FAYMAN

KONSTELLATION
PRESS

Published by Konstellation Press, San Diego

Cover design: Corey Lynn Fayman

Author photo: Bruce Fayman

Editor: Lisa Wolff

ISBN: 978-0-9991989-8-8

*To all of Rolly Waters' fans and friends.*
*Though they be but little, they are fierce.*

*In Memoriam Hunza Kotas*

# 1

## THE FIRE

J.V. Sideman had just finished playing the saxophone break for the band's rendition of "This Magic Moment" when a twenty-one-foot Bayliner speedboat skidded across the beach outside the Admiral's Club ballroom and crashed through a large picture window. Partygoers screamed as glass shards exploded into the room and the boat landed with a deep and frightening thump on the carpeted floor. They scattered into the back corners of the room before turning to stare in disbelief. The band stopped mid-song, as if the power had gone out.

The crash of the boat had already dampened the crowd's exuberance, but when a woman with a bright red gash on her forehead crawled out of the boat's cabin, a nervous silence fell over the room. The woman walked to the edge of the boat and addressed them.

"Save the dolphins!" she said. "Save—"

Someone interrupted from the back of the room, a woman's voice, maternal and demanding.

"Young lady!" she said. "Come down from there immediately."

"No, Mother," said the woman on the boat.

"I demand that you come down from there *now*."

The crowd gasped as the woman on the boat began to pour the

contents of a red gasoline can onto the deck. A bald man in a dark suit took charge of the scene.

"Everyone out," he ordered. "Everyone out now. The party's over."

As the guests rushed to the exits, the woman's mother moved toward the boat. The man who'd sounded the alarm followed two steps behind her.

"Now, dear," said the man, taking a more conciliatory tone. "Is this really necessary?"

"Lies," the woman on the boat said in response. "Lies, lies, lies!" She lifted the gasoline can above her head and poured the last of its acrid contents over her curly blond hair until it lay flat and soggy against her skin. She tossed the can aside, reached into the folds of her sweatshirt and pulled out a fat, stubby pistol.

"That's a flare gun," said Conway, the band's drummer, rising from his throne. "We gotta get out of here."

"What about the equipment?" said Sideman.

"Fuck the equipment," said Conway. "If she shoots that thing off, this whole place is going up. I used to work here. The kitchen's on the other side of that wall. It's all gas lines and grease."

"I'm not leaving without my axes," said Sideman, but Conway had already abandoned the stage, hell-bent for the patio exit, along with the rest of the band. Sideman started after them, then stopped. He couldn't leave without his saxophones. He had another gig tomorrow and three more next week, some good-paying gigs. He retrieved his cases from under the stage, then glanced back at the room, keeping a nervous eye on the family drama that was unfolding.

"Why are you doing this, honey?" said the bald man, sounding like a college professor quizzing a mediocre student.

"It was a lie, Father," said the woman on the boat. "You both know it."

"What was a lie, honey?"

"My life. It was all a lie."

"Now, dear," said her mother. "We've talked about this before. You're suffering from delusions. You agreed to take your medications."

"I've seen him."

"Who, darling?" said the man.

The woman waved the flare gun toward the water outside the shattered window.

"Arion," she said.

"That's ridiculous," said her mother. "Arion doesn't exist. He's a figment of your imagination. You know that. You've told me you know that. Let's put an end to this infantile behavior right now."

Sideman locked his two saxophones inside their cases, picked them up and headed toward the patio. The woman's mother continued to try and talk her down from the boat, but her daughter would have none of it.

"Lies," she repeated. "It's all lies."

"That's enough, young lady," said her mother. "I'm ordering you to come down from there. Your father and I are very disappointed in you."

The woman on board faltered for a moment, then pressed the flare gun against the side of her head. Sideman stopped in his tracks.

"Don't—" he said.

"Save the dolphins!" the woman shouted and pulled the trigger. The flare cartridge ricocheted against her skull and shot up toward the ceiling, its concussive energy knocking her head sideways like a bobble-head doll. She toppled onto the deck in a limp heap. The flare hit the ceiling in a sparkling rush, then dropped back onto the boat, igniting the gasoline. A curtain of flame rose from the deck.

Sideman leapt back from the heat, upsetting the buffet table behind him, where a carved ice sculpture of a scuba diver and two dolphins loomed over platters of crab claws and jumbo shrimp. The sculpture wobbled, tumbled and fell to the floor, breaking into chunks of jagged ice. Sideman picked himself up, grabbed his saxophone cases and ran for the patio door. The door opened and caught him full in the face. Sideman tumbled backwards onto the floor as a long-haired, bearded man wielding a fire extinguisher rushed into the room.

Sideman stared at the ceiling a moment, then rolled to his knees and reached for his saxophone cases. The bearded man broke the seal on the extinguisher and sprayed foam onto the boat, but it had little effect on the flames that now licked at the ceiling. The extinguisher ran out of foam. The man tossed it away. He stepped back, put his hands on his hips and stared up at the flames. The woman's parents had abandoned the room.

A long, terrifying howl filled the air. Sideman's guts twisted into a knot as he saw the woman rise from the deck of the boat. She was on fire, burning in front of him, engulfed in the flames. The bearded man raised his right hand and waved it across his chest, like a priest giving last rites. The woman raised her arms, reaching, reaching. She toppled back onto the deck.

The sprinklers in the ceiling popped on, dousing the room in rusty water like some kind of sick joke. Sideman stood up, collected his saxophones and ran toward the patio. He'd seen a lot in his musical career, thirty years of performing in clubs and hotels and theaters. He'd seen fistfights and stabbings and blood on the bar stools. But he'd never seen someone burn. He was wet now, sopping wet from the sprinklers. He opened the exit door. It was dusk, almost dark out, but the air was dry and warm, like so many autumn nights in San Diego. He could see cars crossing over the water on the Harbor Drive bridge. Christmas lights hung from the bridge, long strings of red and green.

"Hold the door, horn man," said a voice from behind him. Sideman tossed his saxophone cases onto the patio and looked back into the room.

The bearded man stood at the seafood buffet, stuffing his overcoat pockets with shrimp. The boat was still burning. The water had done little to tamp down the fire. Sideman recognized the man with the beard.

"Harmonica Dan?" he said.

"How you been, J.V.?" said the man.

"What the hell are you doing?"

"I thought I'd stock up, since I was here," the man said, grabbing handfuls of shrimp and stuffing them into his pocket. "My dolphins love these things."

A ball of blue flame lit up the room as the Bayliner's fuel tanks exploded. Sideman shut his eyes, felt the heat. When he opened them again, he was outside on the patio. He lay on his back, staring at stars in a dark purple sky.

# 2

# THE FAN

It was Monday night. Tuesday morning, really, because Monday night was the blues jam at Winstons Beach Club in Ocean Beach and now the jam was over. It was twenty minutes past one on Tuesday morning. Rolly Waters sat at the bar, nursing a club soda with lime while he waited for Moogus to pack up his drum kit. A young woman in a tie-dyed halter top walked up to the bar and sat down next to him.

"I'm looking for someone," she said.

"Aren't we all?" said Rolly, as the scent of patchouli oil rolled over him. Not much had changed since he and his band had lived in a house four blocks away from Winstons, in the neighborhood the locals referred to as the War Zone. Fifteen years later, Ocean Beach girls still smelled the same. Patchouli. Or was it sandalwood?

"I'm serious," said the woman.

"So am I," said Rolly. The woman had long blond hair and a lithe, tanned body, but she looked sandy at the edges. The sand was relentless in OB. It found its way into your house, abrading the finish on your guitars. It got into your lungs and corroded your heart. It scraped your soul to a coarse nub.

The woman leaned her elbow on the bar. She rested her head on her hand and narrowed her eyes.

"Someone told me you were a detective," she said.

"Who told you that?"

"Is it true?"

"I do some work as a private investigator," said Rolly. "When I'm not strangling cats."

"What?" said the woman, squinching her nose as if Rolly smelled funny.

"Playing guitar," said Rolly. "It's a musician joke."

"I don't get it."

Rolly turned his head toward the stage, looking for an escape, but Moogus hadn't finished packing his drums yet. The woman continued to stare at him. He turned back to face her. Twenty years ago, he might have been flattered by her intensity. Now it just made him nervous.

"So who are you looking for?" he asked.

"A man."

Rolly resisted the impulse to make another smart remark. He restrained himself these days, more than he used to. The woman wouldn't get his jokes anyway. She didn't seem all that bright.

"Is this man someone you know?" he said.

The woman grabbed the chain necklace that hung from her neck and lifted two shiny rectangles from under her shirt. They were aluminum dog tags, like the ones Rolly's father had worn in the Navy.

"I want to find him," she said, displaying the tags for Rolly's perusal. He leaned in toward her and squinted at the letters embossed on the tags. The dim light in the bar didn't help his aging eyes any.

"Butch Fleetwood," said the woman, sensing his difficulty. "That's his name."

"Yes," said Rolly, pretending his eyes weren't as old as they seemed. "Butch Fleetwood. Was he a friend of yours?"

"My patron gave these dog tags to me."

"I see. Who's your patron?"

"Janis Withers."

"That name sounds familiar," said Rolly, searching his brain for a connection. He found it. "There was a Janis Withers who ran our fan club. The Creatures. My old band. That was a long time ago."

The woman nodded.

"Janis gave me the dog tags. She asked me to find you if something happened to her. She asked me to give them to you."

"What happened to Janis?"

"She died."

"I'm sorry to hear that."

"The police say it was suicide."

"When did this happen?"

"Three days ago. Friday."

"How did . . . excuse me, what's your name?"

"Melody Flowers."

"Hello, Melody. I'm Rolly."

"I don't believe them, you see."

"Who?"

"The police. Janis didn't kill herself," said Melody, her eyes getting brighter. "I have a strong intuition about these things. I can read auras."

Rolly stared at the bubbles in his glass. If the police said Janis Withers had killed herself, she probably had. The cops were usually right about that kind of thing. It wouldn't do him any good to challenge Melody on her instincts, thought. That only made people mad. Her intuition might be as strong as the rip currents off the Ocean Beach Pier. It might be as dangerous, too. He paddled off to the side.

"What's your interest in Butch Fleetwood?" he said. "What will you do if I find him?"

Melody twisted one end of her hair and stared at it.

"I want to save the Lemurian Temple," she said.

"Oh," said Rolly, picturing an animal in his head, some kind of monkey that looked like a raccoon. He remembered a travel show he'd watched on TV where lemurs had taken over a temple in Thailand, someplace like that. He doubted it was the same kind of temple. The zoning laws wouldn't allow for live monkeys, even in Ocean Beach.

"Janis and I founded the temple," Melody continued. "I'm the priestess. My Lemurian name is Merdonis. I live in the back."

Rolly sipped his club soda, wondering how the weirdos always managed to find him. Six months ago it had been a bunch of UFO freaks. He wasn't sure he wanted to deal with more weirdos, no matter how attractive and sandy they might be.

"Lemurians worship dolphins as spirit beings," said Melody. "Dolphins act as our guides to higher consciousness."

"I see," said Rolly. It wasn't monkeys, at least.

"When I met Janis," said Melody, "I could see right away how spiritually in tune she was. I talked to her about swimming with the dolphins in Hawaii one time, you know, with a friend of mine. I told her how it put me on another spiritual plane. She asked me if I knew about Lemuria and the dolphins. She said he was Arion, the dolphin king."

"Who was?"

"Butch Fleetwood. The guy on the dog tags. Arion. That's what she called him sometimes. I think it was him anyway. It was kind of confusing, the way she talked about people."

"Fleetwood was a Lemurian?"

"He was in the Navy, I think. A long time ago. He did something with dolphins. Janis promised she would leave the temple to me."

"Did she put it in writing? Did she leave a will?"

"I don't know. Her mother came to the temple the day after Janis died. She told me I'd have to leave, that they'd be selling the house. The temple, I mean. I thought maybe this Butch guy could help me."

"What about other family?" said Rolly. "Maybe they'd know something about a will."

"Janis never said much about her family. I think she was in love with him. Butch."

"She told you that?"

"I could just tell," said Melody. "The way her aura lit up when she talked about him. They took a lot of her stuff."

"Who did?"

"The guys who came to the temple."

"What guys?"

"The police, and some people in suits. A man and a woman. They took stuff out of the closets."

"What kind of stuff?"

"Papers and photographs. Janis kept some old boxes in there."

"Hmm," Rolly said. It was unusual procedure for a suicide case. He might be able to get some information from his friend Bonnie Hammond at SDPD, if she was feeling generous. He looked at the dog tags again. Below the name was a number, with the letters *USN* at the end. You couldn't go into a bar in San Diego without running into someone who'd worn Navy dog tags. There were women and men all over this city who'd hooked up with a sailor on shore leave. His mother had married one of those sailors. And divorced him when Rolly was twelve.

"My father's an old Navy man," Rolly said, indicating the dog tags. "He might be able to tell me something about these. Did you show the police the dog tags?"

"Janis said I could only show them to you."

"When did she give them to you?"

"The day before she died."

"And when did the police come?"

"The day after. They were rude to me. Those people in the suits were even ruder. Her mother was the worst of them all."

"Did any of them mention Butch Fleetwood?"

"No."

Rolly nodded. He looked back at the stage. Moogus had almost finished packing his drums. Melody lifted the dog tags over her head and placed them on the bar.

"I need you to find him," she said, putting her hand on top of Rolly's. "I think he can help me. Her mother says I have to move out of the temple next week."

Melody looked into Rolly's eyes, the way women did when they wanted something, when they thought you were easy. Her hand on his wasn't sandy, but soft.

"I charge fifty dollars an hour for this kind of thing," said Rolly. It was the best way he knew to get rid of potential clients. "And I'd need an advance."

"I don't have any money," she said. "Janis said you were chivalrous."

"Chivalry doesn't pay like it used to."

"She showed me a photograph. She's in the photo with you and your singer friend. She told me about your friend, how he died."

"That was a long time ago."

"You all look so happy. In the photo."

"We were probably drunk," Rolly said. He and Matt were almost always under the influence of alcohol or some other controlled substance in their Creatures days. Janis might've been too. She put up with their substance abuse, anyway. She had to.

"Did you pay Janis to run your fan club?" said Melody.

"No. She did it for free. She liked helping out."

"Don't you think you owe her something?"

"Okay, okay," said Rolly. He picked up the dog tags. "I'll see what I can find out. That's all I can promise. I can't spend a lot of time on this. I have paying jobs."

"Hey Rolly," shouted Moogus from the stage. "Is the chick coming home with you or not? I want to get out of here."

Rolly pretended to scratch the back of his head while extending his middle finger at Moogus. Melody put her hand on his knee. She was full of sand. She knew he was sandy, too.

"I knew you'd help Janis," she said. "I knew you'd help me."

"How do I get in touch with you?" Rolly said.

"When I'm not at the temple, I waitress at the café on the pier," said Melody. "Late breakfast and lunch. You can call my cell, too, if you want."

They exchanged phone numbers. Rolly slid off the bar stool and put the dog tags in his pocket. Melody grabbed his arm as he started to leave, pulling him back like a rip current.

"There's something I forgot to tell you," she said. "Something Janis told me. Maybe it's why the police came to the temple and took all that stuff from the closet."

"What's that?" Rolly said.

"Butch Fleetwood. Arion. Janis said he was a spy."

# 3

# THE TAQUERIA

R olly and Moogus sat on the patio outside Miguel's taco shop, sharing a plate of carne asada nachos, indulging in an edible memory from their younger, leaner days. Miguel's was two blocks from the beach, four blocks from Winstons. It had been a regular late-night stop for the band when they lived in OB.

"So who was that chick harassing you at the bar?" said Moogus, wiping a gob of guacamole from his chin.

"Her name's Melody," said Rolly. "She wasn't harassing me."

"You didn't look like you were buying what she was selling."

"She's looking for someone."

"Mr. Right? Mr. Wonderful?"

"Mr. Fleetwood."

"Who?"

Rolly ate a tortilla chip loaded with grilled meat and onions. He took a swig of horchata to wash it down.

"Do you remember Janis Withers?" he said. "The girl who used to run our fan club?"

"She was the one with those scars on her face, right? Like she got burned or something?"

"I'd forgotten about that."

"She wasn't bad looking, even with the scars. Kind of quiet and shy. Carried that funny little backpack around with her all the time. She was one of those little rich girls from over the hill, the kind that liked to take us home so they could frighten their parents."

"Did Janis ever take you home to her parents?" said Rolly.

"Hell, no. She was afraid of me."

"Smart girl."

Moogus laughed.

"Yeah, well, you had your own little rich girl back in those days. If you'd married Leslie, you could be catching rays in Cabo now instead of sitting at Winstons getting your ears abused by the local skank. What'd this Melody woman want with an old fart like you, anyway?"

"She was friends with Janis. Janis died a couple of days ago. She killed herself."

"That's fucked up," said Moogus.

"Yeah."

They sat for a moment, munching their nachos in silence. Rolly thought about the late-night phone calls he used to get from Janis, after Matty died and the band fell apart. She'd just ring him up and start talking. He'd listen, not saying much in response, letting her ramble. It was a weird kind of therapy for both of them. She'd never mentioned Butch Fleetwood, though, as far as he could remember.

"You still think about Matt?" said Moogus.

"Every day."

"It could have been any of us, buddy."

"But it wasn't."

"I don't blame you, Rol. Never have and never will. Shit happens."

"I know," said Rolly. "But it happens to some people more than others."

Moogus and Rolly stared at each other a moment. Moogus raised his Styrofoam cup.

"Here's to Matty," he said. "Every band needs its asshole."

"I thought *you* were our asshole."

"Nah. I was the muscle. Matt was the asshole."

"What was I?"

"You were the brains. You're always the brains."

"What about Derek? What was he?"

"He was the bass player. He wasn't anything."

"Yeah, I guess so," said Rolly. "Here's to Matty, our asshole."

He tapped Moogus's cup with his own, drank another slug of horchata. In the old days, he would have spiked it with shots of bourbon from the bottle he kept in his gig bag. He didn't enjoy sobriety all that much, but the alternative was worse.

"Enough of this serious stuff," said Moogus. "I got some news for you. Apparently, hell has frozen over. Or if not, it's pretty chilly down there."

"What happened?"

"I'm performing at an engagement with Mr. J.V. Sideman."

Rolly looked at Moogus a moment. The feud between Moogus and Sideman was legendary among local musicians. They hated each other. No one knew why. The origin of their quarrel had been lost in the mists of time, drifting out to sea like a late-morning fog bank.

"How did this miracle come about?" said Rolly.

"We're both adults now," said Moogus.

"That's debatable," said Rolly. "In your case, anyway."

"It's time to bury the hatchet."

"If you say so," said Rolly. The only place Sideman and Moogus would bury a hatchet was in each other's skull. "I'm guessing there's money involved."

Moogus smiled.

"You got that right," he said. "Double-scale and paid rehearsal."

"What's the gig?"

"It's that new water park they're opening. Ocean Universe."

"Never heard of it."

"You know that painter guy, Wendell?" said Moogus.

"Never heard of him," said Rolly.

"He paints whales and dolphins, murals, that kind of shit. Guy's worth millions. They're opening this new water park on the bay, over by the airport. This guy Wendell's got something to do with it."

"When's the gig?"

"Saturday. Wendell's singing with us."

"Is he any good?"

"Who cares? He's paying double-scale."

Rolly had seen it before, rich people paying a lot of money for their vanity music projects. A good band was a kind of insurance against embarrassment. Moogus and Sideman were two of the best players in town. And the most mercenary. Paying them well ensured their devotion and professionalism.

"You got a guitar player yet?" said Rolly.

"Sorry, buddy. They got some guy from LA."

"Well then, how do mere mortals like me go about witnessing this miracle?"

"It's a benefit concert. Tickets are five hundred dollars."

"Guess I'll have to miss it."

"Sideman said there might be a guest list. I'll get you in if I can. Unless it's only one ticket."

"I'm not your first choice?"

"I got a hard-on for this cute barista at the Better Buzz. There's got to be a blow job in there for me if I get her into a show that costs five hundred dollars."

"Didn't you say you were an adult now?"

"Hey, I'm just speculating. I didn't say I was gonna bargain for one specifically. That's more adult, right?"

Rolly shook his head in dismay.

"Well, don't expect one from me if I get a ticket," he said.

"Nah," said Moogus. "Besides, I hear you give terrible blow jobs."

"Yeah? Who told you that?"

"Your girlfriend."

"I don't have a girlfriend."

"Now you know why."

"That doesn't even make sense."

"Yeah, well . . ." Moogus said. His eyes moved from Rolly to something beyond Rolly's left shoulder. Rolly turned. A police car had double-parked on the street. He turned back to Moogus.

"Something wrong?" he said.

"I forgot to contact my PO last week," said Moogus.

"You're still on parole?"

"Yeah. Shit. It's only two more months. But I'm supposed to check in once a week."

"You want to leave?"

"Nah. I'm just being paranoid. It's being in the old neighborhood, I guess. The cops were always getting on our ass."

"One of the many things I don't miss about living here."

"C'mon, your pitiful little life has never been as awesome as it was when we inhabited the Creature Cave."

"If you say so."

"I'm not saying I want to go back there," said Moogus. "Holy cow, the smell of that place alone would probably make me pass out—Eau de Skank. We were living large, though. And then we weren't. How did that happen?"

"You know how it happened. One of us crashed into a tree and killed the lead singer."

"Yeah. Shit. Sorry. I didn't mean nothing." Moogus pointed at the depleted nachos platter. "Are you done?"

Rolly nodded. Moogus got up from the table, cleared the plates and dumped them in the trash can, then started toward the alley. Rolly hesitated.

"You okay with taking a shortcut?" said Moogus, sensing Rolly's reticence.

"Yeah, I guess," said Rolly. They set off down the alley. It wasn't the darkness of the alley that worried him. It was the house that stood at the end of it, the shadows and memories and unsettled feelings the late hours brought with them. Moogus had convinced him it would be fun to go back and host the blues jam at Winstons again. The show had gone fine, but something had changed when Melody told him about Janis. Nostalgia got sucked out of the room, replaced by timeworn regrets, dark thoughts that popped in his head like noxious balloons. Matt's ghost haunted these streets, more present than it had felt for Rolly in a long time.

"There it is," said Moogus, when they reached the end of the alley. "The Creature Cave."

They stood in the shadows and stared across the street at their old house. The current occupants had strung Christmas lights around the windows. A balloon Santa, his sleigh and four reindeer sat on the lawn.

"What a crappy little place," said Rolly.

"Yeah," said Moogus. "A crappy little place with a legendary history of rock-and-roll debauchery. This brings back a lot of memories."

"Too many, maybe," said Rolly. He glanced over at Moogus, alone in his reveries. Adulthood had a sentimental effect on everyone, even mad crazy drummers.

"Moog?" said Rolly.

"Yeah?"

"Do you remember a guy named Butch Fleetwood ever hanging with Janis?"

"Nah, I don't think so. That's the guy you're supposed to be looking for?"

"Yeah. Janis wanted me to find him if something happened to her."

"Whoa. That sounds kinda ominous. You think you can find him?"

"I told Melody I'd give it a try." Rolly shrugged.

Moogus shifted his feet and scanned the street. He seemed nervous.

"What is it?" said Rolly. "You still worried about the cops?"

"There's something I never told you, about Janis. And Matty. They had a thing going on, near the end. I guess it was kinda serious. This was after you moved out, when you got engaged and moved in with Leslie. Like a month or two later."

"I never knew about that," said Rolly. "Why didn't you tell me before?"

"I only found out after the accident," said Moogus. "Janis came by the house. I had to tell her what happened. You were in the hospital. Matt was dead. She got really upset, started crying, said they were supposed to get married. I couldn't handle it. I had my own problems to deal with, scaring up gigs just so I could eat. When you and I started talking again, it didn't seem all that important. You had plenty to handle just getting back on your feet."

"Yeah, I guess so," said Rolly. There were still ghosts in this neighborhood, more than he'd realized. Had Janis blamed him for Matty's death? She'd never talked about it in her phone calls.

"Let's get out of here," he said.

"Yeah," Moogus said.

As they turned to leave, a police car pulled up in front of them and flashed its lights. Rolly shaded his eyes and watched as an officer stepped out of the car and walked toward them. He couldn't see the officer's face, but he recognized her purposeful gait. She stopped and put her hands on her hips.

"Well, if isn't my two favorite miscreants," said Bonnie Hammond. "Lurking in a dark alley at two in the morning."

## 4

## THE CAVE

"Good evening, Officer Hammond," said Moogus. "You look fashionably hard-ass in that khaki pantsuit ensemble."

"Shut up," said Bonnie. "I could haul you in right now, if I decided to."

"What for?"

"When was the last time you contacted your PO?"

Moogus twisted his mouth, fighting to keep it shut. He and Bonnie had a long history of mistrust and antagonism, but she had him dead to rights. He couldn't afford to pop off. Bonnie folded her arms and waited for Moogus to respond. Rolly stepped in to fill the awkward silence.

"Moog was just saying he was going to call his parole officer tomorrow," he said.

"You're three days overdue, Mr. Ludwig," said Bonnie. Rolly couldn't remember the last time he'd heard anyone refer to Moogus by his last name. He'd known Moogus for twenty-five years and it still caught him by surprise when he heard it.

"C'mon, Bonnie," said Rolly. "Moogus isn't a criminal. He knows he screwed up."

"If he's not a criminal, then why is he on parole?"

"He served his time."

"Parole is considered part of his sentence. You should know that as well as anyone."

"Yeah. Well . . ."

A hard glance from Bonnie cut Rolly short. When their friendship conflicted with Bonnie's law enforcement duties, the job always won. Bonnie was a good police officer, better than most he'd dealt with, but she could be a pain in the butt.

"C'mon, Officer," said Moogus. "I only got two months left."

"That's your problem, not mine."

"You said it yourself, I'm only a couple of days late."

"You know the rules. Let's go."

"I want to talk to my PO."

"You'll get your chance. He clears you, you can be out by noon."

"Can I call him now?"

"You want to call your PO at this hour?"

Moogus nodded.

"He knows I'm a musician. He's used to it."

"Okay," said Bonnie. "Get in the back of the car first."

"Oh, c'mon," said Moogus.

"It's that or I cuff you and take you downtown right now."

Moogus sighed and slumped his shoulders. He nodded. Bonnie walked him to her patrol car and opened the rear door. Moogus climbed in. Bonnie slammed the door shut and returned to Rolly.

"You enjoyed that, didn't you?" he said.

"Yes, it was remarkably satisfying."

"That was you, wasn't it, double-parked at the taco shop?"

Bonnie nodded.

"You ran us both, didn't you?" said Rolly.

"Standard procedure. Two known offenders observed in consultation. You never know what'll come up."

"Is Moogus in trouble?" said Rolly.

"Not much. Not if his PO clears him."

"Then why are you being such a b . . .?" Rolly trailed off.

"Was that the 'B' word about to cross your lips, Mr. Waters?" said Bonnie. "Were you just about to disrespect a female police officer?"

"No," said Rolly. He smiled. "But the thought crossed my mind."

"I'll probably let the jerk go, even if he doesn't reach his PO."

"You really need to let go of this thing."

"What thing?"

"You know, the feud you have with him, that whole Joan-and-Moogus thing. It was a long time ago. You won."

"I just like to remind him who's in charge," said Bonnie. "When I get an opportunity like this, it's too good to pass up."

Years ago, Moogus had managed to hit on Bonnie's girlfriend, Joan, at just the right emotional moment. Every heterosexual man in every band that ever played the Bacchanal nightclub had tried to seduce Joan, the slinky blonde who ran the soundboard. Every one of them failed. Except Moogus. It was only one night. Joan and Bonnie moved in together a month later.

"He's always such a freakin' distraction, anyway," said Bonnie. "I wanted to talk to you."

"What about?"

Bonnie reached in her pocket, pulled out her phone, tapped it a couple of times and showed him the screen.

"That's you, isn't it?" she said, pointing to the photo. "With the guitar?"

Rolly squinted at the photograph.

"Yeah, that looks like me," he said. "A long time ago. Where'd you get this?"

"Found it on a boat."

"Whose boat?"

"You recognize anyone else in the photo?"

Rolly squinted again. Bonnie zoomed in on the picture. Everyone was trying to help him to see better. He looked at the photograph. It was the Creatures, at Winstons, back in their heyday—Moogus on drums, Rolly on guitar. Matt wasn't in the photograph, but he would have been somewhere on stage. Without Matt, there was no Creatures.

"Who's the guy making goo-goo eyes with you?" said Bonnie.

"Harmonica Dan. That's what we called him, anyway."

"Was he in your band?"

"He sat in with us sometimes. That looks like the blues jam at Winstons. Same as tonight. Monday night. Dan always sat in with us."

"Was he there tonight?"

"No. Moogus and I were reminiscing before the gig, wondering if he'd show up."

"You think Moogus has had any contact with him?"

"I doubt it. It's been, like, a hundred years since we played here."

"A hundred years, huh?"

"Okay, more like fifteen. What's this boat you mentioned?"

"It's registered to Daniel Piper. That's the guy's legal name. He lives on a boat. That's where I found the photograph. He's got a mooring in America's Cup harbor."

"Did something happen to Dan?" said Rolly, hoping he wouldn't have to add one more ghost to his list. Bonnie shrugged.

"Daniel Piper's a person of interest in a case I'm working on."

"I didn't know he had his own boat."

"I want you to go over his personal effects with me. You might notice something I didn't, make a connection. This is a weird case. You handle weird better than anybody I know."

"Thanks, I guess." Rolly said. He and Bonnie had worked together before. He had a knack for getting people to talk to him, people who wouldn't talk to the police. Bonnie had backed him up on a couple of his own cases, with muscle and a gun. He didn't carry a weapon. Bonnie also had access to data resources he didn't. She might be able to help him find Butch Fleetwood.

"Okay," he said. "When do you want to do this?"

"How about now?"

"Not now. I'm exhausted. Besides, I'd have to bring Moogus along. We carpooled."

Bonnie looked back at her police cruiser.

"Well, I don't want him around, gumming up the works. How about tomorrow morning?"

"I guess I could do that. What time?"

"First thing, say eight."

"That's kind of early for me."

"Nine."

"Nine thirty?"

Bonnie pulled out her phone, tapped a few times on the screen.

"Okay," she said. "Nine thirty at Driscoll's Wharf in Point Loma. Gate Two."

Bonnie put her phone back in her pocket. She turned and walked back to her car. Rolly took a step forward.

"Are you going to let Moogus go?"

"I'll consider it."

"He's my ride home."

"I'll consider it."

Bonnie opened the back door of the patrol car. She said something to Moogus, but Rolly couldn't hear what it was. Moogus nodded a couple of times, then Bonnie stood to the side and Moogus stepped out. He walked back to Rolly. Bonnie got in her car and drove off.

"God dammit," said Moogus. "Bitch got me by the short hairs."

"You'll survive."

"Nothing's changed since we lived here. Cops still roust Obceans with impunity."

"You're not an Obcean anymore, remember?"

"You remember the riot in the park, when that cop gave me a stick upside the head?"

"Everybody remembers the riot."

"I got laid twice that day. Two different girls."

"So police brutality was good for your sex life?"

"It was the day I learned how to play the sympathy card."

Rolly shook his head.

"It drives you crazy, doesn't it?"

"What?"

"With Bonnie. None of your shit works, does it? You're frustrated as hell. She won't even smile at you."

"Yeah, well, that bitch is barely female, if you ask me. Let's get out of here."

They walked up the street, crossed over to Moogus's truck and climbed in. Moogus drove down to the beach and they cruised along next to the boardwalk.

"What did Bonnie the Copper want to talk to you about, anyway?" said Moogus.

"She wants me to look at some boat with her tomorrow. Oh shit."

"What?"

"I forgot. I'm supposed to have breakfast with my dad in the morning."

"Take him along," said Moogus. "Maybe you'll get lucky and that bitch will arrest his ass."

"Yeah," said Rolly. "I guess that's a possibility."

"I hope it's okay," Moogus said. "Me not telling you about Matty and Janis before."

"You really think Matt was going to marry her?" said Rolly.

"Janis thought so."

"You think maybe she was pregnant?"

"Hell, how would I know? Everything got weird after you moved out. Matt resented it when you had somewhere you could go, someone outside of the band. He'd lost control of the situation. He thought Leslie was our Yoko or something. People always said you were the talent. You never realized how jealous that made him."

Rolly looked over at Moogus.

"When did you become Dr. Freud?"

Moogus chuckled.

"Like I said. I'm an adult now. I understand some things better."

They stopped at the red light on Sunset Cliffs Boulevard. Rolly turned his head and looked out the window. There was a church on the corner, with a steep roof and a steeple. He didn't know what kind of church it was. He didn't remember the church, but it looked like it had been there a long time. He stared up at the red light.

"Do you think Matt hated me?"

"Matt hated everyone and everything," said Moogus. "Like I said, he was our asshole."

The traffic light changed to green. Moogus turned left onto Sunset Cliffs Boulevard. They headed away from Ocean Beach, leaving the ghosts of the War Zone behind.

# 5

# THE BOAT

"Who's this woman we have to see?" said Dean Waters as Rolly pulled into the parking lot near Driscoll's Wharf.

"You don't have to see her," said Rolly. "I do."

"Is she one of your lady friends?"

"No. She's a detective with the San Diego Police Department."

"Are you in some kind of trouble with the cops?"

"Only if I don't look at this boat with her."

"What kind of boat is it?"

"A sailboat."

"What kind of sailboat? A sloop? A cutter? A ketch?"

"I don't know. This won't take long. You can stay in the car."

"I'm your father, not your damn dog."

Rolly found a parking spot and pulled in. So far the morning had been a disaster. He'd overslept, which made him late getting to his father's house, and now he was late meeting Bonnie. He cut the ignition and turned to his father. They hadn't had breakfast yet and it was making them both cranky. Like father, like son.

"No, Dad. You're not my dog. I just meant you could stay in the car if you wanted. This shouldn't take long."

"Great. I'll go with you."

"It'd be easier if you didn't."

"This is your work, right? I want to see what my son does for a living. Is she good looking? I like a woman in uniform."

Rolly stared out the front windshield. He didn't want to quarrel with his father. He always lost the argument, one way or another.

"Maybe I can help," said his father. "I know more about boats than you do."

"I don't need to know anything about boats. She wants me to look at the guy's personal effects."

"The way a man keeps his boat can tell you a lot about his state of mind."

Rolly rubbed his forehead.

"Okay, okay," he said, "Just don't get cute with Bonnie. Don't antagonize her."

"I know these women playing around in a man's job. They're not so tough."

Rolly cleared his throat.

"This is my work, Dad. It's professional. All I'm asking is that you try to restrain yourself."

Dean Waters stared at Rolly, sizing up his son's resolve with blood-shot eyes, the visible manifestation of the intemperate seas he continued to sail.

"I get it," he said. "It's your job. I'll put on my duty face."

"Thank you," said Rolly.

They climbed out of Rolly's Volvo and followed the sidewalk along the eastern edge of the marina, passing two men who were pushing a large wagon filled with fish, hauling freshly caught albacore, yellowfin and corbina to the parking lot where a crowd of sport-fishermen stood waiting to claim their catch.

A row of run-down warehouses crowded the end of the marina like a herd of shabby old elephants—peeling gray paint, rust-spotted doors, and cataract-clouded windows. The railings on the seaward side of the boardwalk had rusted through as well, exposing jagged points of corroded metal. There was a large sign on one of the buildings: OTTER.

"Did I tell you I got my own boat?" Rolly's father said as they passed the first of three locked gates that led down to the boats in the marina.

"You said you were thinking about it," said Rolly.

"I sold the Tioga and picked up an old Chris-Craft. Twenty-two feet. I don't know what I was thinking buying that damn RV. I'm a Navy man. I need salt air in my face, not air-conditioning."

"How does Alicia feel about the boat?"

"She likes it better than the Tioga, except the wind messes up her hairdo. We should all go out sometime. Bring your girlfriend along."

"I'm not really seeing anyone now," said Rolly.

"What happened to that little Macy girl? She was a pistol."

"Too big an age difference."

"You having man troubles?"

"What?"

"You're older now, you got some weight on you, maybe things aren't functioning like they used to. You know, droopiness. A woman her age and temperament has pretty strong needs."

"Everything is functioning just fine," said Rolly. "That wasn't an issue."

"I'm not above telling you that little blue pill made a difference for your stepmother and me. I had to take a break for a while, because of the heart attack, but the doctor cleared me last week. I'm back in the saddle again."

"Can we just drop the subject?" said Rolly. He spotted Bonnie ahead, standing outside the second security gate. She was dressed in plain clothes—a white shirt, khaki pants and a dark green jacket.

"Sorry I'm late," he said when they arrived at the gate. "I had to pick up my dad."

"Captain Dean Waters," said Rolly's father, extending his hand to Bonnie. "United States Navy, retired."

"Pleasure to meet you, sir," said Bonnie, returning the handshake. "Detective Bonnie Hammond, San Diego Police Department. Active duty."

Bonnie turned to the gate and pressed four numbers on the security keypad. The latch clicked. She opened the gate.

"Dad knows a lot about boats," said Rolly as they walked down the gangplank. "He thought he could help us."

"Twenty-eight years in the Navy," said Dean Waters. "I can tell the cut of a man's jib by the set of his trim."

"Appreciate the offer," said Bonnie. "I'm not much of a sailor, myself."

They continued along the pier until they came to a decrepit-looking sailboat with yellow crime tape stretched along one side.

"Thirty-footer?" said Rolly's father.

"Thirty-five," said Bonnie. She lifted the tape. Rolly and his father stepped on board.

"Hey," someone shouted. "You can't go on there."

Rolly saw a man two berths down, standing on the dock with his hands on his hips. Bonnie pulled out her badge as the man approached them.

"San Diego Police," she said, holding out the badge for his perusal.

"Oh," said the man. "Harbor Police put that tape there. Did something happen to Dan?"

"Do you know Mr. Piper?" said Bonnie.

"Everybody knows Dan around here," said the man. "He's like the mayor of the marina."

"When was the last time you saw him?" said Bonnie.

"A month ago, before our trip. We only got back from Baja last week. The wife and me. Sailed down to La Paz."

"Uh-huh," said Bonnie. She pulled a card from her pocket, handed it to the man. "If you see Mr. Piper around, or talk to someone who has, please contact me."

"There were some guys here a couple of days ago, with the Harbor Police. Guys in suits."

"There are several agencies involved in the search for Mr. Piper."

"Geez, what'd he do?" said the man. He laughed. "Don't tell me the Harbor Police are finally going to nail him for living on board?"

"Just give me a call if you see him," said Bonnie.

"I'll do that, Officer," said the man. "Everybody likes Dan. He's the soundtrack for this place, playing for everybody. It sounds kind of lonesome sometimes, the way he plays that harmonica, but I enjoy hearing him."

The man stood looking at them, as if expecting a response. When none came, he turned and walked back to his berth. Bonnie joined Rolly and his father on the deck of the boat.

"Mr. Waters—*Captain* Waters," she said. "You can look over the deck. Let me know if you see anything that seems unusual. Your son and I will be in the cabin going through Mr. Piper's personal effects."

"Aye, aye, ma'am," said Rolly's father and he fell to his task. Rolly followed Bonnie into the cabin. She flipped on a light, illuminating the cabin.

"What is it you want me to look for?" said Rolly, surveying the cramped quarters. The interior of the cabin was far from shipshape. Charts and papers were spread out on the table, anchored in place with cans of soup and packets of ramen. Old magazines were stacked on the seats—*Yoga Journal, Sailing* and *Blues Blaster.*

"All his music stuff's back here," said Bonnie, leading Rolly through the tight hallway into the bedroom. Cabinets and drawers had been built into all four sides of the room.

"That's his harmonica case," said Rolly, identifying the leather box sitting on top of the bed. He leaned over and flipped the latch on the case. There were two rows of harmonicas inside, nestled in a dozen felt slots. "There's one missing."

"What's that?" said Bonnie.

"One of his harmonicas is missing."

"Okay. What else?"

Rolly picked up a scrap of paper that sat in the missing harmonica's slot. It had a single name written on it, an unusual name that set off alarms in his head. The dolphin king, the name Janis had given Butch Fleetwood.

"Arion," he said, reading the block letters.

"Yeah," said Bonnie. "Does that mean something to you?"

"Should it?" he said, volleying back with his own question. He needed a moment to compose himself. Was the name just a coincidence or were he and Bonnie working two sides of the same case? Did Janis Withers have some connection to Harmonica Dan?

"I don't know," said Bonnie. "The FBI got their undies all in a pinch when they saw it."

"The FBI?" said Rolly, feeling the acid rise in his stomach. Men in suits had been to Melody's temple along with the police. One note didn't sound like much by itself. Now there were chords to go with it. "You didn't tell me the FBI was looking for Dan."

"Didn't I?" said Bonnie. "Sorry. Captain's on my ass about this case, wants me to get out ahead of them—you know how that gets. It's kind of a clusterfuck. I needed a different approach. I was hoping it might start with you. Does that Arion thing mean something to you?"

Rolly didn't want to tell Bonnie anything. She'd sandbagged him with the FBI information and it ticked him off. Melody might not be paying him for his work, but she was still his client. He'd keep her information confidential, at least for now.

"Arion starts with an *A*," he said.

"So?" said Bonnie, putting her hands on her hips.

"It's the A harmonica that's missing," said Rolly. He pointed at the harmonica case. "Key of A. There's twelve harmonicas in the set, one in each key. You see—G, then G sharp, and then the A slot is empty. That's where the note was."

"You think that means something?"

"I'm just mentioning stuff that I notice, like you asked me to."

Rolly put the note back in the slot and closed the harmonica case. He took a stack of CDs out of one of the cabinets and scanned through them while Bonnie made notes in her book. The CDs were exactly the kind he expected to find in Harmonica Dan's collection—Little Walter, Paul Butterfield, both Sonny Boy Williamsons. Harmonica-playing bluesmen. The last CD in the stack was different. It wasn't a blues album.

*Gobfish* was the title of the CD, by a band named Rude Abortion. A close-up of the band's singer adorned the cover, the windscreen of a Shure SM58 microphone jammed hard against his gaping lips. A large blob of drool hung from the corner of the singer's mouth. Rolly opened the CD case. An inscription had been scrawled on the inside cover in broad silver ink.

"'To Harmonica Dan,'" he said, reading the inscription out loud. "'Thanks for the blow job. We're all headfucked. XOXO. Dick Nazi.'"

"Dick Nazi?" said Bonnie. "That's some guy's name?"

"These guys are local," Rolly said. "Surf punks."

He pulled his reading glasses out of his coat pocket and looked through the credits listed in small print.

"It looks like Dan played harmonica on one of the songs. That's probably the blow job this Nazi guy's referring to. Musician humor."

"Cute," said Bonnie. "I assume that's some sort of stage name, Dick Nazi?"

"Sure. Like Jello Biafra or Johnny Rotten."

"You know this guy?"

"No."

"You know how I can get in touch with him?"

"Sideman's listed on the credits. You could ask him."

"Who?"

"J.V. Sideman. He's a saxophone player I know. Moogus is playing with him on Saturday."

Bonnie flipped through the pages of her notebook, looking for something.

"John V. Sideman?" she said.

"Yeah, that's him. Why?"

"I talked to him already. He's on my list."

# 6

# THE CUTOUT

"What's J.V. got to do with this?" said Rolly. "Why'd you interview him?"

Bonnie tilted her head, giving Rolly a look.

"Your friend Sideman performed at the location where the disturbance took place. Mr. Sideman claims to have talked to Daniel Piper shortly after the incident. No one else remembers seeing Mr. Piper and no one's seen him since."

"What exactly is this incident you're referring to? What happened?"

Bonnie looked at her notebook again, buying time, which meant she had to think before giving him an answer. Rolly waited. She looked back at him.

"You hear about that thing at the Admiral's Club, on the Navy base?"

"I think I heard something," said Rolly. There'd been a report on the TV a couple of days ago, but he was practicing his guitar while he watched, with the audio muted. "There was a fire."

"Somebody ran into the place with a boat. It wasn't an accident."

An attack on government property. That explained why the FBI was involved. It didn't explain why they'd shown up at the Lemurian Temple and gone through the closets, though.

"Who else did you talk to?" said Rolly. Had Bonnie interviewed Melody? Was there anyone else he knew on her list?

"Not important," said Bonnie. "I just need you to look at this stuff, tell me everything you can about Daniel Piper."

Rolly's father stuck his head inside the room.

"How's it look up there, Captain?" said Bonnie.

"Topside is shipshape," he said. "Couldn't keep it better myself. It's an old boat, but everything's tied down neat as a whistle. Can't say the same for what I'm seeing here in the cabin."

"It was neater before the FBI started pulling stuff out of the cabinets," said Bonnie.

"FBI?" said Rolly's father. He looked over at Rolly. "Sounds like you've stepped in some serious shit, son."

"I hope not," said Rolly, knowing he had. "Bonnie's the one who deals with the Feds."

"I did find something unusual up top," said Rolly's father.

"What is it?" said Bonnie.

"There's a cutout in the stern. And some kind of underwater speaker."

Bonnie looked over at Rolly. He shrugged. They followed Rolly's father out of the bedroom and into the main cabin. He stopped and looked at the nautical charts on the kitchen table.

"What's up, Dad?" said Rolly.

"We used to go down there sometimes," said Rolly's father, pointing at the map. "The Coronado Islands. We cruised the whole coast of Baja one time. Your mother and me in a thirty-foot sloop. That was before you came along."

"Sounds . . . adventurous," said Rolly.

"It was. Those were the good times."

"There was something you wanted to show us on deck?" said Bonnie.

"Yeah," said Rolly's father. "This way."

They climbed out of the cabin and onto the deck. A light breeze fluttered through the rigging as they made their way to the rear of the boat.

"You see that?" said Rolly's father, pointing toward the back end of the boat.

"What is it?" asked Rolly, hoping for further elucidation.

"That line there, the curvy line in the stern that runs from the top edge down to the deck?"

"Uh-huh," said Rolly.

"It's a cutout. Kind of unusual on a boat like this."

"What's it for?" said Bonnie.

"The whole thing lifts out, along with the rudder. Leaves a big gap in the stern so the end of the boat is just above waterline. Not a standard feature since you generally want to keep water out of a boat. The guy must've added it later."

"What's it for?" Bonnie repeated.

"I don't know exactly. It would make for easier access to and from the water, I guess. A diver might use it. Or if you were hauling something in and out of the water. That's not the weirdest thing, though. Look at this."

Rolly's father pointed at a box sitting on the deck.

"I think this is some kind of waterproof speaker," he said. "It's got a line attached so you can lower it into the water."

"What's that for?" asked Bonnie.

"Your guess is as good as mine. You see that plug there, in the wall?"

"It looks like an XLR connecter," said Rolly. "For a microphone."

"Exactamundo, son. That's what I think it is too."

"You think he's broadcasting under the water?"

"It could be a hydrophone, I suppose."

"What's a hydrophone?" Bonnie asked.

"It's a special microphone that allows you to listen underwater."

"Like sonar?"

"Sonar is for echolocation. A hydrophone just listens for whatever sounds are in the water. I suppose this guy could be broadcasting and listening at the same time if he hooked it up right."

Bonnie and Rolly looked at each other, as if checking the other's understanding of what Dean Waters was saying. Rolly still wasn't sure.

"So it's like an underwater telephone?" he said, turning back to his father.

"Yeah. Exactly. You'd have to have somebody smarter than me look at the electronics in that box to tell you for sure."

"Who would he be talking to?" said Rolly. "Scuba divers?"

His father shrugged.

"I don't think so. Unless they're using some sort of special high-frequency signals. Human voices don't travel well in the water. The sound would have to be higher pitched."

"What about dolphins?" said Bonnie.

Rolly's father pressed his lips together, looking thoughtful.

"Could be," he said. "Dolphins hear better than humans, especially underwater. Is this guy a marine biologist or something?"

"Not that I know of," said Bonnie.

"What made you ask about dolphins?" said Rolly. Twice in the last twelve hours someone had brought up dolphins. It was an odd coincidence, to say the least.

"Hold on a minute," said Rolly's father. "Does this guy have something to do with that thing at the Admiral's Club?"

Bonnie looked unfazed, but Rolly was taken aback at his father's deduction.

"Holy shit, Dad," said Rolly. "How'd you figure that out?"

"FBI. Dolphins."

"I don't get the connection."

"The party they crashed at the Admiral's Club. It was the Dolphin Divers."

"Where'd you hear that, Mr. Waters?" said Bonnie.

"I hang around with a bunch of ex-Navy guys," he said. "You hear things sometimes. Is that why the FBI's looking for this guy?"

"I can't talk about the FBI's case," said Bonnie. "I'm doing my own due diligence here. Mr. Piper has been reported missing and I'm looking for him. Since your son knows Mr. Piper, I thought he could be of some help to me."

"Was he?"

"Your son has been very cooperative."

Bonnie pulled out her notebook again and jotted some notes. Another sport-fishing boat pulled into the docks. A crowd had gathered near the parking lot where the crew would unload their catch. Rolly's stomach growled. He hadn't eaten anything since the carne asada last night.

"Are we done?" he said. Bonnie looked up from her notebook.

"For now," she said. "Thanks for your help. Both of you. Nice meeting you, Captain."

She nodded and returned to her notebook. Rolly and his father exchanged glances, then walked to the side of the boat and stepped onto the dock.

"Captain Waters?" said Bonnie, still scribbling.

"Yes?"

"Can I get your phone number?" said Bonnie. "I might need to talk to you later."

"Sure." He recited his number for Bonnie. She thanked them again. Rolly and his father walked back to the wharf.

"I guess your old man's still got it," said Rolly's father.

"Don't flatter yourself. Bonnie's going to run your name through every database she's got when she gets back to her office. You just made yourself a person of interest."

"Guess I caught her attention, then, didn't I?"

"I'm not joking. She almost threw Moogus in jail last night."

"Good for her. That dope should be in the hoosegow. You think she knows I'm married?"

"I expect so. You're wearing a ring."

"She's better looking than I expected. Tight and athletic. I'll bet she's ferocious in the sack."

"Stop it."

They opened the gate, turned and headed toward the parking lot.

"Of course, any woman younger than forty looks ferocious to me," said Rolly's father.

"Can we change the subject?" said Rolly.

"You jealous?"

"I just don't like to hear you talking like this. It's rude to Alicia."

"Just because I ordered already don't mean I can't browse the menu."

"Some things aren't on the menu."

"What do you mean?"

"Bonnie isn't interested in you, or me. She likes girls."

"Really?" said his father.

"Really. She's in a committed relationship."

"With a woman?"

"Yes."

They continued down the sidewalk, past the rockfish and yellowfin that had been laid out on the concrete sidewalk, past the crowd of buyers and fishermen and casual onlookers perusing the day's catch. They climbed into the Volvo. Rolly put the key in the ignition and fastened his seat belt. His father stared out the front window, watching the fishermen lay out their catch.

"How do two women get it on, anyway?" he said. "I mean, I understand some of it, but how do they replace the schtupping part?"

"I wouldn't know, Dad," said Rolly. "I guess you could look it up on the Internet."

"Yeah. Maybe I'll do that."

Rolly closed his eyes and leaned his head back against the headrest.

"Put on your seat belt," he said.

"Yeah, yeah," said his father, attaching the buckle. "You sure are cranky today. Are you feeling okay?"

"I'm just tired. We had a gig last night. I was out late. I got up late. Where do you want to get lunch?"

"How about the Shack?"

"That'll work," Rolly said. He put the car into gear and pulled out of the parking lot.

"Maybe we should check out the Admiral's Club afterwards," said his father.

"I thought it was closed, because of the fire."

"It's just the kitchen that's closed. I was thinking we might want to follow up on our investigation."

"It's not our investigation. It's Bonnie's. And the FBI's."

"I thought we did a pretty good job back there, the two of us, working together. Maybe we can help these folks out."

"I doubt the FBI needs our help."

"Doesn't mean you can't offer to help. You're a private investigator, right? That's what you do for a living?"

"Half a living," said Rolly. FBI work was above his pay grade. They dealt with killers and kidnappers and high-level white-collar crooks while he chased after lowly scofflaws, liars and cheats. He'd put himself in peril more than once when his cases crossed paths with the police. Working with the FBI sounded even more dangerous and up-tempo. He preferred cruising the slower lanes of human trespass—tracking down runaways, insurance swindlers and two-timing creeps. It's what PIs did. He was okay with it.

"I bet you'd be good at undercover work," said his father.

"What do you know about undercover work?"

"Nothing. I just think you'd be good at it. You've got street cred."

Rolly chuckled.

"I think you've been watching too many TV shows."

"There's been a terrorist attack on the Navy base in your hometown and you won't offer assistance? Is that what you're telling me?"

"Hang on, hang on. Who said anything about a terrorist attack?"

"That's the scuttlebutt I've been hearing."

"Where does this scuttlebutt come from? Your drinking buddies?"

"I know a guy who knows a guy used to work in NCIS. He told me the FBI is looking into the terrorism angle. That woman on the boat was connected to one of these eco-terrorist groups."

A thought flickered in Rolly's brain, like fluorescent lights blinking on, not yet fully illuminating his consciousness.

"It was a woman?" he said.

"Yeah, this chick blows through one of those picture windows in her boat, then pulls out a can of gasoline and sets herself, and the rest of the place, on fire. That's why they're calling it a suicide attack."

"What was the woman's name?"

"They haven't released that information yet."

"But it was a woman? You're sure of that?"

"That's what I heard. Ask your policewoman friend. She could tell you."

"Janis Withers," said Rolly. The connection had been there, at the back of his brain, but he'd been resisting it. What had happened to Janis to make her do something like that?

"What's that?" said his father.

"I think I know who it was." Rolly rubbed his stomach, trying to fend off the acidic buildup. "I wish I didn't."

"You want to go back and talk to your cop friend?"

"I'll call her later," said Rolly. He turned the key in the ignition and started the car. "Let's get some breakfast."

7
_____

# THE SHACK

A great white shark blasted through the ceiling of the Seaman's Shack, threatening the restaurant's patrons with its gaping mouth and dead black eyes. The shark had loomed over the room for the last forty years, which explained why no one paid much attention to it. A baby doll in powder-blue pajamas hung from the shark's lower jaw, its pajama belt snagged on one of the shark's razor teeth. A fluffy pink rabbit had been stuffed into the back of the shark's mouth. One floppy rabbit ear dangled from the corner of the shark's mouth like a cigarette.

The rest of the restaurant was decorated in various forms of nautical effluvia—ropes, nets, brass fittings and deck pins. A large wooden ship's wheel separated the dining area from the lounge. It was the kind of place where you could still get a glass of beer and a plate of eggs, bacon, biscuits and gravy for less than a ten-spot. Navy officers and enlisted men, commercial fishermen, sailing enthusiasts and powerboat owners were all regular customers, people who spent time on the water. Old-timers referred to the place as the Semen Shack. The bar's reputation as a hookup location for bayside singles had waned over the years, but the nickname had stuck.

"We could eat at the bar," said Dean Waters, indicating the lounge area.

"It's nice out," said Rolly. "Let's eat on the patio."

This was how it always went at their breakfasts, the old man angling for his first drink, Rolly strategically guiding him away from it, staving off the inevitable. Even in his most dissolute years, Rolly had never been able to match his old man's dedication to alcohol.

Rolly guided his father to the back patio. It was empty. He grabbed two menus from the stack by the door and headed for a table near the patio exit. With planning, and a little luck, they might avoid an encounter with one of his father's lubricated acquaintances. Rolly took a seat, with his back to the exit. His father slumped into the chair across the table. The old man had dropped twenty pounds since the heart attack six months ago. His jowls sagged and his eyes had gone rheumy, but there was still a ruddy energy in his bearing. He looked like an old prizefighter, beaten down but still not to be fucked with.

A waitress came out to take their order. Rolly ordered bacon and eggs. His father ordered a Denver omelet because it had vegetables.

"Can I get a beer with that?" he said.

"Dad," said Rolly.

"What kind of beer?" said the waitress. "We've got Ballast Point Sculpin on special today."

"None of that weird homemade stuff," said Rolly's father. "Just a Bud." He looked over at Rolly. "That okay with you? If I have one Budweiser?"

"You're not supposed to drink this early in the day."

"This is my son," his father said to the waitress. "He's supposed to keep an eye on me, make sure I don't enjoy myself. Whattya think about that?"

The waitress looked over at Rolly, then back at his father.

"I think it's nice you have a son that cares about your health," she said.

"I think he needs a girlfriend," said Rolly's father. "You single?"

"You'll have to excuse my father," said Rolly. "He likes to embarrass me." The waitress was attractive, at least ten years younger than he was. He'd sworn off picking up waitresses a long time ago.

"Hey," said his father. "I care about you too, son. You can't catch a fish if you don't throw out some bait."

"You can't catch a woman if you think she's a fish, either," said the waitress.

Rolly glanced up at the waitress. She winked at him.

"You may bring my father a Budweiser," he said. "But only one."

"You want anything to drink?" she said.

"Just coffee for me. Thanks."

Rolly smiled at the waitress. The waitress smiled back. She turned away. Rolly watched her walk back into the restaurant. Ten years' difference wasn't that much. She wasn't wearing a ring. It was a relief to think about something besides suicide and terrorist attacks.

"Only one beer," said Rolly, turning back to his father. "Or I tell Alicia and she keeps the cabinet locked the rest of the day."

"Is my babysitter going to squeal to my nanny?"

"Let's try to enjoy our breakfast. What's new with you?"

"Same old, same old. Sitting around the house, taking a walk every day, following doctor's orders and taking my pills. Your stepmother's teaching me how to knit."

Rolly pictured his father sitting on the couch with knitting needles and a ball of yarn. He stifled a laugh.

"She's got this new project," his father continued. "Knitting wool beanies for Navy sailors, some kind of charity she joined. She gives them away."

"Sounds like a nice thing to do."

"The woman drives me crazy."

"You're lucky to have her. Lucky she puts up with you."

Rolly turned his head and looked through the scratched Plexiglas window that formed the top half of the wall separating the patio from the alley behind the restaurant. A long-haired blond girl passed by, riding a bicycle. He thought of Melody. How was she involved in all this?

"She's a good woman, Alicia," said his father. "Your mother's a good woman too, in her way."

Rolly sat back in his seat. He couldn't remember the last time his father had said anything nice about his first wife, Rolly's mother. He adjusted his chair, making sure the earth hadn't moved.

"Sounds like you've been doing some thinking," he said.

"Bah," said his father. "I'm not saying things could have worked out between me and your mom. All that hocus-pocus she's into. But we had some good times together."

"You've both mellowed," said Rolly. "A little bit, anyway."

His father laughed.

"I can't argue with that. We were young and crazy kids, the two of us, when we got married. Hot as napalm torpedoes."

The waitress returned with their drinks. Rolly took a sip of coffee, then reached for the cream and sugar. By the time he'd finished stirring, his father had downed half his beer. Rolly pulled out the dog tags from his pocket and placed them on the table. He'd promised Melody this much. She only had a week until Janis's mother threw her out of the house. He needed to get back to her soon. Butch Fleetwood had some connection to dolphins and the Navy. He'd get what information he could and get out. If something problematic turned up, he'd pass the whole thing over to Bonnie.

"What're those?" said his father.

"Dog tags."

"I know they're dog tags. Why are you showing them to me?"

"I got hired to look for a guy. I thought you could help me."

His father picked up the tags.

"Butch Fleetwood," he said, reading them. "Navy man."

"Right. USN. That's his social security number below it, right?"

"Yep."

"I wasn't sure about the rest."

"Blood type and religion. This guy is an A-positive atheist."

"That's what 'none' means at the bottom?"

"Yeah. Or he never bothered to tell them his religion."

"Is there anything I can do to find out more about the guy? Are there records somewhere?"

"National Archives has the records, but only through Dubya-Dubya Two. You have to go directly through the Navy if you want to pull a more recent DD214."

"What's that?"

"Service record. All veterans receive one when they separate from the service. You think this guy's living or dead?"

"Haven't had a chance to find out yet. I'll run his social later today."

"You can do that?"

"Sure. I can find out if the social security number's legitimate, if the name matches. I can see current and former addresses, criminal records, anything that's in the public record. Anybody can do it, if you pay for the service."

A light breeze stirred the leaves of the potted plants that stood in one corner of the patio. The waitress stepped through the door and asked if they needed anything. Rolly waved her off.

"If you don't mind my asking," said his father, "what do people need you for?"

"Records aren't always accurate," said Rolly. "Sometimes you have to knock on some doors, make a few calls, before you actually find the guy."

"So you're boots on the ground."

"Yep. Boots on the ground. That's what I get paid for."

"Like I said. You got street cred. How much do you get paid for this kind of work?"

"Nothing on this one. I owe somebody."

Rolly thought about Janis again, and what he might owe her. If she'd married Matt, maybe she wouldn't have killed herself. Or, being married to Matt, she might've killed herself sooner.

"What about helping your cop friend on the boat?" said his father. "Do the police pay you some kind of consulting fee?"

"That was a favor, too. Bonnie and I have a reciprocal arrangement."

"What's she do for you?"

"Mostly she doesn't arrest me," said Rolly, which was true. Bonnie had threatened him more than once and hauled him into the station a couple of times for questioning, but never officially charged him for anything. If it got to that point, he usually told her everything she wanted to know. That was their unofficial arrangement. It had worked so far.

"You sure do people a lot of favors," said Rolly's father.

"Yeah. I do."

"Who gave you these?" said his father, twirling the dog tags in his hand.

"My client."

"I know that. Is your client related to the guy on the tags?"

"No. I don't think so. Why?"

"You're supposed to give these tags back to the government. If you're not family."

"I'll let her know."

"Is she good looking?" said his father.

"That's not why I'm doing the favor. She's a friend of an old friend of mine, a friend of my old band, the Creatures, the woman who ran our fan club."

"You had a fan club?"

"The band did."

"I didn't know that."

"You never came to any of our gigs."

"I was gone a lot."

"You could have come later, after you started the desk job."

"That was after the divorce. Didn't want to run into your mother."

Rolly nodded. He wasn't going to get in an argument about the past. Bygones were excuses masquerading as reasons. He didn't want to tell his father any more about Janis, either. His father would press him for more information. He didn't have any.

"Anyway," he said. "My client wants to get in touch with this Fleetwood guy."

The waitress returned with their breakfast. The two men fell silent as they got down to the business of eating. Rolly picked up a piece of toast and stabbed the corner into one of his egg yolks.

"What're you looking at, buddy?" said his father.

Rolly looked across the table. His father was glaring past him at something out in the alley. Rolly turned and looked over his shoulder. A gaunt man with a salt-and-pepper beard stared back at them through the Plexiglas screen. The man wore a Greek fisherman's hat and a navy-blue overcoat. There were ribbons on the breast of the coat, gold epaulets on the shoulders.

"You got some kind of a problem, you bum?" said Rolly's father.

"Harmonica Dan?" said Rolly.

The man blinked, then turned his head and pedaled away on a bicycle. Rolly jumped from his seat and rushed to the exit. He pushed open the gate as the man on the bicycle disappeared around the corner. Rolly ran down the alley to the street. He stopped, looked left and right, but there was no sign of the man. He considered running back to his car, setting out in pursuit, but the man could have traveled in any direction. He walked back to the patio and sat down at the table across from his father.

"What the hell was that all about?" said his father.

Rolly pulled out his phone and tapped Bonnie's number.

"That was the guy from the boat, the guy the police are looking for. Harmonica Dan. Daniel Piper."

"No shit," said his father.

"What color was his bicycle?" said Rolly. "Did you notice?"

"Why the hell would I be looking at what color his bicycle was? Wait. It was green. Kind of a metallic green."

"Did you notice anything else about him?"

"He had Navy patches on his jacket, with all that other crap. Lieutenant's bars, I think. There was a diver's badge, too. I used to know all this stuff. What are you doing?"

"Calling the police," Rolly said. Bonnie's voice mail came on. He left her a message, telling her his location and how he'd seen someone who looked like Harmonica Dan. He described the man's clothing and the bicycle. He disconnected his phone and placed it on the table.

"You sure it was him?" said his father.

"Pretty sure. I haven't seen the guy in fifteen years, though."

"Ask the waitress when she comes back."

"Ask her what?"

"Maybe the guy's been in the alley before, Dumpster diving."

Rolly nodded. The waitress arrived and poured him some coffee. He described the man they had seen. The waitress thought she'd seen him before, but she had little to offer beyond that. She didn't know the man's name.

They finished their meal. Rolly paid the check and walked his father out the back exit so they could avoid passing by the bar. In the parking lot, he found a flyer on his old Volvo's windshield, stuck under the driver-side wiper blade. Rolly lifted the blade and removed the paper. It wasn't an advertising flyer like he'd assumed. It was the front page of the *OB Enquirer*, an alternative political weekly published in Ocean Beach. The headline at the top of the left column caught his eye.

"You feeling okay?" said his father. "You look like you might chunder."

Rolly read the headline again. He read it out loud so his father could hear it, so his own ears could hear what he was reading.

*Who Killed Butch Fleetwood?*

# 8

## THE CLUB

Rolly and his father entered the lobby of the Admiral's Club on the Naval Base in Point Loma. There were no signs of fire damage in the lobby of the club, no smoking timbers or charred walls. A fake Christmas tree had been installed near the door, but there were no lights on it yet. A small man in a dark blue suit walked over to greet the two men.

"Captain Waters," he said. "And Mr. Waters. It's nice to see you."

"Thank you, Alphonso," said Rolly's father.

"I must tell you the kitchen is closed, because of the fire."

"We heard," said Rolly's father. "We just wanted to stop by, take a look at the damage."

"The lounge is still open, of course. You may have a drink if you wish."

"As long as there's grog, this sailor's happy," said Rolly's father.

"Yes, indeed," said Alphonso. "There are bar snacks—nuts and chips—and some pre-made sandwiches if you require something more substantial."

"Can we look at the ballroom?" said Rolly.

"There's not much to look at," said Alphonso, "between the fire and the water damage. I'm not supposed to let people in."

"This is an official investigation," said Rolly's father. "My son is working as a consultant to the San Diego Police Department. Give him one of your cards, son."

Rolly pulled out his wallet and handed Alphonso a business card.

"See? He's legit," said his father. "Check with the police if you want." He turned back to Rolly. "What was the name of that detective friend of yours I just met?"

"Bonnie Hammond," said Rolly.

"Yeah, Bonnie. Short, blond hair. Lean and mean looking."

"Yes," said Alphonso. "I think I've met her."

"My son's working with Detective Hammond on this."

"I suppose it's all right," said Alphonso, taking Rolly's father at his word or, at least, not wanting to argue with him. "Anything I can do to help. Follow me."

The diminutive maître d' escorted them to the center doorway of the ballroom. They stepped inside and surveyed the scene. The right side of the room was black and burned. There was a hole in the roof where charcoaled stubs of timber poked through. The picture window on the right side of the room had been shattered. A large plastic sheet had been tacked to the window frame to keep out seagulls and weather.

"The kitchen is an even bigger disaster, I'm afraid," said Alphonso. "I don't know when we'll be open again. We're just thankful no was killed. Except for that unfortunate woman on the boat, of course."

"Did you know anyone at the party?" asked Rolly. Alphonso had been at the club for as long as he could remember.

"Not really. No one I can recall. It was those dolphin people. They had a lovely ice sculpture of two dolphins and a scuba diver set up at the seafood station. They even had caviar. We had to throw all the food away, I'm afraid."

"Our tax dollars at work," said Rolly's father.

"Oh no," said Alphonso. "Tidewater footed the bill for the whole thing."

"Who's Tidewater?" asked Rolly.

"A defense contractor. They do a lot of business with the Navy. This was a farewell party. The dolphin program's been downsized, I guess. The Navy's getting rid of them."

"The dolphins? Where are they going?"

"I don't know the details. You'd have to ask someone in the program."

"How do I get in touch with them?"

"The holding pens are just down the road, as you approach the Harbor Drive bridge. There's always someone working there."

"Is the head still functional?" asked Rolly's father.

"Oh, yes," said Alphonso. "The bathrooms are open."

"That's the problem with drinking beer in the morning," said Rolly's father. "You gotta drain your lizard the rest of the day."

Dean Waters excused himself and left the room. Rolly turned back to Alphonso.

"Do you know J.V. Sideman?" he said.

"Who?"

"He plays the saxophone. He played with the band at the party."

"Oh yes, I think I know who you mean. I've seen him here on several occasions. He gets around."

"Yeah, he does pretty well for himself. How about Daniel Piper? Harmonica Dan?"

"Is that someone in the band?"

"Long hair, beard, might have been wearing a navy-blue overcoat with gold epaulets."

"I don't remember anyone like that," said Alphonso. "Once the guests were evacuated from the ballroom, I had to focus on the kitchen. I wanted to make sure all our staff got out safely."

"Have you ever heard of a man named Butch Fleetwood?"

Alphonso looked thoughtful for a moment.

"No," he said. "I don't think so. I have a list of the party guests on my computer. Would you like a copy?"

"I'd appreciate that."

Alphonso toddled off to his office. Rolly walked across the floor, stepped onto the bandstand and stared out the window. On the far side of the bay a cargo plane lumbered into the air from the Naval Air

Station North Island. He thought about the headline from the *OB Enquirer,* "Who Killed Butch Fleetwood?"

The article was a reprint from the paper's archives, originally published twenty-three years ago. Last week's edition of the paper had carried the reprint. It was the story of Butch Fleetwood, an Ocean Beach surfer, hustler and beach rat, an athletic young man who could swim farther and faster than anyone else on the beach. In his late teens, Fleetwood had joined the US Navy. After basic training, he'd been assigned to the dolphin team, but disappeared during a training exercise off Ballast Point, near the entrance to the bay. His body had never been found. There was more to the article, but whoever had placed the newspaper on Rolly's windshield had only left him the first page.

"Mr. Waters?"

Rolly turned. Alphonso stood just inside the doorway.

"I printed a copy for you," he said, waving a piece of paper.

Rolly crossed the room.

"Thank you," he said, taking the list.

"I didn't see anyone named Fleetwood," said Alphonso, as Rolly scanned through the list.

"No, I'm not surprised."

Alphonso looked down at the ground. He shuffled his feet.

"Captain Waters is with some friends in the bar," he said. "I thought you should know."

Rolly sighed. "How many has he had?"

"His friends are encouraging him to catch up."

"Thanks for telling me," said Rolly. He stuffed the guest list in his pocket and headed for the lounge. Three men sat together at the end of the bar. His father was the one in the middle. He spotted Rolly and swiveled around on the bar stool to greet him.

"There's my boy," he said, raising his glass. "The splendiferous offspring of my ample loins, the man who will track down terrorism in our midst. A toast, gentlemen, to my son, Roland Waters."

The other two men swiveled on their seats to look at Rolly. All three men raised their glasses.

"To Roland Waters," they said, downing their drinks before banging their glasses down on the bar.

"I'm finished, Dad," said Rolly. "We should go home."

"You remember my buddy Figgis?" his father said, putting his hand on the first man's shoulder. He pointed the thumb of his other hand toward the man behind him. "And this is my new friend, Mitchy."

Rolly nodded.

"Hello," he said.

"Join us for a drink?" said Figgis.

"No thanks," said Rolly. "I'm here on business."

"Working hard, or hardly working?" said Mitchy. They all seemed about one sheet short of what old sailors were allotted. Rolly wanted to stop his father from unfurling that last sail.

"The captain here says you're working on a matter of national security," said Figgis. "That you're getting to the bottom of this attack on the heart and soul of our precious Navy, the Admiral's Club."

"I'm doing what I can," said Rolly. Figgis turned to address the other two men.

"You know what that is?" he said. "Humility. You don't see enough of that these days, what with all this boasting and showing off, those football players doing some stupid dance every time they make a tackle. A man should do his job right and not make a big deal out of it."

"You raised him right, Captain," said Mitchy.

Rolly wanted to tell them that his father had barely raised him at all, but it didn't seem worth the trouble.

"Chip off the old block," said Figgis. He raised his right arm straight into the air with his index finger extended. "Bartender, I demand another round."

"Dad," said Rolly. "It's time to go."

"One more for the road," said his father. "Then we'll go."

"You said you'd show me the dolphin pens."

"Oh man," said Figgis. "That brings back the memories. I used to take my daughter out to see the dolphins when she was a little girl. Before that bitch I called a wife and her lawyer took her away from me."

"That's beautiful, Figgy," said Mitchy, with a catch in his throat. "I never had kids."

"Best thing in the world," said Figgis. "Your kids. Tears you up inside to see 'em go. To have them turned against you. You must have done something right, Captain, to have a son who values your counsel and company."

Rolly and his father looked at each other for a moment, weighing the other's interest in disputing Figgis' assessment.

"Just one more drink," said his father. "Then we'll go see the damn dolphins."

"One more," said Rolly, taking a seat at the bar on the other side of Mitchy. He had too much on his mind to care anymore. He pulled the guest list out of his pocket and flattened it on the bar. There were twenty or so names on the list, with spouses or companions listed beside each name in parentheses. Two names caught his eye: Tammy and Henley Withers.

Mitchy pointed at the list.

"Whatcha got there?" he said.

"It's a guest list," said Rolly, "from the other night, when they had the fire."

"Terrible thing, terrible," said Mitchy, staring into his empty glass. "I saw a guy burn up once. On a carrier over in Guam. Jet fuel got on him. Guy lit up like a torch. Hard to believe someone would burn themselves like that on purpose. That girl must've been really messed up."

"Yeah, I guess so," said Rolly.

"What was her name again? The woman in the boat?"

"They haven't released the name yet."

"Oh yeah, they did. I heard it on the radio just this morning." Mitchy frowned, trying to find the information in his sloshy memory bank.

"Janis Withers?" said Rolly, hoping he was wrong. "Was that her name?"

"Yeah," said Mitchy. "How old was she?"

"Late thirties, maybe early forties," Rolly guesstimated. Janis was a few years younger than him.

"Yeah," said Mitchy. "Not the same gal I was thinking of, though. She'd be a bit older."

"What's that?"

"There was a gal used to hang out here at the bar in the old days. Last name was Withers. I got to know her a little bit."

The bartender returned with the men's drinks and placed them on the bar. Mitchy took a sip from his new glass. The drink inside looked dark and fizzy, maybe a rum and Coke. Rolly looked back at his list and found the name again.

"Was it Tammy?" he said "Tammy Withers?"

Mitchy turned and looked at Rolly.

"Yeah. Tammy Withers. How'd you know that?"

"She's on the guest list. She was here at the party."

"You think they're related?"

"Probably."

"Oh shit. That's tough. She could be that girl's mother. Tammy Withers was a little older than me. She was something."

"What do you mean?"

Mitchy looked over at Rolly's father, who was in close conversation with Figgis, then turned back to Rolly and lowered his voice.

"Can you keep a secret?" he said.

Rolly nodded.

"Well," said Mitchy. "I was young man, twenty-two when I came through here the first time. I hung out a lot at this very bar. There were always some gals hanging around on the weekends, you know, gals with husbands who were deployed overseas for a while. Gals looking for a little sympathy and companionship, if you know what I mean."

"I get the picture," said Rolly.

"Yeah," said Mitchy, with a glint in his eye. "Tammy Withers. She was a hell of a gal. She took me out on her boat a couple of times. Out to those islands. She had a really fast boat."

# THE PENS

Rolly and his father leaned against the hood of Rolly's old Volvo, observing the dolphin pens just off the shore. There were dozens of pens, thirty-foot squares of water surrounded by floating wood boardwalks. The boardwalks connected three rows of pens into one central pier that led back to a large prefabricated shed on the shore. A dolphin leapt from one of the pens and dove back into the water.

"I'm bored," said Rolly's father. "That's why I drink too much."

Rolly glanced at his father, then back at the dolphins.

"I mean it," said his father. "Retirement sucks."

"You were drinking long before you retired," said Rolly.

"It got worse when I moved to that crappy desk job. That's when it started. I needed to be manning a boat, not shuffling papers around in an office. Had to stick with it, though, so I could move up the next pay grade, get a better pension."

"How did you lose your commission?"

"Ah hell, I don't remember. We had that little accident in Singapore Harbor, bumped another boat."

"Yeah, you've told me about that."

"I guess the drinking had something to do with it too."

"Were you drunk when the accident happened?"

"No alcohol is allowed on board a US Navy ship. No sir. Not since Sir Josephus laid down his edict."

"Who's that?"

"Josephus Daniels. Secretary of the Navy. Banned alcohol from all US Navy vessels. July 1, 1914. The day the US Navy went dry."

"You didn't get a rum ration?"

"Not in the US Navy, son. Not in the last hundred years. I guess they allow the boys a beer or two these days, on special occasions, but only on captain's orders."

"You didn't really answer my question."

"What's that?"

"Were you drunk when you ran into that other ship?"

"All my drinking was off duty. On shore. Where it should be. Never drink and drive a boat, son."

"Or an automobile," said Rolly.

"We've both made some mistakes."

"Yeah."

They were quiet a moment. Two more dolphins jumped out of the water, playing around. Rolly wondered if they ever leapt into the bay and tried to escape. Probably not. They were spoiled, fat and happy. If Janis was a rich girl like Moogus had claimed, she might've been spoiled too. She wasn't fat, at least when Rolly knew her, and she'd seemed happy enough, behind that shy smile. Moogus remembered the scars on her face, the burn marks. Rolly could picture them now too. Perhaps the scars had run even deeper.

The door to the storage shed opened. A man in tall rubber boots appeared in the doorway, pulling a cart. He stopped and waved at the two of them.

"Beautiful day, huh?" said the man.

"Sure is," said Rolly.

"It's feeding time," said the man, indicating his cart. "You want to join me?"

Rolly lifted himself from the hood of the Volvo.

"What's that?"

"I been here all night and could use some company," said the man. "And you guys looked like you could use some cheering up."

"It's okay for us to go down there?"

"Oh, sure. We give tours all the time."

Rolly and his father walked down to the shed. The smell of fish wafted into Rolly's nostrils, rising from the plastic orange buckets the man had arranged in the cart.

"Are you a trainer?" said Rolly.

"Assistant trainer one," the man said. "Entry level. I don't cost much. That's why the Navy keeps me around."

"Were you at the Admiral's Club party the other night?"

"Nah. I missed all the excitement."

"My son's investigating the incident," said Rolly's father.

"Are you a cop?" The trainer looked at Rolly.

"Private detective," said Rolly. He reached in his wallet and handed over a business card.

"I saw the smoke," the man said, as he looked over Rolly's card. "I heard the sirens, but I didn't know what had happened until somebody told me about it the next morning."

"You were working here?"

"Yeah. I pulled night duty. The fish started chattering just before it went down. More than they usually do."

"The fish?"

"The dolphins. They get to talking at night. Chirping and squeaking with each other. They were really raising a racket that night. I went out to see what the fuss was about. That's when I saw the smoke. There was something in the water, out there in the channel, maybe a harbor seal. Seals usually bark at the fish, though. This guy was quiet and stealthy-like."

"Have you told anyone else about this?" said Rolly. "The police or FBI?"

"Oh yeah. I talked to some guys. We get seals around here all the time. They smell the fish. My name's Hunza, by the way. Come on. We can keep talking down there."

They followed Hunza out to the farthest corner of the pier, the cart clattering as it bounced across the wood slats, jiggling the buckets of fish. A large dolphin circled the surface of the water inside the far pen, keeping an eye on them. Hunza parked the cart and stood facing the pen. He made a fist with his right hand, brought it to his right shoulder, then made a slashing motion across his chest, down and back. The dolphin submerged, then leapt from the surface in a graceful arc and splashed back into the water. When it returned to the surface, Hunza tossed it a fish.

"What's that little hand thing you did there?" said Rolly's father.

"It's called the DS," he said. "Stands for discriminative stimulus. We teach them to associate different signals with different actions. When they get it right, they get a fish."

Hunza squatted down. He signaled the dolphin with a come-hither wave of his hand. The dolphin swam over to him and propped its head on the deck. It opened its mouth and showed all its teeth as if submitting to a dental exam.

"You want to pet him?" said the trainer.

"What do I do?" said Rolly's father.

"Get down here by me," said Hunza. Rolly's father lowered himself to his knees. Hunza gave a new signal, making a clockwise, circular motion with two fingers. The dolphin rotated onto its back, exposing its belly.

"Go ahead, you can give him a rub," said the trainer. Rolly's father leaned over the water and stroked the dolphin between its flippers. The dolphin closed its eyes. It chirped at him.

"Fifteen years on a ship, I never been this close to one," said Rolly's father as he petted the dolphin. "It's just a big, wet ocean dog."

"They're social animals," said the trainer. "They like to be touched. We use touch for positive feedback sometimes, in addition to feeding them."

Rolly's father leaned back and extended one arm, reaching for support. Rolly grabbed his father's hand and helped him climb to his feet. Hunza fed the dolphin another fish. He looked over at Rolly.

"You want to try it?" he said.

"Sure," Rolly said. He lowered himself onto the deck next to the trainer as the dolphin circled the pen. The trainer waved the dolphin over again and twirled his fingers. The dolphin came to the dock, flipped over and offered its belly. Rolly leaned down and rubbed the dolphin's skin. It felt like a wet inner tube. The dolphin chirped and gurgled. Rolly's father laughed.

"He likes you," he said. "And if that's what I think it is, he really, really likes you."

Rolly turned his head and saw a tumescent pink slug extruding from a slit in the dolphin's body, down near the tail. He lifted his hand from the dolphin's belly and looked back at the trainer. Hunza chuckled and tossed in a fish.

"Sorry about that," he said. "They're horndogs. We give 'em rub ropes, but it's not always enough."

"I know the feeling," said Rolly's father.

The dolphin returned to the water. Rolly stood up and surveyed the pens.

"Are they all males?" he said.

"We train females too. But we have to keep them separated."

"The boys get distracted, right?" said Rolly's father.

"Yeah, there's that. The males are bigger, too. They'll gang up on a female."

"Really?"

"Yeah. Everybody thinks dolphins are cute and adorable, but they can be bastards. Males, especially. They're basically rapists. That's not the only reason we keep them apart, though. The females are smarter. They learn a lot faster. The boys can't keep up with them."

"Someone told us the Navy was getting rid of the dolphins," said Rolly.

"It's only the special projects unit they're downsizing. My dolphins do regular duty. Stuff like mine identification and object retrieval."

"What do the special projects dolphins do?"

"I couldn't tell you even if I knew. It's top secret, mostly research projects." Hunza pointed down the length of the pier. "You see those pens on the other side of the fence? That's where they keep the special project dolphins. Tidewater's the contractor for all that stuff."

"That's the company that hosted the party, right?" said Rolly, recalling Alphonso's comments on the food and festivities. It was funded by Tidewater, no tax dollars at work.

"Yeah," said Hunza. "Tidewater's got offices on the other side of the bridge there. In Liberty Station."

Rolly looked across the water and watched a small sailboat pass under the bridge. There had been an attack on the Navy base. That's why the FBI was involved. But the party had been sponsored by Tidewater. Its employees had been at the party. Henley and Tammy Withers were both on the guest list. They must be related to Janis. Did they know anything about Fleetwood?

"Have you ever heard of a man named Butch Fleetwood?" he said.

"No." Hunza shook his head.

"Janis Withers?"

"Nope."

"How about Daniel Piper? Harmonica Dan?"

"I don't think so."

Hunza moved the cart farther down the boardwalk and repeated the feeding ritual with another dolphin. Rolly and his father followed along. Rolly looked back toward the special dolphin pens on the other side of the fence.

"If they're getting rid of those dolphins," he said, "where do they go?"

Hunza turned and pointed across the channel.

"They're moving them over there," he said. "Ocean Universe bought 'em."

Rolly looked at the gleaming new structures, across the channel on the opposite shore.

"We work a lot with places like that," Hunza said. "SeaWorld. Marineland in Florida. Anytime we retire a dolphin, it goes to one of those parks."

"Why don't you just set them free?" said Rolly's father.

"Believe it or not, they'd starve to death in the ocean," said Hunza. "Once they're trained like this, they don't know how to catch fish on their own anymore. We could retrain 'em, I suppose, but it takes too much money and time. More than the Navy wants to spend, anyway."

Rolly and his father thanked Hunza for letting them feed the dolphins and returned to Rolly's car. Rolly didn't start the car right away, but sat looking out at the bay. His father didn't object.

"Did your mom ever tell you about the dolphin pod that followed us in our boat?"

"No," said Rolly. "Not that I remember."

"It was on that trip I was telling you about earlier, when we went down the coast in the sailboat. Something I'll never forget. I was at the tiller. Your mom was beside me. We were out pretty far, nothing but water in sight, and this pod of dolphins shows up, hundreds of them, maybe thousands. They traveled with us for at least half an hour, then disappeared just as quick. One of my favorite memories of that trip."

Hunza had finished feeding the dolphins. He returned the cart to the storage shed, looked up and waved at them. Rolly waved back. He lifted his hands to the steering wheel and started the car.

"You're getting sentimental in your old age, Dad."

"Maybe I am. It wasn't all bad between us, you know, your mother and me. What do you think this guy wants?"

Rolly looked up to see Hunza walking toward them. Hunza waved again. Rolly lowered the window.

"I thought of something," said Hunza. "I don't know if it's important. You know that harmonica guy you asked about, what was his name?"

"Harmonica Dan."

"Yeah. There was this guy on a sailboat, maybe a week ago, early evening. He parked it out in the bay, about midway between our pens and Ocean Universe on the other side of the channel there."

"You think it was him?"

"I don't know. I never met the guy. But the dolphins started going crazy, squealing and leaping up from their pens. It didn't last long. The guy had turned his boat around and was headed back into the bay by the time I got down to the water to check things out. What's this Dan guy look like?"

"He looks like a bum," said Rolly's father.

"Long hair and a beard, somewhere around my age," said Rolly.

"That could be him, I guess. He was pretty far away, so I didn't get a good look. The thing is, well, that's why I thought I should tell you."

"What?"

"I think he was playing a harmonica."

# 10

## THE NEWS

Rolly sat at his old Formica table, nursing a cup of late-afternoon coffee and staring at the screen on his old laptop computer. He'd dropped his father off in Coronado three hours ago, no worse for wear, then drove home to the granny flat he rented from his mother, who lived in the Victorian mansion that occupied most of the lot. A two-hour nap on the sofa had improved his outlook on life. The nap and the coffee helped him process the news stories he'd read on the computer. The authorities had released the attacker's name, making it official. Janis Withers was the woman who'd crashed her boat into the Admiral's Club. She'd burned to death. That was how she had killed herself.

No one knew why she'd done it. There was no suicide note. The FBI was investigating the possibility that it was some kind of eco-terrorist act. Janis Withers had donated a good deal of money to animal-rights organizations, including something called the Ocean Mammal Underground, which had a history of aggressive protests against dolphinariums, research facilities and water parks—any place that kept dolphins in captivity. The OMU's opposition to the Navy's dolphin program was well known and documented.

An obituary for Janis had also appeared in the paper. It was brief and made no mention of the circumstances of her death. Her parents, Henley and Tammy Withers, were listed as survivors, along with a brother named Richard. The obituary said Janis would be missed by the students and staff of Ocean Beach Academy School. It didn't say why. There was no mention of Butch Fleetwood or Melody Flowers.

Rolly heard his mother's car pull into the gravel driveway. A few seconds later, she knocked on the door. Her unannounced visits were the hidden cost of his cheap rent.

"Come in," he said. The door opened and his mother walked in.

"What happened to your hair?" Rolly said.

"Isn't it a kick?" she said, taking a seat at the table across from him. "The checker at Henry's Market inspired me. Her hair was all green. My hairdresser tried to talk me out of doing it all over. This is our compromise, just a streak. How is your father doing?"

"He's fine."

His mother sighed.

"That's what your father would say. I expect more illuminating discourse from you."

"I'm a little distracted. Let's see. Dad bought a boat."

"How does Alicia feel about that?"

"She likes it better than the Tioga, I guess."

"I never did understand how he talked her into buying that big old RV."

"He sold the Tioga. That's how he paid for the boat."

Rolly's mother nodded.

"Your father always did love sailing."

"I think it's a powerboat."

"In the early days, before you arrived, he'd take me out sometimes. One time we sailed down to those islands, those ones you can see, off of Mexico."

"Yeah, he told me about that, about the dolphins that swam along with your boat."

"Oh yes. I remember them. That was quite an adventure we had, in that little boat. There's a hidden bay on the other side of the southern island. And an old casino up on the cliffs. We stayed overnight. It was quite romantic."

"You stayed at the casino?"

"Oh no. We camped out on the beach. The casino had been closed a long time by then. It was a relic from the nineteen-twenties. No one went there after prohibition was lifted. Walking through it felt like we were visiting old Greek ruins. I don't think I ever saw your father more in his element than when he was out on the water. The Navy ruined it for him. When it became a job. Your father's whole personality changed when he had to take on that kind of responsibility."

"Is that when he started drinking?"

"Your father always drank too much. It only got worse after the divorce. Your father has a problem with alcohol."

"*I* have a problem with alcohol."

"You don't drink anymore."

"I ran into a tree. It was a sign from the universe."

"Some people don't notice the signs, dear. Was your father drinking today?"

"We stopped by the Admiral's Club. Dad ran into a couple of his buddies at the bar. He was only out of my sight for a few minutes."

Rolly's mother sighed and shook her head.

"I understand, dear. I know it's not easy. I always hated that place. I never fit in with the other Navy wives. Some of them were nice enough, pleasant women, you know, but I was just too independent for that kind of environment. If I didn't like how the Navy treated us, I let people know. You heard about that poor woman who killed herself?"

Rolly nodded at the computer screen.

"I knew her," he said. "Janis Withers. She used to run our fan club."

"I'm so sorry. Had you stayed in touch?"

Rolly shook his head. He felt tired again.

"She used to call me sometimes, after the accident, but I never saw her again. I didn't see much of anyone for a long time after the accident."

"You did what you had to. You removed yourself from a harmful environment. It was the only way you could find healing."

"She and Matt had some kind of relationship, I guess. Moogus told me about it last night. Sounded like it might have been serious. I didn't know."

"And you think it would have changed things if you did?"

Rolly shrugged. He couldn't bring Matt back. He couldn't save Janis. He looked at the dog tags that lay on the table. Butch Fleetwood's dog tags. Butch was important to Janis. He didn't know why.

"You can't blame yourself for someone else's life, dear," said his mother.

"Didn't you once tell me you blamed yourself for Dad's drinking?"

His mother looked away from him, searching the room for something that didn't exist.

"Perhaps you should see a counselor about this," she said.

"Guilt sucks," Rolly said. He shrugged. "I'll manage it."

His mother rose from her chair and walked out, returning to her own house across the way. Rolly felt surly and mean. He read through the articles again. He read the obituary. Janis Withers was still dead.

He picked up his phone and scrolled through his contacts. He tapped one of the names and put the phone to his ear. No one answered. Leslie's voice message came on the line—cool, calm and dusky. He disconnected. He wanted to ask if she'd known about Matt and Janis, if everyone in the world knew about it except him.

Rolly had been driving the car when the accident happened, when Matt flew through the front window, into the black forever night. They'd all been drunk, celebrating their promotion from local bar heroes to big-time recording artists, driving back from the Columbia Records office in Hollywood where Rolly and Matt had just signed a contract. It felt like the Creatures were headed straight to the top.

But a dark seed had been planted, before the contract was signed, before the celebrations began. Leslie and Matt had broken the rules. They'd slept together, Rolly's best friend and his fiancée. Rolly knew why Leslie had done it. He'd never been faithful to her, even after they moved in together. She was hurt. She was angry. Leslie's infidelity was retribution, an eye for an eye. They'd forgiven each other in time. With Matt it was different. And then Matt was dead and Rolly had killed him.

In the still unexplored crevices of his soul, Rolly wasn't sure if he'd lost control of the car that night or simply aimed it into the trees, acting on a dark impulse to destroy all the chaos between them, testing the limits of their mortality. That night was far away now, fading like a dark stand of trees in life's rearview mirror. But last night at Winstons, visiting the old neighborhood and hearing about Janis, brought it back again. There was more to it now, because of Janis, another soul injured because Rolly got drunk and ran into a tree.

He turned his attention to other things, searching for information on Tidewater, the defense contractors who had sponsored the party at the Admiral's Club. There was plenty to read. Tidewater Defense Systems was a large defense contractor, based in Newport News, Virginia. Most of their work involved building ships. Tidewater had a satellite office in San Diego. Two names were listed under the office— Tammy and Henley Withers, both with PhDs after their names. Rolly copied their numbers to his phone.

A further search turned up some articles on corruption and bribery charges brought against the company years before. There were congressional hearings, and the CEO resigned amid stories of his personal involvement in influence peddling. Witnesses provided lurid accounts of booze, girls and parties held at the CEO's Virginia country mansion.

The information Rolly found on Ocean Universe was decidedly less sensational. The company was based in Japan. They owned several water parks around the world, including the newest one, which would open on San Diego Bay in less than a week. The company stressed its humane treatment of dolphins and education as key components of its corporate mission. To that end, the Wendell Amphitheater and Dolphin Education Center was featured. A small photo of Wendell standing next to one of his murals was included in the article.

Rolly's phone rang. It was Moogus.

"What's up?" said Rolly.

"We've got rehearsal in three hours," said Moogus. "Can you make it?"

"What rehearsal?"

"I told Sideman you could do it."

"What are you talking about?"

"The gig with this Wendell guy. I told you about it last night. The one at the water park. Ocean Universe. It's yours if you want it. The guitar player dropped out."

"What happened to him?"

"I don't know. He lives in LA. Maybe he lost one of his chakras. There's a rehearsal tonight, another one at the water park two nights from now and a performance the day after."

Rolly sifted through the schedule in his head. There weren't any conflicts he could remember, only an accident scene he needed to photograph for an ambulance-chasing attorney who kept him on a bargain-level retainer fee. That was half a day's work, at most. He didn't have another gig until the blues jam at Winstons next Monday.

"Double-scale, buddy," said Moogus. "I hooked you a big one."

"I'm in," said Rolly. "Where's the rehearsal?"

"The OTTER building," said Moogus.

"Where's that?"

"Driscoll's Wharf in Point Loma. You know where that is?"

"I think so," said Rolly, picturing the OTTER sign on the ramshackle building near the marina. "I was out there this morning."

"See you at seven."

"Great. I need to ask Sideman about some stuff, anyway."

"There you go. Sideman said he wanted to talk to you about something too."

## 11

# THE REHEARSAL

Rolly turned his guitar down, seated himself on his Fender Deluxe amplifier and ran through Steve Cropper's guitar part for "Soul Man" while J.V. Sideman discussed some of the finer points of the song's arrangement with the other guys in the horn section. Sideman had mapped out two sets of blues and soul standards for the band to run through. Everyone in the room had played the songs at least a hundred times. All they needed to work on were the keys and the arrangements, who took the solos and breaks. Wendell, their employer and the band's vocalist, wouldn't be attending this rehearsal, which suited Rolly just fine. Singers always complicated the situation, especially when they were the boss. They often had trouble translating their wishes into musical terms. This gig was easy money so far—no charts to bother with, no flyspecks to read.

The inside of the OTTER building was a large, lofty space, as big as a barn. It served as a garage for the OTTERs, amphibious vehicles that were half bus and half boat. Tourists would pay fifty dollars for a one-hour tour in the oversized vehicles, surveying the big bay from both water and land.

A short raised stage had been installed in the back corner of the OTTER building along with a small PA system. The eight members of the band filled the confines of the stage, which was just large enough to contain them. Sideman's girlfriend, Linda, sat on a sofa in front of them clutching a pencil, notebook and stopwatch. She clicked the stopwatch every time the band started a song. She clicked it again when they finished and noted the time in her book. Linda was on Wendell's tab too, working as the band's stage manager. Sideman had perfected the art of double-dipping.

The band ran through two more songs and took a break. Sideman descended from the bandstand and walked over to Linda. They talked for a couple of minutes while Linda took notes. Sideman gave her a kiss on the top of her head and walked over to Rolly.

"Smoke break?" he said, as he pulled a pack from his coat pocket.

"Only one," said Linda, calling after them as Sideman led Rolly out the front door. They walked to the edge of the water and looked out at the boats in the marina. Sideman lit up a cigarette, took a couple of puffs.

"I thought you quit," said Rolly.

"I did. Started again after that chick blew up the Admiral's Club."

"I heard you were there."

"That was some sick shit. Lit herself up like a torch."

"You saw it happen?"

"Saw the whole thing, start to finish. Everybody ran like hell when the fire started. Conway hightailed it out of there, yelling at me how the place was gonna blow up. I wasn't leaving without my gear, though. You know me. Save the saxophones first. Before the women and children."

"Anybody else in the band that I'd know?"

"Nah. Just Conway. He got me the gig. It was all white-bread stuff, you know, limp-dick wedding reception tunes. Cornball."

"I heard Harmonica Dan was there."

Sideman glanced sideways at Rolly.

"Where'd you hear that?"

"I have a friend on the police force. Her name's Bonnie Hammond."

"Yeah, she talked to me. What's your spike in this thing?"

"The girl that died, Janis Withers. She ran our fan club, back in the day."

"The Creatures?"

Rolly nodded.

"I'm looking for information on someone she might've known," he said. "A guy named Butch Fleetwood."

"The FBI asked me about that guy too."

"They did?"

"Yeah. I never heard of him. Her parents were there when she torched herself. They were talking to her, trying to stop her from doing it. She seemed really pissed."

"What'd she say?"

"She said it was all lies."

"What was all lies?"

"Dunno. She wanted to save the dolphins. She said that a couple of times too."

"Anything else?"

"Lemme see. There was some weird name she said. Aeron?"

"Arion?"

"Yeah. That was it. She said she'd seen Arion."

"You're sure that was the name?" said Rolly.

"I'm pretty sure. Does it mean something to you?"

"Maybe," said Rolly. He nodded. Sideman flicked his ashes into the water.

"I told your cop friend Bonnie all that stuff," he said. "And the FBI agents. They showed up at my house yesterday morning real early, a man and a woman, bugging me with all sorts of questions. Real hard-asses. It freaked Linda out. She thought I was going to jail or something. That's why I started smoking these damn menthols again. There was a reporter, too, called me on the phone, asked the same bunch of questions."

"You remember his name?"

"Tom Cockburn for the *OB Enquirer*. That's exactly how he said it. Real old-school kind of news guy, sounded like he was in a movie."

Rolly remembered the headline about Fleetwood in the *Enquirer*. It was in last week's edition of the paper, which had been published before the events at the Admiral's Club. Had Janis seen the article? Had it been some kind of trigger for her?

"This reporter, he asked you about Butch Fleetwood?"

"Yeah. I told him like I told everybody else, I never heard of the guy. Nada. They were wasting their time on that line of questioning."

"Tell me about Harmonica Dan."

"Last I saw him, he was stuffing his pockets with shrimp from the buffet table."

"He was stealing food from the party?"

"Yeah. After everyone else was gone he came running in from the patio, knocked me on my ass. He had a fire extinguisher with him. He tried to put out the fire, but that little thing couldn't do much. The woman on the boat started screaming. Bloodcurdling. I know what that means now. Bloodcurdling. One of the worst sounds I ever heard in my life."

Sideman took a puff on his cigarette.

"Look at that," he said, holding the cigarette away from his face. "My hand's shaking just talking about it."

"Did the FBI say anything about Dan? Why they were looking for him?"

"They asked how I knew him, if I was sympathetic to his political views."

"I didn't know Dan *had* any political views."

"That's pretty much what I said. I told 'em I only knew Dan as a homeless guy who plays harmonica. I don't know nothing about his politics."

"Did they say he was a suspect?"

"They didn't say much of anything. They might've been looking into some kind of animal rights angle, I guess. Save the Whales and that kind of stuff that maybe Dan was involved with."

"What makes you say that?"

"They asked about something called the OMU. Wanted to know what I knew about it. I gave 'em a big, fat zero on that line of questioning too."

"Did they ask about Arion?"

"Yeah, but I didn't know nothing about that either. Those guys struck out with me. Nada times three."

Rolly rubbed his chin, staring out at the dark boats tied up in their slips.

"I think Dan knows something about Arion," he said. "That's why they're looking for him. One of the reasons, I think."

"Well, he didn't mention it to me."

"But he did talk to you?"

"Sure, he called me by name, asked me to hold the door for him. He was stocking up on the shrimp from the buffet table, said his dolphins loved them."

"His dolphins? What'd he mean by that?"

"I don't know. That was just before the gas tank blew up. Next thing I know I'm seeing stars. Conway is slapping my face outside on the patio and forcing a shot of Jack Daniel's down my throat."

"You didn't see Dan after that?"

"No. Nobody else saw him either, I guess. Not before and not after. Nobody but me."

"How well do you know Dan?"

"Just from playing at Winstons, when he'd show up for the blues jams."

"Yeah, me too. I noticed he played on that punk band's album, Rude Abortion?"

"Yeah, that's right. I played on that album too."

"I saw that. Dan had a copy of the album on his boat. The lead singer signed a copy for him. 'Thanks for the blow job.'"

Sideman laughed.

"Dick's a real joker," he said. "He wrote that on mine too. The guy's a little off. Those are his boats in the garage, you know. Those OTTER things."

"Dick Nazi owns the OTTER boats?"

"Yeah. That's his day job. This is his place. We recorded that album here. Sounds like it, too. 'Stay primitive,' that's their whole vibe, their aesthetic. The CD's not even in stereo. Only one microphone hanging from the ceiling to record the thing. Just went in and blasted away for an hour. Dick would point at me or Dan when he wanted us to come in and signal again when we should stop."

"Sounds amusing. Did he pay you?"

"Fifty bucks. Not something I'd want to do every day, but it was good for some grins."

"Do you know if they're playing tonight?"

"Yeah. Winstons, I think. Check the calendar on the wall."

"I will. Thanks. Moogus said you had something you wanted to talk about?"

"Yeah." Sideman nodded. He took a last draw on his cigarette and flicked it into the water. He pointed out toward the entrance to the marina.

"You see that boat out there in the channel? The one with the lights?"

"That big catamaran?"

"Yeah. That's Wendell's boat. I was out there yesterday, going over the set list with him."

"Looks pretty nice."

"A million dollars nice."

"Wow."

"Yeah. Wow. He's got a guy that takes care of the boat for him. Acts as his bodyguard, too. Big, scary dude rowed me out to the boat, kept his eye on me all the time I'm talking to Wendell."

"Have you heard him sing? Wendell, I mean?"

"He played me a CD he made a while back. Nothing special, but nothing terrible, either. He's a real fan boy when it comes to all that old jump blues stuff—Louis Prima, Jay McShann, Big Joe Turner."

"Yeah, I haven't played that Wynonie Harris tune in a while."

"Doesn't matter how he sings with what he's paying me."

"Yeah. Thanks for getting me the gig."

"That's what I wanted to talk to you about. Wendell's the guy you should thank. He asked for you by name."

"He did?"

"Yeah. You met him before?"

"I never even heard of the guy until yesterday."

"He's heard of you, I guess."

"Really? He asked you to hire me?"

"He texted me this afternoon," said Sideman. He reached in his back pocket and pulled out his phone. "Look."

Rolly looked at the message Sideman displayed.

*Guitar player out. Can U get Roland Waters?*

"Bit of a surprise to me," said Sideman. "When Wendell hired me to put the band together, he said it was all in my hands. Then he sends me this text. My guy's out and he wants you instead. I was a bit chuffed."

"I thought the other guy quit."

"Yeah. He did." Sideman shrugged. "But I didn't hear from him until after I got the message from Wendell. Something's funky. I mean I'm cool having you in the band, but . . ."

"Yeah," said Rolly. "It is a bit strange. Let me see that text again."

Sideman showed Rolly the phone screen. There was something funny about the wording of the message.

"Nobody calls me Roland anymore," said Rolly. "Not even my parents."

"Are you still on the union rolls? They might have you listed under that name."

"I haven't paid union dues in years," said Rolly.

"Yeah, you and half the guys I know," said Sideman. "Anyway, I just wanted you to know—the boss man thinks you're special."

"He must've heard me playing somewhere," said Rolly. He looked out at Wendell's yacht. One million dollars seemed like a lot of money to spend on a boat. To spend on anything. Wendell was paying the band double-scale. Wendell had money to burn.

# 12

# THE PUNK

Rude Abortion blasted away on the stage at Winstons, playing fast and loud, mixing up Dick Dale surf riffs, Ramones power chords and Black Flag aggression. What the band lacked in subtlety, they made up for with aggressive commitment. Rolly sat at the end of the bar, watching the dancers mosh around in front of the stage. The band's singer screamed out the song's refrain, borrowing a cadence from the US Marines in Vietnam.

> Yes it's really lots of fun
> Dropping bombs and shooting guns
> How we like to see them run
> Napalm sticks to kids
>
> Dow, Monsanto and DuPont
> Dirty children no one wants
> We must obey, Mein commandant
> Napalm sticks to kids

The band ended the song and took a break. Rolly watched as the singer, Dick Nazi, fought his way through the crowd on his way to the bar. He took a seat three stools over from Rolly, ordered a shot of Jack Daniel's and a glass of Pabst Blue Ribbon, then dropped the shot glass into the beer and chugged half of it down. He turned his head, spotted Rolly sitting at the end of the bar. Rolly smiled and raised his glass of club soda.

"Do I know you?" said Nazi.

Rolly shrugged.

"I've played in some bands around town," he said.

"You were that guitar player in Creatures, weren't you?" said Nazi. "The one who cracked up his car and tried to kill himself?"

"Reports of my death have been greatly exaggerated," said Rolly. He'd heard all sorts of versions of his accident over the years, some funny, some cruel, some both funny and cruel. The stories were rarely accurate. He'd learned how to distance himself from it. He pretended he was in on the joke.

Nazi picked up his drink and sat down next to Rolly.

"Rolly Waters, right?" he said, extending his hand. "You may not believe this, but I really dug you guys when I was a kid. My sister took me to one of your shows. You're part of the reason I started a band."

"I'm honored," said Rolly. "And a little surprised."

"Yeah, well, you guys could actually play your instruments. I don't see the bunch of fuckups in my band getting to that level of sophistication. We're just brutal and loud. More in keeping with our general nature."

"I'll take what you do over smooth jazz any day," said Rolly.

"Yeah. Kenny G blows."

"Agreed."

"That's one of our songs. It's called 'Kenny G Blows.'"

"Where can I buy a copy?"

Nazi laughed. He was shorter than Rolly, leaner, younger and more muscular. His sweaty T-shirt sported a crude drawing of a Mohawk-coifed rabbit holding a smoking machine gun. The words *Bad Hare Day* were printed below the rabbit's feet. Nazi had shaved his head. He had tattoos that covered both arms. His front teeth were crooked and his right incisor was missing.

"I was hoping to talk to you," said Rolly. He was hoping to talk to Melody, too. He'd left a message on her voice mail, letting her know he'd be at Winstons if she wanted to stop by. He told her he had new information, but he hadn't told her Fleetwood was dead. That seemed like the kind of news that should be delivered in person. Melody was a no-show so far. She hadn't called him back, either. "I'm looking for a guy named Daniel Piper. Harmonica Dan."

"Yeah, I know Dan. Haven't seen him for a while."

"He's gone missing."

"You mean like missing-missing?"

Rolly nodded. Nazi gulped down the rest of his boilermaker. He looked back toward the stage, then turned to Rolly.

"Dan's a little out there, you know, kind of a tinfoil-hat guy."

"What do you mean?"

"He's got a lot of theories about how the government's spying on us. That part's true, I guess, with the NSA stuff and all, but Dan's got his own version of how the world works."

"What is it?"

Nazi shrugged.

"I can't really figure it out. He talks about government agents a lot. He calls them the listeners. Why are you looking for Dan?"

Rolly reached in his pocket, pulled out his phone and showed Nazi the photograph Bonnie had sent to him, the one of Dan playing harmonica with the Creatures.

"I have a friend. She's a cop. She sent this to me, wanted to know if I could help her."

Nazi looked at the photo.

"That's you with Dan, isn't it?" he said. "What a fuckin' poser. Can't believe I was into you guys."

"She said the police found this photograph on Dan's boat," said Rolly. "They found one of your CDs, too. You signed it with a personal message to Dan."

"Oh yeah? What did I say?"

Rolly put a finger to his temple and recited the inscription.

"'To Harmonica Dan. Thanks for the blow job. We're all head-fucked. Hugs and kisses. Dick Nazi.'"

Nazi grinned.

"Yeah, that sounds like me, all right."

"I assume the blow job referred to his harmonica playing."

"Yeah. He played on *Headfucked*. We're all headfucked, one way or another."

"When was the last time you saw Dan?"

"Are you trying to be a cop now or something?"

"No."

"You sound like a cop."

"I'm a private investigator," said Rolly. He reached in his wallet, pulled out a card and handed it to Nazi.

"Man, I don't know if this is cool," said Nazi, looking over the card. "Or just pitiful."

"What's that?"

"You being a cop."

"I'm not a cop. I'm a private investigator."

"Like I should talk. Your day job is way cooler than mine."

"What do you do?"

"I perform a trained seal act for fat tourists from Iowa."

"I was at a rehearsal tonight with J.V. Sideman. He said we were using your place, the OTTER garage, that you drove those boats."

"Yeah, that's me. The OTTER man," said Nazi. He switched to an enthusiastic announcer voice. "OTTER Boats. A unique and exciting amphibious tour of San Diego Bay. Your whole family will love it!"

Rolly tried to picture Dick Nazi at the wheel of one of the large, brightly painted vehicles he'd seen in the garage, guiding tourists along the harbor and into the bay, pointing out landmarks and telling bad jokes. It seemed like a stretch.

"I assume you tone down your act for the tour," he said.

"Oh yeah, we put together a script. I save the f-bombs for the band stuff."

"How long have you been doing that?"

"A year and a half now," said Nazi. "The weird part is, I kind of enjoy it. I'm an attention whore. Give me an audience and I'll put on a show. Come to think of it, the last time I saw Harmonica Dan was on an OTTER boat ride. Yeah, I remember now. I comped him a ticket. He really wanted to see the Navy's dolphin pens."

"Those ones near Harbor Drive Bridge?"

"Yeah. Tourists love it when we cruise by the dolphins. It's a big photo opportunity. Dan got kind of quiet after we passed the dolphin pens, but when we got back to the garage he started talking my ear off. He said I had my information all wrong. He said the Navy tells everybody the dolphins are used for noncombat jobs, but it wasn't true. He said that it was all a government smoke screen. He told me they train dolphins to kill people."

"Where'd he hear that?"

"He used to work there, I guess."

"When? What kind of work did he do?"

"He didn't get into all that. He just told me one of the divers that worked with the dolphins got killed when he was there. He said the Navy covered it up."

"Did he tell you the guy's name, the one who was killed?"

Nazi looked thoughtful.

"Bruce somebody," he said, looking at the bar. "It started with a *B*, anyway."

"Butch Fleetwood?"

"That could've been it."

Rolly rubbed his chest. This was the first real connection he'd made to Butch Fleetwood. If he could find Dan, he could learn more about Fleetwood, maybe something to connect him to Janis. Then he'd have something to take back to Melody, something more than just telling her Fleetwood was dead.

"They got all sorts of weird top-secret shit going on at the Navy base," said Nazi. "They used to store nukes on North Island, you know. They're experimenting with all that Star Wars stuff in those bunkers on Point Loma. I wouldn't be surprised if the Navy tried to attach a nuke to a dolphin. 'Hello, Flipper! You're so friendly and nice. Oh, what's that on your back? It looks like a low-level thermonuclear device. Isn't that cute?'"

"They're shutting down part of the dolphin program, I guess."

"Dan told me they got robot fish now that look like a tuna. They don't need dolphins."

"The dolphins are going to Ocean Universe."

"Fucking eyesore. That Wendell guy's full of shit."

Rolly gave a slight nod of his head, as if he agreed. Just because Wendell was paying him double-scale, it didn't mean he had to defend him. He'd meet the mystery man himself soon enough, at the next rehearsal.

"I don't know much about the guy," he said.

"He's like the Kenny G of painters, you know what I mean? The guy's a hack. He's a self-promoting douche bag."

"How do you really feel about him?"

Nazi gave Rolly a lopsided grin.

"Fuck corporate art," he said. "Am I right?"

"Fuck it," said Rolly, nodding in approval.

"I mean, I know our music's not for everybody, but it ain't boring."

"Definitely not boring," said Rolly.

Nazi looked back at the stage, surveying the crowd. He turned back to Rolly.

"Do you know a woman named Janis Withers?" said Rolly.

Nazi froze. He glared at Rolly.

"Fuck you, Waters," he said.

"I'm sorry," said Rolly. "What'd I say?"

Nazi slammed the beer glass down on the counter an inch away from Rolly's hand. He stuck his face in close to Rolly's.

"Leave her alone, fuckhead," he hissed at Rolly. "Leave my sister alone. Let her rest in peace."

He shoved Rolly in the chest, causing Rolly to fall off his seat, taking the bar stool down with him. Nazi leaned over him, his muscles fully flexed, glaring down at Rolly like an enraged bull. Rolly put his hands up to protect himself.

"I'm sorry," he said. "I didn't know she was your sister."

Nazi curled his lip. His shoulders twitched. He turned away from Rolly and stormed back through the crowd to the stage.

"Break's over, motherfuckers!" he screamed into the microphone.

The rest of the band stumbled onto the stage, surprised by the call to action that had cut short their break. The drummer seated himself and counted to four. The band slammed into a new pogo rhythm. Nazi made a gargling sound in the back of his throat and started to sing.

*Headfucked, headfucked*
*I'm in the cockpit*
*Headfucked, headfucked*
*They say I'm legit*
*Headfucked, headfucked*
*Taking what they emit*
*Headfucked, headfucked*
*I'm choking on it*

Dick Nazi was right about the band's music. It wasn't for everyone.

# 13

## THE SCHOOL

The next morning, Rolly sat on a low bench outside the principal's office at Ocean Beach Academy School watching the kids on the playground. A half-dozen young women—teachers and classroom assistants—kept watch over the four-square courts, hopscotch, and games of tag.

The door to the office opened. A short, cheerful-looking woman stepped out and glanced at him. She had his PI ID card in her hands. He'd left it with the receptionist. The woman looked at him more closely, then checked the photo on the card again.

"Mr. Waters?" she said.

"Yes?"

"I'm Principal Boyle."

Rolly struggled up from the bench, which was sized for an average fourth grader. He smiled at Principal Boyle. They shook hands. She handed his ID card back to him.

"Thank you for seeing me," he said, placing the card in his pocket.

"Do you mind if we walk?" said Boyle. "I like to get out and interact with the children when I can. I don't want them to see me only when they're in trouble."

Rolly followed the principal out to the playground. They circled the periphery of the young mob. Boyle smiled and waved at children as they caught her eye.

"I understand from your call you had some questions about Janis Withers?" she said.

"Yes."

"You were a friend of hers?"

"Not exactly. But I knew her."

"That sounds a bit vague."

"I'm a private investigator. I'm doing this for a client."

"Yes, I saw your ID card."

"I'm trying to find a man Janis knew. Someone special to her."

Boyle smiled.

"Was this man a spy?" she said.

"Sounds like you've heard this before."

Boyle nodded.

"Yes. I brought Janis into my office once, to express my concerns. She was a classroom volunteer, not a teacher, so I couldn't officially reprimand her."

"What was the issue?"

"She'd been telling everyone about her secret boyfriend, the mysterious spy. She said he went on secret missions and worked with the dolphins. It sounded crazy. I didn't know what to make of it."

"Did she tell you the man's name?"

"She said his name was a secret."

"Did she ever mention the name Butch Fleetwood?"

"No, I don't think so. Is that the man that you're looking for?"

"He was a Navy diver who worked with the dolphins. He died in a training accident twenty-three years ago."

"So he was real, then?"

Rolly nodded his head.

"He was real."

"She would have been awfully young if she knew him twenty-three years ago," said Boyle. "Just a teenager, I imagine."

"Fourteen," said Rolly. He'd worked out the numbers after reading Janis Withers's obituary and comparing it to the date of the original article about Fleetwood in the *OB Enquirer*.

"She couldn't really have been married at that age, could she?"

"Not in California," said Rolly. "Not without parental consent."

"Have you talked to her parents?"

"Not yet. Do you know them?"

"No. They must be devastated. It's a terrible tragedy, such a hard thing to understand when someone takes their own life. The children were all fond of her."

"How long did Janis work here?"

"Well, technically she didn't work here. I mean she wasn't an employee. She was a classroom assistant. The assistants are all volunteers. Parents, usually."

"Did Janis have any children at the school?"

"None that I'm aware of."

"Why do you think she became a volunteer?"

"I don't really know. She was here when I arrived. That was five years ago. Perhaps she'd had a child here at one time. The teachers gave me generally good reports, so I let her continue."

"They weren't all good reports?"

"Janis had an ingenuous quality the children responded to. She seemed to be able to communicate at their level. She was sweet and kind to all, and fully capable of handling the responsibilities assigned to her in the classroom."

"Is there a qualification to all this?" said Rolly.

"Oh no, not really. I'm sure all the teachers would agree. She was easy to have in the classroom. Much better than some parents. Parents can be a bit meddlesome sometimes."

Rolly nodded. Boyle continued.

"Janis had a unique outlook on life that she shared with the children. Naturally, the children told their parents. Some of the parents complained to me."

"What was the issue?"

A blond-headed boy broke from the pack and ran up to Principal Boyle. She leaned down to greet him.

"Good morning, Thomas," said Boyle. "How are you today?"

Thomas wiped his nose with the sleeve of his shirt. He looked at the ground.

"Is there something you wanted to tell me?" said Boyle.

The boy glanced up at Rolly, then back at Boyle. He twisted the hem of his T-shirt in his fingers.

"Principal Boyle," he said, "do you think Mr. Wendell will let us put a starfish in the painting?"

"Well," said Boyle, "do you remember the sketch we showed everyone in school assembly?"

Thomas put his hand to his chin. He thought hard for a moment.

"I don't remember," he said. He put his hands on his hips. "When was that assembly?"

"It was two weeks ago," said Boyle. "Wendell was there. He showed us that big scroll of paper. You remember that, don't you?"

"Oh yeah, I remember," said Thomas, but he didn't look too sure of himself.

"Well," said Boyle, "I think I saw some starfish in the lower corners of the sketch, and I'm pretty sure there are some starfish outlined on the wall."

"That means they're going to be in the mural?"

"Yes."

"I want to help paint the starfish."

"You'll have to ask Mr. Wendell, but I think he might allow you to help him with that."

"Can I ask him today?"

"Yes, you may."

"Okay," said Thomas. He ran back to his playmates. Boyle turned back to Rolly.

"Pardon the intrusion," she said. "Everyone's in a rather high state of excitement today."

"What's going on?"

"The artist Wendell is going to be here. He's painting a mural for the school. He finished the outline a couple of days ago, and he's going to have the kids help him fill in some of the painting today. It's so sad about Janis. She helped raise the money."

"She liked art?"

"She liked dolphins. That's what it was about, you know, the parents who complained."

"They complained about dolphins?"

Boyle clasped her hands in front of her. She looked as thoughtful and serious as Thomas had a moment ago.

"Did you hear anything about the yoga-in-schools controversy they had in Encinitas recently, Mr. Waters?"

"Vaguely," said Rolly, recalling a bit of news his mother had passed on to him, something about parents up in arms over yoga classes being taught in school, claiming they were a form of religious indoctrination. Boyle sighed.

"It isn't easy being a principal these days," she said. "There are so many opposing interests. Everyone feels they have a right to do things their way. When I started in this business, we were encouraged to be open-minded. We presented as much as we could to children. Now you can barely bring in a speaker without being accused of indoctrinating students into some sort of religious belief or political ideology."

"I wouldn't want your job," said Rolly.

"I even got some resistance to going ahead with this Wendell mural," said Boyle. "There were some in the community who felt he was too corporate, too much of a self-promoter. They questioned his motives. Then there were the animal rights people."

"Why don't they like him?"

"It's all about that theme park he's building, the one on the bay, Ocean Universe. One group in particular seemed to have a problem with it. They don't want to see any dolphins in captivity, regardless of how well they're treated."

"Was it the OMU?" Rolly said, recalling the name of the organization J.V. Sideman had mentioned, the one the FBI had asked him about.

"Yes, that's the one. They managed to get the local press on their side. The *OB Examiner* ran a rather critical article. I'm for animal rights as much as anyone, Mr. Waters, but sometimes it gets a bit much. It's just a mural."

Rolly nodded, trying to appear understanding and sympathetic. The conversation had moved away from his original topic. He wanted to get back on course before Principal Boyle ran out of time.

"What was the complaint about Janis?"

Boyle stopped, clasping her hands together again. It was a well-practiced pose that communicated seriousness.

"Janis Withers was a member of a religious organization, some kind of a new-age thing, the Lemurians."

"I've heard of them," said Rolly. Melody's temple. Dolphins, not monkeys.

"I'm not up on the details of their beliefs," said Boyle. "But apparently dolphins are a large part of the orthodoxy. They believe an ancient civilization, Lemuria, was destroyed thousands of years ago, and it fell into the sea, like Atlantis. The people who escaped were transformed into dolphins. Janis shared her cosmology with the children, rather too enthusiastically, I'm afraid. I talked to her about it, after I heard from some of the parents. They were worried we had some crazy woman working with their kids."

"Do you think Janis was crazy?"

"Janis Withers was a sweet-tempered woman, but she never seemed quite an adult. Her disposition, I mean. She carried this pink dolphin backpack around with her like a security blanket. I guess if anything was a little off, it was that, and her fascination with dolphins, the whole Lemurian thing. She tended to go off on that sometimes, and her secret agent boyfriend, of course. Aside from that, she was quite well behaved and dependable. As I said, the kids loved her. She didn't seem to have any meanness in her. She was just a bit . . . unusual."

"There's a lot of unusual in OB," said Rolly.

Principal Boyle chuckled.

"Well said, Mr. Waters," she said. "It took me a couple of years to get used to this community, but I've become rather fond of it now."

"I lived here when I was younger," said Rolly. "Rented a house with my band, in the War Zone."

"You could probably make all the noise you wanted down there."

"I don't think I could handle it now. I was younger then. Much younger."

"Mr. Wendell sings, you know. He's very nice. There's a kind of radiance to him. Would you like to see the mural?"

"I thought it wasn't painted yet."

"He came by a few days ago and completed the outline."

Rolly wasn't all that interested in viewing Wendell's outline of a mural, but it was easier to get your questions answered when you showed an interest in other people's projects.

"Sure," he said.

Boyle led him out of the playground toward the street. They turned into the back parking lot. A vegetable garden grew at one end of the lot. A colorful mural of butterflies and flowers had been painted on the wall behind the garden. A second mural ran along a wall perpendicular to the butterflies. Dolphins and other sea life had been outlined in chalk.

"I don't understand why Janis killed herself," said Boyle. "She was so excited, so happy about this. And I simply can't believe this terrorist talk. Are they sure it wasn't some sort of horrible accident?"

Rolly shrugged his shoulders.

"They're still investigating. Did Janis ever mention a brother to you?"

"No. I didn't know she had a brother. What's his name?"

"Richard Withers. His stage name is Dick Nazi."

Boyle lifted her eyebrows.

"Another colorful Obcean, I take it?" she said.

"He's in a punk band. He drives one of those big amphibious tourist boats you see around the bay."

"The OTTER?"

"Yes."

"Janis came to school in one of those boats. This man dropped her off, three days a week. She only worked three days a week. He'd pick her up at the end of the day too."

"Shaved head and tattoos on his arms?" said Rolly.

"I'm not sure," said Boyle. "He wore a captain's hat."

"It must be him," said Rolly.

"I expect so," said Boyle. "They certainly seem to be a colorful family. Janis lived at the Point Loma yacht club, you know. She lived on her boat."

"Did she ever mention someone named Daniel Piper?" said Rolly. "Or Harmonica Dan?"

"What did he look like?"

Rolly described Dan's appearance, the trench coat and gold epaulets. Boyle furrowed her eyebrows as he spoke.

"I did see a man like that," she said. "The first time Wendell was here, when we made the announcement."

She pointed out toward the street. "I was here by the wall, with Mr. Wendell. This man was standing behind the fence, out on the sidewalk staring at us. I considered calling security, but he wasn't on school property."

"Was Janis here that day? Did she see him?"

"I don't remember, but . . . oh my goodness."

"Yes?"

Boyle swiveled around. She pointed up at a second-story window.

"It was later that day. I was walking the halls and I looked out that window. Janis was down here in the garden next to the fence. She was talking to that man."

Rolly looked from the window back to the fence. Principal Boyle had now connected Janis to Harmonica Dan, here at the school. Dick Nazi had dropped Janis off at the school three days a week. Last night at Winstons, Nazi had connected Dan to Butch Fleetwood. In music, three notes were the minimum needed to identify the type of chord being played. A chord wasn't a song, though. It was only a place to start. He still needed to search for the melody.

# 14

## THE RAG

The offices of the *Ocean Beach Enquirer* were located on the second floor of one of the old commercial buildings on Newport Avenue in the central business district of Ocean Beach, four blocks from the school. Rolly had a full morning's work still ahead of him, starting with a visit to the newspaper office to talk to the man who had written the article about Butch Fleetwood. After that, he planned to visit the Lemurian Temple, where he hoped to find Melody. She still hadn't returned his phone calls. He climbed the stairs to the newspaper office and opened the front door.

"Can I help you?" said the young man sitting at the front desk. The man wore a sky-blue tank top and tangerine beach trunks. He was short, thick and muscular, with light mocha skin. A small scar ran from the corner of his mouth up to his left nostril.

"My name's Rolly Waters," said Rolly, handing the man a business card. "I'm looking for Tom Cockburn. I talked to him on the phone earlier."

"Yes, Mr. Waters," said the man. "I'm Ferdy, short for Ferdinand. Tom told me you would be stopping by." He shoved his bare feet into a pair of flip-flops and stood up. "He asked me to pull some old editions for you. They're over here."

Rolly followed the man past the front desk to a large melamine table in the middle of the room. Fluorescent light from the ceiling shone down on the table.

"These are the editions he asked me to pull," said the young man, indicating a half-dozen copies of the newspaper arranged on the table.

"Is Mr. Cockburn around?" said Rolly.

"He stepped out for a cup of coffee."

Rolly nodded.

"I wanted to show him something."

"He should be back soon. You're welcome to stay as long as you like."

"Thank you," said Rolly.

"I've arranged the articles you requested in chronological order. Both the original series and the updated companion piece we ran recently."

"How long have you worked here?" asked Rolly.

"I've been Mr. Cockburn's assistant for a while now."

"Did you work on any of these stories?"

"Only the recent one. The follow-up to the original article. Inside, page three. I researched what was publicly available and filed the FOIA request."

"What's that?"

"The Freedom of Information Act. That's how we got the transcripts from the Navy."

"From the court-martial?"

"Technically it was an inquiry. Not a court-martial."

"Sounds like you know the difference."

"Six years a blue shirt. Would you like anything? Some coconut water?"

"No thanks," said Rolly.

"Helps keep your electrolytes and potassium levels up," said the man. "Good for your complexion and your heart."

"Maybe later," said Rolly. The man started to leave, then hesitated.

"Tom told me you were famous around here at one time. In Ocean Beach, I mean."

"I had a band."

"You were a musician?"

"We did pretty well for a while. Locally. Around town."

"Well, it's nice to meet you Mr. Waters. Let me know if you need anything."

"Thanks. I will."

Ferdy walked back to his desk. Rolly sat down at the table. He read the complete copy of the reprinted article that had been left on his windshield—"Who Killed Butch Fleetwood?" The follow-up on page three provided additional information gleaned from a newly available transcript of the inquest into Fleetwood's disappearance. According to the article, the transcript had been heavily redacted, but some new facts had come to light.

Butch Fleetwood's last training exercise had tested the efficacy of a system that helped dolphins distinguish between friendly and enemy divers. If an enemy diver approached the vessel, the dolphin would bump the diver, discharging a weapon it carried on its snout. Specific information about the functionality of the device had been redacted from the transcript, but anonymous sources suggested it might attach a flotation device to the diver. The device would inflate and pull the diver to the surface, immobilizing him and making his position known to observers on board a ship.

Butch Fleetwood and his diving partner played the parts of friend and foe during the exercise. Fleetwood's partner was tagged by a dolphin almost immediately and was picked up by the chase boat two minutes after the start of the exercise. What little was known about Fleetwood's final minutes came from his partner's testimony.

According to the other diver, Fleetwood had violated training protocols almost as soon as the exercise began, diving faster and deeper than the guidelines allowed. If a flotation weapon really existed, it was a dangerous thing for him to do. The deeper a diver went, the longer he stayed underwater, the greater the chance he'd suffer decompression sickness when he was hauled to the surface.

Fleetwood's oxygen tanks held thirty minutes of breathable air. Emergency operations commenced on the stroke of the thirty-first minute and continued through the night, but to no avail. A second problem presented itself during the rescue operation. One of the dolphins had gone missing as well. Neither Fleetwood, the device, nor the dolphin were ever seen again.

The inquiry concluded with the theory that one of the dolphins had jolted Fleetwood hard enough to disorient him or knock him out. Many of the divers, including Fleetwood's partner, had sustained bruises and contusions from dolphin bumps during previous training exercises. The missing dolphin was known for its erratic and some-times aggressive behavior. Butch Fleetwood had a less-than-perfect record himself. He'd been disciplined several times for not following Navy procedures.

Nighttime conditions contributed to Fleetwood's disappearance as well, making search and recovery more difficult. The exercise had taken place near Ballast Point, at the entrance to the harbor, where strong underwater currents came into play. Fleetwood's body could have been pulled out of the harbor into the depths of the Pacific Ocean. The conclusions of the report seemed reasonable to Rolly, but it was still speculation. Without a body or an eyewitness to the dolphin's attack, there was no proof of what happened to Fleetwood. There was no mention of Arion, either.

Rolly turned his attention to the other articles, which had appeared in the paper a few weeks before Fleetwood's disappearance twenty-three years ago. The articles were part of a series exposing secret government programs conducted at the Point Loma Naval Base. A deep and exclusive source had provided copies of plans and diagrams for weaponizing the dolphins. The most disturbing was a $CO_2$ injection cartridge that would cause a diver to explode, literally turning him inside out.

"The FBI visited me after that one was published," said a voice behind Rolly. "That's how I knew I'd hit close to home."

Rolly lifted his head from the table. A man stood behind him, looking over his shoulder.

"Tom Cockburn," the man said, extending his hand. "Chief muck-raker, editor and owner."

Rolly stood up and they shook hands.

"Rolly Waters," he said.

"Oh, I remember you," said the man. "With your band. You were much prettier then."

"I forgot to put on my makeup today."

Cockburn grinned. He was older than Rolly, and shorter, with curly brown hair touched up with gold highlights. He had a beard, but no mustache. The beard was neatly trimmed, running from ear to ear in an elegantly clipped line. A dark purple beret and a gold loop in one ear completed the look and gave him the rakish air of an Amish movie director attending a film festival. Cockburn lifted the newspaper from the table and scanned the page.

"That wasn't the first time the FBI came to visit, mind you," said Cockburn. "I always take it as a sign that I've touched a nerve when they do, that I'm on to something they don't want the public to know."

"Were you on to something with that?" asked Rolly, indicating the drawing of the $CO_2$ delivery system included in the article.

"Well, it did bring the FBI into my office, but I have to admit, I've never found any evidence that a weapon like that, or even a prototype, was ever built. My feeling is it never got past the drawing board, like so many of the idiotic ideas that come out of military research. Have you had a chance to read through the other articles? Were they helpful?"

"Yes. Thank you."

"You mentioned when you called that you had something that might be of interest to me, something about Butch Fleetwood?"

"Yes," said Rolly. He looked around the office. "Can we talk in private?"

"Certainly," said Cockburn. "Let's go to my office." He led Rolly to one of the small offices in back and closed the door.

"I have to say if you're trying to keep something from the FBI or the NSA, it won't do you any good. They can listen in just about anywhere these days. Cell phones, satellites, Internet. I just assume now that everything I say is being listened to. I've decided not to give a damn."

"I haven't done anything illegal," said Rolly. "Not recently." He took a seat across from Cockburn.

"Well, it's our government stooges that get to decide that, isn't it?" said Cockburn. "What have you got for me?"

Rolly reached in his pocket, pulled out Fleetwood's dog tags and placed them on the desk. Cockburn picked them up. He clucked his tongue against the roof of his mouth.

"My, my," he said. "Where'd you get these?"

"A client gave them to me. As I mentioned on the phone, I'm a private investigator. I can't reveal the client's name." Rolly handed Cockburn his card. The newspaper editor clucked his tongue again.

"Please continue," he said.

"These were found in the personal effects of a friend of mine, a friend who died recently."

"I see. Can you tell me anything about this friend?"

"You know about the incident at the Admiral's Club last week?"

"Of course. What's your interest?"

"The woman who killed herself, she was in charge of my band's fan club many years ago."

"You knew Janis Withers?"

Rolly nodded.

"I talked to J.V. Sideman," said Rolly. "He said you called him and asked about Fleetwood."

"What else did he tell you?"

"About the party?"

"About anything."

"Off the record?" said Rolly.

"Certainly," said Cockburn. "You're a secondary source. I can't report what you say he said. That would be hearsay."

Rolly ran through J.V. Sideman's account of the incident at the Admiral's Club and the death of Janis Withers.

Cockburn leaned back in his chair. He pushed his fingertips together and flexed his hands a couple of times.

"You've done some top-notch detective work, Mr. Waters," Cockburn said when he finished. "Worthy of a good journalist."

"Thank you," said Rolly.

"Arion? What do you think Janis Withers meant by that?"

Rolly shrugged.

"I don't know. There's a Greek myth about a guy who gets saved by dolphins. His name was Arion."

"You've heard of Tidewater Defense Systems?"

"That's the company that sponsored the party, right? They have some kind of contract with the Navy's dolphin program?"

"Correct. Tidewater is a very large, very successful defense contractor. Their headquarters are in Newport News, Virginia, hence the name. Janis Withers's grandfather is majority owner. He founded the company."

"Are Henley and Tammy Withers her parents?"

"Yes. Have you spoken with them?"

"Not yet."

"Let me show you something," said Cockburn. He pushed his chair back, opened a file drawer and fished out a piece of paper. He placed it on the desk in front of Rolly.

Rolly picked up the piece of paper. It was a copy of Tidewater Defense Systems stationery with ARION spelled out in block letters in the center of the page with a "TOP SECRET" stamp next to it.

"Advance Reconnaissance Interception Observation and Nullification," said Rolly, reading the words under the acronym.

"I have the rest of the document," said Cockburn. "It was a research project at Tidewater. For twenty-three years I've been trying to figure it out. The documentation doesn't make sense. No one's been able to explain it to me."

"You think this is the ARION Janis was talking about?"

"The thing is, Mr. Waters, we journalists collect lots of little bits of information. But we can only use confirmed facts. If two facts are connected by a third fact, I may have a story. But I need the connection."

"You think these dog tags are the connection?"

"They could be. Where did you get them?"

"I can't tell you that."

"What I'm trying to tell you, Mr. Waters, is the articles I wrote all those years ago contain all the information I could responsibly print at the time. Coincidences don't make a story, not for a reputable journalist. If I knew where these dog tags came from, I might see it as more than a coincidence."

"What's this coincidence you're talking about?"

Tom Cockburn stroked his beard a few times, then looked at the dog tags again.

"The same night Butch Fleetwood disappeared, Janis Withers checked into the emergency ward at the Naval Hospital. She had burns on one side of her face."

# 15

## THE TEMPLE

The morning fog had lifted by the time Rolly left the newspaper office. It was warm and sunny outside, the kind of day when the ragged, funky charm of Ocean Beach beckoned more brightly, when a strong dose of sun, waves and cold beer seemed like a prescription for all of life's ailments. The salt air tickled his nostrils as he walked down the street. He didn't drink beer anymore and his skin burned easily in the sun. And a horde of jellyfish had invaded the local beaches.

He turned off Newport Avenue and walked four blocks to the address he'd found for the Lemurian Temple. It turned out to be nothing more than a one-story beach bungalow, painted sky blue with dark navy trim. A pair of midget palm trees stood like sentinels on either side of the entryway. Calligraphic gold letters spelled out "Lemurian Temple Pacifica" on the top edge of the door frame. A large man sat in one of the metal garden chairs at the end of the porch. He was tanned and muscular with a graying beard, long blond braids and deep lines on his face.

"Anybody home?" Rolly said. The man didn't say anything. Rolly knocked on the door. It opened. Melody Flowers greeted him with a quizzical smile.

"Hello," said Rolly.

"Hello," said Melody. Her face looked blank.

"I need to ask you some questions," said Rolly.

"Who are you?" said Melody.

"Rolly Waters."

"Oh yes," said Melody. She seemed unsure.

"You talked to me at Winstons a couple of nights ago, after the blues jam?"

A strange light went on in Melody's eyes. Her smile disappeared.

"I thought you were going to call me," she said.

"I did," said Rolly. "I left messages. You never called back. I was in the neighborhood, so I thought we might talk."

"Okay."

"Can I come in?"

Melody hesitated. A man's voice called out from the back of the house.

"Hey babe," he said. "Do you know where I left my sandals?"

Melody turned her head toward the room.

"They're here, by the door."

The man entered the front room. He was dressed in long, baggy shorts and a pink Hawaiian shirt. He buttoned the shirt as he crossed the room and stood behind Melody. He put one hand on her shoulder for balance as he slipped into his sandals.

"Hey, buddy. What's up?" he said, looking out at Rolly.

"Not much," said Rolly.

"You here for an aura reading?"

"Just exchanging some information with this young lady."

"Oh yeah? What kind of information?"

"I'm a building inspector."

The man wrinkled his brow, giving Rolly a chance to register his striking facial features—high cheekbones and a strong chin, deep green eyes with slightly hooded lids. His skin was light brown, almost shiny, with a smattering of light freckles. Rolly felt like he'd seen the man before, but couldn't place where or when.

"Well, honey," said the man, addressing Melody. "Looks like you've got some business to do, and I've got a bunch of kids waiting for me. I'll see you soon."

The man squeezed the back of Melody's neck.

"I left something for you," he said as he stepped over the threshold onto the porch. "I signed it this time."

The large, ponytailed man on the porch stood. His left arm hung against his side as if it were paralyzed.

"Are you next?" Rolly said, thinking the porch might serve as some kind of waiting room.

"Happy's my shadow," said the smaller man. "He follows me wherever I go."

The two men walked out to the sidewalk and headed into the main part of town.

"I guess we can talk now," said Melody. "Come on in."

The front room was larger than Rolly expected, with a plank wood floor and Craftsman-style built-ins. Glass curios filled the shelves and cabinets. Tabletops were crowded with polished crystal globes and dolphin statues carved out of glass, stone and wood. A painting hung over the mantel, a reproduction of some classical piece, men drowning at sea.

"I'm sorry if I was rude," said Melody. "I get very focused when I'm working."

"I didn't mean to interfere with your business," said Rolly.

"Did you find him?" asked Melody. "Did you find Butch Fleetwood?"

"Yes and no. Do you read the *OB Enquirer*?"

"What's that?"

"It's a local newspaper. A weekly."

"I don't really read much. I don't watch the news. Negative information interferes with my aura cleansing."

"There was an article in last week's edition. I thought you should see it."

Rolly handed Melody the newspaper. She cried out when she read the headline and collapsed into the rattan chair next to the fireplace.

"When did this happen?" she said. "When did he die?"

"Twenty-three years ago. That article is a reprint."

"Oh," said Melody. She sat up in the chair. "I thought it just happened."

"They're not sure what happened. He might have been killed by a dolphin."

"That's impossible. Dolphins don't kill people."

"It was an accident, a training accident. He worked for the Navy. The dolphins were trained to attack divers."

"That's terrible, that's sickening."

"The dolphin didn't mean to kill him. They think it just bumped him too hard."

"Dolphins are gentle beings. They're spiritual creatures."

"It happened here, in the bay, near the Navy base. They never found his body."

Melody leaned forward. She picked up a crystal globe that lay on the table and placed it on her lap.

"Poor Janis," she said. "She must've been so young when he died."

"Fourteen," said Rolly. "I did some figuring."

Melody closed her eyes. She turned her face to the floor.

"Poor Janis," she said.

"I need to ask you something," said Rolly. Melody didn't respond. He asked anyway.

"Did Janis know anyone named Daniel Piper? Harmonica Dan? He lives on sailboat."

"Misery," said Melody. "Misery and corruption."

"What's that?" said Rolly.

Melody rocked back and forth in her chair as she fondled the crystal globe. She shouted at the floor in a deep, mannish voice.

"Misery and corruption. Death and despair. The great clouds have broken over Lemuria. We must go to the temple. We must go to the sea."

She turned her gaze from the floor to Rolly.

"Are you an emissary of the ocean king?" she said.

"Uh . . . no, I don't think so," said Rolly. "What are you doing?"

"Why have you come here?"

"I'm Rolly Waters. I'm a private detective. You hired me."

Melody's body went still. Her hands looked like talons clutching the crystal ball. Her face tightened into a rictus of dark intensity. Alarmed and uncertain, Rolly approached the chair where she sat. He squatted down in front of her and smiled. A smile had helped him with crazy women before. With angry women. With crazy angry women. He softened his voice.

"Hello, Melody," he said. "It's me. Rolly Waters. I'm here to help you."

"Rolly. Waters."

"Can you talk to me?"

"I answer to the entreaties of the ocean king."

Rolly nodded. Melody appeared to be having some sort of psychotic episode. It might be temporary, like an epileptic fit, if he could just get her through it.

"What's your name?" he asked.

"I am Merdonis," she said.

"Merdonis? Your name isn't Melody?"

"Merdonis is my Lemurian name."

"I see," said Rolly. "This is your temple then, isn't it?"

"It is a temple for all who worship the dolphin kings."

"I see. Am I a Lemurian?"

"Have you swum with the dolphins?"

"No. I don't think so. I'm not a very good swimmer."

"You are human. A despoiler of the natural world."

Rolly looked around the room.

"Well, I try to recycle as much as I can, but point taken. Are you a human being?"

"I am a shaman who speaks for the Lemurians."

Rolly nodded.

"What else can you tell me about Lemurians?"

"They come from Lemuria."

"Yeah. I got that part. Where is Lemuria?"

Melody pointed at the painting on the wall, the one of the shipwreck.

"Lemuria was a great continent, in the time before mankind's consciousness arose. It sank into the ocean. Pieces of the ancient land still exist underwater. Dolphins are its emissaries, moving between the water world and the land, carrying messages of enlightenment and peace. They are our allies against the power of global tyranny."

"I see," said Rolly. He resisted rolling his eyes or making a joke. He held his gaze steady and stared into Melody's eyes. She blinked. Her body relaxed and she slumped into the back of the rattan chair.

"What happened?" she asked.

"You had some sort of spell," said Rolly. "A seizure or something."

"Did I say anything?"

"You said your name was Merdonis. You wanted to know if I was an emissary from the ocean king."

"Why would I say that?"

"I don't know."

"Only dolphins can be emissaries of the king."

"Oh," said Rolly, wondering if Melody had really come out of her spell, or if she'd only replaced it with a new one.

"I'm sorry," said Melody. "This doesn't usually happen to me, not in these kinds of circumstances."

"It's happened before?"

"I call on my spirit self when we conduct Lemurian ceremonies."

"That where the shaman stuff comes in?"

"Excuse me," said Melody. She rose from the chair. "I need to lie down."

"Yes," said Rolly. "Have you heard of him?"

"Who?" said Melody.

"Daniel Piper. Harmonica Dan. I think Janis may have known him."

"I don't know his name," said Melody. "I'm tired now. I need to lie down."

She walked away, disappearing into the back of the house, leaving Rolly by himself. He looked around the living room, studying the crystal globes and dolphin debris. It was all very strange. He walked over to look at the painting that hung over the mantel. There was more to the painting than he'd originally noticed. Naked men with fishlike tails swam in the waves. There was a sinking ship in the background. Strange-looking fish with doglike faces swam with the men. A man in red robes and holding a lyre sat on the back of the largest dogfish.

Rolly squinted his eyes at the small print along the lower edge of the poster. For a brief second the characters came into focus, just long enough to read the title before it went blurry again. The title under the painting was *Arion and the Dolphin*. There was a signature, too. He couldn't read the name, but it started with a big *W*. Melody's mystical fits were disconcerting, but there was something else about his visit that bothered him too, something he couldn't quite put a finger on. He looked at the painting again. Arion. It was everywhere now. He had an appointment with Janis's parents later in the day. Maybe they could explain why.

# 16

# THE SHRINK

L ate that afternoon, Rolly climbed the stairs to the offices of Tidewater Defense Systems in Liberty Station and read the names listed on the directory at the top of the stairs. There were only two names: Tammy Withers, PhD in Suite 201 to his left and Henley Withers, PhD in 202 to his right. He'd called both their offices that morning. No one had answered. No one had returned his calls.

He decided to try Tammy Withers first and knocked on the door of 201. No one answered. He turned the doorknob and let himself in. A pug dog lay on a small mattress in one corner of the room. It barked at Rolly and climbed to its feet.

"Who's there?" It was a woman's voice from down the hall.

"My name's Rolly Waters. I'm looking for Tammy Withers."

"I'm with a patient. Sit down."

"Thank you," said Rolly. The pug eyed him as he took a seat in a chair on the opposite side of the room. There was a magazine rack mounted on the wall next to him displaying old copies of *Boating*, *Shooting Life* and *Pet Therapy*, none of which interested him. A woman entered the room from the back office. Rolly stood up.

"Mrs. Withers?" he said.

"Oh no," said the woman. "She's with Pookie. I had to leave. I was telegraphing my aspirations."

The woman sat down in the chair next to the pug.

"This is Snookie," she said, looking down at the dog. "Pookie and Snookie don't get along. That's why we're here. What kind of dog do you have?"

"I don't have a dog," said Rolly.

"Are you a cat person?"

"I don't have any pets."

"Don't you like animals?" said the woman.

"I like animals fine," said Rolly. "This is a business call."

The woman looked down at Snookie. The pug looked back up at her.

"She was a champion, you know," said the woman, indicating the magazines. "Dr. Withers."

"What's that?"

"Racing boats. Target shooting. She's got a bunch of trophies in her office."

"She must be quite an accomplished person," said Rolly. People who displayed trophies made him nervous.

"Oh yeah. She's done all sorts of stuff. Not like me. I've never accomplished anything. I got two dogs with different dads. Neither of the guys wanted to marry me, so they left me with the dogs. I have zero boyfriends now and two dogs that fight all the time."

The woman opened her purse and fished out a Kleenex. She wiped her eyes.

"Excuse me," she said.

"It's okay."

"Control yourself and you control your animal. That's what Dr. Withers always tells me."

A strident voice interrupted them, a call to attention.

"Annie!"

A tall woman dressed in a tan pantsuit stood at the entrance to the back hallway. A second pug dog, presumably Pookie, stared out from between the tall woman's legs.

"I think we've made some progress, Annie," she said. "Are you ready?"

"Yes, Dr. Withers."

Annie stood up. She nodded and took a deep breath, pulled a leash out of her purse and attached it to Snookie's collar.

"Now call Pookie over," said the tall woman.

"Pooks," said Annie. "Come here, Pooks."

The second pug walked into the room.

"Maintain your indifference," said Dr. Withers. Rolly glanced over at Annie, who looked physically taxed by the effort. Pookie stopped in her tracks, facing Snookie. The two dogs stared at each other for a moment, and then seemed to lose interest. Annie looked to Dr. Withers for approval and the tall woman nodded her consent. Annie took a second leash out of her purse and attached it to Pookie.

"Very good, Annie," said Dr. Withers, opening the front door. "I'll see you next week."

Annie and her dogs walked out the door. Dr. Withers shut the door and turned her attention to Rolly.

"I got your message, Mr. Waters."

"I'm sorry to intrude at this difficult time."

Dr. Withers turned to the magazine rack, rearranging the order of things.

"Yes, well, this . . . event was not completely unexpected," she said. "My daughter had been committed to her self-destruction for some time. This was the simply the most spectacular in a long line of suicide attempts. And the most successful. My daughter was unhappy and sick, and, in the end, simply unreachable."

"I'm sorry."

Dr. Withers finished her magazine rearrangement and turned back to Rolly.

"Let's get on with it, shall we?" she said. "I understood from your message that you knew Janis?"

"She was the head of my band's fan club."

"You're a musician?"

"I played guitar in a band called Creatures."

"Did you have a sexual relationship with my daughter?"

"No. But . . ."

"Yes?"

"A friend of mine, the singer in my band. They were involved."

"What is your friend's name?"

"Matt DiFranco."

Dr. Withers brushed something from the lapel of her suit.

"Dog hair," she said in distaste. She looked back at Rolly. "I've never heard of your friend. Are you acting as his agent? Does he plan to make some kind of claim on my daughter's estate?"

Rolly remembered Moogus telling him Janis was a rich girl. Rich people thought everyone else was after their money. Maybe they were.

"I don't know anything about your daughter's estate," he said. "My friend Matt died in a car accident many years ago."

"I see. What is your interest, then?"

"I was driving the car."

Tammy Withers extended her long neck like a heron preparing to strike at a fish.

"Come back to my office," she said. "I prefer to conduct business there." She turned on her heel. Rolly followed her down the hall. Two cheap plastic chairs faced off against each other in her office, like boxing opponents on the black linoleum floor. There was no desk in the room. There were no filing cabinets or drawers. Professional certifications and trophies were displayed on the wall. Little gold boats and gold pistols.

"Take a seat, Mr. Waters," said Dr. Withers, indicating the chair on the left. They sat down and faced each other, a body length apart.

"Truth chairs," said Dr. Withers. "That's what I call them. I'm an animal behaviorist by training, but humans exhibit many similar psychological responses. It is important to remove external stimuli so that we may concentrate on reinforcement and punishment."

"I see," said Rolly, wondering if he'd become part of a clinical experiment.

"Ninety percent of pet therapy is addressing the behavior of the pet's owner," said Dr. Withers. "I need to observe their interactions with the animal."

"I don't have any pets," said Rolly. "I wanted to know more about Janis. And Matt."

"Yes, of course. You're looking for some kind of closure."

Rolly sighed. He'd heard that word a thousand times from therapists, family and friends. But closure was meaningless. It was an illusion. Guilt was a bitter coat on the hollow body of grief. Tammy Withers had sidetracked him into thinking about Matt. She didn't seem to feel any guilt, or grief, about what had happened to her daughter.

"Mr. Waters?"

"Hmph," said Rolly, stirring from his thoughts.

"You're sure this has nothing to do with my daughter's estate?"

"Not at all," said Rolly. "It's a personal thing."

"I'm inclined to believe you, but I doubt I can help. Janis moved out of our house the day she turned eighteen. We had no other hold over her at that point. She didn't need money, as my father had set up a trust. We saw each other sporadically since then. I don't know if she was married. I don't know if she had any children."

"Would your son know?"

"You're speaking of Richard?"

"Yes. I met him last night. He got very upset when I asked about Janis."

"Richard gets upset easily. He has poor impulse control."

Dr. Withers stood up. She walked around the room, then paused at her trophy wall.

"My husband and I were not very successful parents, Mr. Waters," she said, staring at her shinier achievements. "We were both too involved in our work. Our children's lack of fealty is the price we paid for our professional success. The simple truth is neither of our children has given us the time of day since they moved out of the house. We never asked for it, either."

She turned back to the room.

"So there you are," she said. "I can't really tell you about my daughter and your friend or their level of intimacy. I simply don't know. I doubt Richard knows anything. Our children led separate lives from each other, as well. Richard is quite a bit younger."

"Did you know Janis volunteered at an elementary school in Ocean Beach? That Richard drove her there three days a week?"

"No, I didn't know that. As I said, we lost touch."

Dr. Withers returned to her truth chair.

"Will that be all, Mr. Waters?" she said. "I do have some work to attend to."

"Just one more thing," said Rolly. "Did Janis know anyone named Arion?"

Dr. Withers sighed.

"Arion was a figment of my daughter's imagination," she said. "An imaginary friend, I guess you might call him. It's not unusual for children to have imaginary friends, of course, but Arion became a stronger presence when she was fighting depression. She would insist he was real and that we were all trying to kill him."

"Arion was a man?"

"Yes."

"Was he some sort of spy?"

Dr. Withers gave a dry chuckle.

"It was quite remarkable from a psychological point of view," she said. "All the details Janis filled in. Most children give up their imaginary friends as they grow older. Arion kept coming back to her, even in adulthood."

"Was there ever a Tidewater project called Arion?"

Dr. Withers blinked hard, paused a moment, then blinked again.

"That's a rather spurious connection you're trying to make, Mr. Waters, and a rather ill-informed one."

"So there isn't one, a connection I mean?"

"The ARION project was top secret, Mr. Waters. I can't discuss it."

"I understand. I just wondered how Janis came up with such an unusual name for her friend."

"My husband and I were heavily involved in the project, perhaps to the detriment of our attention to Janis when she was a teenager. It's possible she heard the name around the house and took emotional ownership of it, as a way to connect with us. As I've said, we didn't give her the guidance she needed."

"I'd like to speak to your husband," said Rolly.

"He'll tell you the same thing."

"There are some other things I'd like to ask him about."

"Such as?"

"I understand he worked with the Dolphin Divers program."

"We both did. My father founded this company, Tidewater Defense Systems. Tidewater builds ships for the Navy, parts of ships anyway, but the company has bid on other government contracts over the years, including the dolphin work. That was our specialty, my husband and I."

"What was your involvement with the Dolphin Divers?"

"As an animal behaviorist, my job was to work with the trainers to develop and codify best-practice training techniques. My husband developed physical prototypes for dolphin/human interfaces. He's a brilliant engineer. That's all I can tell you. Our work was top secret. Much of it is still classified."

Rolly shifted in his seat. He needed to poke Tammy's memory more directly. He hoped the truth chairs worked both ways.

"Did you know a diver named Butch Fleetwood?"

Dr. Withers looked into the corner of the room.

"That was a tragedy," she said. "It could have been avoided."

"But you knew him?"

"Yes. As did my husband."

"And Janis?"

"Why are you asking me this?"

Rolly pulled Fleetwood's dog tags out of his pocket and handed them to Dr. Withers.

"Where did you get these?" she said, with even more ice in her voice.

"My client gave them to me."

Dr. Withers glared at Rolly.

"Whom are you working for?" she said.

"I can't tell you that."

"Is it the FBI?"

"No."

"The OMU, then? Hoping to discredit us?"

"No. I'm a private investigator. I don't think my client means any harm."

Dr. Withers stared at the floor. She played with the ring on her left hand.

"I apologize, Mr. Waters. You've brought up some old memories. Some painful accusations were made. We were all under a cloud. I take the blame. I tried to take Mr. Fleetwood under my wing, to improve him, to give him some sense of family and belonging. By the time I recognized his true psychological nature, it was too late."

Dr. Withers stood up. She walked to the office door, then turned back to Rolly.

"My daughter was fourteen years old when she met Butch Fleetwood," she said. "She was naive and trusting. She didn't understand how exploitative some adults can be. Butch was in his early twenties, a physically attractive young man with a highly manipulative personality, a true sociopath. My daughter couldn't help but develop a crush on him. He led her on. He built up quite a fantasy in her head, none of which had any basis in reality. I didn't realize the full extent of it until after Butch's death. My daughter was devastated when she realized how he'd used her, how he toyed with her affections. That was when Janis first tried to kill herself."

# 17

# THE ENGINEER

R olly followed Tammy Withers across the hall to Suite 202.
"Does anyone else work here?" said Rolly. "Besides you and
your husband?"

"It's just us now," said Tammy. "We've downsized considerably.
Our budget isn't what it used to be. The dolphin program's been
cancelled."

"I heard they were moving the dolphins to Ocean Universe."

"Yes."

She opened the door to 202. They stepped inside.

"Henley?" she said. "I'm with someone. Are you here?"

No one answered. The space inside was a pile of junky chaos, filled
with metal tools, electronic circuit boards and mechanical gadgetry—a
mad inventor's workshop. Blueprints and mechanical drawings
covered the walls.

"He's probably in the tank room," said Tammy.

"What's that?"

"We've got two hydraulic tanks downstairs, for testing fluid
mechanics. That's Henley's specialty. Hydrodynamics."

"Sounds way beyond me."

"Yes, I imagine it would be. Let's try downstairs."

Tammy's jibe rolled off Rolly like rain on a tin roof. In the early days of his musical career, the slightest indignity would sometimes set him off, but now he'd grown used to it. Insults were the expression of someone else's discomfort and fears. He followed Tammy out of the office and down the stairs. She pulled out a key, unlocked the double door under the stairs and led Rolly into a large open room with a concrete floor.

"We have a large tank and a small tank," said Tammy. "The larger one includes a wave maker and beach."

They walked toward the two tanks of water in the middle of the room. The larger one looked to be a hundred feet long, the smaller one about eight feet in length. The tanks had thick glass walls on all sides. You could see inside from any angle.

"What do you use these for?" said Rolly.

"Testing prototypes."

"I thought you worked with dolphins."

"Dolphins are remarkable from a fluid dynamics view. My husband is an expert on dolphin mechanics. Where is he? Henley!"

"Yes, dear." A man walked out from the shadows of the tanks. He was old, shriveled and naked, but there was a vitality in his posture, without awkwardness or shame.

"For God's sake, Henley, put some clothes on," said his wife.

"Oh," said Henley. "I didn't know you had someone with you."

He turned back to the corner. When he returned he wore a short-sleeved blue dress shirt and a pair of black swimming briefs, his feet were still bare.

"Who's this fellow?" he said.

"This is Mr. Waters," said Tammy. "He'd like to talk to you. About Butch Fleetwood."

"Fleetwood? Christ," said Henley. "I was just going to test a new model."

"This should only take a few minutes," said Rolly.

"I can't spare more than ten," said Henley.

"Mr. Waters and I have already spoken," said Tammy. "I'm leaving him with you. My husband may be able to tell you more about Mr. Fleetwood than I could, Mr. Waters. Goodbye."

Tammy turned and walked back to the door. Henley watched her go. There was a formality in their manner that Rolly couldn't explain, a cool distance between them.

"Well, what is it?" said Henley after the door closed.

"I was sorry to hear about your daughter," said Rolly.

"It's no use being sorry. She gave up on herself a long time ago."

"I knew Janis," said Rolly, taking step closer. "She was in charge of our fan club."

Henley pulled a pair of glasses out of his shirt pocket, placed them on his face and inspected Rolly through the thick lenses. Whereas Tammy bore a resemblance to a crane or a heron, her husband looked more like a short-tempered owl.

"You had a fan club?" said Henley. He didn't sound impressed.

"I had a band," said Rolly. "I'm a guitar player."

"That's your story, huh? You make a living at that?"

"Not much of one. I'm also a private investigator."

"It's original, I'll give you that. A guitar-playing detective. Never had anyone use that story before."

"I'm not sure what you mean."

"Same old baloney on a new slice of bread. Who are you with?"

"I'm not with anyone."

"Well, you're not FBI. I can spot an FBI agent twenty yards away. They couldn't look like you if they tried."

Rolly wasn't sure if the last remark was meant as an insult to him or the FBI. It didn't matter. He had nine minutes left. He reached in his pocket and pulled out the dog tags. He handed them to Henley.

"These belonged to Janis," he said. "She left them for me."

"They belong to the US Government," said Henley. "The man who wore them is dead. And now my daughter's dead. What does that tell you?"

"You think they're cursed?"

"Anyone who knew Butch Fleetwood was cursed."

"Does that include your daughter?"

"My daughter was fourteen when she met Butch Fleetwood. She was an impressionable teenager who didn't know any better."

"What about you?"

"The Navy dumped Butch Fleetwood on me, on our program. He was a strong swimmer. He could hold his breath underwater for a long time. Aside from those aptitudes, he had zero qualifications for the job to which he'd been assigned. The Navy sent us some real dopes in those days, but Fleetwood was the dopiest. He flunked out of SEAL training, you know."

"A lot of guys flunk out of SEAL training."

"Not if they pass the physical tests. Butch Fleetwood drove the damn Navy crazy. He drove us all crazy. Just as soon as you thought you had him trained to do something properly, he'd screw it up. I don't know how he ever made it through boot camp."

"What was Arion?" said Rolly.

Henley pulled off his glasses. His eyes looked smaller now, but more dangerous.

"Are you a reporter?" he said. "Is that it? A member of the so-called fourth estate who thinks he's entitled to fuck around in our lives because my research isn't politically correct?"

"I'm not a reporter."

"Whom are you working for?"

"I can't tell you that."

"Is it that jerk-off Tom Cockburn and his oily rag?"

"I'm not working for Tom Cockburn. I only met him today."

"So you talked to the old queer, huh?"

"I think he'd prefer the term *gay*."

"You talked to that gay queer?"

"I went to the newspaper office. I read those articles, the ones he wrote about Butch Fleetwood and the dolphin program. He told me about the FBI interrogations."

"Did he tell you he sucked Butch Fleetwood's dick?"

"Excuse me?"

"Fleetwood and Cockburn were buggering each other. I don't suppose Cockburn mentioned that little fact, did he?"

"No, I can't say that he did."

"The FBI went after all of us. No stone unturned for the American Gestapo, even when the obvious answer was right in front of their faces. Wal-Mart has better security than the US Navy."

"You think Fleetwood leaked those plans to Tom Cockburn's newspaper?"

Henley scrunched his mouth like he'd swallowed hot lemons.

"Have you ever been interviewed by an FBI agent, Waters?"

Rolly thought for a moment. He shook his head.

"No, can't say I have."

"Well, they don't say much. They just sit there and ask questions, write things down in their little pocket notebooks. Anytime you tell them something they ask another question. 'Why do you think this? Why do you say that?' Fleetwood got himself killed through his own bullheaded stupidity and the rest of us suffered the consequences. The Navy canceled a lot of our contracts after that stuff that came out in that newspaper, Cockburn's little socialist rag. We couldn't do any real-world testing for years."

"What kind of things were you testing?"

"What do you care?"

"Your wife says you're an expert on dolphin mechanics."

"So what?"

"She said you were brilliant."

"She's supposed to say that. She's my wife."

"You don't think you're brilliant?"

"I'm smarter than you."

"Probably. I'm not that smart. I'm just trying to figure out why Janis wanted me to have these dog tags."

"You'd have to ask my wife. She's the psychiatrist."

"Do you think Fleetwood was killed by a dolphin?"

"It's rare, but they're certainly capable. A man's got no chance against a dolphin. Whatever happened to Fleetwood, it was his own damn fault. If Butch Fleetwood had followed protocols, he might have survived. He thought he could play around with the rules. Dolphins aren't a problem. People are the problem."

Rolly didn't argue the point. People were always the problem. His job was to figure out how and why particular people became a problem. Butch Fleetwood was Rolly's problem right now, even though he was dead.

"Why do you think they never found his body?"

"Now you sound like Cockburn. He tried to make a big deal out of that, the body not showing up, like we covered up the whole thing. They got blue sharks and makos there off Point Loma, even great whites. Fleetwood's body was fish food, probably stripped to the bone within twenty-four hours of his death."

"I understand from your wife that Janis was very upset after Butch Fleetwood died. That it was the first time Janis tried to kill herself."

"Yes. I believe that was the case."

"You don't remember?"

"My wife moved to Virginia for a year after it happened. She took Janis with her."

"When was this?"

"Soon after the incident. The situation was impossible for all of us, especially Janis. We thought it would be best if she were removed from that environment. Especially after . . . when she injured herself. The increased scrutiny wasn't healthy for any of us. My wife was pregnant, as well. She and Janis went back to stay with her father while I dealt with the inquiry."

"Was that your son, Richard? I mean your wife being pregnant?"

"I suppose you know Richard too?"

"Not very well. I don't think he likes me."

"Richard doesn't like anyone. A real misanthrope."

"I got that feeling. I went to hear his band."

"I wasn't aware Richard had any musical talent."

"It's a punk band."

"That sounds plausible."

"He seemed very upset when I asked him about Janis."

"Richard was always emotional. I don't know where he gets that. My wife and I have always stressed good analytical thinking to our children. You have kids?"

"No."

"Don't. They never turn out as expected."

"Richard took Janis to work three days a week."

"Janis didn't need to work."

"It was volunteer work. Your wife told me Janis had some sort of trust fund?"

Henley gave that lemon rind look to his mouth again.

"My father-in-law set up a trust for Janis after her accident," he said. "After the first time she burned herself. Richard probably found a way to get money out of her, driving her around. Janis was what people call big-hearted. She was a soft touch. She was foolish. Anyone can be foolish when it comes to money, I suppose. Have you heard the term 'golden handcuffs,' Mr. Waters?"

"I think so," said Rolly. He thought of his engagement to Leslie, years ago, his little rich girl from Point Loma. "Never got a chance to try them on, though."

"I have," said Henley. "Believe me, they're not worth it."

# 18

# THE SHIP

Rolly stood near the top of the Harbor Drive Bridge, looking out toward the bay and ruminating on the geography of his investigation. The Tidewater offices were behind him, on the other side of the bridge. On a jutting point of land off to his left stood the completed structures of the new water park, Ocean Universe. On his right, directly across the channel from Ocean Universe, he could see the Navy's dolphin pens. Farther down the shoreline was the Admiral's Club and beyond it the bayside entrance to the Driscoll's Wharf marina, where Harmonica Dan kept his boat. There was an orange glow on the horizon. The sun had just set. He looked at the water below the bridge, contemplating the curlicues that swirled around the concrete pillars, hypnotized by the beckoning currents.

He thought about Janis Withers and her brother Dick Nazi, her parents Tammy and Henley. He wondered how families got so twisted up, what made family members abandon each other. No flashes of insight or wisdom materialized in his brain. No signs appeared, so he considered his options for dinner instead, thinking about where he might pick up something to eat on the way home. The slap-water rhythms of the bay modulated into a dusky evening refrain.

A Mustang convertible whooshed by on the road behind him, its top down, blasting Van Halen and breaking the spell. David Lee Roth shouted from the car's stereo, encouraging him to go ahead and jump, but the bridge wasn't high enough and the water wasn't deep enough to bestow on him the watery oblivion it had given Butch Fleetwood.

He crossed the street, walked to the bottom of the bridge, and took a shortcut through a stand of trees to get down to the parking lot where he'd left his old Volvo. He stepped out of the trees next to a large structure that looked like a Navy ship. The USS *Recruit* had served as a training platform for new enlistees at the old Naval Training Center, its top deck and tower fitted with the same rigging and cleats found on more seaworthy vessels. The below decks were empty and hollow. Dubbed the USS *Neversail* by former recruits, the training ship had been decommissioned years ago, then sold to developers as part of a transfer of Navy land to the city.

When Rolly was ten, his father had taken him on board the *Recruit*, sharing his memories of boot camp and sea voyages, hoping to pass on his enthusiasm for Navy life to his son. He gave Rolly lessons in rigging, how to tie knots and use the marlinspike, but it hadn't turned Rolly into a sailor. Their disappointment in each other might have started that day.

Music drifted through the air as Rolly walked past the ship. It sounded like someone playing harmonica. Rolly stopped in his tracks, listening to determine where the music came from. A light wind rustled the magnolia trees along Harbor Drive on the other side of the ship, but he couldn't see anyone. The harmonica continued to play, a familiar blues tune, "One Way Out" by Sonny Boy Williamson. Rolly looked up toward the ship.

"Harmonica Dan?" he said. "Is that you?"

The safety chains on the edge of the deck swayed gently. Rolly heard a faint clink from above.

"Hello?" he said, calling up to the ship. "Is someone there?"

No one answered. He heard a light pad of footsteps on the deck. He called out again.

"Who's there?"

"Ahoy, matey," came a low grizzled voice.

Rolly moved away from the ship, trying to get a better view. He saw a man standing next to the front gun turret, silhouetted against the burnt-orange sky.

"Halt and identify," the man said. Rolly stopped.

"It's me, Rolly Waters. The guitar player from Creatures. You used to play harmonica with us, on blues night at Winstons."

"Roger that."

"The police want to talk to you, Dan."

"Radio silence must be maintained until the mission is complete. Run silent, run deep."

"What kind of mission?"

"Top secret."

"The police want to talk to you about Janis Withers. They want to know why you left the party."

"I have to complete the mission."

"What is your mission?"

Dan didn't answer. Rolly scratched his cheek. He didn't like talking to someone this way, at a distance.

"Can I come up there?" he said.

"Nay."

"Can you come down?"

"Nay again, sailor."

"I don't like shouting like this. Someone will hear us."

"You are an unidentified agent."

"I told you who I am. Rolly Waters."

"The guitar player."

"Yes."

"You went on my boat."

"Yes. Did you see us there?"

"I have eyes on the harbor."

"The policewoman that was with me, she wants to talk to you."

"And the other one?"

"The other one?" said Rolly.

"A boatswain. A man of the sea."

"That was my father. He's a Navy man. Retired. Twenty-eight years."

"He was checking her trim."

"He said you had some kind of speakers that could be lowered into the water."

Dan played a strange little melody on his harmonica, a set of high-pitched, squeaky notes, quite different from the blues riffs he'd played earlier.

"That's the dolphin reveille," said Dan. "For my friends."

"Am I your friend?"

"You're a bogey. Intent undetermined."

"Was Janis Withers your friend?"

"Roger that. Janis was a friendly."

"What about Butch Fleetwood?"

There was no answer.

"You know something about Butch Fleetwood, don't you?" said Rolly. "You left that newspaper on my car, didn't you?"

"Evasive action required," said Dan.

"What?"

No one answered. Someone shouted from behind Rolly.

"Hey you!"

Rolly turned to see a rotund little man trotting toward him.

"What're you doing there?" said the man.

"Nothing," said Rolly. "Just looking at the ship."

"I heard you. You were talking to someone. I heard you."

The man drew close. He was a security guard. The guard stopped three feet from Rolly, put his hands on his hips and unsnapped the can of mace on his belt.

"Who's up there?" said the guard.

"I don't know what you're talking about," said Rolly.

"We've had reports," said the man. "Some guy's been living in there. We found trash, and some old clothes."

"I don't know anything about that," Rolly said.

A crashing sound came from inside the ship.

"We got him this time," said the guard. He pulled a walkie-talkie from his belt. "Hey, Barney," he said. "I'm at the boat. I think our bogeyman's here."

There was a crackle of noise on the walkie-talkie. Barney's voice came through.

"On my way," he said. "Hold tight."

"Roger," said the guard.

"You should call the police," Rolly said.

"Can't wait for the cops," the guard said. "We'll call 'em once we've got the suspect in custody."

"I know who's in there."

"Oh yeah?" said the guard, placing his walkie-talkie back in his belt. "I thought you said you didn't talk to anyone."

"His name's Daniel Piper. Also known as Harmonica Dan. The police are looking for him."

"How do you know all this?"

"I'm a private detective," said Rolly. He pulled out his wallet, handed a business card to the guard. "I'm trying to get him to give himself up. To talk to the police."

The guard handed the card back to Rolly.

"You think this guy's dangerous?"

"You know that fire they had at the Admiral's Club?"

"Geez," said the guard. "Is he wanted for that?"

"He's a person of interest. The police want to talk to him."

"This could be a big deal, nabbing the guy."

"He's not a suspect. They just want to talk to him."

"You wait here for my boss," said the guard. "I'm going in after this guy. I don't want to lose him."

"I'm going to call the police."

"You do what you want," said the guard as he fumbled at a large ring of keys on his belt. "I'm making the apprehension."

The guard found the key he was looking for. He advanced on the door in the side of the ship, opened it, pulled his flashlight from his belt, shone it inside the hull and announced himself.

"This is station security," he announced. "I have backup and police on their way. Surrender yourself."

For a moment, Rolly thought he heard a harmonica. The guard moved his flashlight around inside the ship, then looked back at Rolly.

"Wait right there," he said. "Wait for Barney."

"I don't think—" said Rolly, but the little guard had disappeared into the hold of the ship. Rolly pulled out his phone and called Bonnie.

"What's up?" she said.

"I found Harmonica Dan," said Rolly. "He's inside a ship."

"You mean his sailboat?"

"No. It's the *Recruit*, that training ship in Liberty Station."

"Can you keep him there?"

"I don't know. A security guard just showed up. He's trying to apprehend him."

"I'm on my way."

Rolly hung up. A golf cart whined across the parking lot and pulled up behind him. A security guard climbed out of the cart. He was older and taller than the first guard.

"Are you Barney?" said Rolly.

"Yeah, that's me," Barney said. "Where's Eddie?"

"He went inside."

"I told him to wait for me."

"I called the police. They'll be here soon."

They heard a crash from inside the ship. Barney grabbed his flashlight and aimed it at the door, then moved it up to the tower. A face appeared in the window of the tower. It was Eddie.

"What're you doing up there?" said Barney.

"I can't find him," said Eddie.

"You checked inside already?"

"Yeah. He's gone. Hey! What the . . .?"

Eddie's face disappeared from view, dropping into the tower like he'd been yanked on a string. Barney called to the ship.

"Eddie? Are you okay?"

There was no answer. Barney called again.

"Eddie?"

"Haaalp! Haalp!"

Barney ran to the ship. He looked back at Rolly.

"Stay there," he said. "And wait for the police."

Barney opened the door on the side of the ship and stepped inside. The door closed behind him. Rolly pulled his phone out of his pocket and started to dial 911, then stopped and put the phone back in his pocket. Bonnie would be on the scene by the time he explained the situation to an emergency operator. He'd let Bonnie decide if they needed more backup.

He paced back and forth, crunching gravel under his feet as he looked out toward the parking lot, then back at the ship. A man pushed a bicycle out from behind the ship.

"Dan!" Rolly called. The man stopped and looked over at him.

"The boys are a little tied up," said Harmonica Dan. He climbed on his bicycle and pedaled away. Rolly ran to the side of the ship and pulled the door open. A flashlight lay on the ground, illuminating the dirt floor. Rolly leaned down and picked it up.

"Are you guys okay?" he said.

"Over here," said a voice.

Rolly stepped inside the ship. He passed the flashlight beam over the room, illuminating the dirt floor and a forest of vertical wooden studs crosshatched with lateral supports. There was a man on the floor, propped against one of the posts. His shirt had been pulled over his face, exposing a fleshy belly. The man's hands were behind him, tied to the post with his belt. Rolly knelt down behind him and loosened the belt.

"Where's Eddie?" said Barney, as he pulled his shirt down over his stomach. He stood up and threaded his belt through his pant loops. "Did you find Eddie?"

"I'm over here," a voice quivered.

"Gimme that," said Barney, taking the flashlight from Rolly. He searched the room with the light until it came to rest on his partner, who'd been tied by his wrists to a wooden ladder. Eddie's pants were pulled down to his ankles.

"Holy cow, Eddie," said Barney, shining the flashlight on Eddy's stubby legs and luminescent pink buttocks.

"What is it? What is it?" said Eddie, turning his head as he tried to look over his shoulder.

Barney took a step closer, focusing the light. There were black marks on Eddie's rear end.

"What the hell is that?" said Barney.

"What did he do to me?" said Eddie, almost squealing. "What did he do to my ass?"

"He wrote something on it," said Barney. "Let's see. *A . . . R . . .*"

Rolly heard the long wail of a police siren approaching.

"Arion," he said. "It says Arion."

# 19

# THE AMBULANCE

Rolly stood by the USS *Recruit*, watching as an ambulance, two Harbor Police cars and a fire truck turned in by the parking lot. They passed him and continued down the road to the building where Tidewater Defense Systems was located. A dark sedan pulled up in front of Rolly. Bonnie Hammond got out of the sedan.

"What's going on?" Rolly said, indicating the flashing lights farther down the road.

"Somebody called in an eleven-eighty," said Bonnie. "Where's Daniel Piper?"

"He got away. Took off on his bike."

"What about the security guards?"

"They're nursing their wounds back at the office. What's an eleven-eighty?"

"Accident. Serious injury. Call came in a few minutes ago."

"Who called it in?"

"I don't know the details."

"Those are the Tidewater offices," said Rolly.

"Tidewater like the company that sponsored the dolphin party?"

"Yeah. I was over there earlier."

"What were you doing there?"

Rolly sighed. He should have called Bonnie earlier, once he'd made the connection between Janis and Dan.

"Listen, Bonnie," he said. "I used to know Janis Withers. She ran our fan club. I talked to her parents a little while ago. They work over there."

Bonnie's jaw tightened like a steel cable.

"When were you planning to tell me this?"

"I told you just now."

"Get in the car," said Bonnie, shaking her head.

They climbed into the sedan. Bonnie gunned the engine and sped down to where the emergency vehicles had gathered in front of the Tidewater offices.

"Stay here," she said, climbing out of the car. "Or I'll bust your ass back to the disco era. I mean it."

Rolly nodded. Bonnie walked toward the front door, paused to talk to a patrol officer standing outside his car and then walked into the building. She returned a few minutes later and motioned for Rolly to get out of the car.

"When were you here?" she said.

"An hour ago, maybe forty-five minutes."

"Tell me exactly what happened while you were here."

"What happened?"

"Just give me a timeline of what you did while you were here."

Rolly described his visit to the building, his conversation with Tammy Withers and her client with the pug dogs.

"You talked to the husband, too?" said Bonnie. "Henley Withers?"

"Yeah. In that tank room downstairs. I talked to him for maybe ten minutes before I left."

"Did you see anyone else hanging around the place?" said Bonnie.

"No. I don't think so. What happened?"

A black Ford Explorer pulled in behind the rest of the emergency vehicles. A man and a woman in blue suits climbed out of the Explorer.

"Dammit," said Bonnie, under her breath. "How did they find out so fast?"

The man and woman walked over to Bonnie.

"Officer Hammond," said the woman. "What's our status here?"

Bonnie put her hands on her hips.

"We've got a drowning victim inside, looks like a drowning anyway. He was found in one of the water tanks, wave machines I guess they're called."

"ID?"

"Henley Withers. His wife found the body."

"Is she still on scene?"

"She's upstairs in her office waiting to be interviewed."

"Any sign of breaking and entering, theft or robbery?"

"I just got here," said Bonnie. "I haven't had time to survey the situation."

The two agents looked at each other. The female agent turned back to Bonnie.

"We need to lock down the scene," she said. "Essential personnel only. All requests for evidence removal will need to go through me. Under no circumstances are computers, storage media, files, photographs or any written media to leave this building without my express consent. Is that clear?"

"What's going on?" Rolly said.

"Who are you?" said the male agent.

"Mr. Waters is a private investigator," said Bonnie. "And a former associate of Daniel Piper. He's been assisting me in trying to locate Mr. Piper."

"I see," said the male agent. He reached in his pocket and pulled out a small notebook. "May I have a contact number for you, Mr. Waters?"

Rolly pulled out his wallet and handed the agent a business card.

"Mr. Waters," the agent said, after he looked at the card. "Do you understand that you are not to enter this building or discuss anything you've heard here with anyone?"

"Cross my fingers and hope to die," said Rolly.

The agents stared at him, narrowing their eyes. They didn't like his attitude.

"I promise I won't say anything," said Rolly.

The female agent turned her attention to Bonnie.

"Officer Hammond, what's your initial assessment of the cause of death?"

"Like I said, I just got here," said Bonnie. "I don't think it was an accident, though."

"Your reasoning?"

"There's a note you'll want to see, some kind of confession, but I doubt this is a suicide."

"Why?"

"The deceased appears to have drowned in a water tank. The tank is less than three feet high and has a locking cover on top. According to his spouse, the tank was locked when she found the body. Locked from the outside. If that's true, there's no way this could be an accident. And if it isn't true, she's lying to us. For now I consider this a possible murder scene and the San Diego Police Department will be investigating it as such."

"Understood," said the female agent. "The FBI stands ready to assist you in any way with your investigation. Our interest here is in protecting documents and assets related to Tidewater Defense System's work with the US Navy."

"I'll want to get my forensic inspectors out here ASAP," said Bonnie.

"Only in the crime room for now; no one goes in the other offices."

"Yeah, I get it," said Bonnie.

"I think we can send the rest of these folks home, including Mr. Waters."

"He came with me," said Bonnie. "He'll have to stay a while."

Both agents looked at Rolly. They didn't protest.

"Wait in the car," said Bonnie. "Let me get this fixed up."

Rolly got back into Bonnie's car. The female FBI agent followed Bonnie into the tank room while the male agent took the stairs up to the second floor, presumably to secure the contents of Henley Withers's office. One by one, police cars and other emergency vehicles left the scene until Rolly sat alone in Bonnie's sedan. The burnt-orange sky had turned to dark purple. Safety lights on the exterior walls of the building came on, illuminating the sidewalks and casting frail shadows across the concrete walkways to the edge of the lawn.

A faint tremor passed through the car, as if something had bumped it. Rolly turned his head and looked out the back window. The fronds on a pygmy palm near the corner of the building fluttered in the wind. He turned and looked out the front window. None of the plants by the stairway fluttered at all. There was no wind.

He opened the door, stood up and looked across the roof of the car. The front lawn was dark now, but you could see where it ran to the water, where the holiday lights from the Harbor Drive Bridge reflected off the surface of the bay. Something moved near the far edge of the lawn. The watery reflections flickered. Rolly stepped around to the other side of the car and shaded his eyes. Something moved into the water, rippling the surface. He dashed across the lawn. By the time he arrived at the shore, the ripples had dissipated into the currents.

He stared out toward the bay, watching for movement. In the water below the center arch of the bridge he saw something break the surface, something sleek and black, like a seal or a sea lion. He waited and watched, but the animal never returned to the surface. By the time he started back for the car he wasn't sure he'd seen anything at all. He felt hungry and tired. It had been a long day.

Something bright and hard kicked off the toe of his left shoe as he walked back across the lawn. A silver twinkle of reflected light bounced across the grass in front of him. He squatted down and stared at the rectangular object for a moment, wood and silver. He reached down and picked it up by the edges, placing it in his back pocket. He walked back across the lawn to the Tidewater offices. As he approached the building, the male FBI agent exited Henley Withers's office and walked down the stairs. The agent stopped at the foot of the stairs and glared at Rolly.

"Where did you go, Mr. Waters?" said the agent. "You were supposed to stay in the car."

"I saw something out there," said Rolly.

"What?"

"I don't know," said Rolly. He moved toward the offices. The agent stepped in front of him and put his hand on Rolly's chest.

"Hold on, Mr. Waters," he said. "This area is on lockdown. You're not allowed in."

"Where's Bonnie?"

"Officer Hammond is upstairs interviewing Mrs. Withers."

"I need to show her something."

"Until we have fully secured this area, you are not permitted in the building. Only authorized personnel are allowed. There are matters of national security in play here. You are not authorized."

"I found something," said Rolly. "Out there. I think it might be important."

"What did you find?"

"I want to show it to Bonnie."

"You're not showing Officer Hammond anything unless you show it to me first."

"Okay, but if I show it to you, you have to let me talk to her."

The agent nodded. Rolly reached in his back pocket and extracted the item, holding it at the edges so as not to smudge the rest of the surface with his fingerprints.

"Is that a harmonica?" said the agent.

"That's right," said Rolly. In the light he could see a letter engraved in the silver top. "Key of A."

# 20

# THE PARTNER

Tammy Withers paced the floor of her back office, wearing a groove in the floor. She was dressed in the same tan pantsuit she'd had on when Rolly talked to her an hour ago, but the outfit seemed drab and dingy now. She looked even more underfed than the last time he'd seen her, her long frame disappearing into the clothes as if they were camouflage. Her eyes were the color of dull steel.

Bonnie spotted Rolly in the doorway and waved him in. Tammy looked up at him. The dull steel in her eyes sharpened to titanium daggers.

"Do you know this person, Officer?" she said, returning to Bonnie.

"Yes, ma'am," said Bonnie. "He's a private detective."

"I don't want him here."

"Is this the man you told me about?"

"Yes. He's been nosing around in my family's affairs and harassing us."

"I can wait outside," said Rolly. Bonnie raised a detaining finger in his direction and continued her conversation with Tammy.

"Mrs. Withers, do you have a specific complaint about Mr. Waters's behavior? Has he done anything illegal?"

"I'm a trained psychiatrist. His body language begs of iniquity."

"I'm not sure what that means, Mrs. Withers. Do you have a specific charge you'd like to make against Mr. Waters? Has he done something in your presence you believe is illegal?"

"No. I don't have any charges. As I told you, he was the last person I saw with my husband."

"I've asked Mr. Waters about that. He says he had a short conversation with your husband and left the building soon afterward. I know this is a difficult time for you, Mrs. Withers, but I've known Mr. Waters for twenty years and I can't imagine him doing physical harm to anyone. Unless you have a specific complaint against him, I'd like to include him in our conversation."

"He makes me uncomfortable," said Tammy.

"He makes me uncomfortable sometimes too, but I've learned to live with it. He may have seen or heard something relevant to the death of your husband. Please tell me again why you think someone killed your husband."

Tammy eyed Rolly again.

"Wipe that stupid smirk off your face," she said.

"I'm sorry," said Rolly. "I didn't know I was smirking."

"I disdain male smirking. It smacks of arrogance and entitlement."

"I just look like that sometimes. It's not smirking."

"You're not very bright, are you?"

"Mrs. Withers," said Bonnie, "let's leave our assessment of Mr. Waters's intelligence for another time. Please repeat what you said to me."

Tammy looked at Rolly again, presumably to check for further signs of smirking. She folded her hands together in her lap.

"My husband was in excellent health," she said. "So I doubt cardiac arrest or stroke were contributory. He was of sound mind. Self-annihilation is unthinkable. That wasn't his style."

"Did your husband express any remorse over the death of your daughter?"

"My husband was not a very expressive person."

"He didn't indicate any regrets?"

"Why would he do that?"

"In my experience, people often blame themselves when something like that happens."

"Yes, well, I'm sure that's true of ordinary people. My husband and I are ratiocinative and highly educated human beings. Regarding Janis, my husband . . ."

"Yes?"

"It's not important."

"Everything is important, Mrs. Withers."

"That's not true, Detective. Winnowing pertinent facts from the inessential information is an important human skill."

"Let me do the winnowing, then. What were you going to tell me?"

Tammy glanced at her wall of trophies and diplomas.

"What I object to," she said, "is society's judgment that our marriage might have been less robust or dutiful than a traditional union. Henley and I rejected the notion that biological impulses are the basis of the marriage dynamic, when in many cases they serve as an obstacle. We believed a rational and pragmatic assessment of intellectual skills and interests provided a better foundation for mutual productivity and satisfaction."

"I don't have a traditional marriage myself," said Bonnie.

"No," Tammy said, looking Bonnie over. "I don't imagine you do."

"But your husband must have had some feelings for his daughter," said Bonnie.

Tammy scrunched her mouth to one side, impatient with explaining her views on matrimony to the less enlightened.

"Janis was Henley's daughter in name only," she said. "He consented to her adoption as part of our marriage agreement, so we could avoid social complications. Henley had very little involvement with her upbringing."

"He wasn't her biological father?"

"No."

"Who was her father?" said Rolly.

"That's irrelevant," said Tammy. "I made certain decisions as a young woman. They were purposeful and informed. I accepted my responsibilities. Henley played no part in them."

"Did Janis know Henley wasn't her father?" said Bonnie.

"She had no information to indicate otherwise. Why aren't we talking about the people responsible for all of this?"

"All of what?"

"My husband's murder. My daughter's suicide."

"You think their deaths are connected?"

"We've been on their list for a very long time."

"Whose list?"

"The animal rights people. The OMU. From the moment the ARION project became public we've been on their hit list. Henley especially. They caricatured him as some sort of evil genius promoting barbaric experiments. They've harassed us incessantly. And I think they're using Mr. Waters here to further provoke us."

"You think I'm working for the OMU?" said Rolly.

"Not directly, Mr. Waters. I don't think you're bright enough to think those things up."

"That's true. I'm not."

"Ask yourself this. How much do you know about the person who hired you?"

"I rarely know my clients that well."

"Well, don't you think it's convenient that in this particular case they hired the one private detective in town who had a personal relationship with my daughter?"

Rolly rubbed the back of his neck. He didn't like Tammy Withers. She was cold, arrogant and conceited, but she had a point. He'd accepted Melody's story at face value. He'd accepted it because of the Janis connection. Because of the guilt and the ghosts it had raised.

"Why would the OMU care about Butch Fleetwood?" he said.

"They think there's a story there," said Tammy. "They're rooting around in our trash, trying to find dirty laundry, something they can wave around in the air to discredit us. Aided and abetted by the cockroach crusaders of our local press."

"You're referring to Tom Cockburn?" said Rolly.

"The biggest cockroach of them all. Mr. Cockburn hounded us mercilessly for years. The OMU and Tom Cockburn are in bed together."

"You think the OMU is responsible for your husband's death?" said Bonnie.

"I think this is the work of some radicalized individual, an unstable member of the organization who's taken it upon himself to eradicate their declared enemies through violence. But the OMU as an organization is responsible for inciting him. Make no mistake about that. Radicalism leads to fanaticism, and their campaign of invective is highly inflammatory."

"I see," said Bonnie. "I understand your daughter made several large contributions to the OMU?"

Tammy scrunched her mouth to the side again. She crossed her arms, forming the top half of her body into a rigid wall of tan polyester. She sighed.

"May I sit down?"

Bonnie nodded. Tammy sunk into one of her plastic truth chairs. Bonnie remained standing. Rolly inspected his fingernails. The nail on his right index finger had a crack in it. He needed to purchase some clear nail polish on the way home so he could play his guitar without damaging the nail any more. Two members of the Withers family were dead now. Two people who'd once known Butch Fleetwood. He had no idea why.

"I suppose that's what happens when you provide disposable income to a young woman with a Narcissus complex and no grasp on reality," said Tammy. "I warned my father against it."

"Against what?" said Bonnie.

Tammy cleared her throat.

"My father is a great believer in the economic value of a woman's appearance," she said. "After the accident, when Janis disfigured herself, he set her up with a trust fund so she'd have income for life. My father didn't think she could find a husband, at least a prosperous one, with her face scarred like that."

"What happens to the trust fund now?" said Bonnie.

"I'm not aware of the specific provisions of the trust. My father shared none of its contents with me."

"The trust wouldn't go to you or your husband after her death?"

"Under no circumstances can I imagine my father allowing that particular scenario to take place."

"Could Janis designate where the trust went in a will?"

"I rather doubt it. Knowing my father, I'm sure the trust is completely revocable. He likes to maintain control of his capital. I suppose there might be some provision for a natural heir."

"A son or a daughter, is that what you mean?"

"Yes."

"Did Janis have any children?"

Tammy shrugged. It was a strange way to answer the question.

"What does your father do?"

"He's CEO ex-officio of Tidewater Defense Systems."

"So he's your boss?"

"In a manner of speaking. We have our own fiduciary arrangement with the Tidewater Corporation. Our offices are a satellite branch."

"So Janis couldn't leave the money in the trust to anyone?"

"As I said, I'm not aware of the provisions of the trust. My father did not consult with Henley or me. If you want to know the details, you'll have to check with my father's accountants. In Virginia. They're the ones who cut the checks."

"One last thing, Mrs. Withers," said Bonnie. "Did your husband know anyone by the name of Daniel Piper?"

"I don't think so," said Tammy. "Who is he?"

Bonnie turned to Rolly.

"Let's see it," she said.

Rolly held out the harmonica, which was now in a plastic evidence bag, courtesy of his new FBI friends.

"It's a harmonica," he said.

"Yes, I can see that," said Tammy. "And why are you showing me this?"

"Daniel Piper sometimes goes by the name Harmonica Dan," said Bonnie. "He was seen at the Admiral's Club shortly after the fire began, after everyone left the room. According to our witness, Mr. Piper tried to put out the fire."

"He was that bearded man, the one in the trench coat?"

"You saw him then?"

"Just a glimpse. Henley pulled me out of the room when . . . well, to protect me, I suppose."

"Why didn't you report this before?"

"I don't know. It was all so surreal. There was the explosion. We had to run from the building. Are you saying this man was here tonight?"

"We've been trying to locate Mr. Piper ever since the incident at the Admiral's Club. Mr. Waters reported seeing a man who matched Mr. Piper's description nearby, but local security was unable to detain him."

"I found the harmonica out on the lawn in front of the building," said Rolly.

"Oh dear." Tammy Withers put her hand to her mouth.

"What is it?"

"I remember a man, many years ago. One of the divers. He played the harmonica. I don't remember his name, but . . . I can't be sure."

"You don't remember his name?"

"No, but I do remember, at least I think I remember . . ."

"What?"

"He was Butch Fleetwood's diving partner."

# 21

# THE INVITATION

Rolly sat in his kitchen the next morning, working on his fourth cup of coffee and jittering over the keys of his laptop computer. He hadn't slept well, so he got up early, made a double pot and started researching everything he could think of that might give him some insight into the case, starting with the mysterious name that seemed to be everywhere—Arion.

According to Wikipedia, Arion was an ancient Greek poet and musician, credited with inventing, or at least perfecting, the dithyramb —a style of ancient Greek song that honored Dionysus, the god of wine, fertility and ritual madness. In sixth-century Greece, the dithyramb was rock and roll. Arion was its Chuck Berry and Elvis all rolled into one.

Aside from the dithyramb, Arion's biggest claim to fame was the apocryphal story of his kidnapping at sea and subsequent rescue by dolphins. Arion sailed to Sicily, where he entered a music contest. He won the contest and was awarded a large sum of money. On the boat back home, the crew attacked him and took his money. They gave Arion a choice: he could be murdered on board ship or take his chances and jump into the sea. Arion opted for the second choice, but not before he'd made a deal with the sailors to play one more tune on his lyre. A pod of dolphins heard his music and were drawn to the ship like Grateful Dead fans to a free concert. After Arion jumped into the water, one of the larger dolphins carried him home to Corinth, surrendering its own life by beaching itself on the shore. When the crew of the ship returned several months later with some half-assed story about how Arion had chosen to stay in Sicily, the king had them all crucified.

After reading about Arion, Rolly moved on to reading about dolphins. He found stories of dolphins that had rescued foundering swimmers or guided shipwrecked sailors into safe harbor. The stories weren't all apocryphal. Some of them were true.

Stories like these caused some people, like the Lemurians, to claim that dolphins operated on a higher plane of consciousness than human beings, that dolphin intelligence could be a conduit to greater spiritual knowledge and wisdom if humans were only willing to tune in and listen. There was a lot of dolphin love on the Internet and much of it came with rainbows and crystals and claims of interspecies telepathy, but it rarely mentioned the darker side of dolphin behavior.

Dolphins were horny and promiscuous, Dionysians of the deep who liked to get high on puffer fish toxin. Some of them had been observed committing rape and infanticide. They were temperamental and smart and used all manner of sounds to communicate—clacks and whistles, buzzes and squawks. Dolphins had a form of sonar built into their nervous system, allowing them to locate almost anything underwater, under almost any conditions. Navy trainers had taken advantage of those skills to teach them to locate underwater mines.

Someone knocked on Rolly's front door, three soft taps. He rose from the table and opened the door. His mother stood on the porch, dressed in gray yoga pants and an old yellow sweater. Her long gray hair with its fluorescent green streak was pinned up on top of her head.

"Max wants to talk to you," she said. Max was an old friend and mentor, a retired attorney who had helped Rolly get into the investigation business.

"Okay. I'll give him a call."

"He said specifically for me to come over and get you. You're not to talk to him on your cell phone."

Rolly furrowed his brow.

"Max is holding for me on your home phone?"

"Yes. That's what I'm trying to say. You need to come over and talk to him."

"Okay," Rolly said. He slipped his feet into the pair of old flip-flops he kept by the door, closed the door behind him and followed his mother across the driveway, through the back door of her house and into the kitchen. His mother cut the flame under a whistling teapot.

"Would you like any tea?" she asked. "I can make you some breakfast."

"Not now," said Rolly. He walked into the living room and picked up the phone.

"What's with the cloak-and-dagger stuff?" he said.

"Just a precaution," said Max, on the other end of the line. "I'm guessing they haven't bugged your mom's landline yet."

"What are you talking about?"

"I got a call from a former client today. He's been under surveillance."

"You really think someone's bugged my phone?"

"Given my client's history, I can't discount it."

"Who is this former client?"

"Let's call him Joe. Joe wants to talk to you."

"What does he want to talk about?"

"Not for me to say, or even know about. He said there's more to the story than what he told you before, some things he needs to explain."

"He sounds kind of paranoid."

"Let's call it an abundance of caution on his part. Believe me, he's earned a right to his vigilance."

Rolly thought about the people he'd met in the last two days. A lot of them had expressed concerns about government agents and surveillance. Tammy and Henley Withers had both accused him of being an FBI agent. Tom Cockburn at the *OB Enquirer* had a history of conflict with government agencies. Harmonica Dan thought spies were all around them.

"Okay," said Rolly. "What am I supposed to do?"

"He wants to set up a meeting," said Max. "A different location, not where you talked before."

"Where, then?"

"He'll let you pick. Someplace public. He'll find you there, once you set up a time."

"Today?"

"As far as I know. Where do you want to meet?"

"I don't know. Balboa Park, maybe?"

"He'll need something more specific than that."

"Geez, I'm not used to this kind of thing. Can I call you back?"

"I'll be here another half hour."

"Give me ten minutes."

"Okay. Call from your mom's line. Not from your cell phone."

"Yeah, I get it."

Rolly hung up the phone. He walked back into the kitchen. A teapot sat on the table. His mother had set out two mugs and bowls on the table, along with a box of organic flaxseed cereal and a quart of almond milk.

"Why don't you have some tea?" she said, indicating the pot. "We can talk."

Still bewildered by Max's request, Rolly did his mother's bidding. He sat down at the table and stared at the photo of the flaxseed cereal on the box. It looked like cornflakes studded with birdseed. His mother poured tea into the two mugs and pushed one across the table to him. He put his hands around the mug. The warmth of it felt good. It was chilly this morning, San Diego chilly, maybe 60 degrees.

"What did Max want?" said his mother.

"A friend of his wants to talk to me."

"I see."

"It's just something I'm working on."

"One of your cases?"

"That girl I told you about, the one who used to run our fan club. Janis Withers."

"I wish you wouldn't torture yourself with the past."

"I'm not torturing myself."

"Are you saying this isn't about Matt?"

"No. It's about a man named Butch Fleetwood."

"Who's he?"

"Someone Janis knew. A dead man. A memory. A ghost."

"You're waxing poetic this morning," said Rolly's mother.

"I guess I am, aren't I?" said Rolly. He reached for the cereal and poured some into a bowl. Birdseed or not, he needed something to eat. His mother was right, of course. It *was* about Matt. Butch Fleetwood was a substitute, a proxy. Rolly was using Fleetwood as a pretext for interviewing people who knew Janis, people who might have known Matt. In either case, he was looking for a dead man. A memory. A ghost.

"I was reading about dolphins this morning," he said, looking for a way out of the conversation he didn't want to have with his mother or himself. "Dad and I went to see the Navy dolphins yesterday."

"Oh yes," said his mother. "They're moving some of them, aren't they, to that new water park? Ocean Universe. I'm not sure how I feel about that."

"What do you mean?"

"Some people are protesting. They say the dolphins should be set free, that they shouldn't be kept in captivity."

"We talked to one of the trainers down there. He said trained dolphins have a hard time surviving in the wild, after they've worked with people awhile."

"He seems like such a nice man."

"Who?" said Rolly.

"Wendell," said his mother. "I can't believe he'd allow any cruelty to the dolphins. He's written a children's book, you know. I was thinking of going to the signing."

"Going where?"

"To Cabrillo Monument. In Point Loma. He's signing his new children's book. I've got the invitation around here somewhere."

His mother rose from the table, went to the counter and shuffled through the mail she kept in a basket.

"Here it is," she said. "It's some sort of fundraiser, for the schools."

She handed Rolly the postcard, a stylized illustration of a young boy and a dolphin playing together in the sea with the title *Danni's Dolphin* at the top. Rolly flipped the card over. There was a photo of Wendell on the back, next to the details of the event. Rolly had seen the man in the photo before. Yesterday at the Lemurian Temple. Wendell was the relaxed and confident dude buttoning up his shirt as he walked out from Melody's back room. The man on the porch was Wendell's bodyguard. There was a connection now, explaining why Wendell might've chosen Rolly to play in his band. The connection was Melody.

"He's very attractive, isn't he?" said Rolly's mother. "Unusual looking, but quite handsome."

"Are you going to the book signing?" Rolly said.

"I thought it might be fun. It's always so beautiful out at the monument. I thought it might be interesting to hear what he has to say. Plus all the profits from the book sales goes to the artist-in-residence programs for schools."

"Would you mind if I joined you?" said Rolly. He wanted to see Wendell again, to look him in the eyes and see what was there.

"I think that would be lovely," said his mother.

Rolly stood up from the table and turned back toward the living room.

"Where are you going?" asked his mother.

"To call Max. Maybe his friend can meet me out there."

# 22

# THE MONUMENT

C abrillo National Monument stood on the cliffs at the end of Point Loma, overlooking the Pacific Ocean and San Diego Bay. There was an old lighthouse on the point, no longer in use, but rehabilitated to approximate its original condition. During World War II, military bunkers had been constructed and soldiers had manned radar stations along the cliffs, waiting for the Japanese invasion that never came. Trails ran along the edges of the cliffs with turnouts overlooking the ocean. You could watch passing ships or look for the spouts from whale migrations. The parking lot near the visitors' center was three-quarters full when Rolly and his mother drove up in her green Mini Cooper.

"Oh dear," said his mother as they walked toward the visitors' center.

"What?" said Rolly.

"There are protestors," said his mother. "I hope things don't get out of hand."

The protestors didn't look like they'd be much trouble. Rolly counted only six of them. Either by choice or legal edict, they had confined themselves to a small concrete strip between the parking lot and the visitors' center. The protestors waved signs denouncing

Wendell and Ocean Universe and calling for the freeing of all dolphins in captivity. *Free the OU8.*

Rolly and his mother walked past the protestors and turned down the sidewalk, passing the restrooms and a lecture hall. They entered the main room of the center. Light flooded in from floor-to-ceiling windows on all sides of the room and you could see down the length of San Diego Bay all the way to Mexico. Directly below them, Ballast Point pushed out into the water, constricting the entrance to the bay. Butch Fleetwood had died in those unsettled waters.

The guest of honor sat in the corner with his back to the windows. A line of fans had queued up to meet him. The line snaked around the exterior edge of the room as they waited patiently for a chance to share a few words with the master, express their enthusiasm for his work and get his signature. Rolly's mother purchased two copies of *Danni's Dolphin* at the cashier's desk and gave one to Rolly. He slipped one of his business cards inside the front cover and joined his mother at the back of the line to wait with the rest of the sycophants.

A large man stood behind Wendell, the blond, ponytailed body-guard Rolly had encountered outside the Lemurian Temple, the man Wendell called Happy. As Wendell signed books and chatted with his fans, Happy scanned the room for troublemakers, keeping an eye out for ne'er-do-wells, crazies and protestors, anyone who looked like they might harass his boss. Rolly and his mother moved up in line. The bodyguard stared at Rolly for a moment, as if he recognized him, then moved on, assessing other potential threats.

The line moved at a steady pace, so it wasn't long before Rolly and his mother arrived at Wendell's table. Rolly's mother placed her copy of *Danni's Dolphin* on the table. Wendell glanced up at her and smiled.

"Hello, young lady," he said. The guy was a pro.

"It's Judith," said Rolly's mother.

"Well, Judith, thank you for coming today and supporting the artist-in-schools program."

Wendell opened the book and scrawled something on the title page in large sweeping letters, then passed it back to her.

"'To Judith, *Me ka aloha pumehana*,'" said Rolly's mother, reading the inscription.

"A warm aloha, with kindest regards," said Wendell.

"Oh, that's lovely. You know when my husband was in the Navy, I always hoped he'd get an assignment in Hawaii. I so wanted to live there. But it never happened. Well, not while I was married to him. He went there by himself a couple of times."

Wendell nodded and smiled.

"This is my son," said Judith. "He's an artist too. Well, a musician, anyway."

Wendell turned his attention to Rolly.

"What instrument do you play?" he asked. He glanced up at Rolly, but showed no signs of recognition.

"I play guitar," Rolly said.

"Are you coming to the concert?" said Wendell. He put out his hand for Rolly's book.

"I'll be there," said Rolly, clutching the book to his side. "I know some guys in the band."

"So you know J.V. Sideman?"

"Sure. Every blues player in town knows J.V."

"What's your name?"

"Rolly Waters."

"His real name is Roland," said Rolly's mother, interjecting herself into the conversation.

"Well, Roland, nice to meet you," said Wendell. He gave no indication he'd ever heard of Rolly before, let alone asked Sideman to hire him. "Can I sign that book for you?"

Rolly handed the book to Wendell.

"It's for a friend," said Rolly. "A girl I know."

"What's your girlfriend's name?" said Wendell. He opened the book. Rolly's business card fell out on the table. Wendell picked it up and read it.

"Her name's Melody Flowers," said Rolly.

Happy the bodyguard uncrossed his arms and took a step forward. Wendell backed him off with a relaxed wave of his hand. He looked up at Rolly, then back down at the business card.

"I thought you looked familiar, Roland Waters," he said. "You were just fooling with me yesterday, weren't you? You're not really a building inspector."

Rolly shook his head.

"No, I'm not," he said. "But I'd like to talk to you in private sometime."

"What about?" said Wendell.

"Melody. She's part of a case I'm working on."

"Well, I've got your number now," said Wendell. "I'll be in touch."

Wendell handed the card to his bodyguard and turned his attention back to the business at hand.

"Now," he said, twitching his Sharpie pen over the open book, "how would you like me to sign?"

"Surprise me," said Rolly.

Wendell looked thoughtful for a moment, and then scribbled something onto the page. He closed the book and handed it back to Rolly.

"Thank you," said Rolly, taking the book.

"You're welcome. *Okole Kāmamo*," said Wendell. He smiled. Someone in line giggled. Rolly had the feeling he'd just been insulted, but he let it slide. His ego was Teflon right now. He'd learned what he needed to know. Wendell hadn't looked twice when he read Rolly's name. He'd never heard of a guitar player named Roland Waters, let alone insisted that Sideman hire Rolly to play with the band. But if Wendell hadn't requested Rolly's guitar-playing services, who had?

"What was that all about?" said Rolly's mother, when they got outside the building. "I hope you weren't being rude."

"He knows my client."

"What did he write in your book?"

Rolly stopped. He opened the book and read the inscription.

"'I went home with a waitress, like I always do.'"

"That's an odd thing to write."

"It's a line from a Warren Zevon song."

"It's still an odd thing to write in a children's book."

"I guess he's trying to tell me something."

As they walked back to the parking lot, Rolly considered the inscription and decided it meant exactly what it said. Melody was just another girl to a man like Wendell. She was a groupie, a one-night stand. She massaged his big aura. Perhaps Melody had been with Wendell when the guitar player from Los Angeles canceled. She might've suggested Rolly for the band, but if Wendell had sent the text message to J.V., he didn't remember the name.

They opened the doors of the Mini Cooper and tossed their books into the backseat. His mother looked at Rolly across the roof of the car.

"Aren't you supposed to meet someone here?" she said.

Rolly checked the display on his phone. He had five minutes left before his rendezvous with Max's client.

"Yeah," he said. "Will you be okay hanging out for a while?"

"Of course, dear," said his mother. "It's a lovely day. I'll take a walk up to the lighthouse."

"I'll call you when I'm done."

Rolly watched his mother walk up the trail to the lighthouse, then closed the door of the Mini Cooper, set the alarm and headed back toward the visitor center. There was an overlook on the other side of the center where he'd told Max he'd hang out while he waited for his contact to arrive. He checked his phone again. He still had four minutes. He turned into the men's room.

There was no one in the restroom. He went into the first stall, closed the door, dropped his pants and took a seat. As he did his business, the restroom door opened and someone walked in. A pair of tan loafers with gold buckles walked past his stall. The door to the second stall opened, but the man in the loafers let the door swing back shut. He didn't go in. The loafers returned to the front of Rolly's stall. There was a knock on the door.

"Occupied," said Rolly, staring at the man's shoes.

"Ballast Point Overlook," the man said. The voice sounded familiar.

"Where's that?"

"There's a trail map outside. Give me a two-minute head start."

The man turned on his heel and left the room. Rolly flushed the toilet and gathered himself. He opened the stall door and went to the sink, washed his hands and stared at himself in the mirror. He hadn't showered or shaved for a couple of days. His hair looked plastered to the top of his head. Between that and the stubble on his chin, he looked like some guy in a Wanted poster. He briefly considered the possibility that he'd just made an appointment to give some guy a blow job. This wasn't the weirdest case he'd ever worked, but it was getting there.

He left the bathroom and walked outside, looked at the map of the monument posted near the front door of the visitors' center. He found a spot on the map labeled Ballast Point Overlook and traced his finger along the trail leading up from the overlook to the *You are here* marker. He glanced to his right, spotting a break in the bushes a hundred feet away. It must be the trailhead. He checked the time on his phone again, then took a seat on the bench. The man had asked him to wait for two minutes. Rolly didn't know much about spy craft, but he knew how to follow directions.

# 23

# THE OVERLOOK

T he trail dropped down below the visitors' center and ran down the edge of the cliffs through a set of switchbacks overlooking the bay. As Rolly rounded the third switchback, he could see to the end of the trail, a circular outcropping fringed by a short wall of stacked granite. A man sat on the wall, looking out over the harbor. Rolly checked the trail behind him. No one had followed. He continued down to the end. The man on the wall turned to greet him. It was Tom Cockburn, editor and owner of the *OB Enquirer*.

"Thanks for going through all this trouble," said Cockburn.

"This seems secluded enough," said Rolly.

"Did you see anyone up there?" asked Cockburn. "Anyone suspicious?"

"Men in Black? Not that I noticed."

"Good. We have a little time."

"Are you sure this is necessary?"

"I had visitors this morning, Mr. Waters. Two FBI agents. Agent Goffin and Agent King. I always ask for their names and ID. Have they contacted you?"

"I met a couple of agents last night," said Rolly. "I don't remember their names."

"I told them about your visit yesterday," said Cockburn. "They seemed very interested. I apologize, but it seemed prudent to tell them, given the circumstances. I'm sure they would have figured it out anyway. I've always cooperated with the FBI. The only things I won't give up are my sources. That's the one thing I won't do. My sources are sacrosanct."

"What did the FBI want?"

"They told me Henley Withers was dead."

"Yes. I know. I was there."

"They asked if you worked for me."

"I don't understand."

"Neither did I at first. They weren't willing to tell me much, but I think they've reopened the case."

"What case?"

"The Butch Fleetwood case."

"Do you think it has something to do with your printing that article?"

"I'm sure the updated article caught their attention, as it did yours, but who knows? FBI agents rarely respond to my questions."

"They're looking for someone named Daniel Piper," said Rolly.

"Really?" said Cockburn. "My antennae are all tingly now. We may have dislodged a boulder and let in some light."

"I guess," said Rolly. If they'd dislodged a boulder it was a large one, and rolling straight toward them.

"Let me show you something," said Cockburn. He reached in his shirt pocket, pulled out an old Polaroid photo and handed it to Rolly. There were four people in the photograph: two men, a woman and a teenaged girl. The four of them stood on a beach, next to a sailboat. There was a large pile of rocks on their right and some sort of building behind them, off in the distance.

"The girl is Janis Withers, isn't it?" Rolly said.

"Do you recognize anyone else?"

"The guy on the right looks like her father," said Rolly, pointing to one of the men. "Henley Withers."

"Yes," said Cockburn.

"And the tall woman is Tammy Withers."

"Yes, one happy family. What about the young man?"

A little light came on in Rolly's brain.

"The big guy's Butch Fleetwood, isn't he?"

"Yes. Now look on the back."

Rolly flipped the photograph over.

"ARION," he said, reading the word scrawled in inky block letters. "Where did you get this?"

"It was on the floor of the office this morning when I came in. Someone slipped it under the door."

Cockburn turned to look at the view. He pointed at the Navy base across the bay on North Island.

"You see those concrete structures there, at the edge of the island, those large concrete bunkers?"

"Yes," Rolly replied.

"They used to store nuclear warheads there. Did you know that?"

"I knew they kept nukes on the base. I didn't know which buildings."

"They're empty now," said Cockburn. "They moved all the warheads to South Dakota. Our lovely bay is now nuke-free. At least when there aren't any submarines in port. That's the submarine base down there, just below us."

Rolly knew about the submarine base. On family trips to the monument, his father had pointed out any number of Navy operations over the years. Since the Navy owned most of the bayside at the time, there was a lot of area to cover. Post–Cold War downsizing and changes in deployments had left San Diego less of a Navy town, but the federal government still owned plenty of real estate.

"I like to think I had something to do with it, getting rid of the nukes," said Cockburn. "The *Enquirer* was the first publication to make the information public. I got a visit from the FBI about those articles too. This was thirty years ago. Back in the paper's prime muckraking days."

"Why are you so interested in Butch Fleetwood?" asked Rolly.

"The FBI kept a file on me, Mr. Waters. I've seen it. You'd think I was quite a depraved man if you read through it. Sex and drugs and socialist potluck dinners. There was some information in there that could only have come from one person."

"Butch Fleetwood?"

"Yes."

"Henley Withers told me you had some kind of relationship."

"Yes. That's correct. Butch and I had . . . I don't know if I'd call it a love affair. We had a very intense sexual relationship for two months."

"Fleetwood was gay?" said Rolly. It sounded stupid and he immediately regretted it. Cockburn cleared his throat and continued.

"Butch Fleetwood wasn't gay or straight. He was a rapacious young man who would fuck anyone and anything if it were to his advantage in some way. When I met Butch, he was a seventeen-year-old hustler who hung out on the Ocean Beach boardwalk at night. He was ready, waiting and willing to take me for whatever he could get."

"You picked him up."

"I had originally intended to do a story on the homeless young men who hung around in that area, the lost boys. In retrospect, I romanticized them too much. I romanticized my own desire to make a difference, thinking I could improve their lot by getting to know them. I suppose . . . I don't know. I was younger then and less cautious. Butch Fleetwood was, well, he was beautiful, like a Greek god. He had a gift for flattery and deceit. I took him home with me that night."

"That's what the FBI has in your file?"

Cockburn nodded. "It's one of the things. Butch Fleetwood was a manipulative son of a bitch. He was a brilliant sociopath. He talked me into letting him stay. First it was another night, then a week, then a month. I bought him clothes. I was his sugar daddy, I guess you could call it that, for a couple of months."

"How did you get rid of him?"

"He got arrested."

"For prostitution?"

"For assault. He got in a fight. Late one night, I got a phone call. It was Butch, calling from jail. I guess I was his last hope. He wanted me to come down and bail him out."

"Did you?"

"I told him I would. I got in my car, preparing to go to the bondsman and get him out of jail. I sat in my car for a long time, thinking about what had happened, what he'd done to me the last couple of months, all the turmoil, how I'd lost control of my life. I got out of my car and walked back into the house."

"Did you ever see him again?"

"Once. A few years later."

"What happened?"

"Someone rang the doorbell at my house. I opened the door and there was a man in a uniform standing outside. It was Butch. His hair was short. He told me how he'd managed to avoid jail time by joining the Navy, that he was making something of himself now. This was maybe a week or so before the diving incident, when he disappeared. It was only later, when I found out what had happened, that I put two and two together."

"What's that?"

"Well, you see, Mr. Waters, Butch Fleetwood may have changed his appearance, he might have cleaned up his act and put on a uniform, but he was still a manipulative son of a bitch. He wanted money."

"What for?"

"It was blackmail, pure and simple. He knew the FBI was watching me, after I ran those articles in the paper, when we revealed the Navy's plan for weaponizing the dolphins. The FBI raided our office, trying to find out who my sources were. Apparently I'd set off quite a shit storm amongst the Navy brass. Those plans were top secret. You still can't get access to them. The government took me to court. They threatened me with jail time if I didn't reveal my sources. That's how I met your lawyer friend Max Gemeinhardt. Max heard about my case and offered to help with my defense. He helped me stay out of prison."

"Max helped me stay out of jail once, too," said Rolly.

"I guess we have something other than Butch Fleetwood in common."

Rolly sat down on the granite wall, thinking things through.

"The FBI, those agents who talked to you this morning, did they ask about ARION?"

"Yes, as a matter of fact they did. I told them nothing. Is there anything else you know about ARION?"

Rolly told Cockburn about the note he'd found in the harmonica case on Dan's boat. He told him about the message Harmonica Dan had scrawled on the security guard's butt.

"Sounds like this Daniel Piper has gone round the bend," said Cockburn. "He's loopy."

"Maybe," said Rolly. "He got the drop on those security guards, though. So far he's managed to evade both the police and the FBI."

"I didn't say Mr. Piper was stupid," said Cockburn. "Just crazy. How is he connected to all this?"

"Tammy Withers remembered a man who used to play the harmonica. He was Fleetwood's diving partner."

"Now we're getting somewhere. The diving partner's name was blacked out in the transcripts. I need to do some digging on Mr. Daniel Piper."

"Let's get back to Fleetwood," said Rolly. "You say he tried to blackmail you because of your earlier relationship?"

"The FBI knew about my sexual orientation, of course, but they couldn't do much about that. The sodomy laws in California had been repealed by that time, thank God. Butch Fleetwood was a minor when he lived with me, though. They might've been able to press charges against me for statutory rape, contributing to the delinquency of a minor."

"Did you pay him the blackmail money?"

Cockburn sighed, rubbed his right temple.

"I'm afraid so," he said.

"How much?"

"Two thousand dollars. I must admit I always felt guilty for not bailing him out of jail that night. Some part of me felt responsible, I guess. I gave him the money."

Cockburn took a seat on the stone wall and stared at the scenery. A Navy transport plane approached from over the ocean, making last-minute adjustments before it landed on the runway at North Island.

"This happened just before Fleetwood disappeared, right?" said Rolly. "Do you think he was planning something?"

"It's something that's stuck with me all this time, something he told me. He said if I gave him the money I would never see him again.

There's something else, too. Something I didn't know until I saw that photograph I showed you. The backpack."

Rolly looked at the photo. A backpack sat in the sand at Janis Withers's feet. The backpack had blue and pink dolphins on it.

"It seemed so odd at the time," said Cockburn. "So random. Butch gave me a backpack to put the money in. He gave me the key to a locker down by Driscoll's Wharf. It was rental locker, something the fishermen use. I put the money in the backpack and left it in the locker. I remember that backpack. It had dolphins on it, just like the one in that photograph."

# 24

## THE AGENTS

"You have visitors," said Rolly's mother as they pulled into the driveway between their two houses. A familiar-looking couple, a man and a woman dressed in identical blue suits and aviator sunglasses, stood on the porch of Rolly's house.

"That didn't take long," said Rolly. Tom Cockburn had warned him the FBI would be coming. They'd agreed to share future information in person, so the Feds wouldn't intercept anything from their phones.

"You know these people?" said his mother.

"I've met them before."

"They look rather serious. Are you in some kind of trouble?"

"Only one way to find out," said Rolly. His mother rolled down her window.

"Good afternoon," she said, addressing the visitors. "Can we help you?"

"FBI," said the woman, flashing her badge. "I'm Agent Goffin. This is Agent King. We'd like to talk to Roland Waters."

"Oh dear," said Rolly's mother. Rolly climbed out of the car. He walked around to the passenger side and helped his mother out, hoping the agents would note it in their files.

"We'd like a few minutes of your time, Mr. Waters," said Agent Goffin.

"Sure," said Rolly. He turned to his mother. "I had a feeling they'd show up here, sooner or later."

"Do I need to call Max?"

"I don't think so. It's not a big deal."

His mother pinched her lips together and narrowed her eyes at him.

"Take your Wendell," she said.

Rolly took his copy of *Danni's Dolphin* from his mother. He walked past the agents and opened the front door.

"Come on in," he said. The agents followed him into the house. He placed the book on top of the Formica table just inside the door.

"Have a seat," he said, indicating the table. "Can I get you some water or anything?"

"We'll be fine, thank you," said the woman. Agent Goffin. She sat down at the table. Agent King circled the living room, searching for whatever FBI agents were trained to look for.

"You play guitar?" he said.

"How'd you guess?" said Rolly. Two Stratocasters and a Les Paul Junior hung on the living room wall. There were two guitar cases on the floor, and two Fender amplifiers. A nylon-stringed Córdoba lay on the sofa.

"You mind if I look through the rest of the house?" said Agent King.

"Knock yourself out," said Rolly. The most incriminating things in his bedroom were the dirty socks on the floor. Agent King disappeared into the back. Agent Goffin pulled out a small notebook and a pen.

"Have a seat, Mr. Waters," she said.

Rolly took a seat at the table, across from Agent Goffin. She clicked her pen twice, then reached for the Wendell book.

"You mind if I take a look?" she said.

Rolly shrugged.

Agent Goffin flipped through the first few pages of Wendell's book. She read the inscription on the title page and smiled at Rolly.

"That's a rather odd inscription," she said, clicking her pen again. Rolly shrugged.

"Artists," he said. "My mother talked me into going to his book signing at Cabrillo Monument this morning."

"You have an interest in dolphins?"

"Not particularly."

"This looks like a children's book."

"My mother bought it for me. I'll always be her little boy, I guess."

"Was that your mother outside? Judith?"

"Yes," said Rolly. "How can I help you, Agent Goffin?"

"Do you know a Tom Cockburn?"

"Yes, I do."

"How long have you known him?"

"I only met him yesterday."

"That was your first contact with Mr. Cockburn?"

"Yes. I went to his office. At the *OB Enquirer*."

"What did you talk about?"

"I read through some articles he'd written. About a man named Butch Fleetwood."

"I see. What's your interest in Butch Fleetwood?"

"I have client who wants to know more about him."

"What is your client's name?"

"I can't tell you that."

There was a clunk from the bedroom, Agent King checking the closet. Agent Goffin jotted something in her notebook.

"I understand you're a private detective?" she said.

Rolly nodded.

"When I'm not strangling cats," he said. Agent Goffin frowned. Nobody got that joke. He should stop using it.

"Playing guitar," Rolly said. "I work as a private detective when I'm not playing guitar."

Agent King returned to the room.

"What year is that Telecaster back there?" he said, pointing his thumb over his shoulder.

"Nineteen ninety-three," said Rolly.

"Mexican?" said King.

"The body," said Rolly, trying not to look at the ball chain dangling from Agent King's fingers, the chain Melody had given him. "It's not the original neck."

"Nice color on it," said King. He tossed the dog tags on the table. "I found those on the nightstand." Agent Goffin picked up the tags.

"Where'd you get these?" she asked.

"Someone gave them to me," said Rolly.

"Your client?"

"I'm not at liberty to say."

"Tom Cockburn?"

"No. It wasn't Mr. Cockburn."

"Who, then?"

"I really can't say."

The two agents exchanged glances. Agent Goffin started in again.

"Mr. Waters, it's come to our attention that you've recently met with several persons of interest to the FBI."

"Like who?"

"Tom Cockburn. Richard Withers. Daniel Piper."

"I'm not sure I'd call it a meeting in Harmonica Dan's case. What's this all about?"

Agent King reached into his inside jacket pocket and retrieved some papers. He unfolded the papers and scanned through them until he found the information he wanted.

"According to our records, Mr. Waters, you have a history of criminal infractions, including three public intoxication misdemeanors," he said.

"Only three?" said Rolly. "I thought there were more."

"You don't remember?"

"They were a long time ago."

"You have two felony convictions," said Goffin. "Vehicle code 23152a, driving under the influence, and 192c vehicular manslaughter for which you were sentenced to three years' probation."

"Yes. That was a long time ago, too."

"During your probationary period, you worked under the oversight of the attorney Maximilian Gemeinhardt?"

"Max. Yes."

"Mr. Gemeinhardt was, at one point in his life, a member of the Peace and Freedom party and is a lifetime member of the ACLU. He's also sued the US government on several occasions."

"He beat the IRS once. He loves to talk about that."

"Did you know Mr. Gemeinhardt also represented Tom Cockburn in Mr. Cockburn's trial against the US Government?"

"I might've heard something about that."

"How would you describe your relationship with Mr. Gemeinhardt?"

"He's a friend. A mentor. We go to ball games together. He's my lawyer sometimes. He handled my DUI case."

Agent Goffin scribbled in her notebook. Agent King shuffled his papers again.

"There's a history of substance abuse in your family," said Goffin. "Is that correct?"

"I'm sober now."

"What about your father?"

"What about him?"

"Is he sober too?"

"No," said Rolly. "He's retired."

"From the United States Navy, correct?"

"Yes. Twenty-eight years with the most powerful navy in history, as he likes to remind me."

"Your father was demoted during his time in the service. He lost command of his ship. What do you know about that?"

"Not much, except that it happened."

"Are you aware how rare it is for the captain of a ship to lose his command?"

"I am now, I guess."

"There were several incidents that took place in foreign ports during his tenure. Has he ever spoken to you about these incidents?"

"I've heard a few things."

"Your father consorted with prostitutes during stops at foreign ports."

"I believe that's standard protocol for Navy personnel," said Rolly.

He'd heard enough stories from his father's compatriots over the years.

Agent King stared at Rolly for a moment, then went back to his papers.

"How often do you see your father?" she said.

Rolly shrugged.

"I take him to breakfast once a week."

"How long has this been going on?"

Rolly hummed the melody to the old tune. The agents looked at him like he was an idiot.

"George Gershwin," said Rolly. They didn't get the reference, or care. "Sorry, I didn't get much sleep last night. What were you asking?"

"Have you always met with your father on a weekly basis?"

"No. Only since he had a heart attack."

"When was that?"

"Don't you have that in your notes? You seem to know everything else."

"Just answer the question, please," said Agent Goffin. "When was his heart attack?"

"About six months ago. My mother's been bugging me to see him more, get some father-son bonding going. I finally gave in. We started getting together on a weekly basis about three months ago."

"At these breakfasts, does he ever discuss his demotion with you?"

"He told me he wasn't really demoted, that he resigned his commission to avoid getting railroaded."

"How does he feel about resigning his post?"

"I don't think he was happy about it. He hated his desk job."

"Does he express any anger?"

"He expresses anger a lot, especially when he's drunk."

"Would you call him resentful?"

"Why are you asking all these questions about my father?"

"Just answer the question, please."

"I don't know if I'd call him resentful. Bad-tempered and rude, absolutely. The opposite of my mother."

"Let's talk about your mother."

"Okay. What about her?"

"Is she resentful?"

"Of my father?"

"Of the Navy, of your father's demotion."

"His resignation?"

"Yes."

"No. I don't think she's resentful. A lot of that stuff happened after they were divorced."

"Why did your parents get divorced?"

Rolly shrugged.

"I gave up trying to figure out my parents a long time ago."

"Has your mother expressed any resentment toward the US Navy or the Federal Government?"

"What? No. I mean, no more than you might expect."

"What do you mean by that?"

"Sometimes she says she didn't realize she was marrying the Navy when she married my father. That's all."

Goffin made some more notes in her book. She looked up at King, who flipped through his papers again.

"Your mother has been a member of several dissident organizations, has she not?" said King.

"She likes to join things."

"Greenpeace, ACLU, One World Foundation. OMU."

"OMU?"

Agent Goffin squinted at his papers.

"Yes, the Ocean Mammal Underground. Your mother gave them fifty dollars, three months ago. The FBI considers the OMU a proto-terrorist organization."

"You can't seriously think my mother is some kind of terrorist?"

"We believe the OMU is planning additional attacks on US Government property."

"What do you mean 'additional'?"

"We consider the suicide bombing at the Admiral's Club in Point Loma a terrorist act."

Rolly stared at the table. They hadn't asked him about Janis Withers. Not yet. Agent Goffin clicked her pen.

"Look at this from our point of view, Mr. Waters," she said.

"Help me out," said Rolly.

Agent Goffin put down her pen. She held up the pinky finger of her left hand and counted her fingers as she listed each point.

"One," she said. "Your mother gives money to a suspected terrorist organization. Two, your father carries a grievance against the US Navy."

"I don't think I'd go that far . . ."

"Three," said Goffin, continuing her indictment. "Your former employer and current lawyer has done pro bono work for Tom Cockburn and the OMU."

"I'm not surprised," said Rolly. "Max likes to—"

"Four," said Agent Goffin. "You were observed entering a known meeting place of the OMU two nights ago."

"I don't know what you're talking about."

"Driscoll's Wharf. The OTTER garage."

"I went to a rehearsal there. That's all."

"And five," said Agent Goffin, adding an extended thumb to her finger count. "You had a personal meeting with the head of the local chapter of the OMU that same night. There was an altercation between the two of you at Winstons nightclub in Ocean Beach."

"You mean Dick Nazi?" said Rolly.

"Richard Withers, aka Dick Nazi, is a founding member of the Southern California chapter of the Ocean Mammal Underground. His sister contributed more than fifty thousand dollars to the organization before her death."

"I knew Janis had money. I didn't know it was that kind of money."

"Miss Withers received a sizable income from a trust fund her grandfather established for her."

"I didn't know they were brother and sister when I first talked to him," said Rolly. "I didn't know anything about the OMU or the money she gave them."

"But you knew Janis Withers, didn't you?"

Rolly stared across the table at Agent Goffin. She had a blank look on her face. They taught FBI agents to do that, to maintain a neutral, lackluster facial expression so you couldn't figure out what they were thinking. Standing by the table, Agent King flexed his hands. He made his hands into fists and released them, made a fist again as if warming up for a beating. The FBI taught them to do that too.

"What do you want me from me?" Rolly said.

Agent Goffin clicked her pen again.

"I'm glad you asked," she said.

# 25

# THE CAFÉ

Rolly sat on a bench outside the tumbledown café on the Ocean Beach Pier, waiting for Melody Flowers to finish her lunch shift. There was no one else on the pier, except for a couple of fishermen hanging their lines over the railing. Surfers rode by on the waves below.

The intermingled smell of salt water, fish scales and seagull guano tickled the inside of his nose. A brown pelican flew down and settled itself on the railing across from him. It turned its head, looked at him sideways and clucked a few times, but Rolly didn't feel like engaging in conversation. The pelican decided he was a deadbeat and jumped off the pier, making a guttural squawk as it dropped toward the water. It soared back into sight a few seconds later, drafting on gusts from the breakers below.

The door of the café opened. Melody stepped out. She looked down the pier toward Ocean Beach, then turned and walked over to Rolly. Her scarf fluttered in the breeze like a satin rainbow.

"Have a seat," Rolly said. Melody glanced at the book that lay on the bench next to him.

"Let's walk down to the end of pier," she said. "I don't want the boss to see me out here. One of the other girls called in sick and he wants me to work her shift."

Rolly rose from his seat and picked up Wendell's book, *Danni's Dolphin*. The two of them walked out toward the end of the pier.

"How long have you worked at that place?" he asked.

"Couple of months," she replied.

"Nice location," said Rolly. "My mom used to bring me here sometimes when I lived in OB. I couldn't afford anyplace but the taco shop."

"You must have been pretty poor. It's not that expensive."

"I *was* poor, living-in-a-one-room-apartment-with-two-other-guys-poor," replied Rolly.

"The job's okay. If you don't mind the fish smell. And the grease. I wish I could do better with my aura readings and temple work, but it takes time to develop your own business."

The pier forked in two directions, forming a *T*. Melody took the right fork of the *T*. She leaned over the railing at the end of the pier and stared down at the foaming green water that swirled around the pylons. Rolly stood next to her and leaned in close. Anyone else on the pier would assume they were intimate.

"Two FBI agents came to my house today," he said.

"Really? What did they want?"

"They asked about Butch Fleetwood."

"Whoa."

"Yeah. That's what I thought. A big Clydesdale whoa."

"Was Fleetwood a spy?"

"I don't know. Maybe. Somebody leaked government secrets to the Ocean Beach newspaper about this top-secret Navy dolphin program he was in. The editor of the paper won't say who it was, but the leaks stopped after Fleetwood died. The FBI wants to know where I got the dog tags."

"Did you tell them?"

Rolly shook his head.

"No. As far as I'm concerned you're my client. I won't give them your name. That's why I needed to talk to you. I don't think I can do this anymore."

"You want some money, is that it?" said Melody.

"The FBI wants me to work for them."

"Are they paying you?"

"I didn't take the job," Rolly said. "But I'm on their radar now. If I keep messing around in this Butch Fleetwood stuff, they could come after me. I might have to tell them about you."

"I've got some money," said Melody. She reached in her purse and pulled out some bills. "Here's two hundred dollars. Is that enough?"

Rolly sighed. Melody shoved the two Benjamins at him. It seemed odd for her to be carrying hundred-dollar bills around, but he decided not to worry about it. He took the money and put it in his pocket.

"It helps," he said. "Why is this so important to you?"

"Janis was my friend. She was nice to me, kind of like the mother I never had. I can't believe she killed herself."

"And that's all there is to it?"

"Yeah. Well, not completely. Janis kept my rent really low on that place. The Temple. My rent's a third of what people pay around here for a place half as big. I don't want to move. It's a great situation for me. If there were some sort of Lemurian people she knew, someone with money, maybe they could help."

"I can understand that," Rolly said, thinking of the sweetheart terms his mother gave him for the granny flat in Hillcrest when she could charge anyone else twice as much for the place.

"There's something else you should know," he said. It would be interesting to see how Melody reacted to the news. "Somebody killed Janis's father last night."

"Are you shitting me?" said Melody. "Who did it? Was it Tammy? His wife?"

"Their chief suspect is someone named Harmonica Dan."

"Who?"

"Harmonica Dan. I asked you about him at the temple."

"I don't remember that."

"It was just before you had your little spell."

"Oh, yeah. My vision thing. What was the guy's name again?"

"Daniel Piper, aka Harmonica Dan."

Melody looked serious and thoughtful, as if she might call up her Merdonis spirit again. She didn't. She stayed in the real world.

"There was this guy," Melody said. "He took us out on his sailboat a couple of weeks ago, Janis and me. We went out to those islands, the ones off the coast down near Mexico."

Rolly nodded.

"Where did you board the boat?" he said.

"He had a berth at this marina in Point Loma."

"The one near Driscoll's Wharf?"

"Yeah. That was it. How'd you know that?"

"I've been on Dan's boat. Did they seem close? Dan and Janis?"

"Not like they were lovers, if that's what you mean. I didn't see anything like that. They didn't talk much. Everything was kind of formal and serious. They were really synced up, like they'd done this before. It was a dolphin thing."

"What do you mean?"

"When we got to the island, we went around the other side into this little bay. He circled around the bay while Janis dropped dolphin balls over the side of the boat. It was some kind of ceremony."

"What are dolphin balls?"

"They're these smooth crystal globes. There's some in the temple. Janis told me she was setting up an energy field in the water. She said the dolphins are drawn into the circle of energy because of the crystal power in the dolphin balls."

"Okay. What else?"

"After Janis finished, this guy took the boat into the center of the circle he'd just made. He had these speakers attached to the back of the boat and he lowered them into the water. Then he played his harmonica. It didn't sound like a regular harmonica, though. It was all kind of squeaky and high-pitched. He said he was waking the dolphins."

"Did it work?"

"Yeah. It was crazy. This one dolphin kept swimming in circles around the boat. The harmonica guy opened a door in the back of the boat and the dolphin leapt up into the boat. Janis knelt down close to the dolphin. She started talking to it."

"What did she say?"

"I couldn't hear, exactly. She talked to it real quiet like. The dolphin talked back to her, I swear."

"What did it say?"

"I don't know what it said. It was just dolphin noises to me. But Janis was talking to it, just like you and me. This Dan guy, he rode the dolphin for a while, holding its fins. He even jumped out of the water on it."

Melody fiddled with the end of her scarf. Rolly cleared his throat.

"Harmonica Dan was at the Admiral's Club the night Janis died. They know he was there," he said. "And I saw him last night. Near the building where Henley Withers was killed. I need to find him."

Melody moved over to the bench and sat down. Rolly sat down next to her. Melody looked out at the ocean.

"Where did you get that book?" she asked.

"Out at the lighthouse, the visitors' center. Wendell was signing out there."

"No one's supposed to know about us," Melody said. "He's married."

"He wrote something inside," Rolly said, handing Melody the book. "You might want to read it."

Melody opened the book and read the inscription. She bit her lip, closed the book and looked out at the ocean. Rolly felt like a jerk.

"He told me he's getting divorced," she said.

"They all say that," said Rolly. Melody glared at him.

"He said it would be easier for us once the divorce goes through," she said. "That we could stop sneaking around."

"You think he's serious?"

"I don't know what I think. I know he's rich. I know he's good looking. He's taking me for a cruise on his yacht, after the concert is over. Maybe I don't care if he's serious."

"Maybe you don't."

"You think I'm a slut, don't you?"

"I know guys like him. I used to be one of them. Without the money."

"Were you ever married?"

"Engaged once."

"Did you cheat on her?"

"Yes." Rolly nodded. It was still painful to admit, even now. But women liked it when men admitted their faults. They thought it meant you were honest. Young women thought so, anyway. Older ones knew better.

"What should I do?" said Melody.

"I'm not the kind of guy who should be giving relationship advice," said Rolly. "I just wanted you to know that I know."

"It was afterwards," Melody said. "After the dolphin was gone. Dan and Janis rowed into the beach. They made me promise to stay on the boat."

"Where did they go?"

"There's this old building on the island, up on the cliffs. It looks like a castle. I saw them go inside. I don't know what happened, but when Janis came back to the boat she was really freaked out."

"Did she say anything?"

"No. She just sat out there on the front of the boat all the way home and cried. She wouldn't talk to me or anything. I took her some water, 'cause you know you gotta stay hydrated when you're out on the ocean like that. That was the first time I saw them."

"Saw what?"

"The dog tags."

"You're sure about that? She didn't have them before?"

"It was the first time I saw them. She was holding them in her hands and staring at them."

"What about Harmonica Dan? Did he say anything?"

"They were both kind of gloomy on the way back. Like, you know, thinking about something real serious. I saw him again, you know, the day I met Wendell. That Dan guy was hanging around outside the school."

"You mean the school where Wendell's painting the mural?"

"Yeah. Wendell was doing his outlining that day. Janis was so excited. She invited me over to check it out."

"And Wendell checked you out?"

"I know. I know. He's a dick. After the water park opens he'll never come back and I'm history. Maybe I should dump him first. Before the concert."

"Are you going to the concert?"

"He gave me a ticket. Maybe I should just dump him and sell the ticket. It's worth five hundred dollars. I could pay you with that."

"Two hundred will be fine for now."

"He took me cruising out on his yacht," said Melody. "It's really nice. I don't meet any guys with million-dollar catamarans slinging fish and chips in that roach café."

"Let's get back to Harmonica Dan," said Rolly. "You say he was at the school that day?"

"Yeah. He was standing outside the fence. I don't think he even noticed me. He kept talking to himself, acting like some kind of crazy, homeless guy."

"What did he say?"

"I couldn't understand most of it. Except one thing he said really stuck with me."

"What's that?"

"'I didn't kill him.'"

"Kill who?"

"He didn't say who. He just kept repeating it. 'I didn't kill him.'"

# 26

# THE MEETING

The sun had just set when Rolly pulled into the parking lot near Driscoll's Wharf. A dirty brown haze floated on the ocean horizon and glowing windows reflected the sunset's rusty orange color. The OMU was meeting tonight in the OTTER garage. The FBI claimed that Dick Nazi would be leading the group and they wanted someone at the meeting, someone who didn't look like an FBI agent. That person was Rolly.

As Rolly saw it, he wasn't an FBI informant per se. He was a private contractor making use of information the FBI had provided to him. The FBI would talk to him afterward. They'd want to know what he'd heard, what he'd seen. He wasn't wearing a wire and he wouldn't get paid for his work, but he might get the FBI off his back.

He walked along the edge of the marina until he came to the OTTER garage, and then tried the door. The handle turned. He walked in and took cover behind the large rear tire of an OTTER vehicle parked near the door, hoping to assess the situation before anyone noticed he was there.

A sequence of wobbly harmonica notes rang out, a squeaky melody that sounded like Dan's dolphin reveille. A chorus of other harmonicas repeated the notes, with varying accuracy. The call and response continued, first the solo harmonica, then the chorus. Rolly peeked around the OTTER's oversized tire, hoping to get a look at the musicians, but only managed to thump his head against the hull of the boat.

"What was that?" someone said. The harmonicas stopped playing. Rolly heard the rustle of clothes, the squeak of moving seats.

"Who's there?"

Rolly stepped into the room.

"Hello," he said, greeting the men and women gathered around a long table in the center of the room. A bald, tattooed man took a step toward him.

"What are you doing here, Waters?" said Dick Nazi.

"I had a rehearsal here a couple of nights ago with J.V. Sideman's band."

"Yeah, I know. What about it?"

"I can't find my guitar tuner," said Rolly. "Thought maybe I left it here."

He stretched his index finger and thumb to indicate the size of the tuner.

"It's a little plastic box about this big. It's got a little meter and some LED lights on the front. Anybody seen it?"

"Your tuner's not here," said Nazi.

"Can I take a look around?"

"Not now. Come back tomorrow."

"It'll only take five minutes."

"You need to leave."

Rolly glanced around the room, making a show of searching for his tuner, but he knew he wouldn't find it. The tuner was at home in his guitar case.

"Is this some kind of music class?" he said.

"That's none of your business," said Nazi.

"That song you were playing, I've heard it before. Harmonica Dan plays that tune."

Something invisible ran through the room, like an electrical current passing through the people gathered around the table.

"You can't be here, Waters," said Nazi. "This is a private rehearsal."

Rolly decided to throw a bomb into the room. He didn't have time to finesse this or try and make friends.

"Why does the FBI think the OMU is a terrorist group?"

"Because they're fascist goons doing the bidding of their corporate overlords," said one of the women.

"Quiet, Sissy," said Nazi, looking back at the woman. "I'll take care of this."

"Listen," said Rolly. "I don't care what you do. I don't care about politics. I just want to talk to Harmonica Dan."

"You can't be here," said Nazi. "Get out."

"Butch Fleetwood," said Rolly, looking over the room. "Has anybody here heard that name?"

All he got for his effort was blank faces. No one stirred.

"What about Arion?" Rolly said. "Has anyone heard of Arion?"

Nazi grabbed Rolly's arm.

"C'mon," he said. "Let's go."

"You need any help?" said one of the men. Nazi looked Rolly in the eye.

"Am I going to need help, Waters?" he said.

"No," said Rolly. "I'll go easy. You can walk me out."

Nazi turned back to the others.

"Everybody continue with the rehearsal. I'll take care of this."

Nazi escorted Rolly out of the building, shutting the door behind them.

"Jesus, Waters," he said. "What is it with you? Everybody told me you were cool. Why are you being such an asshole?"

Rolly thought for a moment. He didn't have a good answer. He didn't know what he was doing or why. He couldn't explain it. He took the dog tags out of his pocket.

"Your sister gave these to me," he said. "I think they have something to do with her killing herself."

"What are they?"

"They're Butch Fleetwood's dog tags. Your sister knew him. She might've been in love with him."

"Is this the spy guy?"

Rolly nodded.

"Jesus," said Nazi. "Why didn't you tell me this earlier?"

"You didn't give me a chance."

"I always thought he was someone my sister made up. My parents would leave me with her sometimes, when I was little. She'd tell me stories about him. I never knew the guy's name."

"Did she say anything about him recently?"

"We didn't talk much."

"You drove her to school three days a week. You must've talked some."

Nazi twisted his mouth. He looked away.

"I felt sorry for my sister," he said. "She was even more fucked up than me."

"I talked to your mother yesterday," said Rolly. "I was there with the police after your father died."

"Yeah? So?"

"You don't seem upset about your father's death."

Nazi stomped his boot on the ground, as if he were killing a roach. He took a pack of cigarettes out of his jeans pocket and lit one up. He walked to the edge of the marina and contemplated the boats floating on the dark purple water.

"Here's the deal, Waters," he said. "They're not really my parents. Janis wasn't my sister. Not biologically."

"I don't understand."

"They're not my blood. I was a foster kid."

"The Witherses adopted you?"

Nazi nodded.

"Yeah. My real parents are from Virginia."

"Do you know who your real parents are?"

"Sure. I know. Miss Minor and Mr. Unknown. That's how they're listed on my birth certificate—mother minor and father unknown. No names for either of them. Best I can figure it, Tammy and Henley Withers yanked me outta some holler back in Ol' Virginny, brought me back to California to keep some gap-toothed yokel from drowning his inbred bastard son in the creek. Grandpa Baldry told me as much when I went to visit him a couple of years ago. He made all the arrangements for the adoption. Grandpa Baldry's very civically minded, if you know what I mean. He carries a lot of weight in that town. Hell, he practically owns it."

"You think he knows who your parents were?"

"Probably. 'Course I can't rule out my father was Grandpa Baldry himself, taking care of some indiscretion with one of his backwood Lolitas. Shipbuilder Baldry, the lord of Newport News, VA. Tammy's father. Principal shareholder and chief executive officer of the largest privately held defense contractor in the U S of A."

"Tidewater Defense Systems, right?"

Nazi nodded again.

"Yeah. That's the real joke, you know. Tammy and Twinkie acting like their work's so important."

"Who's Twinkie?"

"That's what I called Henley. A pet psychiatrist and a harebrained inventor. I doubt either of them could run a business of their own. It was Grandpa Baldry who set them up out here, helped them get the contracts for the dolphin show. Grandpa paid for the house. He paid for their boat. He paid my boarding school tuition and fees. Armed Forces Academy. That was Grandpa's idea too."

"You went to boarding school?"

"When I was thirteen. Didn't get out until I graduated high school. Grandpa said it would strengthen my moral fiber."

"My dad used to say that to me," said Rolly.

"Did you go to military school?"

"No, but he threatened me with it sometimes. My mom was dead set against any kind of boarding school, especially military."

"You got lucky. Tammy and Henley were pretty much done with me by the time I hit puberty. They told me the Academy would be great for building character. They were right, I guess, if bullying and buggery build character. That's why I'm so fucked up. I hardly saw them after I graduated. I was done with them. They were done with me too."

"What about Janis? How was her relationship with her parents?"

"She crashed their party and set herself on fire. What do you think?"

"Your mother told me—"

"She's not my mother. Call her Tammy. Or Tams. Tam-O-Shanter."

"Tammy told me Janis tried to commit suicide before. She said this wasn't the first time Janis had done something like this."

"Yeah. I guess. Grandpa bought Janis that house in OB. He set up a trust fund for her, after the first time she tried to kill herself, when she burned her face."

"Does Grandpa Baldry know Janis is dead? Has anyone told him?"

Nazi shrugged.

"Wouldn't make any difference if they did. Grandpa's got dementia. His money can't help him now. He's sitting up there in that old Virginia mansion with a couple of sexy nurses and his brain turning to Swiss cheese."

The door behind them creaked open. Rolly and Nazi both turned to look.

"You okay?" said the man at the door, the one who'd offered to help remove Rolly earlier.

"I'm fine," said Nazi. "Keep practicing. I'll be back in a minute."

The man disappeared back into the building. Nazi tapped the ashes from his cigarette.

"What else you got, Waters?" he said.

Rolly mulled over the list of things he wanted to ask Nazi and sorted them for importance, first things first.

"Harmonica Dan," he said. "You learned that music from him, didn't you?"

Nazi shrugged.

"Maybe. What's it to you?"

"The FBI's looking for him. So are the cops. I want to find him before they do."

"I don't keep the guy's social calendar."

"He's part of your group, isn't he?"

"Dan's not part of anything. He comes and goes. You never know when he's going to show up."

Rolly showed the dog tags to Nazi again.

"Dan took Janis out on his boat a couple of weeks ago. They went down to the Coronado Islands. Janis talked to the dolphins. I think she might've found these dog tags on the island. She left them for me and I want to know why."

"How do you know all this?" said Nazi.

"It's not important," said Rolly. "Listen. I know Dan's got some connection to your group. I don't care about OMU's politics, whatever plans you're cooking up. Protest as much as you want against Wendell and his Ocean Universe thing. Monkey-wrench him to hell. He's a dick."

"That's the spirit, Waters."

"Don't mess with the concert, though. I'm playing in his band."

A look of disgust crossed Nazi's face.

"You are such a sellout," he said.

Rolly didn't care what Nazi thought of his career choices. Double-scale was double-scale.

"I just want to talk to Dan," he said. "This is important to me."

Nazi finished his cigarette and flicked the stub into the bay.

"Was there something special going on between you and my sister?" he said.

"No," said Rolly. "Nothing special."

"You nailed her, though, didn't you?"

Rolly shook his head.

"I never slept with your sister," he said. "She was . . . It just wouldn't have been right."

Nazi narrowed his eyes at Rolly.

"Shit," he said. "You really expect me to believe that? After all that stuff people told me?"

"What kind of stuff?"

"C'mon, Waters. It's not exactly a secret. You guys must've set some kind of record for going through the local groupies."

Rolly rubbed his temples. He didn't know there had been a competition. He didn't know people kept score. But he knew Janis Withers hadn't been one of those scores. This was about something else.

"Our singer, Matt . . ."

"The guy you killed?"

"He was involved with your sister. When he died. I heard he was going to marry her."

"Jesus Christ, Waters. I didn't know that."

"Neither did I. Not until a couple of days ago."

"I can see why you're kind of freaked out."

"Just talk to Dan for me, will you? Tell him I want to help him."

Nazi walked back to the building. He stopped at the door and looked back at Rolly.

"I'm one of the good guys, Waters," he said. "I'll see what I can do."

# 27

# THE SLOOP

Rolly sat on a bench at the end of Driscoll's Wharf, eating a grilled opah sandwich from Mitch's Seafood. The bench faced out toward the water, but he wasn't enjoying the view. He'd turned his back to the bay in order to keep his eyes on the door of the OTTER garage, waiting for the OMU meeting to end.

He finished his meal, crumpled up the paper bag it had come in and looked around for a trash can. There wasn't one near. He dropped the bag onto the bench next to him, stood up and stretched, then walked to the safety rail overlooking the bay. Something moved in the water below him, pushing out ripples. A fat sea lion surfaced. It swam farther into the marina, searching for fish scraps or a vacant section of the dock where it could sleep. The sea lion barked as it slid through the water, announcing its arrival.

The door to the OTTER garage opened. A man stepped out. Another man followed him. Rolly returned to the bench and watched them make their way down the sidewalk, moving away from him. More people followed. Rolly listened in the shadows, catching scraps of conversation. The discourse was mundane—goodbyes and farewells, promises of phone calls and a beer in the future. Dick Nazi wasn't among those who left. Rolly waited another twenty minutes before deciding Nazi had used a separate exit, then picked up his sandwich bag and headed toward the parking lot. As he did so, the light bulb above the garage door went out. The door swung open and Dick Nazi stepped outside. A small knapsack hung over his shoulder.

Rolly stepped away from the sidewalk, removing himself from the hazy halo of light shining down from the streetlamp above. Nazi crossed the sidewalk and entered the marina through gate number two. He walked down the gangplank, out to the end of the pier, turned and boarded Harmonica Dan's sailboat. Disappearing into the cabin for a moment, he soon reappeared and headed back toward the gate. Rolly prepared to confront him when he came through.

Nazi didn't make it back to the gate. He stopped halfway along the dock and climbed into a dinghy that was lashed to the pier, undid the rope attached to the dinghy and pushed out into the marina. Rolly kept to the shadows, watching Nazi row across the water until he disappeared in the dark bay. Rolly looked back at Harmonica Dan's boat, wondering why Nazi had gone there, what he'd done while on board.

He crossed the sidewalk to the marina gate and keyed in the combination he'd seen Bonnie use two days ago, the four corner numbers of the keypad, clockwise from the top left. The latch clicked. He opened the gate and paused at the top of the ramp, considering the wisdom, not to mention the legality, of what he planned to do next. He thought about calling Bonnie or his new FBI friends and telling them what had happened. He thought about going home and getting some sleep. He decided not to do either and walked down the pier to Harmonica Dan's boat. Standing on the pier might be legal, but he could get himself in real trouble if he boarded Dan's boat. The yellow crime tape had been removed, but Bonnie would give him hell if she knew he'd boarded the boat. She might arrest him.

"Hey you," someone called.

Rolly turned. A man approached him from the far end of the pier. It was the same man who'd accosted him two days earlier, the marina's self-appointed watchman. Rolly nodded.

"Hello again," he said.

"What're you doing there?" said the man.

"I'm a friend of Dan's," said Rolly. "I was here a couple of days ago, with the police officer, the blond woman?"

"Oh yeah. I thought you looked familiar. Have you found Dan yet?"

"I talked with him yesterday."

"He's okay, then?"

"Spry as ever," said Rolly. "Still playing his harmonica. I don't think he's coming back here for a while, though."

"Did they arrest him?"

"Not yet. He wanted me to check on his boat."

"Let him know we're keeping an eye on things for him."

"I will. Have you seen anybody else on his boat since I was here? Anyone besides the police?"

"Just the cops, and those FBI guys in the suits. They took down the tape yesterday."

"I saw someone down here just a few minutes ago."

"What did he look like?"

"Early twenties, shaved head, tattoos, kind of a punk rocker look?"

"Sounds like Ricky."

"Who's Ricky?"

"Little bilge pumper who used to work around here. Helped keep the place clean. Janitorial stuff."

"His name's Richard Withers. He works at the OTTER Company up there on the wharf," said Rolly. He pointed back at the buildings.

"I heard Ricky moved up in the world. Good for him."

"Have you seen Ricky lately?"

The man scratched the back of his head.

"No," he said. "It's been a while since I seen him around."

Rolly pulled out his wallet and handed the man a business card.

"If you see Ricky, or Dan, or anyone else near this boat, please give me a call."

"Sure," said the man. "I can do that."

"Thank you," said Rolly.

The man started away, then stopped. He turned back to Rolly.

"There was something strange in the water last night," he said.

"What's that?"

"Last night. Something big swam by my boat."

"I saw a sea lion a few minutes ago."

"This thing was too quiet for a sea lion. They're always chuffing and barking. They're loud. This thing was real quiet-like."

"What about dolphins?" said Rolly. "Do they ever come around here?"

"Out in the main channel, sure, but I never seen one this close to the shore. There's pelicans sometimes. They're kind of big, but I can usually tell them by the clucking."

"You didn't see what it was?"

"Nope. By the time I looked out, there were just some ripples in the water, like something dived under. It wasn't any boat wake, either. I know what those feel like."

"This was last night?"

"Yeah. And a couple of nights before that. What do you make of it?"

Rolly shook his head. He knew next to nothing about the creatures that swam in the bay.

"No idea," he said. "But let me know if it comes by again."

"Can do," said the man. He turned again to leave.

"Wait," said Rolly. "Could it be a scuba diver?"

The man scratched his chin for a moment.

"Well," he said, "I guess that's a possibility. Usually with a scuba guy, you see bubbles coming up to the surface. You can pretty much track 'em by the bubbles."

"You didn't see any bubbles?"

"No," said the man. "I didn't see any bubbles. Some of those Navy guys use rebreathers, though."

"What's that?"

"They're scuba rigs that recirculate the air the diver exhales, then add some oxygen back into the mix so he can breathe it again. There's no venting, no bubbles. Good for sneaking up on your enemies."

"Do the Navy divers ever come into the marina here?"

"I've seen them out in the bay sometimes. More divers use rebreathers now, if they can afford them. It's not just the Navy."

"Well," said Rolly. "Like I said, give me a call if you see anyone."

The man walked to the end of the pier and climbed onto his boat. Rolly surveyed the marina and wharf, checking to see if there was anyone watching. A couple of boats had their lights on, but otherwise the marina looked empty. He stepped onto Dan's boat and ducked down into the well by the cabin door. He felt safer now, out of the line of sight.

He opened the cabin door and crawled inside, shut the door and stood up. A dim glow filtered in through the portholes, but it was too dark to see anything more than general shapes in the cabin. He pulled his phone out of his pocket, found the flashlight button and tapped it on. The light blazed up into his face. He turned the phone over and pointed the light down toward the table, focusing it a few inches from the surface to minimize the amount of light leaking out through the windows.

He passed the flashlight over the horizontal surfaces of the dining room and kitchen. It was the same stuff he'd seen before: charts and magazines, packs of ramen and cans of beans. He made his way to the back of the cabin and ran the light over the bedroom surfaces. Nothing looked any different there, either. The harmonica case sat on the bed just as it had before. He moved the light over Dan's harmonica case. The snaps on the case were loose, so he opened it. Still one harmonica missing. Key of A.

The boat moved. It was just a slight rock, an almost imperceptible dip to the port side. Rolly turned off his flashlight. He held his breath and listened. The cabin stairs creaked. Someone had boarded Harmonica Dan's boat.

# 28

# THE ISLAND

I t was dark out. That was the first thing Rolly noticed when he opened his eyes, how dark it was. The second thing he noticed was the pain along the left side of his body. His neck was stiff. His left shoulder was sore. The last thing he remembered was opening the door of the boat's cabin, peeking out at the aft deck. Now he found himself on the boat's bathroom floor, the back of his head propped against the toilet. A rhythmic slap of water beat against the boat's fiberglass hull. Rolly lifted his head from the toilet. The boat was moving.

He rose to his feet and tried to open the door. The latch clicked, but the door didn't budge. He pushed against it. The door moved a half-inch, but no farther. He stepped back from the door and searched through his pockets. His wallet and keys were gone. So was his phone. He seated himself on the toilet and looked out through the porthole. Black peaks of water passed by the window, reflecting the sparkle of lights from the shore. He remembered now.

A dark shape, a man in a black rubber suit, had jumped in front of him as he looked out the door of the ship's cabin. The man jabbed his fingers into the little depression just above Rolly's left clavicle. There was an explosion of pain along the left side of his body. That was the last thing he could remember, the pain. He wondered what time it was, how long he'd been locked in the bathroom.

He reached in his pockets. They were still empty. He considered pounding on the porthole window and screaming for help, but doubted it would do him much good. It would only alert the man in the rubber suit that his prisoner had become restive. The man would come down to the cabin and jab his fingers into Rolly's shoulder again. He might do something worse.

Melody's conspiracy talk about spies and Janis's death didn't seem so crazy anymore. A man who could knock you senseless by sticking his fingers into the space above your clavicle had training in hand-to-hand fighting techniques. He could be a Navy SEAL or a Special Forces Marine, one of those guys who could kill people ten different ways with just his bare hands, a guy who might have done it before.

The sailboat tossed and pitched. Rolly peeked through the porthole again. The waves had become more agitated and rough. He could still see lights on the shore, but he could also see where the lights ended and a massive outcropping of dark landscape began—the cliffs at the end of the Point Loma peninsula. They were still in the harbor, but they would pass Ballast Point soon and head into the Pacific Ocean. The opah sandwich he'd eaten earlier turned against him. A black rock of fear tumbled around in his guts. The rough toss of the waves didn't help any.

He sat on the floor and rested his head against the toilet seat. A few minutes later, he took his first heave. A second one followed soon after, clearing out whatever was left in his stomach. His insides twisted into a tight knot, but the worst of the purge seemed to be over. The rigging clanked. The floor began to slope. The boat had turned south. It was heading toward Mexico. Rolly curled up on the floor and closed his eyes.

By the time he woke again, the boat had stopped moving. The water was calmer. It was still dark, but a dim glow from the porthole window suggested moonlight. He lifted himself off the floor and took a pee. His mouth felt like an old, sweaty sock. He noticed a jug of water under the sink, took the top off the bottle, sniffed at its contents, and tried a small sip. It was drinkable. He downed a few gulps. He wasn't dead. The boat hadn't burned. It hadn't exploded. The man in the rubber suit had some purpose other than Rolly's demise.

Rolly leaned down and looked through the porthole. The boat appeared to be anchored in a small cove, fifty yards from a moonlit sliver of beach. A towering wall of rocks surrounded the beach. He tried the bathroom door again. It gave a half-inch before it caught on something. The outside handle had been tied off with rope.

He searched through the bathroom cabinets, rifling through toilet paper rolls and old toothpaste tubes. In the bottom of the second drawer, he found a straight razor, the kind barbers used. He pulled the blade open, knelt down by the door, slipped the blade through the crack and sawed at the rope. A few moments later he cut through the last strands and swung the door open.

He closed the razor, put it in his pocket, stepped into the bedroom and listened for signs that someone might still be on board. The only thing he could hear was the soft lap of water on the hull. He made his way out to the kitchen, opened the door to the cabin and paused for a moment, waiting to see if the man in the rubber suit would attack him again. Nothing happened. Feeling emboldened, he climbed the back stairs, stepped onto the deck and surveyed his surroundings.

Beyond the entrance to the cove there was limitless ocean, a flat inky horizon. He didn't see any landmarks by which he could judge his location. Given the direction the boat had taken last night he assumed they were somewhere in Mexico, anchored in some secret spot along the Baja coast. He turned the other way and looked at the land that encircled the cove—steep rock shadows with sharp, pointed peaks that jutted from the water like the craggy fingers of angry sea gods. A long, flat two-story building hung along one side of the cliffs. Turrets anchored each corner of the building, suggesting a medieval castle. Small, square windows ran along the face of the building, evenly spaced every fifty feet. The windows were all empty or broken. The foundational structure of the building seemed intact, but its aging wooden exterior was weathered and beaten. A rocky stairway descended from the corner of the building down to the waterline and a decrepit wood pier. The boat was tied up at the end of the pier.

He heard a splash from the other side of the boat and turned to see a black hand grasp the guardrail. A man in a rubber suit hauled himself onto the deck. Rolly reached for the straight razor folded up in his pocket. The man was at least six inches taller than Rolly, his muscular body pressed tightly into the full-body wetsuit. Moonlight glinted off the dark glass of the man's diving mask, hiding his eyes

"Who are you?" said Rolly, pulling the razor out of his pocket and flipping it open. Its sharp edge wouldn't stop a Navy SEAL, but it might give him pause. The man took a step forward.

"Don't come any closer," said Rolly, waving the blade. The man stopped. "Who are you?"

"I'm everyone's nightmare," said the man in the wetsuit. He dodged to Rolly's left, away from the razor. Rolly raised his arm, preparing to strike, but it was too late. The man ducked and swiveled to block Rolly's right arm with his own. The razor blade clattered onto the deck as the man lifted Rolly and tossed him over the side of the boat. By the time Rolly resurfaced, he'd drifted at least thirty feet. He watched the man untie the boat from the pier.

"Hey!" Rolly sputtered. "You can't leave me here."

The man set the rudder, swiveled the boat away from the pier and headed out to sea, snapping off a middle-finger salute as he sailed away. Rolly struggled against the weight of his clothes, trying to keep his head above water, then turned his head toward the shore, channeling his best freestyle stroke as he swam in toward the beach. The swirling current pulled him in different directions. By the time he'd advanced twenty feet, he felt exhausted. He stopped, dog-paddling, then reached down and pulled off his shoes.

Something moved in the water. A cold shaft of fear ran down his body as a dorsal fin cut through the surface, headed toward him. He was shark bait. The creature circled around him and lifted its head to the surface, rolling one eye. It was a dolphin. The dolphin smiled and chirped at him twice.

"Good boy," Rolly said. It sounded stupid, like he was addressing a cocker spaniel. The dolphin chirped at him a couple more times. Rolly didn't know how to respond.

"Good boy," he said again, trying to sound friendly.

The dolphin moved in closer as Rolly struggled to keep his mouth above water. It nuzzled up next to him and he grabbed onto the dolphin's flipper with one hand, its dorsal fin with the other. The dolphin chirped again, then swam in toward the beach, pulling Rolly along.

As they moved in closer to shore, the dolphin caught a wave breaking into the beach. It chirped again and twisted sideways about ten feet from the sand, dislodging Rolly's grip as it dove and turned back out to sea. Rolly put his feet down, found bottom. He crawled onto the beach and lay on the sand, catching his breath. Once he'd recovered, he rose to his feet and looked out at the water. A dorsal fin cruised the surface just beyond where the waves broke. Rolly brought his hand down across his chest and then up again, imitating the signal the trainer had shown him at the Navy's dolphin pens. Fifty feet offshore, the dolphin arced out of the water and dove back in.

"I am Arion!" Rolly shouted. He raised both arms in the air, exultant. "I am Arion!"

A voice came from behind him, a command.

"¡Detener!"

Rolly turned toward the voice. Two soldiers stood on the beach, pointing rifles at him.

# 29

# THE ANNEX

R olly paced the floor in a windowless room at the Coast Guard headquarters on San Diego Bay, awaiting his interrogation or debriefing or whatever they called the thing that came next. There was a table in the room and three chairs. He couldn't say much for Coast Guard hospitality. No one had spoken to him in the last forty minutes. No one had looked in on him and or asked if he might like a cup of coffee. He really needed a cup of coffee.

The man in the wetsuit had abandoned Rolly on South Coronado Island, west of Tijuana. The island's only inhabitants were a lighthouse keeper and the two Mexican soldiers who had apprehended Rolly on the beach. None of them spoke any English. Rolly only spoke a little Spanish, but somehow he'd communicated to them that he was a stupid American who'd fallen off his boat and washed up on their little island. After marching him up the ridge behind the old casino and down to their barracks on the other side of the island, one of the soldiers got on the radio to his superiors. The wheels of cross-border diplomacy took a while to get rolling, but eventually a US Coast Guard helicopter arrived, touching down on the concrete landing pad behind the soldiers' bunkhouse and whisking Rolly back to this small, windowless room in the good old USA.

208 | COREY LYNN FAYMAN

The door to the room opened. FBI agents Goffin and King walked in. Bonnie Hammond walked in behind them.

"Good morning, Mr. Waters," said the man, Agent King.

"Good morning," said Rolly.

"Sounds like you've had quite an adventure."

"I guess you could call it that," said Rolly.

"What would you call it?"

"Kidnapping. Abduction. I'm the victim here."

"Have a seat," said King.

Rolly sat down at the table. The two agents sat down across from him. Bonnie crossed her arms and took a stance behind the two agents, in the far corner of the room.

"You're in a lot of trouble, Mr. Waters," said the woman, Agent Goffin.

"What for?"

"Interfering with a Federal investigation."

"I'm not trying to interfere."

"What are you doing, then?"

"I did what you asked me to. I went to the OMU meeting."

"Tell us about that."

"They were playing harmonicas."

"Harmonicas?"

"Yes."

"That's not very helpful."

"It was the dolphin reveille."

"And what is that?"

Rolly told the agents about the funny sounds Dan made with his harmonica. He told them about Janis and Dan, the crystal balls and harmonica squeaks they used to call dolphins up from the deep. The two agents listened to his story with dour faces.

"Who told you that story?" said Agent Goffin. "About the dolphins and the island?"

"It's just a story I heard."

"Is that why you chose to go out to the island?"

"I didn't choose to go out there. Someone kidnapped me."

"Who are you working for?"

"I can't tell you that."

"We could get a subpoena, Mr. Waters. We could *make* you tell us."

"I've got a good lawyer. Max has won cases like this before."

"We'll see about that."

"I talked to Dick Nazi," said Rolly. "Richard Withers, I mean."

"What did he tell you?"

"I'm not telling you what he said unless you act nice."

"It's not our job to be nice, Mr. Waters."

"You threatened me and my family."

"No one here has threatened you or your family. We've only confirmed pertinent facts. Officer Hammond has convinced us you're not a credible threat to the government, regardless of your personal history and associations."

"Thanks, Bon," said Rolly. "I guess." He looked over at Bonnie, standing in the corner.

"I'm only here as an observer," she said, shaking her head. "The FBI's in charge of this thing."

"We think you have information that may be critical to preventing a terrorist attack," said Agent Goffin. "Once we're satisfied that you've told us everything you know, you may go."

Rolly turned back to the agents.

"Could I get a cup of coffee, at least? I'm kind of beat."

"We can do that," said Agent Goffin. Agent King left the room.

"Have you found the boat?" Rolly asked.

"You mean Daniel Piper's sailboat?"

"Yes."

"As far as we can tell, Mr. Piper's boat never left its berth."

"But it did. I was on it. A guy knocked me out and locked me in the bathroom. We sailed to that island. That guy pushed me overboard. That's how I ended up there."

"We're not discounting your story, Mr. Waters. But we have no proof Daniel Piper's boat ever left the marina."

"Don't you have somebody watching the boat?"

"Believe it or not, Mr. Waters, the FBI has limited resources available for this case."

"Don't you have cameras or GPS tracker things you could put on his boat?"

Agent Goffin cleared her throat.

"We didn't have eyes on the marina last night."

"Well then, talk to that nosy neighbor two boats down from Dan's berth. Bonnie, you remember that guy who tried to stop us from going on Dan's boat?"

Bonnie nodded.

"Yeah, I remember him."

"He chatted me up, before I got on Dan's boat. He told me he saw me something weird in the water a couple of nights ago."

"What did he see?" said Agent Goffin.

"I don't know, but the trainer at the dolphin pens saw something weird too, the night Janis Withers blew up the Admiral's Club. They both said it didn't look like a seal or a sea lion."

"Hang on," said Agent Goffin.

"It could be that guy who knocked me out. The scuba diver guy. I think he's a Navy SEAL or something. Special Forces."

Agent Goffin held up one hand, palm out toward Rolly.

"Hold on," she said. "Let's backtrack. Who's the guy at the dolphin pens?"

Rolly told Agent Goffin about the trainer he and his father had talked to at the Navy's dolphin pens. As he finished, Agent King returned to the room. King set a Styrofoam cup of black coffee on the table next to Rolly, along with two packets of sugar, then took a seat next to Goffin. Rolly tasted the coffee, then stirred in both packets of sugar. It wouldn't improve the coffee much, but it would boost his blood sugar. Agent Goffin cleared her throat.

"Why did you board Daniel Piper's boat in the first place?" she said.

"Dick Nazi went there after the meeting."

"You saw Richard Withers board Daniel Piper's sailboat?"

"Yes. You guys wanted me to keep an eye on him, right?"

Agent Goffin nodded.

"Did you know he's adopted?" said Rolly. "Janis isn't really his sister, not by blood anyway."

"We're aware of Richard Withers's legal standing in the family. We have a file on him."

"His parents sent him to military school. It really messed him up, I guess. I think he might have been abused there. That could explain some of his attitude, you know, the rebellion thing . . ."

"Mr. Waters?" said Agent Goffin.

"Yes?"

"Let's leave the psychological profiling to professionals. Just tell us what happened."

"Yeah, right. Okay. Dick Nazi. After the meeting, I saw him go on board Dan's boat. He was only there for a couple of minutes. Then he took a rowboat out of the marina."

"Where did he go?"

"Into the bay. Out toward . . ."

"Yes?"

"I just realized something. Wendell's yacht is out there."

"Are you saying Richard Withers rowed out to Mr. Wendell's yacht?"

"No. Not exactly. It was dark. I lost sight of him. But he was headed that way."

"You didn't actually see him board Mr. Wendell's yacht?"

"No."

"What happened after that?"

Rolly told the agents about going into the cabin of Harmonica Dan's boat, feeling the floor sway as someone else came on board. He told them about the man in the rubber suit appearing in the doorway and knocking him out. He told them how he managed to escape the next morning, only to get knocked off the boat and watch the man sail away.

"Can you tell us anything about this man's appearance?" said Agent Goffin.

"He was big, six-four at least. Blue eyes, I think."

"Anything else? What makes you think he was military?"

"He just seemed very . . . professional."

Bonnie's phone buzzed. She checked it and left the room. Rolly looked in his Styrofoam cup. There was a clump of wet sugar still left in the bottom. All the coffee was gone.

"I want to know about Arion," he said.

"Where did you hear about Arion?" said Agent King.

"I saw that note in Dan's harmonica case," said Rolly. "I know that before Janis Withers killed herself, she said she'd seen Arion. I know there was a top-secret Tidewater Defense project called Arion too. Advance Reconnaissance something or other."

Agents Goffin and King looked at each other, then back at Rolly.

"Where did you get that information?" said Goffin. "About the Tidewater project?"

"I can't tell you that."

"Did your client tell you?"

"No."

"Who is your client again?"

"I'm still not telling you."

"Withholding information in a Federal investigation is against the law. It's a felony."

"My client hasn't committed any felony that I'm aware of. Neither have I."

"That's not the point. You do not have clearance to view or access classified government documents, Mr. Waters. Your client, whoever they are, is committing a felony if they made top-secret files available to you."

"It wasn't my client who showed me ARION. I only saw the cover page, anyway."

"Why are you so interested in ARION?"

"I think there's a connection between Butch Fleetwood and ARION. And Janis."

Goffin and King looked at each other again. King shrugged his shoulders as if to say it was the other agent's decision to make. Goffin turned back to Rolly.

"You are aware, Mr. Waters, of the newspaper articles printed in the *OB Enquirer* twenty-three years ago?"

"Yes."

"So you're also aware that top-secret documents were illegally leaked to Mr. Cockburn."

"I guess so."

"And you're aware that Mr. Cockburn was investigated by the FBI in connection with those articles? That we asked him to reveal his sources and he refused to do so?"

"Yes. I know that."

"What you may not know is that FBI agents who worked on the case at that time had narrowed down the list of suspects to a small group of people."

"Who were they?"

"I can't tell you. That information is classified."

"Was Harmonica Dan one of them?"

"What makes you say that?"

"Tammy Withers told me he was Butch Fleetwood's diving partner, so he would have been around at the time. That's why you're looking for him, isn't it? He's one of the names?"

"I can't tell you the names. What I can tell you is that a sting operation was put into place to capture the perpetrator. It was called Operation ARION."

"You're telling me ARION was a trap?"

"Yes. Exactly. A technical-looking set of plans was cobbled together from other projects to make it appear authentic, but the operation itself was a complete fake. It was a deception. The documents were dangled in front of each suspect in expectation that the guilty party would take the bait."

"Did anyone bite?"

"Circumstances suggest a suspect, but we never found proof."

"What do you mean?"

"The plans disappeared the night Butch Fleetwood died."

# 30

# THE OTTER

R olly walked along the Embarcadero, making his way down the sidewalk from the Coast Guard office toward the cruise ship terminal at Broadway Pier. Bonnie disappeared after taking her phone call. The FBI agents had turned him loose, but they hadn't offered him any transportation. His phone was gone. He didn't have any money or identification. There might be taxis waiting outside the cruise ship terminal, looking for fares. If he couldn't find one there, he could walk inland a couple of blocks to the Santa Fe station. There were always cabs at the train station. The walk would give him a chance to stretch his legs and clear his mind.

He heard the rumble of a truck or some other large vehicle behind him and turned to look. It was an OTTER, like the ones he'd seen in the rehearsal garage. He continued to walk. The OTTER slowed, maintaining its position as if it were following him. He stopped, turned and looked again. The OTTER pulled up next to him and came to a stop. A set of steps levered down from the passenger side of the vehicle, leading up toward the driver's seat. The driver wore a short-sleeved white shirt and baby-blue Bermuda shorts. Epaulets on his shoulders and a captain's hat on top of his head completed the outfit.

"Hey, Waters," said Dick Nazi. "I thought that was you."

Rolly stepped off the sidewalk and approached the vehicle.

"Nice outfit, Captain," he said. Nazi laughed.

"Don't tell my fans," he said. "What're you up to?"

"Just taking a walk."

"I thought maybe you were gumshoeing," said Nazi. "Out looking for clues."

"Clues to what?"

"Hell, I don't know. You're the detective."

"I'm walking to the cruise ship terminal so I can catch a cab."

"You want a ride down there?"

Rolly looked down the Embarcadero. The terminal wasn't far.

"No thanks," he said. "I could use the exercise."

"Where's your car?"

Rolly looked back up at Nazi.

"I left it in the parking lot at Driscoll's Wharf," said Rolly. "After I saw you last night."

"You want a ride?" said Nazi. "I could take you there."

"Aren't you working?"

"Lunch break. I'm taking the beast back to the garage. Don't have to be back until two."

Rolly looked back down the Embarcadero. If he caught a cab, it would only take ten minutes to get home. The cab would cost him twenty dollars, but he could eat something when he got home. He could play his guitar, too, maybe lie down and take a nap. He didn't want to chase spies anymore. He didn't want to chase ghosts. He was old and tired and he wanted to go back in his hidey-hole.

"You drive a Volvo, right?" said Nazi, dangling a silver key in his hand.

"Where'd you get that?" said Rolly.

"It was pinned on the door of the garage when I came in this morning. In a little envelope with the initials 'RW' on it. I didn't know who RW was supposed to be, but then I spotted you gumshoeing over here. The light bulb went on."

Rolly climbed the steps of the OTTER boat. He took the key from Nazi.

"It looks like mine," he said, inspecting the key. "I don't suppose anyone left you my wallet or phone?"

"No. Sorry. Just the key. You sure you don't want a ride back to the wharf?"

Rolly looked over the empty seats in the OTTER boat. They were bench seats like you'd find on a school bus. It wouldn't take long to drive to Driscoll's Wharf. And he'd get his car back.

"Sure," he said. "Thanks."

Rolly took a seat behind Dick Nazi as Nazi put the vehicle into gear. He made a U-turn at the signal and headed back toward Point Loma.

"Can I ask you something?" said Rolly, looking into the rearview mirror so he could watch Nazi's face. Nazi needed to keep his hands on the wheel, no matter what Rolly said.

"What's that?" said Nazi.

"Where did you go last night? After the meeting?"

"What do you mean?"

"I saw you rowing that boat into the bay."

"You saw that, huh?" Nazi shook his head. "Well, it's a messed-up world when a man can't take his boat out in the middle of the night without some gumshoe getting suspicious and accusing him of nefarious behavior."

"I'm not accusing you of anything, nefarious or otherwise. I just know Wendell's yacht is out there, in the direction you were headed."

"Everybody in the marina knows Wendell's yacht is out there."

"I also know the OMU isn't too fond of Wendell's involvement with Ocean Universe."

"What's your point?"

"The FBI thinks you're planning some kind of attack."

"How do you know what the FBI thinks?"

"They came to my house. They asked me to spy on you. On the OMU."

"Holy shit, Waters! Are you wearing a wire or something?"

"Calm down. I'm not working for them."

"Then why were you at our meeting last night?"

"Like I told you," said Rolly. "I'm looking for Harmonica Dan. I saw you go on Dan's boat. After the meeting. I went on board after you left."

"Oh yeah? What happened?"

"Some guy knocked me out and locked me in the bathroom."

"Holy crap! You think it was Dan?"

"I don't know. I didn't get a good look at the guy. He was wearing a diving suit and a mask. He's bigger than Dan, though. At least he seemed bigger."

Dick Nazi checked his side mirror, then steered the OTTER into the left lane so they could avoid the traffic approaching the airport. He looked in the rearview mirror at Rolly.

"What is it?" said Rolly.

"Harmonica Dan called me last night, right at the end of the meeting. He asked me to go on his boat."

"Why?"

"No reason. He told me to go in the cabin for a few minutes, then come out and take the rowboat into the harbor. He said I should stay out there until I saw his boat leave the marina."

Rolly rubbed his forehead.

"You were the bait," Rolly said. "And I got the hook."

"What's that?"

"Nothing," said Rolly. Dan had lured him in, snagged him and tossed him into the hold just like an albacore caught by one of the sport-fishing boats. He rubbed the area just above his left clavicle. It still felt sore.

"You okay?" said Nazi.

"I guess," said Rolly. "Just digging my way out of a big pile of stupid."

"Everybody's stupid," said Nazi. "You ever hear that song? By Sparks? We do a cover version."

Rolly shook his head. He leaned against the seat and stared out at the scenery as they drove over the Harbor Drive bridge. He could see out to Ballast Point and the cliffs of the Point Loma peninsula, to the monument where the old lighthouse stood. He had a rehearsal tonight with J.V. Sideman and the band, at Ocean Universe. Wendell would be there. The next night was the concert. Wendell would leave town the day after that and Melody would go with him.

"I met a guy at the marina last night," he said. "He called you Ricky the bilge pumper."

"Yeah, that was me. I pumped out the boat toilets. I got paid to dispose of their shit."

"How long did you do that?"

"A year and a half, two years. After I got out of school, I needed a job."

"So how did you end up with these OTTER things?"

"I got these off of Grandpa Baldry after I went out to visit him in Virginia. He had two prototypes sitting outside on his lawn. They were left over from some military contract that didn't go through, something like that. He gave them to me. Janis gave me the money to rent the garage."

"Did she give the money to you or the OMU?"

Nazi furrowed his brow.

"It was a little bit of both, I guess."

"Did she ever come to your meetings?"

"No. That wasn't her kind of thing."

"Do you remember your parents ever talking about a project called ARION?"

"No. I don't think so. But I pretty much didn't listen to anything my parents said from the time I was thirteen."

"Is that why they sent you to military school?"

"That and other things. You name it, whatever I did, they didn't like it."

"What about your sister?"

"What about her?"

"Janis said something about Arion the night she died."

"I didn't know that. What'd she say?"

"She said he was alive. That it was all lies."

"What was all lies?"

"I don't know. Tidewater Defense Systems had a project called ARION. The FBI says it wasn't real, that it was a setup they were using to find a spy."

"You think that's what she was talking about?"

Rolly shrugged.

"Did they catch the guy?" said Nazi.

"Not exactly," said Rolly. "But the circumstantial evidence points to Butch Fleetwood."

"That's the guy with the dog tags, right? The one Janis said was a spy?"

Rolly nodded. Dick Nazi stared out the front window. They crossed over the Harbor Drive bridge and headed toward the marina.

"Everything about my family—the Withers family—is screwed up," said Nazi. "We've had zero interaction since I got out of school."

"Except for your sister, who wasn't really your sister. You took her to work three days a week. And picked her up afterward."

"I felt sorry for Janis. She was messed up, but she was nice to me."

"She gave you money."

"I'll admit it," said Nazi. He shrugged. "You do what you need to. She seemed kind of happy to give it to me. Like I said, she was nice."

"Not like your parents."

"They're not my parents. Fuck nice, anyway."

"That sounds like one of your songs."

"What's that?"

"Fuck nice."

"Yeah. I might use that. 'Fuck nice.' It's kind of got a double meaning."

They passed the Driscoll's Wharf parking lot. Nazi didn't turn in.

"Where are we going?" asked Rolly.

"There's a guy I need to pick up," said Nazi.

They turned onto a dead-end street, a back alley that ended at the shoreline. Nazi pulled the OTTER boat to the curb and lowered the stairs. A man appeared from behind a closely trimmed hedge of bay laurel. He wore a pair of tangerine-colored cargo shorts and a Hawaiian shirt, yellow flowers on a blue background. The man climbed into the OTTER. He turned to face Rolly. His hair was short with a part on the side and his face was clean-shaven, so it took Rolly a moment to recognize who the man was. Harmonica Dan had a new look.

# 31

# THE FUGITIVE

Harmonica Dan walked to the back of the vehicle, inspecting each row before settling himself in the middle seat of the last row. Rolly leaned in toward the driver's seat and whispered to Dick Nazi.

"What's going on?" he said.

"Be cool, Waters," said Nazi. "Wait 'til we're out on the water. Then go back and talk to him." He put the OTTER into gear and headed down the alley, drove over the curb and angled the vehicle down a dirt slope, heading into the bay. "Hang on."

Rolly braced himself as the OTTER boat splashed into the water. Nazi cut the engine, letting the vehicle's momentum carry them out into the channel. He reached in his pocket, pulled out a small cell phone and tossed it into the water.

"Burner," he said, responding to Rolly's mystified look. "That's how we communicate. He leaves them for me."

Nazi flipped a pair of switches on the dashboard. The outboard motor kicked in. Nazi guided the OTTER into the channel and turned it toward the main part of the bay. Rolly stood up, walked to the back of the boat and took a seat in front of Dan. Harmonica Dan pulled something out of his jacket and passed it to Rolly over the back of the seat.

"Any chance I can get my phone too?" said Rolly, taking his wallet.

"Your phone's in your car," said Dan. He shook his head. "We don't want the watchers listening in."

Rolly stretched out in his seat and leaned against the wall.

"You think someone's tapped my phone?" he said.

"Someone is always listening," said Dan. "Radio waves, microwaves, Wi-Fi. We're safer out here on the water. It will take ten minutes for them to recalibrate and switch over their frequencies. We can talk until then."

"What do you want to talk about?" said Rolly.

"I was a terrible drunk when you knew me before," said Dan. "When I played the blues with you on Mondays."

"I was a drunk back then too," said Rolly.

"Yes, I know. People told me what happened to you, to your friend, that singer."

"Matt."

"Yes. I remember him. That's why you got sober, isn't it? After he died in the car accident?"

"Yeah," said Rolly. "That was a big part of it."

"I killed someone too," said Dan. "Because I was intoxicated."

Dan fell silent and looked out at the water, his thoughts sinking into the depths of the bay. Rolly tried to bring them back to the surface.

"You were Butch Fleetwood's diving partner, weren't you?" said Rolly.

"Yes."

"Were you there the night he died?" said Rolly. "Were you diving with him?"

"It was dark out. A night dive. Dangerous."

"I read the report. They redacted your name."

"It was my job, filling the cylinders, the scuba tanks. I set the mixture wrong. Too much $CO_2$. If you stay down too long with air like I put in the tanks, you get loopy, start seeing pink elephants. You lose track of time. You don't realize until it's too late."

"You think that's what happened to Butch?"

Harmonica Dan nodded.

"I didn't read anything about problems with the oxygen tanks in the inquest report," said Rolly.

"No one else knew," said Dan. "I drained the air from my cylinder so no one would find out. If they'd found Butch's body, or his tank, they would have figured it out. I didn't face up to what I'd done. I was a coward. It was drinking that made me that way."

"Are you sure it was your fault?"

"I checked the machine the next day. I set the mix to different percentages and I tested them all. The final mix always matched the gauge readings. The machine worked. I tried it a dozen times. The gauges were accurate. I must have missed something that day. I was drunk. I didn't follow the protocol."

"If your tanks had the bad air, why didn't you die?"

"I didn't go deep enough. It doesn't affect you at shallower depths. The dolphin saved me."

"You mean the dolphin that tagged you with the flotation device? I read about that in the report."

"The dolphin hit me. The balloon popped and dragged me to the surface. That was the last time I saw him."

"Butch Fleetwood, you mean?"

"Yes. Butch. He talked me into switching. I didn't mind. The dolphins always hit Butch harder than me. They didn't like him."

"What do you mean about switching?"

Harmonica Dan looked down at the floor as Dick Nazi guided the OTTER farther into the bay.

"Two divers," he said. "One friend and one foe. We were testing to see if the dolphins could distinguish between them. It was a new piece of equipment they were testing. The transmitter put out a specific signal frequency, like a sonar fingerprint. We'd tested it a couple of times already. It seemed to work. I was supposed to be wearing the transmitter that night, but Butch talked me into switching. We broke protocol, but if Butch hadn't asked me to switch, I'd be dead."

Rolly thought for a moment. He remembered Tom Cockburn's confession, how Fleetwood had blackmailed him before he disappeared.

"How well did you know Butch, outside of work?"

"A little bit," said Dan. "We went out to the bars a couple of times. Chased girls. I was the one did the chasing. Butch would just stand there and the girls would gather around."

"What about boys?"

Dan smiled.

"I guess I knew Butch flew both directions. All sorts of people would lay down for Butch; they'd do anything because of his looks. Butch took advantage of that animal magnetism he had. He'd talk people into doing bad stuff, twisting things around so you'd do something you might not normally do. I shouldn't have listened to him. I should have followed the protocol."

"You'd be dead now if you did."

Dan reached into his pocket and pulled out a harmonica. He held it in both hands, rubbing the metal sides like a priest with his rosary.

"Survivor guilt," he said. "You ever hear of that?"

Rolly nodded.

"Sure," he said. "I went to a therapist after my accident, after my friend died. She explained it to me."

"How long did it take you to get over it?"

"I didn't. Not really."

"She was a lousy psychiatrist, huh?"

"No. She was fine. Survivor guilt didn't apply to me."

"Why not?"

"The accident was my fault. I shouldn't have been driving. I was drunk and I killed him."

"Was your friend drinking too? The singer guy?"

"Yeah. There were three of us. We were all plastered."

"It could have been your singer friend driving, then, couldn't it?"

"Could have been, but it wasn't."

"When did you stop drinking?"

"I never had another drink after that night."

"You still want a drink sometimes?"

"Sure. All the time."

"You did better than me. Took me ten more years to figure it out."

"What made you stop?"

Dan put the harmonica to his mouth. He blew a few notes of the dolphin reveille, strange high notes that Rolly had never heard anyone play on a harmonica before.

"How do you do that?" said Rolly.

"It's a special technique I taught myself," said Dan. "Overblown harmonics, sympathetic vibrations. You gotta open it up and futz with the reeds a little, if you want to get it right. I figured out how to do it when I was working in Mexico. I had a lot of time on my hands down there."

"What were you doing in Mexico?"

"Working with dolphins. They're why I stopped drinking."

"You'll have to explain that one for me."

"I was a mess when I moved down there, a full-on rummy. I managed to get a job at this piece-of-shit water park, because of my Navy experience. Just janitor work. I felt pretty low. It was the dolphins that saved me."

Dan blew on the harmonica again, a bluesy, musical phrase.

"They had an old shack there for storing stuff. That's where I lived. In my little shack, with my bottles of rum and my harmonicas. Wasn't nobody around at night except the dolphins and me. I'd sit by the dolphin tanks and play my harmonica, just for myself, you know, but after a while the dolphins started coming around, like they were listening. They started to talk back to me. After a while it was like we were communicating. They imitated some of the harmonica sounds. Dolphins can do that, you know, vocalizing. We started doing call-and-response stuff, like you and me used to do with the guitar and harmonica on blues night at Winstons. You remember that?"

"Sure," Rolly said. "I remember."

"I started playing around with my harmonicas, trying out different things, you know, opening them up and messing with the reeds, that kind of stuff. I started finding new sounds. The dolphins went crazy for the new way I played, this overblown harmonics thing. They started jumping out of the water like crazy. That's why I call it the dolphin reveille."

"What's this have to do with getting sober?"

"I got really focused on the harmonica thing with the dolphins. I

226  |  COREY LYNN FAYMAN

got so involved, it started to replace my drinking. Little by little. I
didn't even realize it at first, but when I counted the days since I'd had
a drink it had been more than two months. I never went back. It was
the dolphins that saved me."

Rolly nodded. It was a good story and he was glad for Dan's recovery, but he wasn't sure it was relevant to his investigation.

"It wasn't long after that," said Dan, "I decided I had to do more
with my life. I had a mission."

"What was it?"

"Saving the dolphins like they saved me, setting them free."

"You joined the OMU?"

"I started it."

Rolly stared at Dan for a moment. The plainness of what he'd said
made it feel true.

"I talked to the FBI," Rolly said. "They asked me about you."

"What did you tell them?"

"I told them about my trip on your boat last night."

Dan shook his head.

"That wasn't me. That was a ghost."

"Was it this ghost who gave you my wallet and keys?" said Rolly.

Dan stared at the water again. He didn't answer the question.

"Where did he take you?" he said. "On my boat?"

"Out to those islands. The Coronados. There's a little cove on the
backside of the big island."

"Yes. I know it," said Dan.

"You took Janis there, didn't you?"

"Yes. She liked to go there. We talked to the dolphins."

"Did she find Butch Fleetwood's dog tags out there?"

Harmonica Dan stared at Rolly a moment. He put the harmonica
back in his pocket.

"We need to go in," he said. "We've been out too long."

"Why did Janis want me to have those dog tags?" said Rolly.

"I don't know," said Dan. He whistled. Dick Nazi looked back,
nodded and turned the boat in toward shore. Rolly watched the
surface of the water ripple. Dan had told him a secret, but there must
be more to it than his remorse over Fleetwood's death.

"You left that newspaper on my windshield, didn't you?" he said. Dan nodded.

"We don't have much time," Dan said. "I thought you should see it."

"I talked to the man who wrote the article. He gave Butch some money. Two days before Butch disappeared."

"What was the money for?"

"Butch was blackmailing him. He gave the man a backpack to put the money in. The backpack had dolphins on it."

"Janis had a backpack like that, with dolphins."

"Yes. I know. Is there anything else you want to tell me?"

Harmonica Dan stared at the water. He'd been trying to solve this puzzle for the last twenty-three years. He turned to Rolly.

"Butch waved at me," he said. "We were under the water where no one could see. Just before the dolphin hit me, before the balloon hauled me up, I put my flashlight on Butch. He waved at me like he was saying goodbye."

## 32

# THE CLIFFS

Rolly opened the door of his old Volvo. It was in the same spot he'd left it at the Driscoll's Wharf parking lot. He unlocked the glove compartment and retrieved his phone, right where Harmonica Dan told him it would be. The battery still had some juice, but it needed a charge. He pulled out the charging cable, plugged it in and connected his phone.

Harmonica Dan had told Rolly something he'd never told anyone else. It was a secret, like a koan, an unsolvable riddle he'd been puzzling over the last twenty-three years. Butch Fleetwood had waved goodbye.

Rolly's phone beeped as it came back to life. He checked the screen. Tom Cockburn had called him. He didn't remember adding Cockburn's number to his phone. They'd agreed not to use cell phones to communicate. Rolly's stomach tightened as tapped on the number and put the phone to his ear. He hadn't eaten anything since his fish sandwich the previous evening and now it was past noon. The number rang through on the other end of the line.

"Hello?" someone answered. It was a woman's voice.

"I'm looking for Tom Cockburn," said Rolly.

"Who is this?" said the voice.

"You tell me first."

"This is Detective Bonnie Hammond, San Diego Police."

"Bonnie? It's me. Rolly. I thought I was calling someone else."

"You were," said Bonnie. "Where are you now?"

"I'm in Point Loma, over at Driscoll's Wharf."

"You should come over here."

"Where?"

"Sunset Cliffs. The Pappy's Point pullout."

"Why do you have Tom Cockburn's phone?"

"I found it in the rocks, next to his body. And you've got some explaining to do."

A chill ran down Rolly's spine. He looked out the front window of his Volvo. A gray wall of fog sat off the coast, waiting to roll into the bay.

"Tom Cockburn's dead?" he said.

"We have an informal ID, based on the phone and the automobile registration."

"What happened to him?"

"Just get over here. I would have called you anyway. You're on his contact list."

"Yeah," said Rolly. He rubbed his forehead. It felt like someone had punched him in the stomach. "I'll be right over."

He hung up the phone and started the car. It would only take ten minutes to drive over the hill to the Sunset Cliffs section of Ocean Beach. He needed to eat first. He spotted a drive-in taco shop as he drove along Rosecrans. He pulled in, ordered rolled tacos and a large horchata.

He picked up his food, tore the bag open and arranged it on the passenger seat so he could access his tacos without taking his eyes off the road. He pulled onto Rosecrans, then turned west on Nimitz Boulevard and headed over the hill. That bastard Nimitz, as his father's old Navy buddies liked to say, referring to the admiral, not the street.

At the top off the hill, he turned off Nimitz and on to Voltaire Street, crossing the spine of the peninsula and heading down into Ocean Beach. Even the names of the streets conveyed the difference between the two neighborhoods, exchanging military heroes for philosophers of the Enlightenment, replacing Nimitz and Rosecrans with Voltaire and Bacon. The coastal waters changed too. The shallow ripples of San Diego Bay were replaced by the rough swells of the Pacific Ocean rolling onto the beach.

At the bottom of the hill, Rolly cut back on Sunset Cliffs Boulevard. He didn't remember the location of Pappy's Point, but if there were a body on the beach below the cliffs, an accumulation of emergency vehicles along the shoulder of the road would indicate where it was. He followed the road up onto the cliffs. A quarter-mile on, he spotted a fire truck, an ambulance and three police squad cars parked in a turnout. He pulled in behind them. He didn't see Bonnie anywhere, so he pulled out his phone and called her.

"I'm at the pullout," he said when she answered. "Where are you?"

"In the rocks down below. I'll be up in a minute."

Rolly put away his phone. He walked to the edge of the asphalt parking lot and stepped onto a wide strip of earth overlooking the ocean. None of the emergency personnel mingling about seemed to notice him. He walked to the edge of the cliffs and looked down. The ocean had carved a crescent shape into the land, creating a hideaway beach down below, a small stretch of sand that lay between tumbled-down boulders. There were four people on the beach. Only three of them moved. The fourth one lay on his back, staring up at the sky. Even from this distance, Rolly could tell it was Cockburn. He backed away from the edge and returned to his car. He leaned back in his seat and closed his eyes.

*Dolphins had smiles, but their smiles had razor-sharp teeth. He was drowning, sinking under the surface. Matt was next him. Matt was swimming alongside him. Matt smiled and turned into a dolphin. The dolphin jabbed Rolly with its beak and pushed him to the surface. The dolphin pushed Rolly onto the beach. He lay in the sand, but it was hard like a rock. Something tapped on his head.*

Rolly opened his eyes. Bonnie Hammond stared at him from outside the driver-side window. Rolly brought his seat back up to a straight position and opened the door.

"You okay?" Bonnie asked.

"Just tired," said Rolly. He climbed out of the car. The whump-whump sound of a helicopter fluttered in the distance. "What's up?"

Bonnie shaded her eyes and looked up toward the sky. The sound of the helicopter grew louder. It flew over them, then hovered in the air near the edge of the cliffs. A gurney dropped from its belly down toward the beach. Bonnie turned back to Rolly.

"When did you last talk to Tom Cockburn?" she asked.

"Yesterday. Out at Cabrillo Monument. Wendell was signing books out there, so we arranged to meet."

"You didn't text him at four o'clock this morning?"

"I didn't have my phone with me at four o'clock this morning. As you may recall, I was locked in the bathroom of Harmonica Dan's sailboat at that time."

"You're sticking with that frogman story you told the FBI?"

"I'm not making it up. The guy took my phone. I just got it back a half hour ago."

"Did you check your text messages?" asked Bonnie.

"I didn't see any new ones," said Rolly. He tapped his phone, checked the list. The most recent text had come in at 4:02 a.m., while he was still on the sailboat. It said OK. It wasn't flagged as new, which meant it had already been viewed by someone else. An outgoing message had been sent from Rolly's phone two minutes earlier.

"'Pappy's Point in two hours'?" he said. He looked over at Bonnie. "That guy in the wetsuit must have sent this. He stole my phone."

"How'd you get your phone back?" said Bonnie.

"Harmonica Dan gave it back to me. He found my keys and wallet, too."

Bonnie crossed her arms and scowled at him.

"I guess I should explain," Rolly said.

"I guess you should."

A black Ford Explorer with tinted windows bounced into the parking lot, revving its engine as it came to a stop behind Rolly's Volvo. The doors opened. Agents Goffin and King jumped out.

"What's the situation here?" said Agent Goffin. "Where's the body?"

Bonnie pointed to the helicopter.

"They're hauling it out of there now. Next stop is the Medical Examiner's office."

"What's your preliminary assessment, Detective Hammond?"

"Looks like he fell off the cliffs and hit his head on the rocks."

"Was he pushed?"

"I have no evidence of that, but I haven't ruled it out, either."

"Any witnesses?"

"Not so far."

"Time of death?"

"Sometime around 6:02 a.m."

"That sounds very specific. How do you know that?"

"He had an appointment with someone."

"Who?"

"The appointment was made from Mr. Waters's cell phone."

Agents Goffin and King turned their attention to Rolly.

"How do you explain this, Mr. Waters?"

"I think it's that Special Forces guy who dumped me on the island. He took my phone."

"So in addition to being some kind of ninja, your abductor is also a cryptographic genius?"

"What do you mean?"

"You don't lock your phone?"

"Sure. I mean it locks itself after a while."

"How long is the auto-lock set for?"

Rolly tapped his way through the screen and found the lock setting. He looked back up at the agents.

"The auto-lock's off," he said. "Someone changed it."

"Was your phone unlocked when the man struck you?"

Rolly thought for a moment.

"It wasn't locked. I was using the flashlight app."

"Tom Cockburn's auto-lock was off too," said Bonnie. The agents nodded.

"Am I missing something?" said Rolly.

"It's one of the first things we do now," said Bonnie. "When we get to a crime scene. Check for phones. Switch off auto-lock so we can access the information on the phone."

"Mr. Cockburn was quite scrupulous in his security regimen," said Agent Goffin.

"Watertight," said Agent King. "Mr. Cockburn wouldn't disable the auto-lock."

"What's going on here?" said Bonnie. "What do you know about this?"

"We're not at liberty to discuss our case, Detective Hammond," said Agent Goffin.

"Do you think someone killed Mr. Cockburn?"

"That's your area of expertise, Detective. We'll let you tell us."

"You think it could be this frogman guy, don't you?" said Bonnie. "You think he took Mr. Waters's phone, unlocked it and sent a message to Cockburn?"

"Yes. Assuming Mr. Waters has told us the truth."

"I didn't send that message to Cockburn," said Rolly. "I swear it. He didn't want us to use cell phones when we communicated."

"So this person, whoever he is," Bonnie continued. "He makes an appointment with the deceased, who thinks he's going to be meeting Mr. Waters. And somehow he gets the deceased to unlock his phone before he kills him. And what we find is a record of Mr. Waters and Mr. Cockburn's text exchange shortly before he died. Sounds like a diversion to me, like he's trying to frame Mr. Waters."

"That is a possibility," said Agent Goffin.

"This guy's pretty smart," said Bonnie. "Who is he?"

"Can we see Mr. Cockburn's phone?" said Agent King.

"Sorry," said Bonnie. "It's already bagged."

"We need to see that phone."

"Well, in that case, you can follow me down to the station and we'll go through it together."

"Can I join you?" said Rolly.

"No," said both FBI agents and Bonnie in unison.

# 33

# THE YACHT

That evening, Rolly stood on the stage at Ocean Universe, wiping his guitar down and preparing to put it back in the case. Rehearsal was over. It had gone well. Wendell had proved himself a passable blues singer and the sound system was state of the art. The band ran through two sets of material, pausing occasionally for Sideman and Wendell to confer and make adjustments. Rolly placed his guitar in its case and shut the latches. His nerves were shot. He looked forward to getting some sleep. Someone stepped up behind him.

"The boss wants to see you."

Rolly turned to find Wendell's bodyguard looming over him.

"Okay," Rolly said, drawing out the syllables. Wendell had given no indication he remembered their two previous meetings. Not until now. "What should I do about my gear?"

The bodyguard shrugged.

"Your stuff's not going anywhere. The boss needs to talk to you now."

Rolly followed the bodyguard across the Ocean Universe stage and down the back stairs to a boat ramp. A motorized raft was moored to the ramp. The bodyguard untied the rope from the ramp.

"Get in," he said.

"Where are we going?"

The bodyguard pointed to where Wendell's yacht was moored in the bay.

"Oh," said Rolly. "I thought he was still here. On land, I mean."

"You got a problem with water?"

"No. Not exactly. Sometimes I get sick on boats."

"Give it a rest, fat boy," said the bodyguard. "Get in."

Rolly didn't particularly like the idea of going out to Wendell's yacht, but Moogus and Sideman had both seen him leave with the bodyguard, so it wasn't like Wendell would try to kill him. Threaten him, maybe, but not actually murder him. He climbed into the front of the raft. The bodyguard climbed in after him, started the motor and set out across the water. It was dark on the bay, except for a few buoy lights. Rolly watched Wendell's catamaran grow larger as they approached. It was bulkier and more substantial than he'd first realized. The bodyguard brought the raft up to the rear of the boat. A set of stairs had been built into the back of each pontoon.

"Up," said the bodyguard. Rolly climbed onto the stairs and up onto the deck. The bodyguard tied off the raft and climbed up beside him.

"This way," he said.

Rolly followed the bodyguard into the main cabin. It was larger than Rolly's entire house. Built-ins and appliances were trimmed in gold. The floors had been polished to a reflective sheen. The bodyguard pointed at two burgundy leather sofas next to a round white coffee table.

"Take a seat," he said. Rolly sat on the first sofa. A large-screen TV had been built into a cabinet across from it. Glass aquariums bookended either side of the TV. Tropical fish swam inside the aquariums.

"This is quite a setup," he said.

"What's your deal?" said the bodyguard, reaching across his chest and gripping his left elbow with his right hand.

"I'm just a working stiff," Rolly said. "Guitar player by night and gumshoe by day. Trying to make a living. What's *your* story?"

"I don't have to answer your questions."

"No, you don't," said Rolly, "I'm just trying to keep things friendly. That's how it works. You ask me something. I respond to your question and then ask you something. We go back and forth like that. It's called a conversation."

"Why are you bird-dogging the boss?"

"I'm not after your boss."

"You keep showing up where he's at."

"I can't help it if your boss is a popular guy. I assume that's why he needs someone like you, to make sure he doesn't get too popular."

"What's your deal with that hippie chick?"

"Maybe it's the same kind of deal your boss has."

"A schlub like you? I doubt it."

"You never know. Some girls go for portly men. I might have hidden charms. Maybe your boss doesn't measure up."

The bodyguard snickered.

"You swing a big dick, huh?"

"You said it, not me," said Rolly. He pulled his phone out of his pocket and pretended there was an important message on the screen. "I'm in kind of a hurry. When's your boss going to be here?"

"He's here now," said a new voice. Wendell walked into the room carrying a bottle of beer. "Thank you for waiting."

"I didn't know I had a choice," said Rolly.

"Oh, I wouldn't worry about Happy here, unless you really want to make trouble. He's a peaceable fellow ninety-nine percent of the time."

"What about the other one percent?"

"Under duress he can defend himself rather vigorously. He got me out of a jam once, saved my life down in Panama, left the three men who were trying to rob me in very bad shape. He's a good man to have on your side."

"Better than on your back, I suppose."

Wendell sat down on the second couch, perpendicular to Rolly. He kicked off his flip-flops, took a swig of his beer and put his feet up on the table.

"You've got big cojones, Mr. Waters," he said.

"Just average size."

"I mean showing up tonight after accosting me in public like that."

"You're still paying double-scale, aren't you?"

"I remembered you from the book signing. I didn't say anything because I didn't want to upset the rehearsal."

"Are you planning to fire me?"

"Unfortunately, no," said Wendell. "We don't have time to work in another guitarist. Besides, I dug your chops. I liked what I heard out there."

"Well, thanks for hiring me," said Rolly. "Did you hear me play somewhere before?"

"Not that I can remember."

"Sideman said you requested me specifically to be in the band, after the other guy dropped out."

Wendell frowned.

"No," he said. "I don't think so. You puzzle me, Mr. Waters."

"I puzzle myself half the time."

Wendell pulled Rolly's business card from his pocket and pretended to read it.

"One thing that puzzles me is why someone with your musical talent has to work as a private investigator."

"That's an old puzzle," said Rolly. "And there's a lot of missing pieces."

Wendell took another sip of his beer, put it back on the table.

"You want a beer?" he said. "Longboard Lager. It's Hawaiian. I got plenty in the fridge."

"No thanks."

"No drinking on the job?"

"No drinking period. Not for me."

"Maybe that's a piece of the puzzle?"

"Maybe," said Rolly. "How long have you known Melody?"

"That depends, Mr. Waters," said Wendell. "How long have you known my wife's lawyer? Greg Perry? Of Kawai and Perry? Based in Honolulu?"

"Never heard of him," said Rolly. He folded his arms and leaned back on the couch. "You and your wife are getting divorced?"

"We're separated right now."

"And you think I'm digging up dirt for her lawyer?"

"That's what private detectives do, isn't it? Sneak around taking pictures of husbands cheating on their wives."

"Sometimes we take pictures of wives cheating on their husbands."

"I'm under a lot of pressure, Mr. Waters. I need an outlet."

"Melody seemed to be under the impression she was more than an outlet."

"What did you tell her?"

"I just showed her what you wrote in my book."

Wendell took another sip on his beer. He held the bottle against his forehead.

"That's unfortunate. What did she say?"

"She's selling her ticket to the concert tomorrow. She needs the money."

"I'll call her. Melody's got nothing to lose from this relationship."

"How would you know?"

Wendell rubbed his forehead and sighed.

"I've got a lot on my mind, Mr. Waters. Melody can't always be priority one. She needs to understand that."

"That's your prerogative. If it helps set your mind at ease, I'm not working for your wife's lawyer. You don't have to worry about me reporting on your extramarital activities."

"Who gave me those photographs, then?"

"What photographs?"

Wendell picked up the TV remote on the table, pressed a few buttons.

"I have security cameras on board," he said. "This is from last night."

A black-and-white video feed appeared on the TV screen. The camera was focused along the aft hull of the yacht. Something appeared in the water off to the right, a man in a rowboat. There was something strange about the man's head. It looked like a dolphin. He'd put some kind of rubberized dolphin mask over his face. The man stopped rowing, pulled in his oars and turned to face Wendell's boat. He reached into the well of the rowboat, picked up a knapsack and tossed it onto Wendell's yacht, then took up the oars again and made his escape. Wendell paused the video after the man passed out of the frame.

"That wasn't me," said Rolly. "I don't have a snout."

"This guy's skinnier, too," said Wendell. "With tattoos on his arms. Is he a friend of yours?"

"No," Rolly said. He had an idea who the man might be, but he wasn't going to share his thoughts with Wendell. Not yet, anyway. "Those photos you're talking about. Were they in the backpack?"

Wendell nodded.

"Yes. On a USB drive."

"Was there a note or anything?"

Wendell reached in his pocket and pulled out his phone. He scrolled through the screen and turned it toward Rolly.

"I got this text five minutes later. He wants fifty thousand for the photos," he said. "I destroyed the USB drive, of course. I know the photos are digital and they've got copies, but I don't want something like that lying around."

"Do you still have the backpack?" said Rolly. Wendell looked over at Happy, who shook his head.

"What did it look like?" said Rolly. "I couldn't tell from the video."

"It was a little kid's backpack," said Wendell. "Like something my daughter would carry. Cartoony dolphins, rainbows and stars. Is that important?"

"It could be," said Rolly. "Did you know Janis Withers?"

"Isn't that the woman who crashed her boat into the Admiral's Club?"

Rolly nodded.

"Janis had a backpack just like that one," he said. "She carried it around with her all the time."

"I didn't know the woman personally," said Wendell. "I met her father a couple of times, business things related to the Ocean Universe deal."

"Were you at the Admiral's Club that night?"

"I made a brief appearance, gave a little speech about how we'd take care of their dolphins as well as they did. By 'we,' I mean Ocean Universe. Their PR people sent me some bullet points. I'm licensing the Wendell brand to Ocean Universe. I'm not actually involved in running the place. I left before the attack."

"What do you know about the OMU?" said Rolly. "The Ocean Mammal Underground?"

"I know that ever since I licensed my name for this water park I've been getting threats from them. Emails and letters. They protest at my public appearances. The FBI finally started taking them seriously after the attack on the club."

"You've talked to the FBI?"

"Yes, of course. They want me to cancel the dolphin parade tomorrow. I'm swimming with the dolphins on their way over from the Navy base to Ocean Universe. I've got a lot going on tomorrow, with the parade and the concert. I'll be glad when it's over."

"Have you told the FBI about the photos?"

"I'd prefer not to share this with anyone."

"You shared it with me."

"I assumed you were behind this, that we could make some sort of deal."

"Is that why you wanted me in the band?"

"I'm not sure what you mean. Mr. Sideman did all the hiring."

"Sideman got a text message from you. I saw it. You asked for me by name."

"Why would I do that?"

"That's what I've been trying to figure out."

"This is strange," Wendell said. "Happy, did you text Mr. Sideman?"

"No, boss. This guy's full of shit."

"What about Melody?" said Rolly. "Could she have done it?"

"It's possible, I suppose. Why did you ask about that backpack?"

"Janis Withers donated fifty thousand dollars to the OMU last year. And she was Melody's landlord at the Lemurian Temple."

Wendell whistled. He leaned his head back and stared at the ceiling.

"Holy shit," he said. "You think Melody's in on this with the OMU? You think she's working with that man in the boat?"

"I don't know," said Rolly. Melody might've known all along that

Wendell was leading her on. She might've made a contingency plan. "I think someone's screwing with both of us."

Wendell sighed.

"I'm an environmental good guy, you know," he said. "I've worked my whole life to help dolphins, to make people aware of how special they are. I checked on Ocean Universe after they contacted me. They had a good reputation. I mean, where else are the dolphins going to go? You can't just release them into the wild. It's an educational thing. It's for the kids. I don't know why these OMU people can't understand that."

"Fuck 'em, boss," said Happy.

"That's your answer to everything, Happy," said Wendell. "You don't have a wife and a family to protect. This is personal. I never imagined this Ocean Universe deal would screw up my life like this. Why did I agree to do this damn thing?"

"Same reasons I took the gig with you," said Rolly.

"And what are those reasons?"

"A big payday and a big ego."

# 34

# THE PARADE

A few minutes before sunset the next day, Rolly stood in the back of his father's twenty-two-foot Chris-Craft speedboat, scanning the bay with a pair of binoculars. Crowds of people had gathered along the shore, waiting to see the dolphin parade and the display of holiday-themed boats that would tour the bay shortly afterward. Four Harbor Police boats patrolled the channel, keeping a lane clear for the dolphins to swim from the Navy base to their new home at Ocean Universe.

Rolly swung the binoculars back toward the dolphin pens, looking for familiar faces. He could see Wendell, dressed in a full-body wetsuit, standing at the end of the dock. FBI agents Goffin and King hovered ten feet behind him. Goffin surveyed the water with her own set of binoculars while King had his face stuck into some sort of walkie-talkie. Happy, the bodyguard, was nowhere to be seen. Rolly swung the binoculars to the other side of the boat and found Wendell's yacht parked in the harbor. Happy sat on the deck, protecting the boat from dolphin-headed intruders and watching the proceedings from a comfortable distance away.

Dean Waters eased his boat between two larger ones, maneuvering it into position for a better view of the parade route. Rolly checked the time on his phone. In two minutes Wendell would take to the water and dolphins would carry him across the channel. Wendell had described the event in detail to Rolly last night. It wouldn't take long if everything went right.

Rolly trained his binoculars on the Harbor Police boat closest to the dock. He spotted a woman with short-cropped blond hair standing on the aft deck. It was Bonnie. As a general rule, police detectives didn't get assigned to crowd control. Bonnie was here to keep an eye out for Harmonica Dan. Rolly had told her about the changes in Dan's appearance. Aside from his showing up at the Admiral's Club party, Dan was now a person of interest in the deaths of Henley Withers and Tom Cockburn. He needed to give himself up. Continuing to hide wouldn't help his case any.

Rolly surveyed the boats gathered along the edges of the dolphin route. There were sailboats, motorboats, cruising yachts, catamarans and even a few folks out in kayaks. The larger boats were all packed with partygoers. The Parade of Lights was a holiday tradition in San Diego. Boat owners invited their friends to come out on their boat and cruise the shoreline, displaying Christmas decor and waving at the crowds. Some of the boaters even sang Christmas carols. There was lots of Christmas cheer, much of it in liquid form.

None of the boats had turned on their holiday lights yet. Rolly could make out some of the unlit decorations with his binoculars: snowflakes and reindeer, Santas and Christmas trees, symbols of the winter holiday in a city that hadn't had seen a snowflake in fifty-odd years. He dropped the binoculars and looked at the decorations his father had hung on the Chris-Craft. They weren't going to win any contests. They barely qualified to be in the parade.

He raised the binoculars to his eyes again. A small sailboat in the middle of the channel caught his attention. He adjusted the focus on the binoculars. A speaker box sat on the forward deck of the sailboat. It wasn't unusual for boat owners to play Christmas music over jerry-rigged speakers during the parade, but there was something notable about this particular speaker. It looked just like the one on Harmonica Dan's boat.

The man on the boat looked familiar, too: a barefoot white guy with dreadlocks and a Bob Marley T-shirt who sat with his legs hanging over the side of the boat. The man had his hands cupped around his mouth, as if warming them with his breath. It wasn't cold out. The thermometer had touched 75 degrees earlier in the day. Rolly remembered where he'd seen the man before. At the OMU meeting. It was the same man who'd offered to help Dick Nazi escort Rolly out of the building. A flash of silver winked out from between the man's fingers. He was holding a harmonica.

Rolly turned his binoculars on other boats nearby. He saw three more faces he recognized from the OMU meeting. They all had the same speaker boxes on the front deck of their boats. They'd gathered their boats together near the center of the parade route, making sure they had a front seat.

"What the hell?" said Rolly.

"What's that?" said his father.

"Something's going on."

"Something like what?"

Rolly put the binoculars down. He took a seat.

"Do you feel okay?" said Alicia. "Do you need some water? I know I get awfully dry out here on the ocean."

"It's a bay," said Rolly's father. "It's not the ocean."

"It's still important to stay hydrated," said Alicia.

"They're planning something," said Rolly.

"Who's planning something?"

"The OMU."

Rolly turned and looked back toward the parade route.

"Dad," he said. "Can you get us in closer?"

"Sure."

"Now be careful, dear," said Alicia. "There are a lot of boats out here. And people are drinking."

"I can take a destroyer through the Philippine Islands, I think I can manage this."

"You were younger then, dear. And islands don't move, or drink beer."

Rolly's father grumbled to himself, revved the motor and nudged the boat forward. Rolly pointed at Bonnie's boat.

"You see that Harbor Police boat, on our side, near the Navy center?" said Rolly. "Get as close to them as you can."

"Aye, aye, captain," said his father. The breeze picked up. Alicia grabbed her Christmas tree scarf and retied it under her chin. Rolly looked through the binoculars, but it was hard to keep focus on anything with the boat bouncing on the water.

He didn't know what the OMU was planning to do, but he felt sure the harmonica lessons in the OTTER garage had been some kind of rehearsal for the event. The dolphin reveille. That's what Dan called it, the squeaky set of notes the OMU members were playing that night. Melody had told him about Harmonica Dan calling dolphins up out of the water and onto his boat. It seemed crazy to even consider the possibility, but he had to tell Bonnie.

His father brought the boat to within a hundred feet of the Harbor Police boat where Bonnie stood. Rolly cupped his hands around his mouth and called to her.

"Hey Bonnie!"

She didn't hear him. He called again. Then he realized how stupid it was trying to shout. He pulled out his phone and tapped Bonnie's number. He watched her answer.

"Where are you?" she said.

"I'm behind you, about a hundred feet," Rolly said. Bonnie turned and scanned the water. Rolly waved. She waved back.

"What's up?" she said.

"The OMU people, there's a bunch of them out here. On the water. I think they're planning something."

"Yeah, well, no surprise there. But I can't really arrest anyone until they do something illegal."

"They've all got harmonicas."

"What?"

"Harmonicas."

"I can't arrest 'em for that, either."

"They've got those speakers, like the one on Dan's boat. I think they're going disrupt the parade by playing their harmonicas."

"Is that even possible?"

"Harmonica Dan knows how to do it. He calls dolphins into his boat with his harmonica. Janis Withers went out with him one time."

"Okay, okay, I get where you're coming from, but I can't arrest them for playing harmonicas."

"I know, I know. I just thought I'd warn you."

"Where are these guys?"

"The first one's across from you, right at the middle of the course. The little blue sailboat with the white Rasta guy."

"Let me look," said Bonnie. She lifted a pair of binoculars and scanned the scene.

"Yeah, I see him," she said. "He's definitely got one of those speakers on the bow. We'll keep an eye on him."

"Or an ear," said Rolly.

A rocket shot into the air, a smoking flare that arched above the bay. It came from the dolphin pens on the Navy side of the pier.

"That's the signal," said Bonnie. "This circus is about to get started."

A second flare arched into the air from across the bay at Ocean Universe. A motorized Navy raft started across the bay. Wendell dove into the water behind it. A few seconds later he emerged from the water, riding the dolphins. They were bunched in a pack, staying close to the surface. Wendell lay on their backs at first, but he soon rose to his knees and then stood. He moved side to side, riding the pod as if it were some kind of living surfboard. It was quite a show. People started cheering.

Just before the dolphins reached the midpoint of the channel, a screech of noise blasted across the water. Even from a distance, Rolly recognized the sound of amplified harmonicas bashing out the squeaky high notes of the dolphin reveille.

He punched in Bonnie's number. She answered immediately.

"You hear that?" said Rolly.

"Yeah, I hear it. What the hell . . ."

Rolly looked back at the dolphin pod as it hit the midpoint of the channel and passed in front of the OMU boats. A dolphin at the edge of the pack leapt from the water and spun in the air. Wendell wobbled a bit but maintained his stance. Two more dolphins peeled off from the pod and spun into the air. They were all going crazy, jumping in different directions, breaking away from the pod as amplified squeaks of the harmonicas filled the air. It was chaos.

"Oh my goodness," said Alicia. Rolly watched Wendell fly twenty feet through the air, propelled by one of the dolphins. Wendell whirled his arms and legs as he tried to manage his landing. It didn't go well. He belly-flopped onto the water. The dolphins continued to jump all around him, leaping and spinning like crazed water dancers.

The police boats swung into action, navigating around the orgy of dolphins and heading toward the harmonica boats. Bonnie had passed the word on to their crews. The Navy raft leading the parade turned around and headed back toward the dolphins. The man at the bow ran through a set of hand signals, trying to get the dolphins' attention. Some of the dolphins moved toward the raft and away from the blast of harmonicas.

"Oh no!" said Alicia. She pointed. "That boat! It's going to hit him."

Rolly saw an OTTER boat headed toward the patch of water where Wendell was floating. The Harbor Police boats had moved to the other side of the parade route to intercept the harmonica boats. They had their backs turned. They didn't see what was happening.

"Dad?" said Rolly.

"I got him," said his father. He gunned the motor and sped toward the OTTER boat. "I got him."

# 35

## THE CONCERT

Wendell was a trouper. Rolly had to give him credit for that. A mere three hours after he had been tossed in the air by a dolphin and nearly run over by Dick Nazi's OTTER boat, the world-famous painter of sea life sat on the stage of his eponymous amphitheater at the Ocean Universe water park and sang old rhythm-and-blues hits for an appreciative audience. The benefit concert went on as scheduled.

With his left ankle in a cast, one arm in a sling, and splints on the fingers of both hands, any Jagger-like stage prowling Wendell might have contemplated was out of the question. He sat on a wooden stool in front of the band. The stage crew set up a boom stand in front of him. Wendell's voice started strong, but as the concert went on a lazy enunciation crept into his vocalization.

"I'm a shoal man," he sang, sounding like a drunken sailor with an affinity for running aground on sandbars. Rolly suspected the slurring came from the pain medicine kicking in. The rapidity of Wendell's discharge from the emergency ward required some compromises.

If the OMU hoped to set the dolphins free with their harmonica-playing intervention, the plan had been a dismal failure. After the Harbor Police shut down the protestors, the Navy trainers rounded up the stray dolphins and guided them to their new home at Ocean Universe. Rolly could see the dolphins now, cavorting in their pens. Large windows embedded into the back walls of Wendell's Ocean Amphitheater provided the audience with an underwater view of the dolphin activities.

The OMU protesters had been apprehended. Unless they'd made plans for bail, they'd all be spending the night in jail. Dick Nazi would face the most serious charges. He'd organized the whole thing. He was their leader. And he'd almost run over Wendell with his OTTER boat. It was still unclear if Nazi had been aiming the boat at Wendell or just didn't see him, but the sudden appearance of Dean Waters's Chris-Craft had forced him to alter his course and Wendell had suffered only a glancing blow. Rolly expected Dick Nazi would be busy the rest of the night, answering questions from the police and FBI interrogators.

The band finished playing "Soul Man", or "Shoal Man," as Wendell had intoned the chorus. After the song ended, Wendell held up his bandaged hand, indicating he had something to say to the crowd before they continued.

"Thank you, everyone," he said. "And thank you for coming out tonight and supporting the Arts in the Schools program. Let's have a big hand for this great band up here."

Rolly looked out over the audience as they applauded. He wondered if Melody was in the crowd or if she'd scalped her ticket to the highest bidder. Wendell continued to address the audience.

"Seriously, folks," he said, lowering his voice. "I know there are people out there who object to keeping dolphins and other sea mammals in captivity." He held up his bandaged fingers. "As a matter of fact, I ran into a few of them this afternoon."

The audience laughed. Wendell continued.

"I want you all to know that I've dedicated my life to increasing global awareness of dolphin culture. I would not have allowed my name to be attached to this enterprise if I felt it was in any way detrimental to the health and well-being of our ocean friends. When the folks from Ocean Universe contacted me about synergy opportunities, I wanted to make sure we created something of value, something I'd be proud to have my name on. The Wendell Amphitheater and

Dolphin Education Center you see here is the result of those discussions."

The audience applauded again.

"And last, but not least," said Wendell, "all the dolphins you see here were already in captivity and have been for many years. They are highly trained and socialized to human contact and interaction. They are not wild dolphins. It would take years and years of retraining to make them capable of living in the wild again. For the record, I do not support the capture and enslavement of wild dolphins for use in ocean parks and aquariums."

There was a smattering of applause.

"Thank you," said Wendell. "You've been a great audience. We've got one more song for you before we close out the night. Take it, drummer."

Moogus clicked his drumsticks four times. The band launched into their version "Sea Cruise," the Huey "Piano" Smith song made famous by Frankie Ford. It was a bit corny, not something Rolly would choose to play on a regular basis, but the horn section was hot and he was getting paid double-scale tonight. He smiled and joined in on the *ooo-eee* background vocals like he was having the time of his life. He could be a trouper too.

Backstage after the concert, Wendell hobbled his way toward the exit as Happy, his shadow and bodyguard, cleared the way. Rolly stood talking to Moogus near the stairwell. Wendell paused to address them.

"Thank you, gentlemen," he said. "It was a pleasure working with you. I'd offer a handshake, but as you can see it's a bit complicated."

"You're a good soldier," said Moogus. "Thanks for the gig."

Rolly nodded his agreement. Wendell looked him in the eye.

"Mr. Waters," he said, "I take it we're done with all those other matters between us."

"I think so," said Rolly.

"I've been told you may have saved my life this afternoon. I'm sorry if I didn't recognize you. I was a bit disoriented at the time."

Rolly shrugged.

"I give my dad most of the credit. He was driving the boat."

"Well, thank him for me. Was he here tonight?"

"He doesn't like music that much."

"One of your missing puzzle pieces?"

"What?"

"I was thinking of our conversation last night."

"Oh, yeah. Sure. It's a piece of the puzzle."

"There's nothing else we need to discuss before I go?"

"Nope. Not that I can think of."

"Our mutual friend wasn't out there tonight, was she?"

"I didn't see her."

"No. I didn't either. Well, I'm sorry to leave on a sour note. She's an attractive young woman. Let her know that I'm sorry for any . . . misunderstanding."

"I'm sure she'll get over it."

"Yes. We all get over things, don't we? We all have our disappointments."

"Some more than others," said Rolly. "Will you be leaving town soon?"

"My business here is done," said Wendell. "It's back home to the Big Island for me. I'm on my way to the airport right now."

"You're not taking the catamaran?"

"Too little time and too much to do," said Wendell. "It takes two weeks to sail to Hawaii from here. I've got a commission in two weeks, a new mural in Japan that I haven't even visualized yet. I want to get back home, see my wife and family before I have to go to work again. I rented a private jet."

"What do you do with the boat?"

"Happy will sail her back to the Big Island for me," said Wendell, glancing over at his bodyguard. "That's why I hired him, to keep my boat shipshape and deliver her wherever and whenever I need her."

"I thought you hired him for protection."

"I won't need protection for a while," said Wendell. "Not when I'm at home."

"Did you get any more information on that . . . financial request?"

"The sellers have set a date for turning over the artwork, if that's what you mean. I won't be meeting with them personally. Happy will handle that bit of business for me."

"Another kind of protection," said Rolly.

"Yes, well. What about you, Mr. Waters? Any new developments in your pursuit of . . . whatever it is you're pursuing?"

"Just a lot of dead ends," said Rolly.

"I'm sure that's frustrating," said Wendell. "Have you ever considered giving up this private detective thing and going back to playing guitar for a living?"

"I've considered a lot of things."

"I like you much better as a guitar player than as a private detective."

"Most people do."

"I've got friends in the music business."

"I have friends in the business too," said Rolly. He glanced over at Moogus. "I played with some of them tonight."

"I'm serious. You should consider a full-time career."

"I tried it for a while. It didn't work out for me."

"Follow your bliss, Rolly Waters. Follow your bliss."

"Yes, well . . ." Rolly said, but Wendell had turned away. Happy the bodyguard cleared a path for him through the backstage riffraff. Wendell climbed into a limousine parked outside the back exit. The limousine drove away. Happy turned and stared at Rolly for a moment, then walked to the dock, climbed in the raft and headed out to the yacht. Happy would be handling the blackmail business. It sounded like a threat the way Wendell had said it. Rolly wondered if he needed to warn Melody. He wondered if Wendell knew more than he'd said about Janis, or Ricky, or the OMU.

"What was that all about?" said Moogus.

"Nothing," said Rolly. "It's nothing."

He reached in his pocket, pulled out his phone and switched it on. There was a message from Bonnie. She'd called twenty minutes ago. He tapped on her number, put the phone to his ear.

"We have to talk," said Bonnie when she answered the phone.

"What about?" said Rolly.

"Henley Withers," said Bonnie. "Something's come in from the coroner."

"What is it?"

"It looks like he had a heart attack."

"So he didn't drown?"

"No."

"He seemed to be in pretty good shape."

"Yeah, the coroner thought so too. Withers had elevated levels of adrenaline in his blood, though."

"What does that mean?"

"He had some kind of stress event, like a panic attack, which might have led to the heart attack. Even healthy people can have a heart attack if they get scared enough."

"You said the top of the tank was locked, right?"

"Yeah."

"That would scare me."

"Yeah. I guess. But there was plenty of oxygen in there. The coroner did a quick calculation. Withers had enough air for another hour or so. He was a smart guy. He would've known that. The FBI found a note in his office."

"What did the note say?"

"The FBI won't release it."

"Is it a suicide note?"

"More in the line of a confession, from what I've heard."

"You know what he confessed to?"

"I thought you might have some idea."

"Do I win anything if I guess right?"

"Nope."

"I'll let you know if I think of something," said Rolly. Bonnie was dangling bait, but he wouldn't bite. "Thanks for the call."

He disconnected. His phone rang again. It was Max. Max was usually in bed by this time of the night.

"What's up?" Rolly said.

"Hey," said Max. "I figured you'd be up. You want to take a bail job?"

"Tonight?" said Rolly. Posting bail for Max's clients had been one of his regular jobs, back when he worked in Max's office, after the accident, during recovery. If the clients needed some TLC, Rolly would show up to make sure they got through the process. Sometime he'd buy them a meal, drive them home.

"Yeah, tonight," said Max. "One of those kids from the OMU protest. They dropped charges against everybody but this one guy."

"Is it Dick Nazi?"

"Who?"

"Richard Withers," said Rolly. "His stage name's Dick Nazi."

Max chuckled.

"Yeah, that's him. I should have figured you'd know the guy. Anyway, his girlfriend will be down at Etta's Bonds in about half an hour. I told her I'd send somebody to hold her hand and walk her through the process."

"What's her name?"

"Let's see. Here it is. Melody Flowers."

Rolly rubbed his forehead. He stared at the dark ripples of water crossing the surface of the bay.

"You still there?" said Max. "You want the job?"

"Oh, yeah," said Rolly. "I'll take the job."

## 36

## THE BAILOUT

Melody and Rolly sat in the outtake room at the downtown jail early the next morning. Dick Nazi's bail payment had been processed. The wheels of the justice system had been greased rather easily, and for quite a bit less than Rolly expected. He guessed the government would have difficulty proving harmonica playing was a terrorist act, and that Nazi's boat hitting Wendell could be seen as an accident. Rolly wondered, though, if the wheels had been greased for other reasons. Maybe Nazi was more valuable to the FBI if he were free. At any rate, he would slide out of the machine soon and walk out to greet them. "Soon" was a relative term, of course. If the police or FBI were still interviewing him, they might find a way to delay his release. If they decided on additional charges, they could process him back into the system without letting him out of the building. Max would have to set up another round of bail bonds with Etta.

Melody looked tired. Or pissed off. Probably both. She hadn't look surprised when Rolly walked into Etta's Bail Bonds and told her he was the man Max had sent to hold her hand while she bailed out her boyfriend. She'd just looked at him and declared in a flat monotone voice, "Oh, it's you."

There was nothing for them to do now but wait. Rolly had a lot of questions for Melody. It seemed like a good time to ask them.

"When did you meet Dick Nazi?" he asked.

"Couple of months ago, I guess."

"You know he's Janis's brother, right?"

"Yeah, I know. You got some kind of problem with that?"

"You told Max you were Dick's girlfriend."

"So?"

"Is that true?"

Melody gave Rolly a dull stare, then turned away.

"I got a lot of dicks in my life right now," she said. "He's one of them."

"Does he know about Wendell?"

Melody snickered.

"Why do you think he tried to run him over?"

"You know about that?"

"Sure. It was the first thing he told me when he called me from jail. He said he would have done it, too, if some old boozer in a speedboat hadn't got in his way."

"That was my dad. I was on that boat too."

"You're a pain in the ass, Waters, you know that?"

"Maybe you shouldn't have hired me."

"Maybe I shouldn't have. I'm out two hundred dollars and I got nothing to show for it."

"What would you like to be able to show?"

"A profit. I'd like to see what that looks like sometime."

"You and me both."

Melody sighed. She fiddled with the bracelets on her left wrist and stared at the wall.

"I spied on him, you know."

"Who?"

"Wendell. Ricky knew about Wendell and me. He encouraged it."

"Who's Ricky?"

"His real name is Richard. I call him Ricky."

"Right," said Rolly. Richard Withers aka Dick Nazi aka Ricky. The man had three names. It was hard to keep up. "What do you mean you spied on Wendell?"

"I told stuff to Ricky, things Wendell told me. Wendell talks a lot. He told me about all the stuff he was doing—the book signing, the concert, the mural at the school. There's nothing Wendell likes better than talking about Wendell."

"What about the dolphin parade? Did he tell you about that?"

"He loved to tell me about that. He was totally stoked about it. He told me the plan. I told it to Ricky."

"Did you know what Ricky and the OMU were planning to do?"

"That's Ricky's thing, that protest shit."

"I thought maybe there was a connection, because of Janis and the Lemurian Temple."

"I'm not really into politics. I'm a spiritual person."

Rolly contemplated the linoleum floor for a minute, the seemingly random pattern of silver and brown blocks set against the off-white background of each tile. The pattern wasn't random. If you looked across the whole floor you could see how the design was repeated. You had to expand your view to recognize it.

"I can't figure you out," he said.

"Ditto," said Melody. "I figured you'd try making a pass at me at least once by now. What's your deal?"

"I don't have a deal. I'm too old for you."

"You got a girlfriend or something?"

"No. I'm still single."

"Yeah. Whatever. You ain't interested."

A buzzer went off and the security gate opened. Rolly and Melody both turned to see if it was Ricky. It wasn't.

"Did you have something going with Janis back then?" said Melody. "I've been wondering about that."

"No. Janis used to call me, though, late at night. After the band broke up. She was lonely, I think. I was going through a rough time myself. Some bad things had happened. I let a lot of people down. Janis was one of them. I felt like I owed it to her, just listening to her talk. Running our fan club made her feel useful, I think. Like she was valued. I took that away. I messed up."

"You're kind of a sap, aren't you?"

"Yeah. I'm a sap," said Rolly. He rubbed his eyes. "Can I ask you something?"

"You're going to start asking permission now?"

"Different topic. Did you say anything to Wendell about me?"

"Why would I tell him about you?"

"You didn't go to the concert, did you?"

"I was going to and then . . . this. Fucking Ricky."

"I was there. I played with Wendell's band."

"Wait, what?"

"This friend of mine put together Wendell's backing band for the concert. He got a message from Wendell a couple of days ago telling my friend to hire me."

"Wendell wanted you in the band?"

"Yeah. My friend showed me the text message. It came directly from Wendell. I thought maybe you gave him my name."

"It wasn't me. Wendell's kind of feeble with his phones. He's got more than one, you know. One for calling family and friends, one for business. One for calling special girls like me. He loses his phones all the time, or uses the wrong one."

"I guess he can afford to lose stuff."

"He could afford to lose me."

"We talked about you after the concert. He asked me to tell you something."

"Oh yeah? What'd he say?"

"He said he was sorry for any misunderstanding."

"What a dick."

"He said you were an attractive young woman, if that helps any."

"No. It doesn't. I'll get over him."

"You've still got Ricky."

"Yeah. One dick's as good as another, right?"

"That's not what . . . Oh, forget it."

"I like Ricky okay. He's just not very practical."

"What do you mean?"

"His family. They've got all that money. I talked to him about letting bygones be bygones, but he doesn't want to have anything to do with them. He's into this whole disowning thing, being the black sheep of the family. That's where all this political protest comes in. He says he's never going to accept money from the military-industrial complex, whatever that is. I say, who cares? Take the money. You can still protest against whatever you want. You can still sing your songs."

"For someone who claims to be spiritual," said Rolly, "you have a pretty acquisitive outlook on life."

"What does that mean?"

"You care a lot about money."

"I'm spiritual, not stupid."

Rolly scratched the back of his head. He looked at the floor. The pattern hadn't changed any.

"Someone's trying to blackmail Wendell. They have photos of you together."

"Oh yeah? How do I look?"

"I don't know."

"Am I naked?"

"I assume you're both in some state of undress. In flagrante delicto."

"In what?"

"Nothing."

"You haven't seen the pictures?"

"No, I haven't. Wendell just told me about them."

"Why'd he do that?"

"He thought I'd taken the pictures, that I was working for his wife's lawyer. He thought he could bargain with me."

"Do you know who took the pictures?"

"I don't know who took the pictures, but I saw who delivered them. The guy was wearing a dolphin mask, but I could tell it was Ricky."

"Really? How much money did he want?"

"Fifty thousand dollars."

"Yeah, that sounds like Ricky. Setting the bar low, as usual."

"You think he could get more?"

"Is there any video?"

"Not that I know of."

"Video's where the big bucks are. He could sell the video to one of those websites. Wendell's pretty famous. People like it when you're famous. They all want to see a famous guy's dick. I bet Ricky could make more if there was a video."

"You've given this some thought, I see."

A wistful look came into Melody's eyes, as if she were flying over mountains of money. She shrugged and fell back to earth.

"People are assholes," she said. "They can't help themselves. It's easy to pull someone's chain. Hard to make money doing it."

"Are you pulling my chain right now?"

Melody brushed the hair out of her face.

"Ricky and I have a strange relationship," she said. "He likes to watch me with other guys. I didn't know he was taking photos."

"So you're not part of this shakedown, that's what you're telling me?"

"I'd be asking for more than fifty K if I was."

"Ricky can't go through with this," said Rolly. "Whatever he's got planned. I don't care if he hates Wendell. Blackmail is illegal. It's wrong and it's dangerous."

"Are you going to squeal on him?"

"He shouldn't worry about me. He should worry about Wendell."

"Is Wendell going to pay him?"

"They set a date and a time. Wendell told me Happy was going to take care of things. That's the part that makes me worry."

"Yeah. Happy's a creep."

"What's his story?"

"I guess he saved Wendell's life a couple of years ago, down in Panama. Wendell decided to go out walking one night, someplace he shouldn't have been. Some bad guys surrounded him. They were going to rob him. Happy showed up, saw what was going on and kicked their asses. Wendell figured he owed Happy something after that."

"What happened to Happy's left arm?"

"It's an old war injury. That's what Wendell told me, anyway. Happy was in that war in Iraq. The first one, a long time ago."

"Desert Storm?"

"Yeah. He was one of those Special Forces guys and got shot during a mission. I think he's got a little PTSD, too."

"What makes you say that?"

Melody shrugged.

"I don't know. Just the way he stares at the wall sometimes, like his brain's somewhere else. Like there's bad stuff going on his mind. His aura is really messed up."

"What was he doing in Panama?"

"He had a job down there, bartending at some rinky-dink gringo shack. That's where Wendell found him, anyway."

"I thought he saved Wendell's life?"

"It happened outside the bar. Happy disappeared after he saved Wendell's ass. Said he didn't want to hang around and deal with the police. Wendell went back to the bar the next day to thank him. Happy didn't want any reward money, so Wendell ended up buying him dinner in a nicer part of town, after Happy got off work. They started talking. Wendell found out about Happy's military background and offered him a job."

"How long ago was this?"

"Maybe a couple of years. Wendell's career was really taking off then, a whole new level, you know. People started recognizing him, coming up to him on the street. He figured he needed somebody like Happy to help keep an eye out and protect him from the weirdos. Happy had already saved his ass once. He figured he could do it again."

The buzzer went off again and the security gate opened. A jail guard escorted Dick Nazi into the room. Nazi blinked his eyes, adjusting to the glare of the overhead lights.

"Hey Mel," he said.

"Hey Ricky."

"Hey Waters," said Nazi. "What're you doing here?"

"We need to talk," said Rolly.

"Totally," said Nazi. "I'm starving. You want to get Mexican?"

# 37

# THE ENCHILADAS

"I guess we owe you an apology," said Dick Nazi, waving a half-empty bottle of Dos Equis at Rolly. The two men sat across the table from each other in a booth at the Villa Cantina, a Mexican restaurant ten blocks from the jail. Melody Flowers sat next to Nazi, nursing a wine margarita. They were an incongruous-looking couple—Melody the mystical girl-child in her tie-dye and beads and Nazi the tattooed social agitator, full of anger and revolt.

"You don't owe me anything except some answers," said Rolly. "Melody paid me two hundred dollars."

"That's all she coughed up, huh?" said Nazi. He chuckled. "It was supposed to be five."

"You said I could work my own angle," said Melody. "Five was too much."

"She didn't offer me any money at first," said Rolly.

"You're beautiful, babe," said Nazi, chucking Melody on the chin with a light-fisted tap. "You got no moral compass at all. That's why I love you."

Melody shrugged.

"I'm tired," she said. "My auras are fucking depleted."

Rolly wasn't sure how his own auras were holding up. He felt pretty damn tired. And hungry.

"I didn't do this for the money," he said. "I did it for Janis. I felt like I owed her something."

"You're full of it, Waters," said Nazi.

Rolly stared at Nazi for a moment. He thought about leaving, sticking them with the bill, but he'd already ordered a plate of cheese enchiladas with eggs over easy. He'd give these two jokers just as much time as it took to finish his meal.

"If you want any more information from me," he said, "you'll have to pay me the five hundred dollars. You'll have to answer some questions. If you don't want to do that, you can buy me breakfast, say thanks for the help and I'll call it a day. You decide."

Nazi and Melody looked at each other. Melody shrugged.

"It's your call," she said. "I'm the bait. You're the switch."

"It was my idea, Waters," said Nazi. "To hire you. I didn't want you to know it was me, so I made up that story for Melody, about my sister asking for you, like it was her dying wish or something. I heard about you being a detective. I asked around. People told me you were a soft touch for the ladies, so I figured between knowing my sister and Melody dropping some sexy on you at the club you'd get on the case pretty quick. That way I wouldn't be your client. You wouldn't question my motives."

"What are your motives?"

"The usual stuff."

"And that is?"

"Creating chaos and anarchy."

"You've done a hell of a job of it."

"Thanks. But you really blew this thing up. I just lighted the fuse."

"Why are you doing this?"

"Something stinks in the Tidewater family. I've known it since I was a kid. Janis knew it too. That's why she left her backpack for me. She never went anywhere without that old thing."

Rolly searched his pockets and pulled out the old photograph Tom Cockburn had given him.

"What's that?" said Nazi.

"Nothing," said Rolly, checking the picture. "Did this backpack have dolphins on it?"

"Yeah, that's right. It's a little girl's backpack, with pink dolphins and blue dolphins, hearts and rainbows and stars. It's really old, ragged as shit. I can't remember a time when Janis didn't have it with her. It was like her security blanket."

"She left it with you?"

"Not exactly. I found it the next morning, that Saturday, after she died. I was prepping the OTTER for the first run of the day. The backpack was under the seat. I locked it in my office, figured I could give it to her later. I didn't know what happened to her until Melody called and told me about the police searching the temple. She told me Tammy was there too. That's when I realized there might be a reason Janis left the backpack with me."

"I don't get the connection."

Nazi looked over at Melody.

"Tell him," he said.

"Tammy came over to the house, looking for the backpack," said Melody. "She kept asking about it, saying it had to be there. She got all indignant, calling me names. Said she was going to evict me."

"That made me want to check out the backpack," said Nazi, "to find out what was luffing Tammy's sails."

"That's where you found Fleetwood's dog tags?"

"Yeah. There were some clothes and money in there too."

"How much money?"

"Two thousand dollars. I took five hundred out for Melody to pay you."

"You're sure it was two thousand?"

"Yeah. Two thousand large."

Their meal arrived. The steam rising from Rolly's enchiladas reflected the vaporous heat in his brain.

"That was Tom Cockburn's money," he said.

"You mean that editor guy the FBI asked me about, the one who wrote those articles for the *OB Enquirer*?"

Rolly nodded.

"He put two thousand dollars in the backpack and left it in a locker for Butch Fleetwood. Twenty-three years ago."

"Janis has been carrying that money around this whole time?" said Nazi.

"That's what it looks like."

"Vicious, man. This shit goes deep."

Rolly pushed the photograph across the table.

"You recognize anyone in this picture?" he said. Nazi pushed his chilaquiles to one side and stared at the picture.

"That's Janis, isn't it?" he said. "And Henley. I'd recognize that little twinkie anywhere. And that's Tammy. They're all a lot younger. Who's this other guy? He looks kinda scary. He's got a chain around his neck with . . . oh shit, Waters. Where'd you get this?"

"Tom Cockburn gave it to me," said Rolly.

"That's Butch Fleetwood, isn't it?"

Rolly nodded.

"That's Janis's backpack next to his foot," he said. "I'd like to take a look at it."

"Sorry," said Nazi. "I got rid of it."

"I know. I saw you."

"What?"

"Wendell's got security cameras all over his boat. He showed me the video. The dolphin mask was a nice touch, but you should've worn longer sleeves to cover up those tattoos. I saw you go out in the rowboat that same night, remember?"

Nazi leaned back against the booth cushion and laughed.

"All right, you got me, Waters. You're pretty good at this detective stuff."

"Call it off," Rolly said.

"Call what off?"

"The payment, the exchange. Delete those photos and call it off."

"What are you talking about?"

"You took pictures," said Melody. "Of Wendell and me. You told Wendell you were going to send the pictures to his wife."

"Wait, what? I didn't take any pictures."

"You're telling me you're not blackmailing Wendell?" said Rolly. "That you didn't make arrangements to collect fifty thousand dollars?"

"No. We were trying to scare Wendell a little, I guess, freak him out, make him feel guilty about this Ocean Universe thing. There weren't any pictures. Only a note."

"Who's the 'we' you're referring to? Who else was involved?"

"Harmonica Dan came up with the idea," said Nazi. "He wrote the note and put it inside the backpack."

"What did the note say?"

"'She died for your sins.' That's all that was there. Just the note. I knew about Wendell and Melody, sure, but I didn't take any pictures of them. I just wanted to rile Wendell up a bit."

Melody picked up the photo lying on the table. "So this big ape is Butch Fleetwood?"

"You recognize him?"

"No, but if a guy looked at me like he's looking at Tammy Withers, I'd have a pretty good idea what was on his mind."

"That's because guys look at you like that all the time," said Nazi. "Nobody turns up the heat on The Refrigerator. Am I right, Waters? You talked to Tammy. You've felt the frigidity."

"The photo's from twenty-three years ago," said Rolly, thinking about the secrets Mitchy had revealed to him at the Admiral's Club bar. "Apparently Tammy wasn't so chilly back then."

"Spill the dirt, Waters," said Nazi. "You think there was something between Tams and Butch Fleetwood?"

Rolly shrugged.

"Maybe. He wouldn't be the first boy toy she took out on her boat."

"Roaww!" said Nazi. "Tammy the Cougar. I had no idea."

"Did you know Janis wasn't Henley's daughter? That he adopted her when he married Tammy?"

Nazi chuckled.

"I'm not surprised, I guess. I always knew Henley was in the closet," he said. "Grandpa Baldry told me as much, without really saying it."

"What did he tell you?"

"This was a couple of years ago, same time he gave me the OTTER boats. Grandpa was already having trouble remembering things, getting his words right."

"What did he say?"

"Let's see," said Nazi. "It was something about how he had to prescribe the sissy cure for that whore. He meant Tammy."

"Your grandfather calls his daughter a whore?" said Melody.

"Yeah. He's a real charmer, Grandpa Baldry. He gave me quite an education, Grandpa did, about women. More specifically about whores, but it's kinda the same thing for him."

"What'd he say?" said Melody.

"Grandpa said there's two kinds of whores. The first kind's the traders. Those are the whores who do it for money. He said you can always work with them. They're professionals, real business gals. He admired those girls. They knew how to put a value on what they were trading. Like his first wife."

"What's the other kind?" said Melody.

"It's the natural-born whores you got to watch out for. You can't trust 'em. They got an itch they got to scratch. The only way to make a natural-born whore respectable is to marry 'em off to a sissy. He told me it works to the benefit of both parties, as long as they're both discreet."

"I don't get it," said Melody.

"I bet Waters does," said Nazi. "You can explain it to my sweet Melody, can't you?"

"I can guess," Rolly said. Nazi and Melody stared at him across the table, expecting an answer.

"Well, first off they're married," said Rolly. "That's what makes them respectable."

"I get that part, duh," said Melody. Rolly sighed.

"Well, the husband's gay," he continued. "But he's married to a woman, so he and everyone else can pretend that he's straight. It's a social convention everyone agrees on. If you're doing business with some Bible-thumping bigot, you have a way of pretending you're not a sodomite. You can't possibly be a homosexual because you're married to a woman."

"That's stupid," said Melody. "And totally hypocritical."

"Don't criticize what you don't understand, honey," said Nazi. "A large portion of society would fall apart if we suddenly got rid of all the hypocrisy."

"What's in it for the woman?" said Melody.

"She's not a woman," Nazi said. "She's a natural-born whore."

"What does that even mean?" said Melody. Nazi raised his eyebrows at Rolly, querying him.

"Well," said Rolly, "if I had to guess, I'd say it's a woman who makes her own choices when it comes to her sex life."

"Sounds like most of the women I know," said Melody. "They're not whores."

"No, they're not," said Rolly. "You have to understand, we're looking at this from a patriarchal point of view."

"A what?" said Melody.

"Watch it with the big words, Waters," said Nazi. "They mess up her auras."

"It means the men are in charge," said Rolly.

"Aren't they always?" said Melody.

"Men like Grandpa Baldry are really, really in charge," said Nazi. "A woman who sleeps around is a problem, especially if she's married. If she sleeps with another man, she's emasculating her husband."

"She's what?" said Melody.

"Cutting his balls off," said Nazi. "Which means he might as well be gay."

"Gay men don't have balls?"

Nazi laughed.

"What's so funny?" said Melody.

"I love you, sweetheart," said Nazi. "You have a way of saying something that sounds dumb at first, but kind of nails it. That's exactly what my grandpa and his buddies think. Gay men don't have balls. Not literally, of course, but . . ."

"I get it now," said Melody. "If the wife is fooling around on her husband but he's gay, it doesn't make a difference because he's already ejacuated."

"Emasculated," said Rolly.

"Yeah," said Melody, "so nobody cares."

"That's about it," said Rolly.

"That's exactly it," said Nazi. "The woman is married, so she's respectable. But she can fool around on the side. It's only natural since everyone knows she's not getting any at home. And her husband isn't any less masculine because he never was masculine in the first place. That's the arrangement."

Melody's phone buzzed. She checked the screen.

"Speaking of arrangements," she said, showing the screen to Nazi. "Wendell wants to make up. He's got a present for me."

"That's cute," said Nazi. "How much is it worth?"

"Are you going to see him again?" said Rolly.

"Probably," said Melody. She shrugged. "Like Ricky said, I got no moral compass at all."

She handed the beach photo back to Rolly.

"That photo was taken on the island," she said. "The one I went to with Janis and the harmonica guy, the island with the dolphins."

"Are you sure?"

"You see that building in back with the turrets, like a castle? That's the building where Janis found the dog tags."

"Of course it is," said Rolly, feeling stupid. He'd been there. He'd been to the island. If the soldiers hadn't detained him, he might have figured it out.

"Who took the picture?" said Melody.

Rolly felt stupid all over again. He'd never thought about who was behind the camera, who had gone to the island with the Withers family and Butch Fleetwood that day.

# 38

# THE CRUISE

R olly stood on the foredeck of his father's Chris-Craft, keeping his eyes fixed on the horizon as the boat bounced across the choppy Pacific Ocean waves. Focusing on the horizon helped him ward off seasickness. The breeze in his face helped too. He hoped they could make it to their destination before any queasiness set in. He also hoped they weren't on a fool's errand.

His father stood at the helm of the boat, guiding it across the water. Dick Nazi sat in the passenger seat behind Rolly's father. They were headed to the cove on the other side of South Coronado Island, where the mysterious frogman had taken Rolly in Harmonica Dan's boat, where he'd been saved by a dolphin and arrested by Mexican soldiers. Now he wanted to explore the ruins of the building hanging on the side of the cliffs. Nazi had insisted on joining him. Rolly didn't trust Nazi, but keeping him in sight would also keep the OTTER punk from making more trouble. Nazi had been his real client, after all. Melody was a front.

Rolly didn't know what he would find in the old casino. He wasn't sure he would find anything except rotting timbers and rusty old pipes. All he had was a set of coincidences that pointed back to the island and the old building set in the rocks. He hoped there was something inside the casino, one piece of evidence, one fact that turned those coincidences into a story, a story Tom Cockburn had never been able to finish. What had really happened to Butch Fleetwood?

Dean Waters's Chris-Craft was speedy and agile. It would allow for a quick escape if they needed one. When Rolly called and asked about using the boat, his father had allowed it on one condition: he had to skipper the boat. He wasn't going to let his seamanship-challenged son or some tatted-up punk take his baby out to sea alone. The captain was in his element now, taking charge of an ocean vessel on a strategic mission.

Captain Waters eased back on the throttle as they drew close to the islands. He threaded his way through the channel between the Central and South Coronados, turned south and cruised down the western edge of the southern island. As they approached the little cove on the back of the island, Rolly spotted the tall white spire of a sailboat mast wagging back and forth like an oceanic metronome.

"There's someone here," he said, glancing back at the other two men.

"What do you want me to do?" asked his father.

Rolly crawled back to the cockpit and stood next to him.

"Just creep your way in there," he said. "Let's see who it is."

His father pulled back the throttle and they drifted into the cove. Nazi joined Rolly and his father at the helm.

"That's Harmonica Dan's boat," he said.

"That's what it looks like to me," said Rolly. He thought about the last time he'd been to the island. Three days ago on Harmonica Dan's boat. It had been terrifying, painful and wet.

"Screw your courage to the sticking place, son," said his father.

"What?"

"You looked a little wobbly there."

"We need to be careful."

"It's the guy you're looking for, right? That bum from the Shack? He didn't look dangerous."

"No. Not Dan," said Nazi. "Dan's as chill as they come." He cupped his hands around his mouth as Rolly's father maneuvered them in toward the old pier where the sailboat was moored.

"Ahoy!" Nazi called. "Ahoy to the sailboat."

There was no response from Dan's boat. Rolly's father turned the wheel and tweaked the throttle. They moved to within twenty feet of it. Dick Nazi called ahoy again. There was still no response.

"Put us on the other side of the pier," said Nazi.

Rolly's father nodded, adjusting the controls until he'd pulled the Chris-Craft up next to the pier. He cut the engine. Nazi hopped out and tied the boat to the pier.

"I'll check if anyone's home," he said. He crossed the pier and disappeared into the cabin of Dan's boat, announcing himself as he went in. He reappeared a few moments later, shaking his head.

"No one inside," he said. He nodded toward the casino. "Maybe he's up there."

As if in response, a face appeared in one of the windows of the ruined casino on the rocks. Harmonica Dan looked down at them from above. A look of recognition came to his face. He waved.

"Looks like he's expecting us," said Nazi.

"Yeah," said Rolly. "You know what he's up to?"

"No, but whatever it is, I'm ready. Let's go."

"Yeah. Let's go," said Rolly's father.

"Hang on," said Rolly. He didn't feel so enthusiastic. "You need to stay here, Dad."

"You don't think I can handle this?"

"That's not it. We need to be smart here. You've got a radio, right?"

"Yeah."

"I want you to wait here. Fifteen minutes. If you don't see me give you some kind of OK signal before that fifteen minutes is up, I want you to get out of here as fast as you can. Radio the Coast Guard, send out an SOS."

"What should I tell them?"

"Whatever it takes to get them here fast. If you don't see me within fifteen minutes, something bad has happened. If you see anyone coming out of that building and I'm not with them, it's the same deal. Get out of here fast. Then call it in. You got it?"

"Aye, aye, son. You're in command of this operation."

Rolly looked over at Nazi.

"That includes him," he said, pointing at Nazi. "You can't trust him. Only me."

"He's right, Captain," said Nazi. "You shouldn't trust me. Rooster-tail this skiff like hell if you see me coming back without your son."

Rolly's father shook his head.

"Between the two of you, this is the strangest damn crew I ever sailed with," he said.

"Okay?" said Nazi, turning back to Rolly.

"Okay."

They walked to the end of the rickety pier and up through a twisting stairway of rocks to a wide-open doorway in the front corner of the casino. Rolly paused at the door, wheezing.

"What's up?" said Nazi.

"Just catching my breath. I'm a little wound up."

"You could stand to lose a few pounds, Waters, especially if you want to keep doing this detective stuff."

"Check back with me in twenty years and let me know how your cardiovascular system's holding up."

"I doubt I'll live that long," said Nazi. "You might not either at this rate. You still want to do this?"

Rolly nodded. The two men entered the building.

"This place is really falling apart," said Nazi. There were holes in the rotting wood of the casino floor, a large open room filled with broken-down gambling tables and a smashed roulette wheel. The whole room was covered in sea rot, bird droppings and rust. The floorboards creaked as they crept across the old wood floor.

"There's the stairs," said Nazi, pointing to a grand staircase in the middle of the room. The staircase looked even more rotted and decrepit than the rest of the building.

"You think it'll hold us?" said Rolly.

"Me, maybe," said Nazi. "I don't know about you."

"You first, then," said Rolly. Nazi tested the first step. He gave it his weight, moved to the second step, and the third. Five more steps and he was up on the landing.

"It's not as bad as it looks," he said, looking back at Rolly. "Stick to the right side. The riser seems pretty solid along that edge."

Rolly took the first step. The wood creaked and bent, but it held. He grabbed the railing, what was left of it, and took the next step. The edge of the staircase supported his weight. He climbed up to the landing. The two of them took the next set of stairs and stepped out into the second-floor hallway.

"Which way?" said Nazi.

"I think he was over there," said Rolly, pointing to the right.

They turned and walked down the hall. Faded numbers on dark, stained doors marked the rooms where overnight guests had stayed. They passed room 21. Then 22. Rolly stopped in front of the next door. Room 23.

"This one," he said.

Nazi knocked on the door. There was no response.

"Harmonica Dan?" called out Nazi. "Are you in there? It's Ricky Withers. Dick Nazi. I got Rolly Waters with me."

No one answered.

"What make you think it's this room?" said Nazi.

"Melody told me that Harmonica Dan brought Janis to this island," said Rolly. "They went into this building and when they came out, Janis had the dog tags. She must have found them somewhere in this building. It's like someone's been planning this, deliberately leaving clues. Twenty-three years since Butch Fleetwood disappeared. Room 23."

The floor creaked behind them.

"Very astute, Mr. Waters," said a voice. "You're more clever than I gave you credit for." It was a woman's voice, not Dan's. Both men spun around.

"Hello, Richard," said Tammy Withers. "It's been a long time. I see you've managed to make yourself even more physically repulsive."

"What are you doing here?" said Nazi.

"I asked Daniel to bring me," she said. "I wanted to see what all the excitement was about."

"What's in this room?" said Rolly.

"Take a look for yourself," said Tammy. "It's open."

Rolly turned the doorknob. The door creaked open. He and Nazi walked in. Light streamed in through a small, square window, illuminating a rusty set of box springs on the floor. On top of the box springs lay an old wetsuit, brittle and faded to gray. A ragged hole had been torn out of the front left shoulder. A rusted oxygen tank lay next to the suit, along with a diving mask and a pair of cracked flippers. In the far corner of the room, Harmonica Dan sat on the floor with his eyes closed and his legs crossed in a lotus pose. A harmonica sat on the floor in front of him. Two chairs like the ones in Tammy's office were set up facing each other. Truth chairs.

"Now that you're here," said Tammy, "you'll need to stick around for the final act, the great denouement, as it were."

"I'm not sure we have time for that," said Rolly.

"You're part of this now, Mr. Waters," said Tammy. "I'd like you to stay." She made her request even clearer by raising her right hand. There was a gun in it.

# 39

# THE ROOM

Dick Nazi laughed, a loud and provocative cackle that made Rolly wince. He remembered the awards Tammy had on her wall, testaments to her acumen with a pistol. Rolly was the biggest bull's-eye in the room, and the least agile. Provocation didn't seem like a good game plan, not if they planned to get out of here alive. Nazi didn't seem to care.

"Guess who's coming to dinner?" said Nazi. "Is that what you want us to do, Tams?"

"Shut up, Richard," said Tammy. "We're going to wait here quietly and see what happens."

"You know I can't sit still," said Nazi. "I'm A-D-D. And bipolar. That was your professional diagnosis, wasn't it?"

"Calm down, Richard."

"Let's play a game. Let's tell stories. Like you used to do with Grandpa."

"This isn't a game."

"What'll it be? Charades? Truth or Dare? Maybe Psychiatrist?"

"That's not funny."

"C'mon Tam-O-Shanter, tell me a story."

"I abhor that name," she said. "And you know it."

"Grandpa still calls you that, doesn't he?"

"I haven't spoken to your grandfather in years."

"I have. He told me some stories."

"Your grandfather is a misogynistic, bitter old man."

"He's senile, too. But he's got lots of money. And he'll be dead soon. Don't you think you'd better kiss and make up before he kicks the bucket? You could still get a chunk of the treasure, maybe a spot on the board of directors."

Tammy looked at Nazi as if he were the plague.

"You've never appreciated what we did for you," she said. "And neither did your sister."

"You mean how you saved me from being raised in the backwoods of Ol' Virginny by my poor cracker parents?"

"We gave you a comfortable home and a first-rate education, which you've completely wasted."

"It was an education, all right. I learned that you and Twinkie couldn't stand the sight of me. That's why you sent me away. It's because I reminded you of Grandpa, isn't it?"

"You don't remind me of anyone but your own miserable self, Richard."

"People told me about those parties Grandpa used to have at his house. That's where I come from, isn't it? I'm one of Grandpa's little mistakes."

Tammy waved her gun in the air, as if she were smoking a cigarette at a cocktail party.

"This should be interesting," she said. "Go ahead and spin your little fantasy. We've got time to kill."

"I'm not fond of the word 'kill' in this particular context," said Rolly.

"Shut up, you fat slob," said Tammy, pointing the gun at him, moving it around as if she were marking different targets on his body. "I was a champion shooter in high school, you know."

"Yes, I know," said Rolly. "I've seen your trophies."

"I still can't figure how you fit into this," said Tammy. "Who hired you?"

"I did," said Nazi. Tammy turned the gun back on him.

"Why, Richard?" she said. "Why? What did we ever do to you?"

"I hate you," said Nazi. "And Henley. And Grandpa Baldry."

"That would seem fairly evident from the stunt you pulled yesterday, you and your little band of deadbeat do-gooders."

"I won't be co-opted by the military-industrial complex."

"Where do you think the money Janis gave your little organization came from?"

"I know exactly where it came from. That's the beauty of it, you see," said Nazi. "Janis and I were taking Grandpa Baldry's blood money and using it to fight back."

"Grandpa gave you those OTTER vehicles."

"They were just a tax write-off for him."

"He paid for the academy. He made sure you stayed in school."

Nazi laughed again.

"Yeah," he said. "I can thank him for my brilliant education."

"The tuition was not inconsiderable. Not to mention the additional donations he had to make to forestall your expulsion."

"Blackmail's never cheap, Tams. That's why Grandpa kept you and Henley on the payroll all these years."

"I don't know what you're talking about."

"I've seen the books. You never made any money. Your division was a loss leader."

"Research divisions rarely make money."

"It was nepotism, pure and simple, with a few family secrets kept under lock and key to seal the deal."

Tammy sighed and shook her head.

"All right," she said. "Go ahead and entertain us with your little story."

"I spent some time back there with Grandpa, after I got out of school," said Nazi. "Grandpa might own that town, but that doesn't mean people don't talk shit about him. You can learn a lot hanging out in bars, listening to old stories. I heard about those parties he gave at his house in the country, how he entertained his business associates and those Navy bigwigs. How he'd pay some local girls to attend. Bought them new clothes, too, something nice, to make 'em look pretty."

"I read something about that," said Rolly. "There was some kind of scandal."

"Exactly," said Tammy. "This isn't news, Richard. The stories about those parties came out during the congressional hearings years ago. Your grandfather resigned in order to save the company."

"Not all the details came out, though, did they?" said Nazi with a sick little grin.

"What are you getting at?" said Tammy.

"The girls at those parties weren't the most sophisticated young ladies in the world. They weren't professionals. Sometimes there would be consequences. Grandpa would take care of the girls who found out they had a little consequence growing inside of them afterwards. He'd call on some of the doctors at that hospital to take care of things for him. After hours, of course. Private visits. That was his right, of course. He built the place. He paid for it."

"This is neither edifying nor entertaining, Richard. I'm aware of my father's corruptions as well as anyone. I've been dealing with them my whole life."

"This isn't about you, Tam-O-Shanter. Not this time. This is about me. The lies that you made me live with. About who my real father was."

"Henley was your father. He raised you."

Nazi waved his arms in the air as if warding off gnats. He collapsed into one of the chairs and stared out the window a moment, then turned back to Tammy.

"This is my truth chair," he said. "This is my truth."

"Very well," said Tammy. "Continue."

"Abortion wasn't an option for some of those girls, was it? Some of them wouldn't go for it. They were good girls. They were righteous. They were raised in church-loving families who told them abortion was a sin. Gramps had to handle those girls differently. They gave up their babies for adoption. Grandpa paid for that too. He paid off the agencies. He paid off the girls. He paid off their parents. Grandpa thought he could pay off anybody."

"What's your point?" said Tammy.

"It wasn't just business for Grandpa at those parties, though, was it?" said Nazi. "Sometimes he liked to sample the goods, if there was a girl he took a shine to."

"This is ridiculous," said Tammy.

"I've seen my birth certificate," said Nazi. "'Father unknown.' That's a laugh. You and Henley adopted me as a favor to Grandpa. That's why he kept you both on the payroll. And that's why you sent me away. You couldn't stand seeing Grandpa's face when you looked at me. You couldn't stand having any part of him in your house. Neither could Twinkie. It was a business decision for all of you, just like when you and Henley got married, when Grandpa prescribed the sissy cure."

Tammy glanced over at Rolly, then down at the floor.

"Where did you hear that term?" she said.

"From Grandpa, where else?"

Tammy blinked a couple of times. She pushed Rolly aside, took a seat in the chair across from Nazi.

"My truth," she said. Nazi nodded.

"We both needed a way to get out," she said. "Henley was my friend. He was the only man I'd ever met who didn't try to physically control me. He even loved me, in his way. It wasn't a physical attraction. He appreciated my spirit. He respected my brain."

"He was a poof," said Nazi.

"Your father . . ."

"Stop calling him that. He's not my father."

"Your adoptive father was an abstemious man."

"He was a Friend of Dorothy. Everyone knows it."

Tammy cleared her throat.

"Henley's sexual preferences hardly matter. For all practical purposes, except for a few instances, he was celibate. He acknowledged I had needs he couldn't fulfill. The relationship between us was rational and cerebral. That was our covenant. We loved each other's minds."

"You were a natural-born whore and Grandpa married you off to a sissy. And he paid you to pretend it was a real marriage."

"Why are you so acrimonious?"

"Six years of boarding school made me the asshole I am today."

"You were an impossible child."

"What about Janis? Was she impossible too?"

"Janis was bipolar and prone to depression. What we did, we did for her own good. We couldn't abandon our research. We had government contracts to fulfill."

"What? Some crazy plan to turn dolphins into trained killers? You couldn't give that up to take care of your own daughter?"

Tammy straightened her arm and pointed the gun at Nazi. He flinched, then slid off the seat and down to his knees. He pointed at his forehead.

"Go on, Tam-O-Shanty," he said. "The target's right here. Go on and shoot me. Eliminate the problem."

Tammy's arm trembled. Rolly's heart tightened like the chain on a snare drum. He didn't breathe.

"Shoot me," said Nazi. "I'm the piece of shit your father foisted on you. I'm a child of the beast who came back to haunt you."

"Stop it, Richard. Stop doing this to yourself."

"Every time you look at me you see his face, don't you? You tried to escape from him and his good-old-boy network. You ran away from his patriotic, patriarchal bullshit, but he reeled you back in. He kept you in line by keeping the money flowing."

"You've got it all wrong, Richard."

"Shoot me, Tam-O-Shanty. That's an order from Daddy."

Tammy retracted the weapon.

"I don't take orders from anyone," she said. "Especially men."

The anger went out of Tammy's eyes, replaced by a flicker of something more painful, a dim light exhausted by age and regret.

"Richard, you are not my father's son," she said. "Your suppositions about his trysts with the local trash are not without truth. But you are not the spawn of those unions."

"Who are my parents?"

"I can't tell you that."

"You can't or you won't?"

"Can I tell a story now, Richard? About me? You asked for a story."

"I don't care."

"*I'd* like to hear a story," said Rolly. Tammy looked up at him.

"Compartmentalization, Mr. Waters. Do you know what that means?"

Rolly nodded.

"I wasn't always so good at it," said Tammy. "Not like I am now."

"Tell us the story."

"It's true. What I told you and your officer friend the other day at the office. I was pregnant with Janis when I married Henley. He came to my rescue. It wasn't just the pregnancy from which he saved me. My father could have taken care of that just like he did with the other girls. Richard is correct about that. My father has a lot of power in that town. He could make things disappear. Even an attempted murder."

"Did you see something?" said Rolly. "Is that why he sent you away?"

"Oh yes," Tammy said. "I saw the murder attempt. From beginning to end. I know who tried to kill Janis's father."

"So you were a witness?"

"The prime witness. I was the one who tried to kill him."

## 40

# THE COVER

"My mother died when I was young," said Tammy. "She killed herself. Daddy found her body. There's a history in our family, I guess, something in the genes, maybe it skips a generation. I was ten when Mama died. Daddy didn't know what to do with me. We already had servants, so he just hired more people to take care of me. I hardly saw my father after my mother died. He seemed to be hiding. I thought he blamed me for what happened to Mama.

"I didn't lack for material things. I didn't lack for education. Daddy sent me to the best schools. He paid for horse-riding lessons, for sailing classes and summer camps. Those were the things that he liked to talk about. He'd ask about lessons. My studies. He wanted to know what I'd achieved, what I'd accomplished. We never talked about Mama. I suppose that's where I developed my ambition, my drive. I went to visit him one weekend a month, at his house in the country. I learned to shoot guns at Daddy's place in the country. We practiced together. I wanted to please him.

"Daddy had two houses, the one where Mama and I lived and his house in the country. After Mama died he always stayed at the country house. I stayed in town. My schools were there. I was fifteen when I first heard about the parties. There was a girl in school who'd been to one of them. She talked about the clothes they gave her, about the food and the drinks and the men who were there, how rich and important they seemed to be. She said she'd seen my father at the party, that the other men treated him like a king. It sounded like a fairy tale. I felt cheated. I wasn't invited. She told me it was only the prettiest girls who were invited.

"I was too young to understand, of course. The next time I visited my father, I asked him if he thought I was pretty enough to go to one of his parties. He became angry with me. He said I was going to grow up disciplined and strong-minded, not weak like my mother. That he was spending good money to make sure I grew up strong-minded, that he'd disinherit me and throw me out if I acted like a whore."

"Say what you will about Grandpa, he's consistent," said Nazi. "It always comes back to the whores."

"Yes," said Tammy. She looked out the window at the powder-blue sky. "Your grandfather is quite predictable that way."

"What happened after that?" said Rolly.

"I tried not to think about it for a while. I wanted to be good. I wanted my father's approval. I certainly didn't want to act like a whore. At that age, I wasn't even sure what that meant, but I decided I wouldn't be one. I thought about the girl who told me about the party. I wondered if she was a whore. She didn't look like one, at least from the studies I was able to do on the topic. We didn't have the Internet back then. All I had were the books in our library. Very few of them said anything about whores. On day I heard that girl talking to her friends at school. She said she'd been invited to another party at my father's house that weekend.

"My curiosity got the better of me, I guess. The night of the party, I got myself pretty, at least what I thought pretty was supposed to be. My dress was terribly old-fashioned, even then, a lavender Belle Époque gown with a high lace collar. I made one of the servants drive me out to Daddy's country house. He couldn't refuse me. He knew I could make trouble for him. So he left me there and I walked up the stairs and into the party."

"Don't tell me," said Nazi. "It wasn't what you expected?"

"The first thing I noticed was how girls were dressed, of course."

"More like whores?"

"I wouldn't say that. Not exactly. They had nice clothes, still formal but certainly more daring than mine. Bare shoulders or long slits in the skirts. Deep-cut backs on some of the girls' gowns. Some of the girls were laughing at me. The men were dressed formally too. It was mostly older men, you know. The girls were young, high school and college age, but the men were all older. Henley was the youngest man there. He came to my rescue. The other girls scared him, I think. We were both ducks out of water. He came over and talked to me, got me punch. I think we felt safe with each other."

"Let's get to the point," said Nazi. "Why did you shoot the guy?"

"This is my story, Richard. I won't be rushed."

Tammy looked over at Rolly to see if he had any objections. He nodded his head. Any way Tammy wished to tell the story was okay with him. She had the gun.

"At some point," she continued, "I don't remember why, Henley left me by myself at the party. I saw my father approaching. He hadn't seen me yet, not in any way that indicated he recognized me, but if I didn't move he would run right into me. I left the room and took the stairs up to my bedroom, the room where I stayed when I visited. I needed a break, anyway. The whole event had put me into a state of agitation. I thought I would be safe in my room. I didn't know someone had followed me."

"This is where the shit hits the fan," said Nazi.

"Yes, Richard, as you so eloquently put it. A man came into my room. A Navy officer, in his dress whites. I'll never forget what he said to me. 'Who are you supposed to be? Little Bo Peep?'" I didn't know what to say to him. I was mute. I felt ashamed to be there in the room with him. I knew my father would be angry with me. And, well, not to put too fine a point on it, the man raped me, there in my own bed, in my father's house. I didn't scream. I didn't call out for help. I let him take me.

"When he'd finished, he left me there in the room and went back to the party. I didn't fully understand what had happened to me, but I knew I'd been ruined somehow. I knew this man had made me a whore, that my father would disown me. I'd never felt so angry before.

The gun cabinet was upstairs. Your grandfather was quite a collector, you know. I knew where he kept the keys. I opened the cabinet and selected one of the smaller guns, something that would fit in my handbag so no one could see it. I walked downstairs to the party. I saw the man sitting in one of my father's chairs, acting as if nothing had happened. There were lots of people talking to him. He looked at me. He smirked. I pulled out the gun and I shot him. A single shot to the chest."

Nazi whistled. "This is fucked up. And sort of awesome."

"I've finally managed to impress you, Richard?"

"Yeah. In a weird kind of way."

"Needless to say, it caused quite a panic. Everyone scattered at first. There was blood coming out of the man's chest, staining his white dinner jacket. I stared at him for a moment, watching the blood bloom on his lapel. His eyes were still open, in shock I guess, staring back at me almost as if he wondered what gave me the right to do something like that. I put the gun to my head. I was going to kill myself. I wanted him to see what he'd done to me. Someone called my name. Very quietly. I heard a calm voice saying my name. I turned and saw Henley standing beside me. He put his arm around me, took the gun and escorted me out of the room."

"I wouldn't have thought Twinkie had that kind of nerve," said Nazi. "What happened to the guy you shot?"

"Unfortunately I aimed a bit high and to the right. I missed his heart by an inch or two, assuming he had one. Needless to say, the party was over. My father made everyone leave. There was a doctor present who took care of the man and got him to the hospital. My father's hospital."

"Did anyone call the police?" said Rolly.

Tammy sighed.

"There were never any police. It was all covered up. Everyone had something to lose if the police got involved. I never spoke to any of the other girls. I never saw them again. My father kept me out of school afterward. He told the school I was ill, had one of his doctors write up a fake diagnosis. Henley knew what had happened, though. He knew I was pregnant. He figured it out. He came to visit me a couple of times at the house. He talked to my father. A month later we were married. In secret. My father hired a judge to come to the house. We moved here and opened the satellite office."

"Are you saying Henley blackmailed Grandpa?"

"My father blamed me for what happened. I was a whore in his eyes. I felt like I'd failed him, that it was all my fault. Henley gave us both a way out."

"And Grandpa started sending checks."

"Yes. I was pregnant with Janis, of course. My father knew it. Henley knew too. We were here in California when Janis was born. No one knew us. No one had any reason to think Henley wasn't her father."

Tammy rested a moment. She and Dick Nazi both seemed to be lost in thought. Rolly moved toward the window. He couldn't check the time without drawing attention, but he felt sure fifteen minutes had passed. He hadn't heard his father rev up the Chris-Craft's engine to make his escape and call in the cavalry.

"All right, Tams," said Richard. "I understand about Janis and Henley. I appreciate your situation. But what about me? It still doesn't explain why you adopted me. Why would either of you want to adopt a baby all those years later? You must have been doing Grandpa a favor."

"No. It was different with you. As you've told us, my father had a great deal of power at the hospital there. He did a favor for me."

# 41

# THE ARRIVAL

There was a sound in the hall. Tammy looked up. She pointed her gun at the door. Footsteps came down the hallway. Rolly's father appeared in the doorway, panting and sweaty. He saw Tammy, glanced down at her gun.

"Aww shit," he said.

"What are you doing here?" said Rolly. "I told you to stay on the boat. I told you to get the hell out of here if there was a problem."

"I'm sorry," said his father. "I didn't know what to do. He wants the punk kid to go down there."

"Who does?"

"The guy on the catamaran. He said he would kill the girl."

"Oh shit," said Dick Nazi. He ran to the window and looked out, then turned back to Rolly. "Wendell's got her. Wendell's got Melody."

Rolly looked out the window again. A sandy blond woman in a bikini lay on the deck of Wendell's yacht. It was Melody, put on display so they could see her. She didn't appear to be in any immediate danger.

"It's not Wendell," said Rolly. "Wendell took a private jet back to Hawaii last night."

"Are you sure?" said Nazi.

"I saw him get in a limo after the show."

"Then what's his yacht doing here? Why is Melody on it?"

"Excuse me," said Tammy. "Who is Melody?"

"The woman at the Lemurian Temple," said Nazi. "The one you threatened to evict."

"I have no idea who or what you're talking about."

"That house Janis owned in Ocean Beach. The Lemurian Temple. You went there the day after she died."

"I did no such thing."

"Yes you did. Melody called me after you left. She said you were looking for Janis's backpack, that nasty old thing with the pink and blue dolphins on it."

"I remember the backpack with the dolphins," said Tammy. "But I've never met this woman. I've never been to this temple thing, what is it called?"

"The Lemurian Temple," said Rolly. "Her name is Melody Flowers. Janis rented the house to her."

"Melody called me the day after Janis died," said Nazi. "She said you were tearing up the place and calling her names. She said you were looking for the backpack. But Janis left the backpack for me. On the OTTER. She wanted me to find those dog tags."

"That's quite a story, Richard, but it's not true. How well do you know this Melody woman?"

"I . . . She . . ." Nazi stopped. He glanced up at Rolly with a look of bewilderment. "What do you make of it, Waters?"

"I was hoping you could tell me," said Rolly.

Nazi shook his head. He seemed genuinely baffled. Dim thoughts began to form in Rolly's mind, slow-moving shapes below the surface of a dismal ocean. He looked over at Tammy.

"Do you know who's down there?" he asked. Tammy waved her pistol at the wetsuit that lay on the box springs.

"The man who left this here, I suppose," she said. "The man who gave Janis those dog tags. The man who's been trying to discredit and destroy us. I thought Richard would have revealed their little plan by now instead of continuing on with this farce."

"I don't have a plan," said Nazi. "I'm just fucking with people."

"I know it's you, Richard. I know you're behind this ugly persecution."

"I thought it would be fun, to see if I could get a rise out of you and Henley," said Nazi. "I didn't know people were going to die. It was you freaking out about the backpack that got me going."

"And I'm telling you I've never met this Melody woman and I never went to this Lemurian place."

"It's Wendell's bodyguard," said Rolly. "Happy. That's who's down there."

"That big long-haired goon?" said Nazi. "What's he doing with Melody? Why does he want to see me?"

"It's those blackmail photos of Wendell," said Rolly. "He thinks Melody's part of the shakedown. She knows it was you in the video, that you were the man in the dolphin mask. She must've told him we were here."

"I'm telling you I didn't take any photos," said Nazi.

"Doesn't matter. He thinks it was you. Then there's the small matter of you trying to run over his boss with your boat."

"You think he'd really kill Melody?"

"All I know is that Wendell told me Happy was going to take care of things."

"Oh, man. This is totally fucked."

"Yeah, pretty much."

"Excuse me," said Tammy. "What does this bodyguard look like?"

"Big guy, about my age, but a lot meaner looking," said Rolly. "Long white hair. He has some kind of problem . . ." He looked at the wetsuit lying on the box springs, with a ragged hole in the left side near the shoulder. The dim shapes in his head moved closer to the surface.

"Problem with what?" said Tammy.

"His left arm. He can't move his left arm."

Tammy's face lost what little color it had left. The dull steel in her eyes turned to pinpoints of black light.

"It can't be," she said.

She looked over at Dan, still meditating in the corner of the room.

"When did you know, Daniel?" she said. Dan opened his eyes and looked back.

"I wasn't sure," he said. "Not until now. For the last twenty-three years I thought I'd killed my diving buddy. That was the story I told myself. I was a coward and a drunk. Even after I stopped drinking and committed myself to a consciously aware life, I never forgot that I'd been responsible for Butch's death. It was my load to carry. Until a couple of weeks ago."

"When you saw him at the school?" said Rolly. "Was that it?"

"Yes. I went to see Wendell at the school. His bodyguard looked familiar. Janis noticed him too. I thought it was just my imagination, but the next morning I found some nautical charts on my table. I hadn't put them there. One of my harmonicas had been placed on the map, next to South Coronado Island. The next day the harmonica was gone. I took Janis out to the island to talk to the dolphins. I asked her to walk through the casino with me. We found Butch's dog tags here in this room, along with the wetsuit. Something happened to Janis when she saw the name on the tags. She had some kind of breakdown. She started babbling about Arion. I realized I'd been wrong all those years. There maybe was more to the story. That it wasn't my fault."

"Wait a minute," said Nazi. "Are you saying this bodyguard guy is Butch Fleetwood? That he's alive?"

"That would seem to be the consensus," said Rolly.

Rolly's father broke into the conversation.

"Listen," he said. "I don't know who this Fleetwood guy is that you're all getting worked up about, but we need to do something to stop him from killing that girl."

"He's not going to kill her," said Rolly.

"He sure made it sound like he would," said his father.

"Yeah, Waters," said Nazi. "How do you know what he'll do?"

"They're working together," said Rolly. "That's how I know."

"What the hell are you talking about?"

Rolly crossed his arms and looked at his father.

"Tell me what happened down there," he said.

"What do you mean?"

"When did you first see this guy?"

"I didn't see him. He snuck up behind me."

"How did that happen?"

"I . . . well, goddammit, son, I said I was sorry. All this cloak-and-dagger was making me edgy. I had a couple of nips from the bottle I keep in the cabin, maybe more than a few. Next thing I know this nubile young lady sails into my view. She's standing out on the front deck of this awesome yacht looking like something out of my old-man fantasies. She starts flirting with me and I kind of forgot about keeping my guard up. Next thing I knew some guy was behind me with his arm around my throat, whispering in my ear how he was gonna kill the girl if I didn't come up here and send the punk kid down to talk to him."

"That doesn't prove anything, Waters," said Nazi. "If Melody's acting in league with the guy, it's because she's scared of him. Because he threatened her. I gotta go down there and find out what he wants."

"You can't do that, Richard," said Tammy. "I forbid it."

"You forbid it, huh? The mighty Tam-O-Shanter still thinks she can order me around?"

"It's a trap. You can't let him win."

"What the hell are you talking about?"

"Does Melody have access to the OTTER garage?" said Rolly. "Does she have a key?"

"No," said Nazi.

"Was she there when you found the backpack?"

"No. She'd left by then."

"What do you mean?"

"She stayed overnight. I got a bedroom up in the loft."

"Okay," said Rolly. "Think about this. Was there ever a time you weren't there, when she could have planted the backpack?"

"No. That's ridiculous," said Nazi. "I already told you, she called me later that day, when she told me about Tammy coming by and ransacking the house."

"I wasn't there, Richard," said Tammy. "I didn't do any ransacking."

"Think again," said Rolly. "Was there any time when you weren't in the building, when Melody had access to the OTTER?"

"No," said Nazi. "I swear. Except . . . shit. There's no shower in the garage. I have to go down the street. Melody was asleep, though, that morning, when I got back. She was sleeping the whole time."

"How long were you gone?"

"Twenty minutes, twenty-five tops."

"That would be long enough."

"But that's crazy. Why would she do something like that?"

"She's working with Fleetwood."

"This is crazy," said Nazi. "Janis left that backpack for me."

"He's right, Richard," said Tammy. "We've been set up. He's playing with us. That's what he does, setting people against each other."

"How do you know that it's him?"

"Because Janis told me. She came to my office, the day before she died. She told me Arion was alive. That he'd come to see her. I didn't believe her. How could I? It was preposterous. You have no idea what he did to her, to me, to our family. He tried to destroy us and now he's come back to finish the job."

"Why did Janis call him Arion?" said Rolly.

"It took years of therapy for me to help make Janis functional," said Tammy. "She never matured emotionally, not really, but she could function reasonably well. Arion was a cognitive trick I taught her to use, a way to talk about what happened, to make it less real, to compartmentalize her emotions so she could control the story."

"Cut the intellectual crap, Tammy," said Nazi, "and just tell us the truth."

"The truth is overrated, Richard. It isn't pretty. You may not like what you hear."

"Tell me what happened."

"Very well. I had an affair with Butch Fleetwood."

Nazi shrugged.

"No news there," he said. "Waters figured that out."

"Henley had an affair with him too."

"Twinkie had sex with the guy?"

Tammy nodded. Nazi laughed.

"I didn't see that coming," he said. "No pun intended. Did you sleep with this guy separately or did he bone you both at the same time?"

"Henley and I were unaware of the other's involvement with Butch. At first."

"But you found out?"

"Yes."

"What about Janis? Did she know?"

"Yes. She found out. Butch made sure he told her. After . . ."

Tammy's voice caught in her throat.

"After what?" said Nazi.

"After he raped her."

# 42

# THE MIX

Dick Nazi broke the silence that followed.

"Anybody think this would be good time to join hands and sing 'Kumbaya'?" he said. "Might lighten the mood a bit."

"What the hell is wrong with you, son?" said Rolly's father.

"Sorry, old man. I'm a cynic and a nihilist."

"You're an asshole, that's what you are."

"Yeah. Definitely. Ricky the reprobate. I blame it on my parents. It's all their fault."

"You can't blame your parents for everything, son."

"Sure I can." Nazi shrugged. "I don't even know who they are." He looked over at Rolly.

"What about you, Waters? Do you blame your parents for the way your life turned out? Are they why you're such a fuck-up?"

"Shut up," said Rolly's father. "His mother didn't raise a fuck-up."

"We made mistakes, Richard," said Tammy. "We tried to do the right thing. It wasn't easy. You can't let Butch win, whatever you think of us."

"Why do you keep saying that? That he'll win?"

"He'll lie to you. He'll steal your soul. He'll make you believe things that aren't true."

"Did he really rape Janis?"

Tammy Withers put her hands on the bed and stared at the floor.

"Did he rape Janis?" Nazi repeated. Tammy continued to stare at the floor.

"She was only fourteen," she said. "He took advantage of her trusting nature. She was scarred deeply afterward, both physically and psychologically. It almost destroyed her. Her condition required serious intervention on my part. I had to remove her from an extremely toxic environment. We went back to Virginia to get away. Henley had the FBI and the Navy inquiries to deal with. He had other responsibilities. He had to stay here."

"What does this Fleetwood guy want with me?"

"You can't go down there. You can't let him win."

Nazi crossed his arms and stared at Tammy. A strange light came into his eyes.

"Fuck you," he said. Uncoiling like a whip, he jumped on Tammy, pinning her down and wrestling the gun out of her hand. He held the gun to her head for a moment, then released her and jumped off the bed. He backed out the door, waving the gun at the rest of them.

"I'm going down there," he said. "I'm going to save Melody."

"No, Richard," said Tammy. "You can't let him win."

Nazi ran from the room. Tammy started after him, but Rolly's father stepped in front of her. He blocked the doorway and grabbed her arm.

"Let go of me, you fat old inebriate," she said.

"I'm sorry, ma'am, but you can't go down there. The man said he'd kill that girl if anyone but the punk kid showed up."

"Get your hands off me," said Tammy, trying to squirm from Dean Waters's grip.

"It's too late. You can't stop him now."

"He's right," said Rolly. "It's too late."

"What about you?" said Tammy, twisting away from his father's grip and turning to face Rolly. "My son's your client. Can't you do something?"

"Like what?"

"Don't you have a gun?"

"I don't own a gun," said Rolly.

"What kind of goddamn detective are you, anyway?" said Tammy.

"A not-dead one," said Rolly. He pulled his phone out of his pocket and checked the signal. There was none. They couldn't go down to his father's boat and use the radio without being spotted. There was only one way to call in the cavalry.

"Dad?" he said.

"Yes?"

"I need you to get help."

"How am I going to do that?"

Rolly pulled out his wallet and searched through the cards and receipts. He found the card he was looking for and handed it to his father.

"There's a trail behind this building. It leads to the top of the cliffs and then down the other side. You'll see some buildings down there, a lighthouse and barracks. There are two soldiers stationed there, and a lighthouse keeper."

"You want me to bring the soldiers back with me?"

"I'm not sure you'll be able to. They don't speak much English. They'll probably detain you. We're in Mexico now. Whatever happens, see if you can get a message to the FBI agent listed on that card."

"Agent Carole Goffin?" said his father, reading the card. "What do I tell her?"

Rolly looked over at Harmonica Dan. Dan nodded. He understood what Rolly needed to do. Rolly turned to his father.

"Tell her Butch Fleetwood and Daniel Piper are here. They're on South Coronado Island with me. Tell her I need backup to prevent them from getting away."

"What about these folks?" said his father, indicating Tammy and Dan.

"I need to talk to them," said Rolly. "Can you do this for me?"

"Aye, aye, son. Your old man understands mission critical. He'll get the job done."

"That's what I'm counting on."

Dean Waters winked at his son and left the room. They listened to him tromp across the floor and down the staircase. Tammy turned to Harmonica Dan.

"What about you, Daniel?" said Tammy. "Are you going to help me or are you a coward too?"

Dan rubbed his chin, looking thoughtful.

"It's not really a question of cowardice," he said. "It's a question of principles. Butch saved my life. Maybe it was a twist of fate or maybe he had a plan. I don't know. Butch was an awful son of a bitch, but I owe him my life."

"What are you talking about?"

Dan repeated his story to Tammy, the one he'd told Rolly about Butch Fleetwood switching roles, about Butch waving goodbye. Tammy sat down on the box springs again. She looked at the wetsuit.

"We've got to save Richard," she said.

"From what?"

"From himself."

"Tell me what happened on that dive," said Dan. "Tell me what really happened. I'll figure out a way to deal with Butch."

"We wanted to kill him," said Tammy. "We wanted him dead."

"Who's 'we'?" said Rolly.

"I did. And Henley. And Janis, too, at the end. Butch had humiliated all of us. Do you remember that trip on the boat, Daniel? When we all came to this island?"

"Yes. I remember. You left me with Janis on the beach. I'd been drinking. Butch and Henley were both gone. You went to find them or something."

"I went to find Butch," said Tammy. "He knew I would look for him. I was . . . I don't know how to explain it. My libido overwhelmed my intellectual capacities when I was around Butch, any sense I had of good judgment and reason. I wanted him all the time. Butch made me feel dirty. I debased myself for him. I became the natural-born whore my father claimed I would be."

She paused for a moment, rubbed her forehead, then continued.

"I thought Henley was off exploring the island. He was a scientist. He liked to do that sort of thing. I didn't realize he was looking for Butch too, for the same reasons I was. Neither of us knew about the other's involvement with Butch at the time. We were both fools. Butch didn't care which one of us found him first, which one of us he most debased, as long as one of us witnessed the other's coupling. As it turned out, Henley found Butch before I did. My husband was naked, on the floor, with Butch behind him. I'll never forget the look in Henley's eyes when he saw me. I've never seen him so mortified. Butch just grinned. He was so pleased with himself. He made a vile joke, which I will not repeat, an explicit comparison of our . . . fuckable merits, I guess you might call it. If I'd had my gun, I would have shot him right there."

"You had a gun on the boat, didn't you?" said Harmonica Dan.

"Yes. I considered shooting the bastard when he came back to the beach, or on our way home. I might have done it if you and Janis hadn't been there. Instead, I began my planning for Butch's destruction the next day. As did Henley. Separately from me, of course. I didn't know. We never talked of the incident until many years later, when we were sure Butch was dead. Henley told me he'd killed Butch. He confessed."

"The FBI found a note in Henley's office," said Rolly. "A confession."

"Yes. I made sure they would find it. Henley set Butch up to take the fall for those newspaper leaks. The FBI had been snooping around, interviewing everyone in our group. They were already leaning on Butch pretty heavily. He fit their psychological profile."

"So did I," said Dan. "I was a drunk."

"That's all you were, Daniel. Just a sad drunk. Butch had a far more disturbing history. The FBI honed in on him rather quickly. They found the connection to Tom Cockburn, of course. That's when they set up the sting. Henley was in on it. He drew up the fake plans. He came up with the name."

"ARION," said Rolly.

"Yes. It was just a bunch of unused plans and diagrams cobbled together with a cover page and a 'Top Secret' stamp."

"Did Fleetwood know they suspected him?"

"All Butch knew was that the FBI kept interviewing him, that they were watching him, following him. For the first time in his life, he'd lost control of the situation. He hated the Navy. He hated what was happening to him. I offered him a way out. I saw Butch more clearly after that day. I understood his true character. I knew he was susceptible if I presented my plan the right way."

"What did you do?"

"I pretended I was in love with him. I told him I was leaving Henley. I told him how unhappy I'd been in my marriage, how grateful I was that Butch had revealed my husband's true nature to me. None of it was true. But he believed it. At least I thought he did. I told Butch I wanted to run away with him, that I could provide all the money we needed to live. I suggested we meet on my boat and sail down to Mexico. He went along with the plan. He set the date and the time.

"What I didn't know was that Butch planned to make his escape during one of the training exercises with the dolphins. That was clever on his part. The FBI couldn't follow him out on the water at night. It was the one place they couldn't keep track of him.

"As it turned out, it was also a perfect opportunity for Henley to put the second part of his plan into effect. He knew the details of the dive operation. He knew it would be a long dive, that the divers would be working at greater depths than usual. Henley had figured out a way to reset the dials on the compressors so the gas mixture would be wrong. The air in the tanks was poisonous, just enough that a diver wouldn't notice until it was too late. He adjusted the meters so the readings would look right even though they were wrong. It was brilliant."

"I knew it," said Dan. "I didn't screw up."

"No, it wasn't you, Daniel. We all knew about your drinking problem. Henley figured you'd be drunk or hung over when you showed up that evening, that he could use you as a scapegoat if anyone checked the mixture in the tanks. What he didn't know was that Butch would bolt away from you, that he wouldn't go deep enough or stay underwater as long as he was supposed to. The bad air ended up having little effect."

"But the machine worked when I tested it later," said Dan.

"Henley fixed it after the exercise began. He reset the dials while everyone else was out on the water. If anyone checked, the blame would fall on you. They'd think you did something wrong. Henley had a genius for tinkering with things, taking care of problems. I will miss his keen intelligence."

"He could have killed me," said Harmonica Dan.

"That always puzzled him, Daniel, your escape. He was relieved, I think, that you didn't die. You were considered necessary peripheral damage. Henley didn't want to kill you. He wanted to kill Butch. And he thought he had. For the last twenty-three years, Henley was sure he'd gotten away with murder."

"But you knew he didn't," said Rolly.

"I knew Henley didn't kill Butch," said Tammy. "I never told him, though."

"Why?"

"I thought *I* had killed Butch."

## 43

## THE ESCAPE

"I didn't know about the diving exercise," said Tammy. "I didn't expect Butch to arrive the way he did, in his wetsuit and diving gear. It was only a temporary setback, though. It ended up working to my advantage. No one saw him come into the marina where we kept the boat. There aren't a lot of people on the water at that time of night. He stayed underwater until he reached our boat and hauled himself on board.

"I made him stay in the cabin while I sailed out of the harbor. We couldn't take the chance that someone would spot him. After we cleared the bay I set a southerly course, toward the islands. I had a vindictive end in mind for Butch. I wanted him to know I was going to kill him. I wanted him to see me pull the trigger. I wanted him to know that his arrogance and sadism were responsible for his own death.

"Once we'd reached the island and anchored, I told him he could come out of the cabin. I had the gun in my hands. I told him everything I hated about him, all of the ways he'd destroyed my family and me. He didn't think I would do it. He just smirked and told me about Janis, how he'd deflowered her. It all came back to me, about the man who had raped me, the way he smirked at me when I confronted him. I shot Butch. I kept pulling the trigger until the chamber was empty. I wasn't going to miss my target this time. Butch stumbled away from me. He fell off the boat and into the water. That was the last I ever saw of him. There was no way he could have survived. That's what I thought, anyway."

Tammy rubbed her forehead.

"I heard about the diving incident the next day. As time went by and there was no sign of Butch's body, I felt sure I'd gotten away with murder. I was quite pleased with myself."

"What happened to Janis?" said Rolly.

"I wasn't sure if what Butch had told me about Janis was true. He could have lied to me about what happened between them. It was the next morning, when Janis heard the news about Butch. She went into a frenzy. She was hysterical. As I told you earlier, Mr. Waters, that was the first time Janis tried to commit suicide, when she burned herself and scarred her face. Emotional trauma can lead to self-harming behaviors in adolescent girls. This has been well documented. In Janis's case the compensating responses were quite extreme. I knew we'd both be better off if we left town for a while, at least until the inquiry was over and things had returned to normal. As you might imagine, it was not an easy time for Henley and myself, for our business."

"Janis confirmed her relationship with Butch?" said Rolly.

"I was able to draw the story out of her eventually. Unbeknownst to me, Butch and Janis had met outside of our little family expedition to the island. You have to understand, we gave Janis a lot of leeway in her free time. I had vowed not to overfill her days with activities the way my father had filled mine. As I understand it, Janis attended a street fair in Ocean Beach with some of her school friends. They ran into Butch. Her friends all thought he was gorgeous and encouraged Janis to flirt with him. Butch, in all his warped awfulness, decided this was another opportunity to debase me and my family. 'Going for the trifecta' is how he referred to it."

Harmonica Dan nodded his head.

"I heard Butch say that a couple of times," he said. "I never did understand what he was talking about."

"Well, now you know. To make a long story short, Butch successfully maneuvered my daughter into a position where she couldn't say no to him. He filled her head with romantic ideas. He convinced Janis that he was a spy, that he was going on a dangerous mission and might never return. He told her she had to help him, that she was the only person he could trust. He told her he was in love with her. He pleaded for a chance to consummate their relationship, that he might never see her again. It was all very romantic for someone like Janis. She was a credulous girl, even for a fourteen-year-old. She fell for his lies."

"Did Janis ever tell you about the money she had in the backpack?" said Rolly.

"What money?" said Tammy.

"There was two thousand dollars in her backpack. Tom Cockburn put it there."

"I don't know about any money."

"The money was for Butch. He blackmailed Tom Cockburn. Cockburn put the money into the backpack and stashed it in a locker down by the marina."

"Oh dear," said Tammy. "I never thought that part of the story was real. I thought it was something Janis made up."

"She told you about the money?"

"No, not exactly. It all got very convoluted in her mind, you see, as the years went by. She told me she was protecting Arion's treasure, until he came back. I didn't take it literally."

"So Arion was Fleetwood?"

"Arion was a character Janis created, based on Butch Fleetwood, except Arion was pure and good. He was all the promises Butch had made to her, without the fabrications and depravity. It was a psychological strategy we used, to help her compartmentalize her suffering and torment."

"So she could manage the trauma?"

"Exactly. Needless to say, everything that happened only made Butch's story more real for Janis. The FBI started calling the house after he disappeared. Henley had to testify at secret Navy inquests. That's the great skill of sociopaths like Butch. They pull you into their plans, get you involved. They make you part of their scheme. He convinced Janis he was a spy. He got her to pick up the money for him. Getting

312 | COREY LYNN FAYMAN

the money from Tom Cockburn would make her feel it was even more real, that she was part of the whole espionage plan. My God, it's incredible when I think about it, the level of deviousness the man was capable of."

A single pop like a firecracker came from outside. Rolly looked out the window, then down at the boats in the bay. Melody lay on the deck of Wendell's yacht, still in her bikini. She hadn't moved. Two more pops came from below. They echoed across the water and bounced off the rock walls of the little cove.

"What's going on?" said Tammy. "That sounds like my gun."

A man came out of the cabin of Wendell's sailboat. He looked up at the casino and waved at them.

"It's Dick . . . Richard," said Rolly. "He's waving at us. I think he's signaling us to come down."

"Does he still have the gun?" said Tammy. Rolly checked.

"I think so," said Rolly. "He's helping Melody now."

"Do you see this bodyguard person anywhere?"

"No."

"My God," said Tammy. "He killed him. He killed Butch."

On the yacht below, Dick Nazi put his arm around Melody. They both looked up at the window and waved. Rolly waved back.

"I guess we can go down there," he said. He turned to Harmonica Dan. "What do you think?"

"This isn't your business, Waters," said Dan. "You didn't sign up for this soap opera. Forget about us and take care of yourself. Make like your dad and go out the back way."

"Yes, Mr. Waters," said Tammy. "This doesn't concern you. It's about Daniel and Richard and me."

"What are you going to do, if it's Fleetwood down there?"

"The first thing I'll do is make sure he's dead."

"What if he's not?"

"Then I'll kill him myself."

"What am I supposed to do about that?" said Rolly.

"You don't have to do anything," said Tammy. "You won't be there. You won't be a witness."

"What about you?" said Rolly, looking over at Dan. "Would you go along with that?"

Harmonica Dan rubbed his chin, thinking it over.

"I'm still confused," said Dan. "Something's not right. And it seems like the only way it's going to be set right is if we go down there. Dead or alive, we all need to be there with Butch."

"What are you talking about?" said Rolly.

"Something's not right," said Dan.

"I'm not going to stand around quibbling," said Tammy. "I'm going down there. Daniel. Are you coming?"

Rolly watched the two of them leave the room. He didn't follow. They were right. It wasn't his business. He'd been jerked around enough, by Dick Nazi and Melody Flowers, by Tammy Withers and Harmonica Dan. His interest in Janis was tied up in the past, his own history. She'd been a lost and unhappy girl with a nice smile who sold CDs for his band and collected names for the mailing list. She was already damaged when she arrived in his life. She'd left it the same. There was nothing more to it than that. Janis Withers was dead. She was collateral damage, a blameless casualty in the war between her imperious mother and a home-wrecking sociopath. Janis had died a long time ago.

He waited until the footsteps had faded, then headed out of the room. He walked down the stairway and turned toward the back of the building. He found the back door and stepped outside, then looked up the trail that led over the ridge and down to the lighthouse. Someone stood on the trail, blocking his way.

"Hello, fat boy," said Happy the bodyguard. "I thought you might try something like this."

"We heard shots," Rolly said. He could see it now, the face under the facial hair, how it might've once looked like the face in Butch Fleetwood's photograph. "We thought he killed you."

"That punk kid came up with the idea," said Happy. "He's got a gift for deception, just like his old man."

# 44

# THE RELEASE

"Get moving, fat boy," said Happy. Butch Fleetwood. Whatever his name was.

"The fat boy thing's getting old, you know," said Rolly.

"Just get going."

"Where are we going?"

"Down to the boat."

"What's down there?"

"Satisfaction."

"For who?"

"Shut up and get moving," said Fleetwood, shoving Rolly back toward the door. They walked down the stairs, across the old casino floor and out to the rock staircase leading down to the pier.

"Is Melody working with you?" said Rolly as they stepped through the rocks.

"What do you care?"

"I like to know when I've been duped."

"Doesn't matter. You have to deal with me either way."

"How did you manage to hook up with Wendell?"

"That guy's an idiot. What a sap."

"He's rich. He's famous."

"So?"

"You're not."

"His time will come. I can take him down anytime."

"That's your thing, isn't it, taking people down, knocking 'em off their high horse."

"If they deserve it."

"Like Tammy?"

"Conceited bitch. She thought she could control me with that psychology shit. I took her down a few notches."

"You're still pissed off, aren't you? Because she beat you?"

"She didn't beat me at nothing."

"Isn't that how you got your arm messed up?"

"What are you talking about?"

"She beat you at your own game. She lured you onto her boat and put a few bullets into you before you could escape. You survived, but your arm was never the same, was it? She crippled you for life."

"Is that the story she told you?"

"Mostly. I'm making the inference about your arm."

They'd reached the pier.

"Where's Dan's boat?" said Rolly.

"Out there," said Happy, pointing to the open ocean. Rolly could see the sails of Dan's boat on the horizon. "We made a deal. He delivered the goods."

"Aren't you worried he'll report you?"

"He said he was satisfied."

Rolly stepped onto the deck of Wendell's yacht. Fleetwood shoved him in through the cabin door. Tammy and Dick Nazi stood in the lounge. Nazi still had Tammy's gun in his hand. Dan and Melody weren't there. Neither was Rolly's father, which meant he might've made it to the other side of the island.

"Sorry about this, Waters," said Nazi. "Butch figured you'd try and escape, call for help or something."

"Where's Melody?" said Rolly.

"Butch let Dan and Melody go. We made a deal. If I got Tammy down here, he'd let them go."

"You can do this without me," said Rolly. "Whatever it is you need to get done. It's a family affair as far as I'm concerned."

"More than you know," muttered Tammy.

"Speaking of which," said Nazi, "Butch here told me a different story than Tammy told us."

"Butch is a liar," said Tammy.

"Yeah, I know. So are you. Between the two of you I figured it out. I know what it is you don't want Butch to know. What you've never wanted to tell me. I thought it was Grandpa you saw when you looked at me. I thought that was why you and Henley sent me away. It wasn't Grandpa you saw in me, was it?"

"Stop it, Richard. Please stop."

"You think the big guy's figured it out yet?"

"I doubt it."

"What about you, Waters. You figure it out?"

Rolly looked at Dick Nazi. He looked at Butch Fleetwood. The underwater shapes in his brain rose toward the surface.

"Cut the chatter," said Fleetwood. "We had a deal."

"All in good time, Butch," said Nazi. He pointed the pistol at Fleetwood. "Or should I say Daddy?"

Tammy groaned. Fleetwood looked confused for a moment. He recovered his equilibrium and laughed. He looked over at Tammy.

"Damn, woman," he said. "You told me you were on the pill. I thought all you professor types used the pill, not like those Catholic girls down in Mexico."

"Did you sleep with fourteen-year-olds down there too?" said Nazi.

"What're you talking about?" said Fleetwood.

"Tammy's not my mother."

"Consider yourself lucky you're not in that gene pool."

"Similar genes, but I'm in the kiddie pool," said Nazi. "My birth certificate was correct. 'Minor female.' What I didn't understand until today was the minor female was Janis. Father unknown. That would be you."

"You want violins?" said Fleetwood. He nodded at Rolly. "Maybe fat boy here could play something for you."

"I play guitar," said Rolly. "Not violin."

"Shut up," said Fleetwood.

"The thing is," said Nazi, "I can't decide who I should shoot first, the rapist or the illusionist."

"We made a deal," said Fleetwood. "I let your girl go."

"Yeah, we made a deal. But I've still got the gun."

"Give the gun to me, Richard," said Tammy. "Let me finish what I started. I'll live with the consequences."

"What did he do to her?" said Nazi. "What did he do to Janis?"

"You don't want to hear this, Richard."

"Yes I do. I need to know."

"This woman's been lying to you your whole life," said Fleetwood. "And now you expect her to tell you the truth?"

"Did you rape Janis?"

"Is that what she told you?"

"Did you?"

"I never fucked anyone who didn't want to get fucked," said Fleetwood. Tammy lifted her head. She stared at Fleetwood. He stared back at her. Each waiting for the other to blink.

"My plan worked," said Tammy. "Butch fell for my story. His self-conceit was so blinding, he actually believed I was in love with him. He escaped to my boat. We slipped out of the bay without anyone noticing us. It was when I anchored the boat here, near this island. That's when it went wrong. Butch wouldn't come out of the cabin when I called for him, so I took my gun and walked in. Janis was there, on Butch's lap. He had one arm around her waist and one around her neck. He was stroking her hair, using her as a shield. He would've broken her neck."

"That is some story," said Fleetwood. "But it's all lies."

"Quiet," said Nazi. He wiggled the gun at Fleetwood.

"She's telling it backwards," said Fleetwood.

"You'll get your turn," said Nazi. "Go on, Tams."

"Butch had been sweet-talking Janis for weeks, telling her he was a spy, bewitching her into helping him escape. I told you, Mr. Waters, that I didn't know about that money Tom Cockburn gave Janis. That's not entirely true. Janis brought her backpack with her that night. I knew about the money. I just didn't know where it came from."

"Janis was a good girl," said Fleetwood. "She did what I asked."

"At any rate," said Tammy, "there was nothing I could do by the time I found her with Butch on the boat. I tried to appeal to him. I told him I would take him anywhere he wanted to go, that I'd arrange to get him more money. I would have done anything to protect my daughter from this man. I thought he would kill her. I gave up my gun. It was the biggest mistake I ever made."

"Not as big as the one you're making now," said Fleetwood.

"Once I surrendered the gun, Butch had his way with us. He tied me up. He assaulted Janis. He raped her in front of me. She meant nothing to him. He defiled my daughter in the most obscene ways and I could do nothing to stop him. When he was finished Janis just lay there sobbing, apologizing to me. Butch started putting on his wetsuit again. He took my gun and went outside the cabin. That's when I knew he was planning to kill us. Psychologically, that's what people do, even sociopaths. They remove themselves to prepare. He had to kill us. We were the only ones who knew he was alive.

"I talked calmly to Janis. I told her to find the flare gun and bring it to me. As she started to untie me, Butch came back through the door. Janis fired the flare gun at him. The flare hit Butch in the left shoulder. It stuck to him somehow. He tumbled around on the floor, screaming, trying to dampen the flames. He was on fire. That's how . . . that's how Janis got burned. Even after what he'd done to her, she couldn't endure the sound of anyone in pain. She ran to him, trying to help. Her clothes caught on fire. Her hair started burning. Other parts of the cabin started burning. Butch ran outside and jumped in the water. I finished untying myself and grabbed the fire extinguisher. After I put out the fire, I took up the anchor and started the boat. I gave Janis what first aid I could on the way home and took her to the emergency ward at the Navy hospital when we got back. The next day we left for Virginia. I contacted my father. We took a company jet. I got Janis a private room in my father's hospital."

"Not exactly romantic, was it?" said Dick Nazi. "The night little Richard was conceived?"

"Your sister . . ." said Tammy. "Janis . . ."

"You mean my mother," said Nazi. "Janis was my mother, wasn't she?"

"Janis was traumatized. I had to protect her. She couldn't stay here. It would have destroyed her, all the news going around about Butch, all the inquiries and press. I needed to get her somewhere safe and secure. Until things calmed down."

"Why was I even born?" said Nazi. "Why didn't you get Grandpa's doctors to scrape me out of there? Why didn't you give me up for adoption? Why go through this elaborate scheme and pretend I was your son and not hers?"

"I don't know, Richard. I don't know anymore. Somehow I thought that if I came back with a baby, it would explain everything, why I went away. It would make our family seem normal. It would make Henley look like a father again. The man who raped me at that party had taken something from when I was fifteen, something I never got back. I couldn't let that happen to Janis. I had to make things better for her. I thought I could make her forget the terrible things that had happened that night, instead of having to live with them her whole life. We invented a story together, about an imaginary friend who went away."

"Arion," said Rolly.

"You brainwashed her," said Nazi.

"I only wanted her to be happy. I felt responsible. I understood my complicity. Janis was a sweet girl. Guileless and happy. And then this man came along and tried to destroy her. To destroy us. I couldn't let him do that. I couldn't let him win."

"Winning," said Fleetwood. "It's always about winning for you."

"What was it for you?" said Nazi. "Just a good time?"

"Sure, bud. Maybe I am your father. It could have happened, I guess, but it sure didn't happen that way. Your sister was ready to rock. She came on to me."

"At fourteen?"

"It was Janis's idea to go out on that boat. That's the part Tammy isn't telling you. Janis asked me to go with her on the boat. She's the one who offered me a way out. I took advantage of the situation. I'll admit it. But I didn't rape her. Not like that, anyway. Janis hated her mom. She was running away from this bitch."

"He's lying," said Tammy. Nazi scratched his temple with the butt of the gun.

"Go on, Butch," he said. Fleetwood continued.

"Tammy found us, just like she said. But Janis and I had already set sail when Tammy appeared. She was the one who'd been hiding. She was jealous. She's the one who shot me with that flare, set the whole fucking boat on fire."

"He's lying," said Tammy. "You can't let him win."

Nazi shook his head.

"Why did Janis kill herself?" he asked.

"I didn't mean for nothing to happen," said Fleetwood. "I didn't know about this bullshit story Tammy had been feeding Janis over the years. I noticed Janis still had that backpack, when I saw her at the school. It made me wonder a little. I wanted to see what she had inside the backpack. I didn't know she'd freak out like that."

"You stole it?"

"I didn't steal it. I only asked Melody to borrow it for a while."

# 45

# THE SCAM

"I told you," said Rolly. "They're in this together. Melody's working with him."

"Is that true?" said Nazi, pointing the gun on Fleetwood.

"Sure," said Fleetwood. "That girl's got the touch. She learned from the master."

"What are you saying?"

Fleetwood grinned.

"You should have seen the tricks we pulled when Mel was younger. She could lay that drunk, horny teenager act on a guy like you wouldn't believe. Down in Cabo, that's where we played the scam. She'd let the guy take her up to his hotel room and then I'd show up, acting like I was her daddy. Her mean, angry daddy. You wouldn't believe how much money some guys keep on them, how much they'll give you not to kick their ass or turn them in to the Mexican police. I'd give ten percent to the guy at the desk for the duplicate key. Mel and I split the rest sixty-forty."

"Sixty for you, right?" said Rolly.

"Senior partners get the bigger cut in any business."

"How long has Melody been your partner?" said Rolly.

"Let's see," said Fleetwood. "She was ten when her mother

dumped her on me. Went out to buy groceries and never came back. Left me with the girl."

"Is Melody . . ." said Nazi. "I mean, this other woman and you . . .?"

"Don't worry, kid," Fleetwood said. He winked. "You ain't fucking your half-sister."

"Well, that's a relief," said Tammy. "I think we've had enough Freudian horrors for one day."

"Yeah, huh." Fleetwood continued. "I didn't know what to do with Mel at first. I thought maybe I'd dump her at a church or something. Then I realized she was my ace card. I was big and scary-looking all by myself, but with that cute little blond girl walking beside me, calling me Daddy, tourist ladies fell for whatever I fed 'em. It opened up a whole new world for me."

"What a marvelous accomplishment, Butch," said Tammy. "Turning a ten-year-old girl into a teenaged delinquent. How long was it before you copulated with her?"

"Now that's a funny thing," said Fleetwood. "I never tried nothing like that with Mel. She's like a daughter to me."

"I can't imagine that stopping you," said Tammy.

"Why bother?" said Fleetwood. "I like a challenge, you know, like nailing some stuck-up bitch who says she's going to rescue me from my criminal nature, or maybe her Poindexter fruit husband who goes around telling everyone I'm a half-witted moron. Fuck 'em both. That's what I think. That would be an achievement. There's satisfaction in pulling off something like that."

"And their fourteen-year-old daughter? Was that a challenge too?"

"Just a cherry on top," said Fleetwood. "A little dessert."

"You're a real piece of shit, aren't you?" said Nazi.

"Like I told you," said Fleetwood. "Janis came on to me. I didn't start with the idea. I improvised. It's just the way things worked out."

"Let's get back to Melody," said Rolly. He needed to lower the temperature before a fire broke out. Janis was everyone's flash point. Fleetwood seemed to have softened a little when he talked about Melody.

"Yeah, Mel," said Fleetwood. "It's been a great ride for the two of us. She's all grown up now. This is going to be our last dodge. We hooked a big fish."

"I see," said Tammy. "How much do you want from me?"

Fleetwood laughed.

"You? You're just a minnow. We're on to something much bigger than Tammy Withers, the fucking doggy shrink."

"Then why am I here?"

"I had to make sure no one identifies me. Not until we clear the grift, at least."

"Is that why you killed Henley?"

"That was an accident. The old guy just died on me. Guess I scared him to death. I'm telling the truth about that. He was swimming in that glass tank when I came in. I put my face down there in front of him so he gets a good look. His face looks all quizzical at first, but then it's like he's seen a ghost. His whole body went into contortions."

"What about Tom Cockburn?" said Rolly. "Did you kill him?"

"That one's on you, fat boy," said Fleetwood. "I knew he might be problem, so I messaged him from your phone to set up a meeting. He was expecting to see you. I tried to explain the situation. He kept backing away from me. Then he ran out of steps."

"Everything seems to be going your way, doesn't it, Butch?" said Tammy. Fleetwood chuckled.

"I worked on a sport-fishing boat for a while, back when I was a kid. Sometimes when a customer had hooked a big fish, the boss sent me around to cut other people's lines so they wouldn't get tangled and lose the big one. You have to cut lines if you want the big fish."

"It's Wendell, isn't it?" said Rolly. "He's your sap."

"Fat Boy here's got some meat in his head," said Fleetwood. "How'd you figure it?"

"Those photos, the ones of Wendell and Melody? You sent them to Wendell, didn't you?"

"Sure. Melody came up with the plan. You coming along, that was a bonus, showing up at the temple and the book signing, flashing your private detective bullshit. When you showed up with the band it just about drove the boss nuts. He never even thought about me."

"It was you that texted Sideman, wasn't it, asking him to hire me for the band? You used Wendell's phone to text Sideman."

"Yeah. I sent that one. Melody came up with the idea, though. She had your phone number. She's a sharp knife, that girl. I'm supposed to deliver the payoff tomorrow. Beautiful, isn't it? Wendell just handed the money to me. That's not the best part, though. This was a long con. Took me two years, but it's all gonna pay off."

"Okay," said Rolly. "I'll bite. What's the best part?"

Fleetwood smiled.

"I've got three weeks to deliver this boat to Hawaii."

"Yeah? So?"

"I know a guy up near Long Beach, does some boat modifications, makes it look different inside and erases all the identifiers. I know another guy in Panama, sells used boats at a discount to millionaires who appreciate a good deal, no questions asked. He's got a clerk in the government down there who takes care of the new registration. By the time Wendell wonders why I didn't show up in Hilo, I'll be sitting back and drinking Soberanas in Panama City, counting my money from selling this yacht."

"Melody gets a share of the money too?"

"Sure. Sixty-forty. Just like we always do. This is a good one to go out on. It's a home run."

"Why the fuck are you telling us all this?" said Nazi.

"Melody thinks you've got promise, son. Maybe it's in your blood, knowing what I know now, could be some kind of DNA thing. Melody wants me to cut you in on the deal."

"How much?"

"Half of her share."

"What do I have to do?"

Fleetwood looked over at Tammy and Rolly.

"Keep an eye on these two for me."

"How am I going to do that?"

"You're all coming with me. We're staying together until this deal is done. Once we're in Panama and I've got the cash in hand, I'll let you all go. It would go a lot easier if I had an assistant."

"Don't listen to him," said Tammy.

"It's not a bad deal," said Nazi. "How much would I make?"

"A hundred thousand, hundred and twenty."

"And no one gets hurt, right?"

Fleetwood nodded.

"That's the deal."

"I could never come back here, though, could I?" said Nazi. "To San Diego, I mean, to California? To the freaking United States of America?"

"What you got here that's so special?"

"My family, of course," said Nazi. He laughed.

"I'm your family now," said Fleetwood.

"Yeah. Come to papa." Nazi laughed again, a worn-out, weak cackle. He looked over at Rolly. "What do you think, Waters? What would you do?"

"I don't know," said Rolly. "I don't have the gun."

"Yeah, that's right," said Nazi. "I almost forgot. I have a gun." He pointed the gun toward Fleetwood. "What if I don't go for your plan? What if I shoot you instead?"

"You ever shoot that thing before?"

"Sure. A few minutes ago. Off the side of the boat."

"I mean did you ever shoot somebody with it?"

"Of course not. I don't think I'd miss, though. You're pretty close range."

"That's a twenty-two-caliber target pistol. It's not an automatic."

"So what?"

"I'm fast. If I come at you, you might get off one shot. Now if you're really lucky the shot might go through my eye, straight into my brain. That's about the best you could hope for with one shot. That would drop me. I'll be moving my head when I come at you, though. You might only graze me. The bullet bounces right off my skull. Or maybe the bullet catches my upper torso. That's going to sting for sure, but not enough to slow me down. I'll be coming for you and I'll hit you so hard you'll swallow your teeth."

"Don't be so sure, Butch," said Tammy. "I loaded that clip with hollow points. It won't be like last time. They'll tear you apart."

Fleetwood glared at Tammy a moment, then turned back to Nazi.

"Well, that would be ugly, even on me," he said. "What's it going to be, kid?"

"This is crazy," said Nazi. His gun hand trembled. "This is fucking crazy."

Fleetwood offered his hand.

"Last chance, son," he said. "Let's shake on the deal. It'll put a lot more money in your tank than those stupid OTTER things you drive around."

"Don't do it, Richard," said Tammy. "Let me have the gun."

It was too late. Fleetwood pounced, flicking Nazi's gun hand away with a sweep of his left hand as he stepped in and jabbed Nazi in the solar plexus with his right fist. Nazi crumpled to the floor, and Rolly heard an unpleasant crack as Fleetwood grabbed his gun hand and wrenched the pistol away. Fleetwood spun around to face the room, holding the pistol on them. The whole thing was over before Rolly could even think of escape. Nazi groaned.

"You broke my finger," he said.

"Tough shit, kid," said Fleetwood. "You had your chance."

"What happens now?" said Rolly.

"Guess I'll have to set sail without a first mate. Unless you want the job."

"The pay's pretty tempting, but I don't think we'll make it."

"Why not?"

"The Coast Guard's out there waiting for us. I called the FBI. I told them where I was going, that you and Dan would be here. They'll stop Dan's boat. Then they'll come for us."

"Sounds to me like fat boy's trying to fool the fooler."

"It's true, Butch," said Tammy. "There was another man. He went to get help. You won't get away this time."

A loud thump reverberated through the cabin as if something had bumped into the boat.

"What's that?" said Fleetwood. There was another bump. And a third. Fleetwood looked over at Rolly.

"Who's out there?" he said.

"Navy SEALs," Rolly said. He had no idea. He hoped it wasn't his father, stumbling around drunk.

Fleetwood picked up the remote on the coffee table and turned on the TV. He brought up the indexed screen of the boat's security cameras. There was another bump.

"I don't see anything," said Fleetwood, scanning the camera feeds. Rolly eyeballed the video screens. He didn't see anything either. Then something moved past one of the cameras, down by the waterline. There was another thump on the hull. Fleetwood pressed a button on the remote. The screen zoomed in on a single camera. A dorsal fin sliced through the water in front of it. *Thump.*

"What the fuck?" said Fleetwood.

"It's dolphins," said Rolly. "They're attacking the boat."

"Outside," said Fleetwood, waving the gun at them. "Hook your arms together and stay in front of me."

Rolly and Nazi took positions on each side of Tammy. They hooked arms and walked out the door onto the aft deck. Fleetwood followed them, gun at the ready, using his hostages as a protective shield from whatever might be out there.

"A little farther," he said. They walked toward the stern. Rolly looked down at the water between the two hulls. Two dolphins swam in the water below. More dolphins were circling the boat, all around them. A high-pitched squeal of harmonica notes blasted through the air. The water erupted with leaping dolphins.

"Get down!" Rolly shouted, dragging Tammy along with him. They dropped to the deck and rolled into the corner. A shadow passed over them. A single pistol shot rang out. It reverberated off the rocks, bounced back to the boat and drifted away into the ocean air. Then there was silence. Rolly crawled to his knees. Tammy rose beside him. Nazi lay on the other side of the deck.

"You okay?" Rolly said.

"Yeah. I think so," said Nazi. "What happened?"

Rolly stood up. He surveyed the boat. He looked out at the water. The dolphins were gone. So was Butch Fleetwood.

# 46

# THE BALLAD

R olly and Moogus sat on the patio outside Miguel's taco shop, sharing a plate of carne asada nachos. It was two o'clock Tuesday morning. The last of their scheduled blues jams at Winstons was over. Their gear was packed up. There'd been a good crowd, but the club owners had already decided to try some other form of entertainment for the next three months. Starting next week, Monday night at Winstons would be Trivial Pursuit night.

"Who were you talking to at the bar?" said Moogus. "That guy looked familiar."

"Dick Nazi," said Rolly.

"He's in some punk band, right?"

"Rude Abortion. They broke up."

"Wasn't that the same girl who was dragging your ears a while back?"

Rolly nodded.

"Melody. They're together. They gave me a little gift."

Rolly reached in his pocket, pulled out the check and showed it to Moogus.

"Five thousand bucks?" said Moogus, sounding properly impressed. "Is that for your detective stuff?"

"Yeah."

"What'd you do for them?"

"I brought them together."

"They don't look like they'd have that kind of scratch."

"They do now. Well, *he* does. You remember me telling you about Janis Withers a couple of months ago?"

"Yeah. I remember. She killed herself."

"Dick Nazi's her son."

"Oh shit. Don't tell me Matty's the father?"

Rolly shook his head.

"No. It wasn't Matt."

"That's a relief," said Moogus. "For a second there, I thought this Nazi guy might have inherited some evil lead singer genes."

"Janis got pregnant when she was fourteen."

"Yeeow! Even Matty wouldn't dip his wick in a female that juvenile."

"No. Not even Matt. Anyway, Dick Nazi inherited a house and a very nice trust fund from Janis."

"I told you she was rich."

"He goes by Richard now. He's rethinking his outlook on things."

"Well, a guy can't go around calling himself Dick Nazi his whole life."

"He'd have to be pretty committed to the idea."

"How 'bout his girlfriend? What's her story?"

"She's rethinking her outlook as well."

"Yeah, I'll bet. She's thinking about a diamond ring and getting some documents signed, that's what she's thinking about."

"I was surprised to see them together. I can't figure out that relationship."

"Love is blind, right, buddy?"

"Deaf and dumb, too, I guess."

"Yeah, well, you and I haven't exactly navigated that side of the street to any great success."

"True."

Moogus picked up a tortilla chip, chased the last of the carne asada around the bowl with it.

"Nice to see the captain tonight," he said. "When was the last time your dad came to a gig?"

"Hmm, let's see," said Rolly. "I'm pretty sure it was never."

Moogus chuckled.

"I sure couldn't remember it ever happening. Your stepmom sure keeps him in line. Hey, you know what tonight was?"

"Our last ever blues jam at Winstons?"

"No. Something even better than that." Moogus raised his glass. "Here's a toast to the end of my parole. I became a free man as of midnight."

"Congratulations," said Rolly. They tapped their Styrofoam cups together and downed the last of their drinks.

"Well, I'm done," said Moogus. "You ready?"

"I think I'll stick around for a while, soak up the atmosphere."

"Take a walk on the beach and trip over some bums in the sand?"

Rolly shrugged.

"We won't be playing here for a while. I thought I'd take one more look at the old house."

"Really? I thought you hated that place."

"I do. You want to come with?"

"Nah," said Moogus. "I realized something after we walked around last time. The magic's gone. I'm done living in the past."

"Me too," said Rolly. "I'm saying goodbye."

"I'll see you at Patrick's on Thursday, then. Back to the grind."

"See you there."

Moogus walked out to the sidewalk and headed up the street to his truck. They hadn't carpooled this time. Rolly dumped his leftovers in the trash and headed down the back alley. It wasn't as dark as it used to be. Someone had repaired the safety light over the back door of Miguel's. Its bright glare chased away the old shadows.

They'd recovered Butch Fleetwood's body this time. It had washed up on the shore of South Coronado Island two days after he disappeared from Wendell's yacht. Fleetwood was fully and officially deceased now, although no one could explain how a man with his swimming skills could have faltered in the waters of a protected cove on South Coronado Island. The coroner's report noted bruises on Fleetwood's body, but no other injuries. Drowning was the official cause of his death.

Rolly had his own theory about how Fleetwood died, but he knew FBI agents Goffin and King wouldn't take it seriously, so he never told them about it. He didn't mention it once during the weeks of interviews that followed that day. Butch Fleetwood had managed to get off one shot with Tammy Withers's pistol, one shot with a segmented hollow-point bullet. Harmonica Dan was still missing.

Sometimes as Rolly was falling asleep at night, or when he was just waking up in the morning, he had a vision of Harmonica Dan riding a dolphin as it leapt from the waves. Rolly lay on the deck of Wendell's yacht as the dolphin arced over him and knocked Butch Fleetwood into the ocean. *A man's got no chance against a dolphin.* That's what Henley Withers had said. Butch Fleetwood, the man who couldn't be killed by poisonous gas or bullets or flare guns, hadn't stood a chance either. A dolphin had dragged Fleetwood down into the water and drowned him. It was ridiculous to think it could really have happened. No one would believe him if he said it. He didn't have any proof.

Two Coast Guard ships had arrived within the half hour. One of the ships carried Melody on board. The other had Harmonica Dan's boat in tow, but Daniel Piper wasn't on it. FBI agents Goffin and King arrived by helicopter and presided over the scene. Two Mexican soldiers stood on the shore of the island, protecting their little piece of Mexico from the Americans. Melody, Tammy, Nazi and Rolly were flown back to Coast Guard headquarters for interrogation. Rolly's father was retrieved from the lighthouse two hours later after someone remembered the man who'd called in the alarm was still there. Dean Waters arrived at the Coast Guard compound stinking drunk, having put a serious hurt on a bottle of tequila the lighthouse keeper shared with him while he waited to be rescued. He'd completed his mission, though. He'd followed his orders.

In the end, after hours of interviews and weeks of investigation, no one ended up being charged with any crimes. Fleetwood had acknowledged his part in the deaths of Henley Withers and Tom Cockburn. There were three witnesses to his confession. The FBI finally had its man. Butch Fleetwood had managed to survive his first death for twenty-three years. Now he was dead again. Really and truly dead. Melody told stories of the con games and grifts she and Fleetwood had committed in Mexico, but those crimes were outside the FBI's jurisdiction. Melody had been a minor female most of that time, starting at ten years of age. She played her victim card like a champ and Dick Nazi fell in love with her all over again. Tammy Withers had gone back to Virginia, to care for her dying father in his final days. She might end up owning a big share of Tidewater Defense Systems after all.

Butch Fleetwood's story, along with the fifty thousand dollars in cash found on Wendell's boat, made for a flurry of provocative articles in the media, but the blackmail photos never showed up in the press. Wendell got his fancy yacht back, and his money. He announced he'd be stepping away from public art projects for a while to spend more time with his family.

Rolly walked to the end of the alley and crossed the street. He stood on the sidewalk looking at the front door of the old Creature Cave, the house he'd lived in for three years with Moogus and Matt. The house was dark, as any decent house should be at a quarter past two in the morning. It was quiet tonight. In the old days the War Zone carousing and parties never ended, even on Mondays. The neighborhood had changed. The Creature Cave was just an old house. Someone else lived there now. It was a dream full of sand.

Rolly turned away, walked three blocks to the beach, took a seat on the wall and stared at the waves, ghostly white bursts of lunar gravity exploding on shore. He reached in his pocket and pulled out a harmonica. Dick Nazi and Melody had found the harmonica while going through the items Janis kept in storage at the Lemurian Temple, items returned by the FBI and police.

*Arion. International Pitch.* That's what it said on the harmonica. Every harp man Rolly knew played either Hohners or Fenders or maybe Lee Oskars. He'd never heard of an Arion. He raised the harmonica to his lips and blew a few notes. The sound floated across the sand and disappeared in the roar of the surf. He played the notes again. This time they echoed back at him. He swiveled his head, looking for the source of the reflection. A man sat on the wall thirty feet to his right. The man wore a navy-blue overcoat with epaulets on the shoulders. Rolly blew three notes on the Arion harmonica. The man blew three notes, the same notes, back at him. Rolly blew four notes. The man played them back, then added some additional notes, high-pitched and squeaky, like the notes in a dolphin reveille.

Rolly rose from his seat and walked down the boardwalk. He took a seat next to the man.

"They found this in Janis's house," he said. He handed Dan the harmonica. "Dick Nazi . . . Ricky gave it to me."

"Arion," said Harmonica Dan. "I don't see these much anymore. It's an old brand."

"You used to play them, though?"

"Yeah. I used to, a long time ago."

"Does Ricky know you're his father?"

"I didn't know it myself. Not until . . . How'd you figure it out?"

Rolly looked out at the ocean again.

"I did a little research. I ordered a copy of Richard's birth certificate and compared it with the date Butch disappeared. Something didn't seem right. It was only seven months. Then I realized something. Arion was a musician."

"Do you think Butch raped Janis?"

"I guess he did. One way or the other. Why else would Tammy Withers think he was the father? I guess that's why she did what she did."

"I was a drunk then. I was a mess. I was ashamed of myself."

"How did it happen?"

Harmonica Dan looked at the Arion harmonica, then out at the waves.

"You know that day we went out on their boat, me and Butch and the family?"

"That day in the photograph?"

"Yeah. They left us alone, you know. It was just Janis and me. She seemed upset. I felt sorry for her. She kind of knew what was going on with her parents—not exactly, you know, but just that everyone was acting weird. I didn't have a clue what was going on, myself. That's how out of it I was.

"I played my harmonica for Janis—this one, the Arion—some little songs that I knew. I showed her how to play some things too. We did that for a while. Then we saw some dolphins playing in the surf, riding the waves in toward the shore. I thought we should go out and swim with them. She was kind of nervous about it at first, but I got her to go out with me. I said I'd take care of her. The dolphins were friendly. They even let us catch a ride with them a couple of times. She started laughing and having a really good time.

"Her mom came back, really wigged out, and said we were leaving. Butch and Henley got there a couple minutes later and we headed back home. You could tell something was up. I had a couple more beers and got really drunk. That's how I handled stress back in those days. I sacked out in the bunk in the lower cabin on the way home. Everyone else stayed up on deck. They were distracted, I guess. Janis came down to my bunk. She took off her clothes and crawled in on top of me and it just . . . happened. It was only a couple of minutes."

"Nobody ever knew?"

"I never told anyone until now. I guess Janis never did either."

"Don't you think you should tell Ricky?"

"Seems like he's had plenty to deal with already."

"He might be happier knowing you're his father rather than Butch."

"We'll see. I never saw Janis again after that day, you know. Not until years later at those blues jams with you."

"Were you in love with her?"

"I liked taking her out to see the dolphins. She was different around the dolphins. She was happy. She was free."

"Did you know you were Arion?"

"I wondered about it sometimes, but I wasn't sure."

"Can I ask you something else?"

"What's that?"

"Who leaked those documents? Was it you?"

Harmonica Dan considered the Arion harmonica a moment, then turned back to Rolly.

"Everyone worried about Butch," he said. "No one ever thought about me."

# ACKNOWLEDGMENTS

First off, thanks to Cornelia Feye for offering Rolly Waters a new home at Konstellation Press. He and I are both happy to be here. Also to Celia Johnson and Lisa Wolff for their editing advice and improvements.

To Derek Tarr for his all-around knowledge and advice on scuba diving. To Hunza Kotas, whose personal insights about dolphin behavior and the U.S. Navy Marine Mammal Program were critical to completing this book. Any factual errors on the above topics are strictly mine.

And always to Maria, my wife and first reader, who keeps me on course in any adventure, be it real life or fiction.

# ABOUT THE AUTHOR

Corey Lynn Fayman has done hard time as a musician, songwriter, and interactive designer, but still refuses to apologize for it. His hometown of San Diego, CA provides the backdrop for his mystery novels, including the award-winning *Border Field Blues* and *Desert City Diva.*

"As an independently published author, I rely on the recommendations of enthusiastic readers to help spread the word. If you enjoyed this Rolly Waters mystery, please consider posting a review on Amazon or Goodreads. A couple of sentences and a good rating are much appreciated!"

Sign up on my website or follow him on Facebook for news, giveaways and special offers.

Website: www.coreylynnfayman.com

Facebook: www.facebook.com/coreylynnfayman